"COME HERE, WOMAN."

Caroline's pulse quickened. She folded her arms over her chest and smiled. "No."

She squealed as he leaped off the bed, grabbed her, and threw her over his shoulder. Before she could catch her breath, Garrett was astride her, pinning her thrashing arms to the mattress.

"Do you yield, woman?" Garrett demanded.

"Never." She joined his game eagerly. "No torture can make me yield."

"We shall see about that," he murmured. "I am a master at putting disobedient wives in their place." He kissed the corners of her mouth.

"Mercy," she whispered.

"No mercy."

He cupped her breast in his strong hand, and she gave herself over to the magic of their true wedding night.

Don't Miss the First Two Books
in the "Fortune" Trilogy by
Judith E. French

FORTUNE'S MISTRESS
FORTUNE'S FLAME

If You've Enjoyed This Book,
Be Sure to Read These Other
AVON ROMANTIC TREASURES

ANGEL EYES *by Suzannah Davis*
CAPTIVES OF THE NIGHT *by Loretta Chase*
CHEYENNE'S SHADOW *by Deborah Camp*
FASCINATION *by Stella Cameron*
LORD OF FIRE *by Emma Merritt*

Coming Soon

GABRIEL'S BRIDE *by Samantha James*

FORTUNE'S BRIDE

JUDITH E. FRENCH

An Avon Romantic Treasure

AVON BOOKS NEW YORK

FORTUNE'S BRIDE is an original publication of Avon Books. This work has never before appeared in book form. This work is a novel. Any similarity to actual persons or events is purely coincidental.

AVON BOOKS
A division of
The Hearst Corporation
1350 Avenue of the Americas
New York, New York 10019

Inside back cover author photograph by Theis Photography Ltd.
Published by arrangement with the author
Library of Congress Catalog Card Number: 93-90658
ISBN: 0-380-76866-6

First Avon Books Printing: April 1994

Printed in the U.S.A.

RA 10 9 8 7 6 5 4 3 2 1

For my mother,
Mildred Emma Faulkner Bennett,
who believes that the virtues are
Godliness, cleanliness, and reading

"... Tyranny, like hell, is not easily conquered; yet we have this consolation with us, that the harder the conflict, the more glorious the triumph ..."

—Thomas Paine

FORTUNE'S
BRIDE

Chapter 1

Fortune's Gift Plantation
Maryland's Eastern Shore
December 1777

"Marry you?" Caroline Steele's cinnamon-brown eyes narrowed with contempt. "I'd sooner wed with a red Indian." She stiffened and her naturally husky voice rang with gentle authority. "And take your boots off my father's desk. This isn't a stable."

Captain Bruce Talbot's pocked face flushed an angry red as he pushed back in the chair, put his feet on the floor, and poured himself another glass of port from the Irish crystal decanter. "Unfortunately, cousin," he said sarcastically, "your marrying a savage would do the family very little good."

Caroline's nose wrinkled in distaste. Bruce's red coat was tossed carelessly over a chair; his rumpled white linen shirt showed sweat stains under the arms, and the lace stock at his throat bore traces of the pork gravy Cook had served at dinner. His waistcoat was missing a silver button, and even his scarlet sash seemed the worse for wear. His Majesty must be desperate, she thought, if he was forced to accept an officer such as this in his Light Dragoons.

She didn't miss the slight tremble in Bruce's hand or the bloodred drops that splashed on the polished walnut desk. "You're a drunken pig," she said. "How dare you order me about in my own home? And what lunacy causes you to believe that I'd dine at the same table with you—let alone become your wife?"

One blow from his fist dashed the goblet against the brick hearth. "Damn you, Caroline!" he roared. "You forget your place. I'm here as a representative of the crown. And you are in danger of being declared a rebel and imprisoned for high treason."

She bit back the retort that rose to her lips and forced a wry smile. "I am a loyal Englishwoman. No one can say differently." Strange, she thought, how much Bruce looked like her brother Reed and Papa. All Papa's strengths distorted . . . the fair Talbot complexion marred by disease, the bright blue eyes muddied by drink and loose living. As Papa had looked, she corrected as the familiar pain knifed through her. Over three years had passed since her father's death. And nearly a year since her husband . . .

Bruce's tirade brought her back to the present. "Not so loyal. We both know how and where your dear husband met his end."

"Do we?" She returned his bloodshot gaze squarely. "Wesley drowned. An accident."

"He was a traitor. Killed aboard a rebel privateer."

"Untrue. The Reverend Miles Clark of Lewes bore witness to Wesley's accidental death during a storm on the Delaware Bay."

"And what was he doing at Lewes?" Bruce demanded. "His body was washed ashore with other dead rebels."

"A false accusation, unfairly cast upon an upstanding man who is unable to defend himself against your lies."

"I'll prove it, Caroline," he threatened. "I'll prove it, and I'll strip you of everything you possess."

"Unless, of course . . ." She hesitated, judging the extent of his inebriation. She wouldn't put it beyond Bruce to attempt to strike her if he were drunk enough. After what he'd done to Amanda . . . "If I accept your offer, you'll drop these ridiculous charges against my dead husband."

"Naturally." He rose to his feet and swayed slightly. "I'm thinking of the family name. If Fortune's Gift is confiscated by the crown, you stand to lose a—"

"A king's ransom—as well you know," she lashed back. "Since you took it upon yourself to have yourself appointed my guardian after Wesley's death."

"It was the least I could do," he said. "You were distraught. A woman alone . . . in no condition to administer the finances of your father's estate. Our fathers were brothers, after all. Something should have come to me when Uncle John passed on."

Caroline swallowed the oath that rose in her throat. Wesley's death had come as a shock, but not so great a one that she couldn't manage her own affairs. Bruce had lied and bribed the authorities to get control of her money. "Fortune's Gift came from my mother's family, Bruce, as well you know," she said between clenched teeth. "Whatever my father added to my inheritance, he gained through his own wit and hard work. Fortune's Gift is mine. Even Wesley knew that."

"Yours until you take a husband, cousin." His slack mouth turned up in a smile. "Until we are wed."

She drew her silk wrapper more tightly around her and tried to reach the boy she had once played with as a child. "How could you expect me to come to your bed as a loving wife? Do you think I could ever forget that you raped my sister here in this very house?"

"Amanda is a nigra," he said harshly. "None of your pretty words make her skin any whiter."

"Born black, perhaps, but raised by my parents as a daughter in this house. As a sister to Reed and me. She's a free woman, Bruce, not a slave for you to use as your whore."

"Hardly a little nun, your pet nigra. She didn't get that high-yellow pickaninny of hers in church, now, did she?"

Caroline's hands curled into tight balls as she fought to keep her infamous Talbot temper under control. "She has a name, Bruce," she said quietly. "Her name is Amanda. And don't ever call baby Jeremy by that word again."

"I've always wondered if she was Uncle John's by-blow, but she's dark-skinned to be half and half. Is she my cousin too, Caroline? Sometimes, they say, they turn out dark, if one parent is as black as coal."

"You have a filthy mind. But then, you always did. No, she isn't Papa's natural daughter. He was in England that year; he didn't come home to Maryland until two months before Amanda was born. You know where Amanda came from as well as I do. We heard the story often enough when we were children. Papa picked her up out of a rowboat in the river. Just like baby Moses, he always said."

Bruce scoffed. "Moses or not, she was a good lay."

Caroline's fingers itched to slap his arrogant face. Her voice dropped to a whisper. "Leave her alone, I warn you. You touch her again, and that

British uniform won't save you. I'll shoot you myself, just as I shot that mad dog last summer."

"Save your hysterics for someone who will listen," he said, reaching out and taking hold of a lock of her unbound hair. "Red as a fox," he murmured. "I've always fancied to wake up and find a fox-haired woman in my bed."

She jerked free of his loathsome touch, and he laughed. "Bastard," she cried.

"You will marry me, little cousin. One way or another. And you'll learn to curb that foul temper of yours. Once I'm master of Fortune's Gift, you'll—"

The dull boom of an explosion shattered the night. Stunned, Bruce stared at Caroline. "It sounded as though it came from the river," she said, going to a window and peering out into the darkness. A red ball of light flared in the distance. "Is that your powder magazine?"

For a few seconds, there was utter silence, then hounds began to bay furiously. Shouts rang out. A man's gruff voice barked an order. Suddenly, Caroline heard what could only be a musket shot, followed by the pounding of horse's hooves on the frozen lawn. Another Brown Bess roared, just outside the window.

"Son of a bitch!" Bruce swore. He grabbed his coat and jammed an arm into the sleeve as he rushed out of the plantation office and collided with a young orderly.

"Captain Talbot, sir!" the soldier cried. "Come quick! Someone's fired the powder store!"

Bruce shouted back at Caroline, "Go to your room and stay there. I'll deal with you later."

"We'll see who will deal with whom," she murmured after her cousin's retreating back. She grimaced and glanced around the disorderly room.

Only the library wall lined with the precious volumes collected by her parents and grandparents seemed neat. The rest of the office was a shambles. Official dispatches were heaped on the desk and tables; maps of the Chesapeake and Philadelphia were tacked to the paneled walls. Pewter mugs and a dirty plate holding a half-eaten pork chop stood on a mahogany sideboard. The room smelled of rum, tobacco, and sweat.

As she started for the doorway, she noticed a pair of Bruce's tall, black boots standing on the hearth waiting to be cleaned and polished. Expensive boots they were, too, of Spanish leather, she supposed. Or perhaps they were Hessian. Everything German was the fashion now. She glanced down the hall to make certain she was alone, and edged the boots closer to the fire. With any luck at all, they'd be scorched beyond repair before the orderly smelled the burning leather. "We'll see who gets the best of whom, cousin," she said with satisfaction. "I'd burn Fortune's Gift to the ground before I'd let you be master in this house."

Feeling somewhat better, she left the room and walked quickly to the servants' staircase and up the stairs. Dressed as she was in her nightgown and robe she didn't want to meet any of the occupying English soldiers. She had been making ready for bed when Bruce had sent his orderly to summon her to Papa's office. Even though she'd answered his command without waiting to dress, she'd taken the trouble to strap a razor-sharp dagger to her waist. After what Bruce had done to Amanda, she would take no chances with him.

Her Grandfather Kincaid had given her the knife and its accompanying leather sheath on her eighth birthday. A Scottish skean, he'd called it. "Even a great lady must be able to defend herself against enemies," he'd said with a wink. Her father had insisted she would cut off a finger with the antique weapon, but she never had. Grandfather had taught her the finer points of knife fighting and throwing a blade, and he'd made her practice in the hot Maryland sun for more hours than she wanted to remember—with not only a knife, but also a light rapier.

"This is foolishness," her father had said. "Caroline is a Talbot. Talbot men take care of their women."

"Aye," Grandfather had agreed. "That may be so, John, but ye ken the bairn comes from a long line of warrior lassies. And I'd nay wish to have her grandmother say I'd neglected her education."

Dear Grandfather . . . How she missed his weatherworn face. If he were only here, she thought, he'd make short work of Bruce and his dragoons. But he and her beloved Grandmother Bess were lying side by side in the brick-walled family cemetery. They'd died within hours of each other when she was seventeen.

Caroline sighed and entered Amanda's unoccupied room on the second floor and looked out a window. Mounted troops were searching the gardens with torches. She smiled. Evidently, whoever had blown up the powder magazine hadn't been caught yet. She hoped he had a fast horse. Fortune's Gift was crawling with British soldiers.

Major Whitehead had made the plantation the headquarters for his detachment of Light Dragoons. He had been away for several weeks; she didn't know where. If he had been here, Bruce wouldn't have dared to behave so boorishly in her father's office. Major Whitehead might be an English officer and the enemy, but he, at least, was a gentleman.

She had managed well enough with Major Whitehead until her cousin had been assigned to his staff. The major had treated her with the respect due her station, and since his sexual preferences were definitely male, he'd left her and the women of her household in peace. Now, Amanda and Jeremy were forced into hiding in servants' row. Even Caroline didn't know who had given them shelter this night. Since Amanda's rape, they had moved from cabin to cabin to keep Bruce from knowing where they were.

She looked around Amanda's shadowy room and couldn't keep a lump from rising in her throat. Jeremy's rocking horse stood near a window; his toys were piled in his empty cradle. The house seemed empty without his cooing baby laughter and his sweet smell. "Because of you," she murmured, thinking of her foul cousin. "But it won't stay like this, I promise. I'll bring you home, Jeremy. I'll bring you both home."

Patting the lump under her dressing gown to make certain her knife was still in place, she returned to the dark hallway and made her way to her own bedchamber. She turned the knob and pushed open the door, hesitating for a moment, certain she had left a candle burning on the table beside her tall poster bed.

Caroline froze, listening with her ears, but most of all, listening with her inner senses. Her instincts had never failed her yet, and she had come to depend on her own special gifts for knowing what would happen before it actually occurred. She waited, but no current of fear stirred within her breast. Reassured, she entered the room.

And walked straight into something solid.

A sob of fright burst from her lips. "Oh!" she cried. She stopped, momentarily lost in her own bedroom. Her heart raced, numbness spread through her body, and for an instant she wanted to turn and run. Then, when she realized that she'd heard nothing and that no one human or ghostly had grabbed her, she reached out hesitantly with a trembling hand and touched the back of a chair.

She uttered a nervous giggle. "Damn me for a cowardly jade," she burst out.

Her next thought was: What was the chair doing in front of the door? "If Toby's been rearranging my things again, I'll have his ears on a platter," she murmured, feeling the chair to be certain it was her own familiar cane-back seat.

It was indeed, the very chair she'd toppled off when she was four and cut such a slice in her forehead that Grandmother had had to sew it up with silk thread. Caroline still had the tiny scar. "X marks the treasure," Grandmother had said. Caroline had taken pride in not crying when the wound was stitched up, and her grandfather had bought her a new hound puppy, the best one in Wesley's father's kennel.

She began to take normal breaths again, feeling foolish. She took a step toward the bed table and trod upon a cat. The cat let out a yowl and fled toward the open door. Caroline gasped. I must still need a full-time nanny, she thought, shamed by her silly fears. Gathering her courage, she started across the room again.

Without warning, someone clamped a gloved hand over her mouth. She screamed like an Iroquois captive at a torture stake, but only muffled sounds escaped her assailant's iron grip.

Caroline exploded into a fury of flying fists, thrusting knees, and sharp teeth. She was not tall for a woman, but she had ridden every day since she was a babe, and her muscles were strong from swimming in the river and climbing trees. Terror and tenacity made her a formidable foe.

The man in black was as unyielding as a wall of solid oak. Her furious blows wrung gasps of pain from the specter, but he never loosened his cruel embrace.

Then she twisted and slammed her hipbone into his. He buckled and fell to the floor, carrying her down with him and knocking the breath out of her with his weight.

"Caroline! Caroline!" he hissed into her ear. "I won't hurt you. It's Garrett." Cautiously, he removed his hand from her mouth. "For the love of God, Caroline, don't scream. You'll see us both dead."

Stunned, she struggled to get air into her lungs. Garrett? Who the hell was Garrett? She sucked in a deep breath and opened her mouth to scream again.

His hand hovered over her lips so close she could smell the glove leather, and his urgent words seeped into her brain. "Garrett Faulkner. You know me, girl. You've known me for years. I won't hurt you. Just don't yell."

Caroline opened her eyes wide. There was just enough moonlight to make out his features. He did have the look of Garrett. She nodded. "All right," she whispered. "Get off me. I won't cry out."

He sighed. "Jesus Christ, woman, you nearly killed me." She heard what could only be a groan of deep pain. "You're as game as a cornered badger."

He rolled off her, and she scrambled to her knees. "What are you doing in my bedchamber?" she demanded. "Why—" She sucked in her breath sharply. "You're the one they're looking for—the man who blew up the powder magazine."

"Is that what it was? I heard the explosion. No, it wasn't me. It's a total misunderstanding. I . . . I apologize for coming into your house and frightening you, but it was a matter of life and death. Your brother Reed and I were always friends, and . . ." He groaned. "Has the entire world gone mad, Caroline? This cursed rebellion seems to have addled men's minds."

"You're lucky I didn't kill you." Her heart was still pounding. She wasn't sure her knees were strong enough to keep her standing.

"I know. I'm sorry."

"How did you know this was my room?" she snapped. She didn't know whether to call for Bruce's soldiers or to slap Garrett's face. "How dare you come in here and grab me like that?"

"I didn't realize it was your bedchamber. I climbed the poplar tree and came in the nearest window."

"I can see I'll have to keep my windows bolted."

"This isn't funny, I assure you. I was nearly killed."

"I'm not laughing," she said angrily. Her mouth was dry from fear, and she was suddenly cold. "Do you realize what would come of my reputation if you'd been caught climbing in my window? I'm a respectable widow. I'd either be hanged along with you as a traitor or publicly branded a wanton."

"I said I was sorry. I had little choice."

As Caroline listened to Garrett's explanation, it seemed to her that his speech was oddly slurred, as if he were drunk. The whole of the Eastern Shore was aware of Garrett Faulkner's reputation for wine and women, but now that she knew who he was, she was no longer afraid of him. Garrett had given her rides on his horse when she was a child. She couldn't believe he would hurt her. "You've been drinking, haven't you?" she accused, getting to her feet.

"No. I haven't had a drop. On my word as a gentleman! I was riding by on the road when a masked man burst from the hedgerow and galloped past me. Before I could collect my wits, an English dragoon appeared and shot my horse out from under me."

"And you didn't explain the mistake?" It was plain to her that Garrett was lying. But it wasn't possible he was the rebel. Everyone knew the Faulkners were staunch loyalists. Hadn't Garrett served as an officer in the Royal Navy? She wondered if this could be some plot of Bruce's to trick her into an act of treason. Trembling, she walked to the bedside table and fumbled with flint and steel to strike a light.

"No," he warned, "no light."

She lit the thick beeswax candle and anchored it firmly in the silver holder. "This is my chamber. My cousin, Captain Bruce Talbot, is outside. If he doesn't see a light in my window, he'll suspect something is wrong." She fixed Garrett with a suspicious gaze. "Now, why exactly didn't you tell the soldiers about the man you saw riding away?"

"Logic, woman. I'd just had a blooded mare worth ten guineas killed. A dragoon that stupid wouldn't listen to anything I had to say. If I hadn't leaped off my dying horse and run for the bushes, I'd be as dead as my poor Vixen."

Caroline's eyes narrowed as she took in his black greatcoat, black vest, and black breeches. Even Garrett's stockings and boots were black. His tanned face was surprisingly pale in the candlelight. Garrett Faulkner was still boyishly handsome, almost roguish, despite his age and the thin scar down one cheek. He must be . . . She searched her memory. He must be a good ten years older than she was, and she had celebrated her twenty-fifth birthday. No, she mused, Garrett Faulkner had gone away to England the year she'd gotten her skean. He must be at least thirty-seven.

Papa had never liked Reed to associate with him. The Faulkners were all scoundrels, he'd said. She tried to remember if Wesley had ever had anything bad to say about Garrett. The only bit of information that came into her head was that a branch of the family was related to one of the prominent English generals, and that connection had gotten Garrett his commission in the Royal Navy. Evidently, he wasn't suited for a career at sea, because he was back here working his late father's tobacco plantation. "And what business took you abroad on such a cold night?" she asked him.

"I'd planned to see a neighbor of yours about breeding poor Vixen."

"At this time of night?"

"I'm a bachelor, madame. I keep my own hours."

His breath was coming in short gasps. Despite his arrogant speech, and the danger he was in, she sensed something more was wrong. "I am loyal to the crown," she lied sweetly. "If you are a rebel, it's my duty to turn you in."

"Please," he said. "For the sake of our families' friendship. You must know where our allegiance lies. Mother England is—" He tried to rise, grimaced, and fell back to the floor.

"You're hurt." Forgetting her anger, she ran to him and pulled back his coat. A dark stain covered one thigh. When she touched it, she snatched back a hand sticky with blood. "You've been shot," she said.

He gritted his teeth. "Run through with a sword."

"You forgot to mention that."

"I did," he answered. Trusting gray eyes stared into hers. Garrett's classic features looked strained. A spattering of freckles stood out across his well-formed nose. He looked as though he was about to faint. One lock of light brown hair had come loose from his queue and fallen carelessly over his forehead. To her surprise, Caroline had to restrain the impulse to push it back in place.

She tore her gaze from his and saw the red pool on the floor. Her mind raced. It was obvious he would bleed to death without help. If Garrett was working for the Americans against the British, she couldn't let him be captured. And if he wasn't, he was an innocent man. Could she save him without revealing her own loyalties?

"Just help me stand up," he said. "I was wrong to endanger you. I'll leave at once."

"No, no," she said glibly. "Of course I'll help you. Reed would never forgive me if I let you be arrested when you've done nothing wrong. Lie still. I'll find water and bandages for your leg."

He didn't answer, but neither did he try to rise again. She went to the far corner of the room and returned with a pitcher of water, a bowl, and a clean towel. "I'll have to cut your breeches away," she murmured. There was no time for false modesty. If she waited, there might be no one for the dragoons to arrest.

"This is no job for a lady," he said.

"Nonsense. I've tended injuries before. You forget, I grew up here on Fortune's Gift. I'm no dainty town lass."

"One would think otherwise to look at you, Mistress Steele."

"Save your compliments for those who have need of them," she said, helping him to remove his greatcoat and waistcoat. Secretly, she was glad of his talking. It took her mind off the seeping tide of crimson that slipped through her fingers as she used scissors to cut a section out of the good black wool.

The sword wound was surprisingly small. It was obvious that he had taken only a glancing jab and not a full thrust or a slash. "He must have nicked an artery," she murmured, placing pressure on the injury.

Garrett unwound his stock and wrapped that around his thigh, above the wound. He set his teeth and pulled the stock tight. Immediately, the bleeding lessened.

"I'll have to wash this with soap," she warned. "There may be pieces of cloth in the wound. If I leave them, it will turn septic."

"Have your will with me, woman. It hurts so bad, nothing could make it worse."

Deftly, she soaped the tightly muscled area, then rinsed his skin with a corner of the towel and patted it dry. Only a little blood trickled from the inch and a half slit. "It's a wonder you were able to climb the tree," she said to cover her own nervousness.

She hadn't touched a man this intimately since Wesley had gone away and not returned. Garrett's skin was clean where he hadn't bled on it. Even his hair and his garments smelled fresh. The only odors she could detect were those of leather and pine needles. She couldn't help comparing him with her cousin. It was obvious that Garrett bathed regularly, a peculiarity she apparently shared with him.

When the wound was clean and dry, she poured wine over it. Garrett flinched but made no outcry. Then Caroline cut sections of a linen sheet to use as a bandage. "This will go better if you can help me remove your breeches," she said, hoping against hope that he wore something under them.

"That's not necessary."

"Yes, it is." She glanced up from her work. "I have been wed and widowed. I am not a maiden. If you are shy—"

"Not particularly. I was thinking of your sensibilities."

"Don't bother. The sooner we have this properly bandaged, the sooner we can think of a way to get you safely out of here." She felt her cheeks grow warm. "You do have something on . . . something under your . . ."

"No."

"Nothing."

He shrugged. "Only what God gave me."

She pursed her lips. "Then you must try and make yourself decent with this." She removed her dressing gown and draped it across his thighs, leaving herself shivering in the thin shift.

"You are too kind, mistress," he said.

She was certain she heard a thread of amusement in his voice, but she concentrated on slicing away the rest of his breeches, and binding the wound tightly. "You can loosen the stock now," she said. When he did, both of them held their breath. The bandage turned red, but didn't bleed through the linen. Then she mopped up the rest of the blood from the floor, put the towel in the basin, and pushed the evidence under her four-poster. "If I assist you, do you think you can make it to the bed?" she asked. "I can hardly leave you here on the hard floor."

"There's only one way to find out."

The dozen steps to the bed were pure hell. Garrett was of average height and slim of hip and waist, rather than stocky. Still, she remembered how strong he had been when they'd struggled. He might not be a big man, but there was no softness to him; he was all hard muscle and sinew. "Lean on me," she urged him, trying to support his weight. "Don't put any strain on your leg."

His breathing was loud in the shadowy room as she helped him sit on the edge of the bed and remove his shirt, boots, and stockings, without exposing his loins or harming his injury. Finally, with a sigh of relief, she closed her eyes, whisked away the dressing gown, and covered his naked body decently with a sheet and covers. "Drink some of this of wine," she said. "Too much would be bad for you, but a little may take the edge off the pain."

"I'd not argue with that," he said.

She poured a goblet of wine, handed it to him, and hung his greatcoat, shirt, and waistcoat over the cane-back chair. She had begun to tidy up the room when she heard loud voices and the crash of doors being thrown open. Dashing to the door, she slid the bolt. The hard tread of men's boots sounded on the staircase.

Seconds later, a fist pounded on her door. "Open up, Caroline! We're searching all the rooms," Bruce commanded.

She twisted around and glanced back at Garrett. He was checking the priming on his pistol. She put her finger to her lips and shook her head.

"Caroline!" Bruce called again. "Open up!"

She crept back across the room to the bed. "What do you want?" she asked in what she hoped was a sleepy voice. "There's no one in here."

"Open the door before we break it in!"

Garrett slipped the loaded pistol under the sheets. Caroline looked from him to the door. Sweat beaded on his forehead.

"Go away," she shouted. "You have no right to invade my bedchamber."

The heavy stock of a Brown Bess musket slammed against the door. "What do we do?" she whispered urgently. Garrett shrugged, but his gray eyes narrowed dangerously.

"No," she said. "Not that way." Without thinking, she slid into bed beside him and pulled the covers up to her waist. "Let them think what they will," she said. "I'll not let them have you."

The door shuddered under a second blow.

Garrett's gaze locked with hers and he grinned wolfishly. Before she could stop him, he reached across and seized the neck of her shift with both hands and ripped it to her waist. Caroline cried out with indignation as the door burst open and her cousin charged into the room, followed closely by four armed dragoons.

Chapter 2

Garrett's arm tightened around Caroline's shoulders at the exact instant she yanked a sheet up to cover her naked breasts. "What's the meaning of this outrage?" Garrett demanded of the British officer.

The captain's mouth gaped open in astonishment. When he finally managed to close it, he stammered, "You . . . you common strumpet." The dragoons behind him trod on each others' heels to get a good look at Mistress Steele and her lover caught *in flagrante delicto.*

Garrett silenced Caroline's protest by pulling her facedown against his bare chest and holding her there with an iron grip. "Have you no sense of common decency, sir?" Garrett admonished in his most rigid tones. "I had heard that you were a gentleman." The lady's breasts were warm, full, and deliciously soft. Under any other circumstances, Garrett would have found the situation most pleasurable. As it was, he decided, neither of them could give their predicament the attention it deserved.

The captain's face contorted with anger. "Arrest that man!" he ordered, stabbing a finger toward the bed.

Garrett uttered what he hoped was a convincing laugh. "Since when, Captain . . . Talbot, is it? Since when is it a crime in Maryland to share the bed of a willing widow?"

Garrett's right hand was occupied keeping Caroline pinned down. In his left he held the hidden flintlock, the pistol he dared not use. If he fired, he could kill the officer, but he had only one shot, and there were four dragoons. Not good odds, but a gamble he'd willingly take if it were not for the woman laying beside him. No, the danger to Caroline Steele was too great. He would have to talk himself out of this snare or surrender. The thought was bitter enough to bring bile rising in his throat.

Caroline's lips were in direct contact with his skin, as were her teeth. "Darling," she murmured. Or was it *Damn you?* Her husky voice was muffled by the covers.

Garrett's eyes teared up and he tried not to wince as she nipped him so sharply that he was certain she'd drawn blood. "There, there, sweet," he said. "Let me handle this."

"I said arrest that man!" Talbot repeated. Two dragoons started toward the bed.

"You're making a huge mistake," Garrett warned. Sweat trickled down the back of his neck. The dragoons hesitated.

Talbot drew himself up to his full height. "We are in search of a traitor who blew up a powder storage belonging to His Majesty not sixty minutes past," he declared. "You are under arrest for suspicion of treasonous acts."

"Me?" Garrett laughed again. "The only suspicious acts I've committed were by leave of the lady between these sheets." He looked down at the mass of dark red curls spread across his chest. "I've been here since the clock struck eight, isn't that so, Caroline?" Luck, don't fail me now, he prayed fervently as he loosened his hold on her and flashed his most charming smile. In the split-second before she twisted to face the captain and his menacing soldiers, she shot him a look that would have sunk a man-of-war.

"That's true," she said. Her words came out a whisper, and she repeated her statement. "What he says is true. Garrett . . . Garrett has been here in my chamber all night."

"A pretty story, little cousin," Talbot said. "Nevertheless, we will take the gentleman into custody and—"

Garrett yawned. "I feel it only fair to warn you, sir," he said in a condescending manner. "This act will ruin your career. I have high family connections."

The closest dragoon took one step back and glanced at his captain.

"I care nothing for your family." Talbot frowned. "You are a Faulkner, aren't you? James?"

Garrett shook his head and settled himself against the pillow nonchalantly. Caroline's fingernails were cutting into his good leg, and his injured leg throbbed like all the demons in hell were jabbing it with pitchforks. Not only was he certain he couldn't stand on the leg, but it felt as though it was bleeding again. If they pulled back the covers, the game was over. "I am most assuredly not James. I am his cousin, Garrett Faulkner of Faulkner's Folly, late an officer of His Majesty's Royal Navy. And since you know my family, doubtless you know that my late father was blood cousin to your commander, Lord Cornwallis."

Indecision showed on Talbot's face. "You expect me to believe that?"

"Of course they are related," Caroline said. "It's been common gossip on the Eastern Shore. How else do you suppose a colonial like Garrett received a naval commission?"

"For God's sake, man, you've made a mistake.

While you're harassing me, the real villain is getting away. I live only twenty miles from here as the crow flies. Lord Cornwallis is in Philadelphia. Send a courier to him and ask if he will vouch for me. If you care to arrest me later, anyone can tell you where to find me. It's not as though I'd travel for my health in the midst of rebellion."

Garrett gritted his teeth against the waves of pain, leaned forward, and kissed Caroline's neck. "Meanwhile, you're embarrassing Mistress Steele." He made a lofty gesture of dismissal with his chin. "You might, at least, dismiss your troops. I hardly think you're in any danger from either of us."

"Very well. We will wait and see what Lord Cornwallis has to say." Talbot motioned to the dragoons. "You are dismissed. Pass the word that Mr. Faulkner is not to leave this house until I say otherwise." He scowled at Garrett. "If you aren't telling the truth, it will go very hard on you."

"Not as hard as it will go on you if you embarrass Lord Cornwallis by making outrageous accusations against your commander's relatives," Caroline observed.

Talbot growled an order, and the soldiers hurried out of the room. When they were gone, Talbot moved closer to the bed. "Caroline is my cousin," he said brusquely. "I am also the legal guardian of her affairs. As her closest male relative—"

"I have a brother," Caroline interrupted. "And I am quite capable of managing my own affairs."

Garrett sniffed. "Let the captain finish, darling."

"You have shamed this house," Talbot said, glaring at Caroline. "You sicken me—pretending respectability while all the while you're wallowing with this—this—"

"Careful," Garrett said. "Insulting your own

cousin is a family matter, but if you sully my name, I'll call you out on the field of honor."

"I assure you, Mr. Faulkner, it is only this uniform and my duty to my king that keep me from challenging you to answer for this disgusting behavior."

Garrett reached for his wine goblet and took a long, deliberate sip. "Really? You believe this to be disgusting behavior?" He smiled thinly. "Does your taste lie elsewhere, sir?"

Veins stood out on Talbot's forehead. "Don't try and leave this house," he warned. "And you—" He looked back at Caroline. "I will deal with you later. For now, cover your nakedness and take yourself to another bedchamber as long as this . . . this *gentleman* is a guest at Fortune's Gift." He spun on his heel and stalked from the room.

"I don't believe your cousin likes me," Garrett said as Talbot's footsteps reached down the hallway. Caroline drew back her hand and slapped him full in the face.

"Bastard!" she said as she struggled out of bed on the far side and tried to hold her shift together with one hand while donning her dressing gown with the other.

By sheer will Garrett forced down his own temper and tried not to let her know how much her blow had stung his face and his pride. "I suppose I had that coming," he said slightly. "But it was your idea."

"My idea to save your neck," she retorted hotly. "Not to bare myself for the entire British army." Red spots of fury tinted her cheekbones as she circled the bed. "How dare you?" She seized a blue glass perfume vial from a table and threw it against the nearest wall. The glass shattered, filling the room with the scent of roses. "You bastard," she repeated. "How dare you put me in that position? I'm ruined. I'll never be able to show my face in Oxford again. By tomorrow, this gossip will be all over Annapolis."

"It was your choice." He winked at her. "We were convincing, weren't we? Much more so than with you sitting primly on your side of the bed."

"Damn you to hell." She drew back her hand again.

"No more of that," he said. This time he couldn't prevent his underlying anger from surfacing. "Break all the china you wish, little heiress, but never hit me again." His scorching gaze met her fiery one, and the air sizzled between them. "I have never struck a woman, but I won't be abused by one either."

"I should tell my cousin the truth and let him hang you," she threatened.

"He won't, not if he actually contacts dear Cousin Cornwallis. I was telling the truth, you know. I'm not a rebel," he lied smoothly. Damn, but she was a beauty with those huge russet eyes and that glorious hair. Too bad she didn't have a gentle disposition to go with her looks, he mused. He'd never favored women with uncontrollable tempers . . . perhaps because his own was so bad. "Besides," he added, "if you tell him now, you'll look as guilty as I do."

"Are you a rebel?"

"Good God, woman, of course not. I am as loyal to the king and country as you are."

She moistened her lips. "Then why did you pick tonight to come into my house and destroy my life?"

"It was not by choice. I told you, this was all a misunderstanding."

"Of course." She drew the dressing gown tightly

around her. "There is no one here I can trust," she said. "I will return in the morning to tend your wound again." She started toward the door.

"And the bites on my chest?"

She glanced back and smiled sweetly at him. "I hope they poison you."

Minutes later, in Amanda's bedchamber, Caroline slid a chest of drawers in front of the bolted door. How had she come to this—a prisoner in her own house? Only two years before, she and Wesley had made such plans for the future. They'd even talked about having a child . . .

She brought her knotted fists up to her closed eyes in despair. They had been so happy until the dispute with English rule flared into open rebellion. Wesley had known immediately where his loyalties lay. He had been born here on the Eastern Shore of Maryland; his parents and grandparents had been born here, as had her own family. This was home, and if their neighbors raised weapons against British taxation without representation, against the seizing of American sailors at sea, and against harsh laws, the two of them must join the dissenters. For Wesley, that meant sailing with one of the daring privateers the new Continental Congress had authorized to harry the English warships and run the blockade that kept much-needed military and civilian supplies out of the thirteen Colonies. And two months after Wesley joined the crew of the captain known only as Osprey, her only brother, Reed, had signed on. She was left at home to run Fortune's Gift and to provide as much food and clothing as she could for the Maryland militia.

Despite the many Tories who lived on the Eastern Shore, she had organized women to make stockings, to weave cloth for uniforms, and to tan hides to sew moccasins. She had instructed the workers of Fortune's Gift to raise flocks of geese, pigs, and cattle to be slaughtered, salted, and sent north for the soldiers. And she had accomplished it all while pretending to be a loyal servant of King George. She had entertained Tory leaders and welcomed English soldiers into her home, a ploy that had backfired when Major Whitehead decided to make Fortune's Gift his headquarters. That move had put an end to her provisioning of the Continentals.

For months, Osprey had cut a swath through British sea defenses, robbing English merchant vessels, and once sinking an enemy warship off the Delaware coast. Then the unthinkable had happened. Osprey had betrayed his crew and his country. He had surrendered his ship in the face of British cannon fire and condemned his men to death or imprisonment for piracy.

It had been an act of infamy for which Caroline had sworn to make Osprey pay dearly. "No, you'll not escape my justice," she murmured softly. "If it costs me my immortal soul, I'll see you dead—as cold and lifeless as Wesley."

She had been hosting a birthday party for Major Whitehead the night friends had carried her husband's body home. No one could tell her what had happened to her brother Reed. It was late summer before one of Haslett's Delaware scouts, a Continental, had come to tell her that her brother was reportedly alive and a prisoner of the English in New York.

By that time Bruce had come to Fortune's Gift and his threats had begun. It was no secret that Reed was an American sympathizer, but Wesley had been more cautious. Knowing full well that his actions jeopardized her position as heiress to Fortune's Gift, Wesley had never openly declared that he was a rebel. Caroline had been able to pass his death off to Major Whitehead as an accidental drowning.

Her cousin Bruce believed otherwise and had taken immediate steps to gain control of her finances. Since most of her gold was invested in London, where as an unknown woman she could not hope to prevail against her male cousin, she had been helpless to stop him. And now he was trying to force her to marry him. The thought was revolting. "I'd sooner be dead," she murmured into the empty room.

"Dead is a long time."

She turned toward the soft, lisping voice and saw the familiar ghostly figure standing by the window, outlined by moonlight. "Kutii," she said.

The Incan folded his arms over his bare chest. "And who else would it be, daughter of my house?"

"Where have you been?" she demanded. "You pick the worst times to vanish. Amanda is—"

"Your sister is in great danger."

"Yes, I know. Bruce raped—"

"This one has seen the evil that passed in this room. But the danger is greater than that. I have come to warn you, my heart. You must leave this place. Swiftly."

"What more can Bruce do to her?" Caroline asked, moving toward Kutii. She held out her hands to him, wishing he could take her in his arms and make her safe. Since she was a child, the old ghost had listened to her sorrows and given her wise advice. "He wants to marry me," she said in a strained whisper.

"He wants this land. Like others before him, he

will kill to take it." Kutii turned his hawk face toward her. His eyes were pools of obsidian blackness. "If you become his wife, you will die by his hand, and your sister will be sold into slavery."

"No," she protested. "He can't do that. Amanda is a free woman. Amanda and Jeremy are both free."

"While demons walk this place, there can be no freedom. I, who was once guardian to the royal house of my people, know these things. I have been a slave. I have known the feel of the whip and the taste of dust in my mouth. Flee from this land, child. Take your sister and her little one and flee."

"Leave Fortune's Gift? How could I? Where would I go?"

The purring of a cat sounded loud in the room. Kutii bent and picked up the bedraggled creature, scratching behind the nub of his left ear. "There is a time to stand and fight, daughter of my daughter, and there is a time to run."

Moonlight gleamed off the silver armband encircling his left bicep. She could barely make out the pagan tattoos that covered his face and chest. His hair hung loose to his waist, a curtain of black silk that rippled when he moved. Despite the cold, he wore only a breechcloth around his loins and sandals of twisted rope on his feet. Round disks of gold hung from his ears. The only weapon he carried was a curious stone knife in a feathered sheath at his waist. He smelled of the sea.

"Have you been with her?" she asked him.

Kutii laughed, a comforting sound like wind through the marsh reeds. "The Star Woman," he said. "Her blood runs strong in your veins. Do not forget that it was she who first claimed this land.

You must hold it for those who will come after you, no matter what the price."

"How can you tell me to hold Fortune's Gift and run away at the same time? You're not making any sense, Kutii."

"Use your own power. Do what you must do."

His image flickered.

"No," she protested. "Don't go. I need you, Kutii. You're all I have."

"Her blood," he repeated, but the words were already faint. "Her blood runs in you."

There was a swirling shimmer of color, and then his image faded. Cat and man were gone. Caroline was alone in the room again.

"Don't do this to me," she cried. "Kutii. You stupid ghost. Come back. I . . . I need you."

"Caroline? Is someone in there with you?" Her cousin's voice came from outside the door. "Open up. We need to talk."

"Go away," she said. "There's no one here, and no reason for you to be in my room."

"After what you've done, you can talk to me like that?" He rapped soundly on the door. "Open up, I say."

Caroline closed her eyes. For an instant, the room receded and she saw the dock at Annapolis. It was still winter; there was a crusting of dirty snow on the boards. She sucked in her breath, hard. She could see her sister Amanda clearly. Amanda's wrists were bound, and she was weeping and stretching out her arms. "Jeremy," Amanda cried. "Please! Don't take my baby." Then a strange man slapped her and began to drag her toward a farm wagon. "Jeremy!" Amanda screamed again.

"Caroline! I warn you."

She opened her eyes, shaken by the power of

the vision. Usually, such visions came to her when she tried to think of what was going to happen. The clarity of this scene shocked her. She shook her head, trying to dispel her confusion. Was her *seeing* a warning of a possible threat, or was it a certainty?

"Caroline."

She ignored Bruce and considered what had just happened to her. Caroline had been born with the gift of clairvoyance. It was as much her legacy as Fortune's Gift. Her mother had possessed a sixth sense, not as strong as that of Caroline's Grandmother Bess but real nonetheless. And when she was small, Grandmother Bess had told Caroline that the power came from *her* Grandmother Lacy, whom Kutii called Star Woman, and before that from a wild gypsy woman in old England.

"It's a God-given blessing," Grandmother Bess had explained. "But only those who carry the gift can hope to understand it. Others will fear you and call you a witch. Learn to use your power. Cultivate it, harness it. Never be afraid of it, and never think it to be the devil's work." Her grandmother had warned her against letting outsiders know of her sight.

Seeing Kutii's ghost was part of her gift. Most people couldn't see him, and only her Grandmother Bess had ever admitted to hearing him speak. Her mother had insisted that Kutii was just a story, a tale made up to frighten servants. Mother never denied that Kutii had once lived on Fortune's Gift. A moss-covered stone with his name on it stood in the oldest part of the family cemetery.

"An Incan Indian, to be sure," Mother had said, "but flesh and blood. An old servant, dead and buried and forgotten, at least by everyone except fanciful little girls."

But Caroline knew that Kutii's spirit walked the paths and halls of Fortune's Gift, as surely as she knew she possessed the sight of that far-off gypsy ancestor. Never had a vision come as strong and clear as this one had. And following hard on the heels of Kutii's appearance, it frightened her.

Amanda and Jeremy were in terrible danger. And so was she . . .

"You have one minute to unlock this door, or I'll have my soldiers break it in," Bruce threatened.

"For what purpose?" she asked, moving close to the wooden panel. "Your suspect lies asleep in my bedchamber. You have no business here, and unless you intend to assault me, you'll go away and leave me alone."

"Do you honestly believe your whoring with that popinjay will alter my plans for our marriage? I mean to have you and Fortune's Gift, Caroline. And I mean to have them soon. Now open this door. What you give so easily to another should be offered to your betrothed."

"Go to hell, Bruce!" she flung back. "Try and break this door down and I'll scream my head off. Then you can explain your behavior to both Major Whitehead and Lord Cornwallis."

"How long do you expect to hide in this room?"

"Until tomorrow."

"Until tomorrow then, sweet cousin. Just keep in mind that I have a long memory. And you and your precious Amanda will pay dearly for this rudeness."

She waited, heart pounding, breathless, until she heard him walk away, then turned back toward the window. What do I do now? she wondered. Where do I run, Kutii?

And then her gaze fell on an object lit by a single shaft of moonlight. On Amanda's bedside table next to the candlestand lay a simple conch shell. She picked up the shell and cradled it in her hands. Amanda had always loved the ivory and blue conch. When they were children, they would put the shell to their ears and listen to the echoes of a faraway ocean.

"Arawak Island," she whispered. A shiver passed through her. Was it possible? Could she and Amanda and Jeremy reach Arawak far south in the Caribbean? "There has to be a way. There has to be."

Chapter 3

A faint purple haze glowed in the eastern sky and the moon was still a pale ghost of its midnight glory when Caroline changed into a fresh kersey gown and tied an apron around her waist. She had slept in fitful interludes, and what rest she did find was troubled by dreams of red-coated dragoons and terrible images of Wesley's drowned face. Normally, her maid would help her to dress and arrange her hair, but there was no time for that this morning. She washed her face and hands in icy water and dragged an ivory comb through her unruly curls. After securing the heavy mass with a black velvet ribbon, she pinned a lady's cap of Irish linen over her hair.

Her face took even less time. She had been blessed with her Grandmother Bess's flawless complexion, so she used only a dusting of powder, a bit of rouge for her lips, and the slightest hint of kohl on her thick lashes. Her eyes were her greatest asset, wide-spaced, large, and cinnamon-brown. A shy smile and a sideways glance through those long lashes had caused more than one Tidewater gallant to come to blows with rival gentlemen.

Caroline knew she was no great beauty by fashionable standards that demanded gentlewomen to be delicate and blond. Not only was her hair an impossible riot of rude auburn, but her body was too lush, her mouth too full, and her chin too firm. Vibrant, she had been called by suitors. Caroline chuckled. Vanity was not her chief sin. She could have been squint-eyed and bald, and still the road to Fortune's Gift would have been well traveled by those hoping to raise their station in life by marriage to a land-rich heiress.

No, she did not primp and fuss for the sake of vanity. She used her charms as she did her silks and satins. Her name, her family's wealth, and the honor of Fortune's Gift were all that kept her from being abused by the occupying British army. Amanda had not been the only woman raped.

In late August when the British admiral, Lord Richard Howe, had landed at Head of Elk with over twenty thousand men, there had been widespread rape, murder, and looting by the English troops. Even peaceful Quakers and farmers loyal to the throne had suffered. Benjamin Turner's Irish indentured girl, Tess, had been violated and murdered in Chestertown, and the oldest Dempsey girl on Long Neck had vanished the night a company of Tory soldiers had moved out. And closer to home, a tavern wench in Oxford had been attacked by three British soldiers.

As long as Caroline's class and status protected her, she could use that position to help her servants and friends. As long as she could play the part of a loyal Englishwoman, she could keep her home from falling into the hands of her cousin or being burned to the ground, as the British had burned Thompson's Chance on the Choptank River.

Will Thompson had been declared a traitor because he'd killed a British officer who was trying to abduct his niece. Will had been hanged, his old father beaten senseless, his livestock confiscated, and his surviving children parceled out to loyal Tory families. Will's wife had died in the fire. Some said she ran back into the burning house to rescue her deaf and blind son Edgar; others claimed she had lost her mind. Her younger sister, Abbie, was hidden here in the attic of Fortune's Gift, along with Will's fourteen-year-old niece, Mary.

Amanda, Abbie, Mary, and countless other women, some white, some brown, all depended on Caroline's wit for survival. If she made a mistake, she would take them all down with her.

"Sweet God in heaven," she murmured under her breath as she slid the heavy piece of furniture away from her door. "Garrett Faulkner could not have chosen a worse time to come to my door."

Cautiously, she peered out into the shadowy hallway. Her chamber door was closed. She must order the lock repaired first thing this morning. She'd not sleep a wink, knowing Bruce had access to her room. In stockinged feet, carrying her shoes, she tiptoed down the hall to the servants' staircase.

In the kitchen, Hannah was stirring up the coals to begin the morning's work. "I tole Toby to get Randy to fix yore door right after breakfast, mistress," the black woman said. "It ain't right, Cap'n Bruce comin' into yore house and breakin' up stuff. He ain't got no business here." A single dark eye narrowed in righteous anger. Hannah had fallen into an open fire when she was a toddler, and half her face and one arm were horribly scarred.

What have we come to in Maryland, Caroline thought, when only a woman so afflicted is safe to come and go without fear of molestation? "He's a bastard, Hannah," she agreed. "But then, Bruce always was."

A kitchen boy entered with an armload of wood. "Mornin', ma'am," he said shyly, ducking his head.

"Good morning, Owen," Caroline answered, pleased to see that the Welsh lad was putting some meat on his bones. He'd been little more than a scarecrow when Wesley had purchased his indenture in Chestertown.

Caroline waited until the boy left the kitchen, then gathered bread, a jug of cider, cheese, and some cold chicken in a split oak basket and covered the food with a clean cloth. "I'd like a pitcher of hot water," she said. "And my medicine box, if you please."

Hannah nodded. "Yes'm."

"Amanda—" Caroline began.

Hannah raised a twisted finger to her lips. "She's fine. Baby cuttin' a tooth, but other than that, both fine. Don't worry, Miss Caroline. We keep them safe."

Caroline nodded her thanks. The free blacks on Fortune's Gift were strong, proud people. Many of them still practiced the old religions their ancestors had brought from Africa, and they spoke a mixture of English and their native tongues. They worked for her, but they didn't belong to her. Most, she considered her friends, but she knew she could never really understand them. The chasm yawning between her and a woman like Hannah was too great to be crossed except in times of mutual danger.

Even Amanda's dark skin didn't make her one of them. Amanda was a black Englishwoman, Hannah said. "Too far from the kettle and the gourd." But they loved Amanda just the same—loved her for her caring hands and gentle ways—and they would risk their lives to keep her safe.

Caroline went back up the servants' winding staircase to the third floor, entered a tiny storage room, and opened a hidden door to climb a ladder to the hidden room in the attic. Mary and Abbie were waiting, frantic for a few minutes' conversation. But today, Caroline had no time. She reassured them that she would get them away from Fortune's Gift as soon as she could, left the food, and returned to the kitchen to get the hot water and medical kit with which to tend Garrett.

He came awake as she tiptoed into his room. "Shhh," Caroline warned him. She closed the door behind her, but she couldn't lock it against Bruce's soldiers.

Two of the chamber windows caught the first rays of morning sun. There was no need for a candle to light the way. "How is it?" she asked.

Garrett gritted his teeth and sat up.

She saw the effort he made and compassion flooded over her. No matter how much trouble he'd caused, she reminded herself, she was almost certain that Garrett had been injured in the American cause. She owed him whatever support she could give him for Reed and Wesley's sake. "I've brought you some clothes of my husband's," she said. "I'll tend your wound again, but you'll have to come down to breakfast in the west parlor. If you don't, it will look suspicious."

"You expect me to come down and share breakfast with that barbarian cousin of yours?" he asked.

"No, with me. I don't eat with Bruce." She scowled at him. "They aren't stupid. Whoever ran you through with a sword reported that the suspect is wounded. You can't appear hurt. And if you aren't ill, it's only natural that you'd dine with me."

"Mother of God," he grumbled. "You expect me to walk on this leg and make small talk at the breakfast table?"

"I didn't invite you here," she reminded him. "This mess is all your doing." She went to the bedside and drew aside a lower corner of the blanket, taking care not to bare more of him than was necessary. "Oh," she gasped. The bandage she had applied the night before was stiff with blood. "I'll have to soak this off."

"I was afraid you'd say that."

She made her voice stern to cover her nervousness. It had been a long time since she'd been so intimate with a man. It was impossible not to notice Garrett's sleek muscular shoulders, his well-formed biceps—impossible to forget what it felt like lying naked pressed against him. "I've not forgiven you for what you did last night," she said, trying to tear her eyes from the vee of golden hair that ran down the center of his chest. "I'm doing this because you are my brother's friend, and he would expect no less of me."

Her mouth felt dry, her hands shaky. Butterflies fluttered in the pit of her stomach. I'm scared, she told herself. Afraid of being caught by Bruce's dragoons. But it wasn't just that. It was Garrett.

She had never been shy in the company of men. Her father and grandfather had included her on fishing trips and fox hunts. She had sat up late at night and listened to old war veterans relate stories of wilderness battles with the French and chilling tales of pirates off the Carolina coast. When she was a child, most of her friends had been boys. She had wrestled with them, run races with them, and won her share of rough-and-tumble fistfights. Later, when she had blossomed as a woman, she had delighted in dances, parties, and weddings. Aside from a few girlish crushes, she had never known awkwardness with a man.

Now she was twenty-five, a grown woman, wed and widowed. She had no cause to act like a lovesick goose girl with this rascal Garrett Faulkner.

But she had never been so aware of a man's masculinity before. And she had no defense against him.

Drops of water spilled over the sides of the bowl as she placed it on the floor beside the bed. "I'll try not to hurt you," she said, "but . . ."

He touched her shoulder, and she jerked away as though she had been stung by a wasp. "I'm sorry," he said.

Heat washed through her. She could not meet his eyes. Instead, she concentrated on cutting away the bloody bandage. She heard him suck in his breath, but he made no other sound as she uncovered the gaping wound and began to wash it with warm, soapy water. "It's not closing as it should," she said. "I'll have to sew it shut."

"Wonderful."

She opened her medical kit and took out a needle and fine silk thread, then went to the window to thread it. He's only a man, she told herself. Just because half the women on the Tidewater are all throwing themselves at his feet is no reason for me to play the fool. He probably expected her to fall into his arms. She was a widow, after all, and widows were supposed to be starved for a man's attentions.

It had never been like that for her. Wesley's death had stunned her. And when she'd begun to recover from the shock, she'd had Bruce and half the British army to contend with. No, she'd not thought of bedding with a man. Until this moment . . .

On the third try, the silk thread slid through the eye of the needle. Taking a deep breath, she came back and knelt beside him. "I'll be as quick as I can," she said.

"Just make it neat," he quipped. "I've an image to uphold."

She clamped her lips together and pierced his flesh with the steel needle. Garrett didn't flinch. Carefully, she drew the thread through, mopped away the beads of blood, and took another stitch. Tears clouded her vision and she blinked them away. What had to be done, had to be done. And there was no one else she could trust to do it.

Garrett let out his breath with a low oath as she tied the last knot and cut the thread with her sewing scissors. Then she washed the surface of the stitches with a measure of raw rum and covered it with a dressing of willow bark. She laid a pad of clean linen over the wound and bound it tightly with fresh bandages. After pulling the blanket back over him, she went to wash her hands with lye soap and water from the pitcher.

"Thank you," he said. "I couldn't have done better myself."

She dried her hands on her apron. "I shouldn't think you could do as well," she replied. "I am known for my fine needlework."

"Ah, a lady with practical talent."

"Little use there is for fancy stitching since this rebellion began."

"I suppose not."

She looked at him. The morning sunlight dusted his wheat-colored hair with flecks of gold. She moistened her lips with the tip of her tongue and tried not to think of how hard and muscular his thigh had been under her hands. Like coiled steel . . .

"Don't think that because I've tended your injury you can take further liberties," she chided. "I only did it so you can get well and leave my house."

"I thought you helped me for your brother's sake."

She felt her cheeks grow warm. "Both." She straightened her spine. "Reed will be furious when he hears how you've ruined my reputation."

"Where is Reed?" Garrett's voice was no longer teasing.

"He is . . . away," she lied. She would not tell Garrett that her brother was in prison . . . not yet, anyway.

"But . . ." He hesitated. "There was some rumor that he—"

"Reed is alive and well," she hastened to say.

"I'm glad to hear it." There was no doubt of his sincerity. "And I am sorry about last night. It seemed the only way at the time."

"Easily said, but I must live with the consequences. My cousin will make things very difficult for me now." She removed her apron and bundled up all the soiled bandages and slid them under the bed.

"How long before someone looks under there?" he asked.

"I'll have Toby change your sheets and carry everything to the washhouse this morning. No one will question him."

"You seem to have thought this out very well, Mistress Steele."

"I always do."

"Whenever you're caught with a gentleman in your room?" he dared.

"Every time," she countered, and then laughed. "You're impossible," she said. "No gentleman would ever—"

He flashed a boyish grin. "I rarely call myself a gentleman."

"I can understand why."

"You're not going to leave without helping me get dressed," he said. "I don't think I can manage alone."

A quick retort rose to her lips, but she bit it back. What he said was true. How could he bend over to dress himself? "Very well, this one time," she agreed, "but I am no gentleman's maid."

Smiling, he lay back against the pillows, raising first one arm and then the other as she pulled a white lawn shirt over his head. She had often helped Wesley with his shirt and waistcoat, and usually she had ended up wrapping and tying the stock around his neck. She had done it for him the last morning she saw him alive . . .

It felt odd to be performing this familiar task for a stranger. "You are bigger than Wesley," she said. But it wasn't quite true. Wesley had been heavier and somewhat taller than Garrett, but his shoulders had never stretched the fabric of his shirts so tightly. Again, the queer feeling within her surfaced, and she found herself struggling to keep her breathing even. "Can you manage the breeches alone?"

"No."

It was impossible to miss the amused glint in

his gray eyes. "I don't find this funny," she snapped.

"Nor I," he said. "Usually beautiful women are undressing me, not the other way around."

She ignored the remark. "You'll have to sit on the edge of the bed."

"I'll need your assistance."

She wrapped an arm under his shoulder and helped him slide over. He groaned and turned pale when she eased his legs over the side. "Careful," she warned.

Sweat broke out on his forehead. "I think I'm going to be sick."

"Don't you dare." She averted her eyes and covered his loins with a corner of the sheet. "Your stockings are ruined. You'll have to wear these gray ones." His feet were high arched and clean. Even his toenails were cut straight across. Businesslike, she rolled the stockings over his bare feet and up over his rock-hard calves. "For a seaman you've spent a lot of time on horseback," she commented. The words spilled out before she realized what she'd said. He chuckled, and she blushed scarlet. There was no hiding the fact that she'd noticed and was commenting favorably on his shapely legs.

Getting the breeches on him was worse. She was certain he was deliberately making the task more difficult than it should have been. "Devil take you," she murmured as she leaned behind him to tuck in the tails of the shirt and tie the waistline.

"I have no doubt he'll try," Garrett said.

Seething, she helped him into his own waistcoat and boots. "Next time, I'll send Toby to help you," she said. "You are enjoying this far too much."

"Ouch," he said as she gave a tug on the bottom

of his waistcoat. "You forget I'm a dangerously ill man."

"Believe me, sir, I haven't forgotten. It's all that's keeping you from the king's justice." She picked up his coat and tossed it to him. "There's a clean stock on the table. Surely you can put that on yourself. There's nothing wrong with your arms." She turned toward the door, then glanced back at him. "When you come downstairs, don't anger Bruce unnecessarily. He's a such a fool, it's a temptation, but he is a dangerous man."

"I'll keep that in mind."

Caroline took her green hooded cloak from a peg on the wall and draped it around her shoulders as she left the room. It was growing late, and before breakfast she had to give instructions to her foreman for the day's work. With luck, she would hear word of her sister, but she would not seek Amanda out. It was better that she and little Jeremy remain hidden and out of Bruce's reach.

This time, she took the front stairs, ignoring the armed guard who stood at the bottom of the steps. Instead of leaving by the main entranceway, she turned right and followed the hall to the kitchen wing of the house. She saw Toby had paused long enough to whisper instructions about disposing of the bloody sheets and bandages in her chamber, then hurried on through the winter kitchen and out into the service courtyard of the manor house.

A black and tan hound raised its head as she strode past down the worn brick walk. And from the corner of her eye, Caroline saw a scarred black cat sunning himself on the rim of the well. "Good day to you, Harry," she murmured. The cat yawned and stretched.

"Morning, mistress," Cook called. He balanced a basket of side meat and smoked duck on his shoulder. Behind him, a chubby blond boy carried a bucket of milk, so warm and fresh that steam rose in the crisp morning air.

She smiled at the lad. Jacob might be a deaf-mute, but he was quick to learn and Cook liked him. She'd not be surprised if Cook and his Nanticoke Indian wife, Sara, took the boy into their household. Cook wasn't getting any younger, and Jacob seemed a better prospect to apprentice under the kitchen master than any of his own surly brats.

Caroline followed the path past the smoke and wash houses, through the fallow kitchen garden crusted with crystals of ice, and around the poultry yard where a flock of speckled hens were vigorously scratching the damp earth for worms. Two roosters, feathers ruffled, necks arched, danced around each other in mock battle, while a third clung to a fence rail and crowed mightily.

Caroline stopped at the yellow poplar tree as she and her Grandmother Bess had always done and looked back at the rambling brick house with smoke trailing from the chimneys. Instantly, she felt the warmth of her grandmother's arms around her, and a lump of emotion rose in her throat.

"Fortune's Gift, child." If Caroline listened hard, she could hear her grandmother's familiar voice. "It's yours to love and cherish. Good men died for this land. I passed the treasure to your mother, and from her hands, it goes to you and yours. Hold the land close, child. Hold it until hell grows potatoes, and it will never fail you."

"Until hell grows potatoes," Caroline murmured. With a sigh, she continued on toward the stables and her meeting with her foreman. Fortune's Gift had no overseer and it had no slaves. It was a family tradition. Always, the heiress to the plantation decided when to plant and when to harvest, when to cut new fields from forest, and when to sell the bounty of Fortune's Gift.

Mordecai Brown was waiting for her near the big pound. Within the high board fence a chestnut stallion and a bay mare pranced and chased each other around the enclosure. "I guess it's a love match, Miss Caroline," Mordecai said as she approached.

"Good," she answered, smiling. "As much as we had to pay for the stud, it would be a pity if none of the girls liked him." She laid her fingertips lightly on the top rail. "He's a beauty, isn't he, Mordecai."

"He is that."

For long moments they watched the two horses in silence, and Caroline drank in the peaceful sounds and smells of the barnyard—the rich scents of the animals, the soft lowing of a calf for its mother, and the earthy odors of hay and manure. Here, surrounded by her livestock and the solid barns and outbuildings, she could forget her troubles and for a little while be a much-loved child again.

"Any word of Master Reed?" the foreman asked.

"Nothing new. But I'm sure he'll be coming home soon," Caroline said, as much to keep up her own spirits as Mordecai's.

"Master Reed will love this stallion, certain."

"Won't he?" she replied. "He'll have a saddle on him the first day he gets back."

"I don't doubt it." He nodded and tucked a bit of tobacco under his lip. "Master Reed does love a fine horse."

"Reed will win every horse race on the Eastern

Shore with this stallion," she said. Mordecai grinned in agreement.

Mordecai Brown had been foreman for more years than Caroline liked to think. His curly black hair had turned to gray and his shoulders were a little more bent than they had once been, but other than that Mordecai was as true and solid as good Maryland oak.

The struggle between the Colonies and the mother country had robbed Fortune's Gift of most of her able-bodied men who had gone to fight for one side or the other. The women remained, and when planting time came Caroline was afraid she'd have to call on them to help. For now, they remained out of sight, frightened by the occupying British presence.

This week, Mordecai was rebuilding the miles of fence line that surrounded the plantation and divided it into paddocks and pastureland, cornfields and tobacco acreage. He'd had to hire men and boys from the neighboring farms and villages. Most of the workers Caroline knew, by sight if not by name, but a few were strangers. These men were busy assembling tools and loading wagons on the far side of the yard.

When Caroline finished her conversation with the foreman, she turned to go back to the house. As she did, she heard a crude whistle and the taunt "Lightskirts" from one of the hired laborers.

Her face flushed with anger and she whirled to confront the men. "Does someone have something to say to me?" she demanded. Blank faces were the only reply.

Mordecai, a devout Christian, swore. "Who said that?" he shouted. "By heaven, you'll not come to Fortune's Gift and insult—"

"Never mind," Caroline said, trying to keep her

tone normal. "A man who will not speak his mind openly shows his cowardice. And such a man is as worthless as his opinions." Proudly, she walked away. She kept her back straight and her chin high, but her heart was pounding so hard that she almost missed the faint snicker thrown after her.

So, it's started already, she thought. Some big mouth had been out early to start the rumors flying about her and Garrett Faulkner. Well, they'd not shame her with their whispers and their gossip. She'd done what she'd done to save a fellow American, and no matter what it cost her, she'd do as much again.

She was nearing the smokehouse when Bruce stepped around a corner of the building and blocked her path. "Where to so early, little cousin?" he said. His wig was slightly askew and he wore the same stained shirt he'd had on the night before. From the whiff she got of his breath, he'd already started the morning with a measure of rum.

"Same thing I do every morning, *cousin,*" she replied. "Instructing my foreman. This is a working plantation." She moved to the right, but he took hold of her arm. "Let go of me, please," she said in a low voice.

"Not yet." He released her arm and grabbed the beribboned hair at the back of her neck. "A morning kiss for your betrothed," he threatened.

She lifted her left foot and brought her heel down on the toe of his right boot with all her weight. Surprised, Bruce let out a howl and loosened his grip on her hair. Caroline ducked left, darted around the smokehouse, and seized a long-handled iron meat fork hanging on the outside of the log building. Swearing, Bruce dashed after her.

She faced him, back against the wall, the lethal weapon held waist-high and ready.

"You little bitch," he said.

"Keep your hands to yourself, *cousin*," she warned, "or I'll run you through with this iron and have my staff hang you up to smoke with the rest of the pigs."

"How dare you!" Bruce trembled with white-hot fury. "You little—"

"I'll kill you. You know I can do it," she whispered. "If not now, some night in your sleep. Leave me and mine alone. Get away from Fortune's Gift before I—"

"I'll sell your precious nigra," he threatened. "I can do it. The law's on my side. I'll sell her south to a sugarcane plantation." His eyes narrowed. "Or maybe to a house of joy. You'd like that, wouldn't you, Caroline. Doubtless your black sister is as much a slut as you are."

"Try it," she dared. "Do anything more to Amanda and Jeremy—anything at all—and you'll never live to see her set foot on a boat south." He backed off a step as she raised the iron fork from belly level to his Adam's apple. "Keep your hands off what's mine," she reminded him. She jabbed at him once. He jerked back, and she ran for the safety of the house, slamming the door behind her.

Bruce started after her, tripped over a one-eared black cat, and smacked his elbow against the corner of the smokehouse. When he regained his balance, he cursed a foul oath and drew his sidearm from his holster. "Here, kitty, kitty," he called, looking around for the tomcat, but the ragged creature had vanished into thin air.

Caroline tossed her cloak to Jacob, adjusted her linen cap in the hired man's mirror, and hurried down the hall toward the parlor where breakfast was served. She took a deep breath and forced herself to enter the doorway with the gracious air of the lady of the manor.

The first person she saw was Major Whitehead. Thank God, she thought. No wonder Bruce had tried to ambush her outside the house instead of waiting for her in the hall. "Sir." She smiled sweetly at the major. "What a pleasant surprise. We have all missed you."

"Indeed."

Caroline turned her attention to the Irish hunt table where Garrett was helping himself to fresh fillet of rockfish and a beaten biscuit. "The major and I are already acquainted," Garrett said. "We met in London at a reception for Lord Archer."

Garrett's stock was tied with flawless precision. His sleek wheat-brown hair was drawn back and fastened at the nape of his neck with a black silk ribbon that looked suspiciously like one of her own. Someone, Toby perhaps, had shaved him. She could smell the faint odor of Wesley's shaving soap. The silver buttons on Garrett's black coat gleamed; his borrowed shirt was spotless.

As she stared at him, the corners of his mouth turned up in amusement, and he inclined his head slightly in a salute. From where he was standing, Major Whitehead could not see that arrogant gaze, but she could. Garrett was daring her to give him away.

So, you think to use me, do you? she thought. You may be just what I need.

"I remember Mr. Faulkner well," Major Whitehead said loftily. "Plays a fine hand of loo. I've been trying to convince him to reactivate his commission in the Royal Navy. We need every experienced officer in these trying times."

Caroline crossed the room and reached for

Garrett's hand. "Oh, sir, but I cannot spare him," she proclaimed to the major. "Not for months and months." She flashed a smile at Garrett. "There's no need to keep our secret any longer, darling." Garrett's hand tightened around hers as she went on. "We have been betrothed for months and were only waiting for the proper time to make our announcement. Garrett and I are to be married tomorrow."

Chapter 4

Garrett's gut contracted into a tight fist. For an instant, he stared at Caroline, wondering if she was playing some odd sort of jest. Then her wide-eyed gaze locked with his and he knew this was no joke. The intensity of her challenge jolted him, and in astonishment, he took an involuntary step back on his bad leg. Sweet Jesus! Blinding pain knifed up his hip and white lights danced in his head. He fought the waves of faintness that threatened his balance and covered his dismay with an affected cough.

". . . Garrett's family and mine have shared a friendship for generations," Caroline was telling the major. "Garrett and my brother Reed—"

"Your cousin Bruce will oppose this marriage," Whitehead interrupted. "He has expressed a desire to wed you himself."

Garrett regained his composure, forced what he hoped was an affectionate smile to his lips, and concentrated on what Caroline and the major were saying. He knew enough about Whitehead to suspect that the Englishman had a personal motive for showing such concern for his hostess's marital affairs. Boy-lover or not, Whitehead was a shrewd opponent and an absolutely fearless soldier under fire.

Caroline moved closer to the British officer, and her voice became softer. "Yes, I know." She sighed. "That knowledge has made me decide to accept

Garrett's proposal sooner than I would have, were that not the case. Bruce and I are first cousins. Too close in blood to ever produce healthy children. I realize that in England—"

"Yes, I see your point," Whitehead agreed. "My own uncle is married to his first cousin, and their first child was born with a harelip—a terrible deformity. It has shadowed his entire life. He rarely leaves the country house."

"Exactly," Caroline replied. "Bruce never mentions it, of course, but there is already a weakness in our bloodline. Children have been born that . . ." She trailed off and spread her hands helplessly. "There is a rumor that in my grandmother's time, one male member of the family was kept locked away. How could I—in Christian conscience—be party to another such tragedy?"

Major Whitehead glanced at Garrett with cool appraisal. "And you, sir, you wish to wed the lady?"

Caroline's petticoats rustled as she swept back to his side and took his hand in hers. "Oh, he does, Major." This time, it was her hand that tightened on his. "He loves me, truly."

Garrett barely contained his laughter. Damned if the jade wasn't as artful an actress as any high-priced whore he'd ever paid good silver for.

Whitehead raised his goblet of cider in salute. "You love the lady or her estates?" he asked directly. "It is no secret that Mistress Steele could buy and sell our mutual friend Lord Archer without missing the change."

Garrett glanced down at Caroline and tried not to throttle her. She was smiling at him sweetly but, as she tilted her head up to look into his face, her luminous dark eyes were filled with an unspoken warning. *Agree or be exposed as the rebel they seek!* Amusement turned to a slow-burning anger. He'd never liked threats.

"When has a lady's wealth ever detracted from her desirability?" Garrett asked, draping an arm casually around Caroline's shoulders. "It's true that the captain wants Mistress Steele for himself. That's why he's concocted these ridiculous charges to discredit me, instead of combing the woods and swamps for the real traitor."

"I agree," Whitehead said. "A wanted man would hardly seek refuge in my headquarters." He pursued his thin lips and looked thoughtful.

"We would deeply appreciate your help, Major," Caroline implored.

"You are both serious in this matter of this marriage?" Whitehead asked. He was a tall man, olive-skinned with brown eyes. His wig was neat, simply styled, and expensive; his red and white military uniform was impeccable. His most striking feature was the saber scar that ran from the corner of his left eyebrow across the bridge of his strong nose.

Garrett nodded. He didn't know why Caroline Steele was playing this dangerous farce, but he intended to find out. For now, he would let her move the game pieces.

"You must know that Mistress Steele's brother is a prisoner of the crown, charged with piracy." Whitehead's eyes narrowed. "I have already informed the lady that there is a possibility that Reed Talbot can be released with proper legal counsel, but it will be very costly. Ten thousand pounds sterling to start. Are you willing to part with that much if she becomes your wife?"

Garrett heard Caroline's soft hiss of breath. "Ten thousand pounds?" she echoed.

The major shrugged. "Ten thousand minimum. The barrister is very influential. If he takes your case, it will be strictly confidential. The fees may run much more. Your brother has enemies who wish to make an example of him. Naturally, if I interceded in this, I—"

"Naturally," she said. "Whatever you think is fair. Reed is innocent—a victim of unlucky circumstance. I will give any amount to have him back alive."

"And your cousin . . ." Whitehead left his words hanging in air.

"Bruce would never agree to releasing so much money from my estates," she said, "but Garrett loves my brother. They have been friends for years. Whatever it takes, we will gladly pay."

The major smiled. "Then I believe we can come to some agreement. I would advise you to proceed with the nuptials at once. If Captain Talbot learns of your plans, he will—"

"Thank you, Major Whitehead," Caroline said. "We will take your advice and marry immediately."

"We appreciate your support," Garrett said. He could see why Whitehead would agree to the marriage. He stood to collect an immense bribe. But why, he wondered, why would Caroline Steele want to force him to marry her? She was young and attractive. With her immense wealth, she could have her pick of titled Englishmen. Why not choose someone of her own class—a man who brought more to the union than a single tobacco plantation?

"My congratulations to you both," Whitehead said. He crossed the room and took Caroline's hand, lifting it gallantly and brushing a kiss over her knuckles. "If I were not married, I might have considered courting her myself. It is the rare bridegroom who takes such a lovely and well-dowered widow to his bed."

Before Garrett could reply, a dragoon appeared in the open doorway. "Major Whitehead, sir," the soldier said. "The dispatches you were waiting for have arrived from Head of Elk."

The major nodded. "I'll come at once." He glanced at Caroline and Garrett. "If you two will excuse me, I have official business to attend to."

Garrett waited until he was alone in the room with Caroline before speaking. "We need to talk," he said. "Now."

"I can explain," she began.

"You'd better. But not here, someplace private." He removed his coat and draped it over her shoulders. Outside, where I can be certain we're not overheard."

She nodded. "The maze beyond the herb garden." She shrugged out of his coat and he caught it before it slid to the floor. "I'll take my cape," she said. "It's cold out, and you'll need your coat yourself. Can you walk that far?"

"Your concern is touching, madame," he replied wryly. "After you."

Silently, he followed her from the room, through the kitchen, and around the house to the brick walk that led through the herb garden. Caroline had paused only long enough to put on her green cape and pull the hood up over her auburn hair. Garrett couldn't help noticing that the bottom of the cloak swayed as she walked. The hem brushed the heels of her shoes as she moved gracefully away from the shadows of the brick kitchen past the triangles of lavender, marjoram, and chives, to the formal expanse of lawn and carefully clipped hedges.

As they neared the entrance to the maze, she glanced back over her shoulder to see if they were being followed. "We'll go to the center," she said. "There's a bench there, and shelter from the wind."

Each step was agony as knifelike pain shot up Garrett's hip and down his leg. Sweat beaded on his forehead and he swore under his breath, but he kept walking. Caroline took a right turn, then a left, and then another left, turning and twisting down the crushed oyster shell path that led through the boxwood maze until he had lost all sense of direction. Finally, when he thought he could go no farther, she made one last series of turns into what looked like a solid wall of greenery. He stopped, eyesight blurred by his throbbing wound, not certain which way she had gone. Even when a peal of bubbling laughter drifted through the interlaced boxwood, he still couldn't find the opening. "Caroline," he called. "Where are you?"

To his surprise, a low gate of hedge opened almost at his right hand. "This way," she said.

He ducked his head and stepped into the heart of the maze, a lush oval of lawn, statuary, and flowering shrubs, about twenty feet across. In the center of the clearing stood a carved cedarwood bench, a small peach tree, and a miniature well. The shrubs and the tree were winter barren, but even now he was speechless at the exquisite beauty of the hidden garden.

"Do you like it?" she demanded. Her eyes twinkled with delight as she spread her hands and spun around once like a schoolgirl. "My great-great-grandfather built this maze for my great-great-grandmother. Lacy's Garden, it's called, and the story is that the maze is haunted. On nights when the moon is full and it rides the clouds like a great ship at sea, they say you can see Lacy and James's faces reflected in the well." She laughed again, low and mischievous. "They say you can hear him calling her name sometimes. 'Lacy . . . Lacy.' And they also say—"

Garrett caught her shoulder and jerked her around to face him. "To hell with ghost stories! Why did you tell Whitehead we were to be married?"

The sparkle faded from her gaze, replaced with stubborn will. "We are. And we will be wed today—tomorrow at the latest."

"Have you lost your wits, girl?" The audacity of her! His anger was tempered with admiration. His black stare had been known to intimidate a drunken Carib Indian, yet this spoiled little minx didn't flinch. "I've no intention of taking a bride. And if I did, it would be one of my own choosing."

"Nay," she flung back, twisting free of his grasp.

He couldn't hold her and remain upright without hurting her, so he let her step away. "Nay, indeed," he repeated. "What game is this you're playing? Are you pregnant with some man's bastard that you need to find a husband so quickly?"

She drew back her hand to slap him. He threw up an arm to block her blow. "I warned you never to try that again," he said coldly.

"How dare you insult me!"

He'd seen his share of angry women before—heard his portion of tears and spitting curses. But Caroline offered none of these familiar retorts. Instead, her brown eyes narrowed and darkened to the color of old oak. Her sensual lips tightened to a thin line and her chin firmed. If she'd had a pistol in her hand, he'd have ignored his injured leg and dived for the nearest cover. "What am I to think," he answered, "when you proclaim me your betrothed without so much as a by-your-leave, madame."

"You have ruined my reputation," she said, with only the slightest tremor in her husky voice. "You have ruined *me*, and therefore you must make an honest woman of me. If you do not, I'll be the laughingstock of every decent man and woman in the colony."

"That is hardly my problem."

"No?" She balled her small hands into tight fists at her sides. "But it shall be if I exposed you to Major Whitehead—if I tell him that you forced yourself into my bed."

"What do you want of me?"

She took a deep breath. "Can we sit? It's rather intimidating to have you glowering down at me."

"Why me? A woman of your wealth—"

"You were my brother's friend—*are* his friend," she corrected. "You claim to be loyal to England and you are not already married. Are you?" She looked up at him anxiously.

"No. I'm not married." He followed her to the bench and eased himself down on it. It was all he could do to keep from groaning in relief as he took the weight off his leg.

Caroline sat on the far end and half turned toward him. "I shall be honest with you," she said.

"Thank God for that."

"My cousin has kept me a virtual prisoner in my own home since my husband's death," she said. "Now he is trying to force me into marriage."

"For your money."

She nodded. "Exactly."

"Not to be unexpected, certainly. Women of your class—"

"I am a Talbot by birth," she said proudly. "A

Talbot of Fortune's Gift. This land has been handed down to me from my mother and her mother, back to Great-great-grandmother Lacy. The women in my family don't allow themselves to be manipulated by men, not by their fathers or their husbands."

"An interesting concept. But again—why me? Why not someone—"

"Will you cease arguing long enough to hear what I have to say?" She didn't raise her voice, but her tone became frosty. "You needed my help and I risked my life to give it to you. Now you may pay that debt by marrying me."

He grimaced. "You'd rather give your wealth to me than keep it in the family by marrying Cousin Bruce."

"Not a real marriage, you dunce," she snapped. "A marriage of convenience. We would keep separate beds, and I would keep control of all that is mine."

He stared at her in disbelief. "And what do I get from this one-sided bargain?"

"Your life, for one thing."

"You'd betray me?"

She swallowed. "If I have to," she said softly.

"Your brother's friend."

"We are in perilous times," she answered. "Sometimes it is necessary to do things one would never consider in kinder situations."

"If I was this rebel traitor they've accused me of being, what's to keep me from choking the life from you and making my escape?"

She chuckled. "You're no murderer, Garrett Faulkner. Besides, you'd never find your way out of the maze. You'd be trapped here with the evidence."

A lock of curling red hair fell over her eyes and

Caroline brushed it away, tucking it under the edge of her lace cap. The green wool hood framed her oval face, and he was struck by just how lovely she was. Who would believe a devious mind lurked behind such a facade?

He took a deep breath and tried once more to unravel the mystery. "I can see why it would be to your advantage to marry, but why me? You hardly know me. I could be a profligate, a rogue."

"You are. At least from what I know of your reputation, you are. A scoundrel. What can you say for yourself? The grandson of an indentured servant with a failed naval career behind you? A man with a taste for blooded horses and cheap women? Heir to what? A thousand acres of played-out tobacco land."

"Twelve hundred acres," he replied. "And not all played out."

"You are a poor planter at best, sir, and with our fortunes affected by this rebellion, you are not likely to become any richer in the near future."

"What will you offer me?"

"Money. A great deal of money." She lifted her chin and stared at him with regal arrogance. "You shall have a tenth share of my inheritance—more money than you or yours could imagine."

"And you want in return?"

"I want your name and protection," she said. "I want my brother ransomed, and I want your promise—in writing—that our marriage will be annulled in five years' time."

"Five years?"

"Yes. Naturally, I will give you a living allowance now, but the bulk of your reward will come on the day our annulment is final."

"You think I'm the sort of man who would marry a woman for her money?"

Caroline shrugged. "We'll soon see, won't we?"

Her barb stung like that of a black wasp, and he felt his face flush. The truth was, he found her offer tempting. With Caroline's money, he could buy another ship. And with a ship, he'd find a crew and fight the British again—something he'd not been able to do in the months since his vessel had gone down off Lewes with most of his men. "A marriage of convenience only," he repeated softly. "Does that mean I am to watch while you flit from man to man and perhaps gift me with children?"

It was her turn to flush. "I sleep alone!" she retorted. "I shall continue to do so. No word of gossip has ever touched my name . . . until last night."

"If we did make this bargain, how can you be certain we could obtain an annulment at the end of five years?"

"We will both swear that the marriage has never been consummated."

He scoffed. "You're a widow. That's a difficult point to prove."

"Not for an heiress to Fortune's Gift," she said. "For a high enough bribe, I could find a judge to rule that that you were incapable of functioning as a husband." She smiled and raised a palm to ward off his anger. "Not that I would, you understand. You may put all the blame on me. You may claim anything you like, as long as I remain in control of Fortune's Gift and all its wealth."

"I think the two of us under one roof would soon come to murder," he said.

"There is no need for you to remain on Fortune's Gift. Naturally, your own plantation will require your attention. I need only your name and the title of wife to a man known to be loyal to England. I am quite capable of managing my own affairs."

"I see." He turned his head away. Who would have thought it of Reed's sister? The damnable wench. She had him in a trap and was twisting the bonds. "This is not a decision to be made lightly," he said. She remained silent. Ignoring his pain, he rose and walked to the far side of the garden. A wife . . . It was the last thing he wanted, but if she brought with her the chance of a ship under his feet once more . . .

Caroline had no idea he was Osprey. If she did, she'd not have made the offer. The British had spread the word that he'd betrayed his crew and ship—that he'd deliberately sailed into a trap. He hadn't. He hadn't even been at the wheel that night his ship had gone down; he'd been flat on his back in his cabin with a musket ball in his shoulder. But he'd had only his best friend Noah to confirm his story, and a black man's word meant little. But if Reed Talbot was alive—if he could be ransomed from the British—Reed would vouch for him. His name would be cleared and his honor restored.

The memory of the hearing burned in the pit of his stomach like gall. The Continental high command had charged him with cowardice and treason. They'd demanded to know why forty-four good men had gone to their deaths, and Garrett had been one of only four survivors. He and Noah had lived, Reed had been wounded and taken prisoner. A fourth man had survived the battle and been shot trying to escape.

Garrett sighed. *The captain always goes down with his ship.* But not this captain. His friends and crew had fought bravely and died one by one while he lived to tell about the battle. It was a thing that made for poor nights' sleep, a thing that twisted and turned inside a man and made him want to seek revenge.

"It wasn't my fault," he whispered. The only reply was the lonely cry of a fish hawk high overhead.

In the past months, he and Noah had harried the British, seizing dispatches, cutting loose moored vessels, doing whatever they could to harm the English military. Even though he had gone to every friend of his and his father, no one would help him get another ship—no one would let him sign on to fight aboard another captain's privateer. Now Wesley Steele's widow might give him that opportunity.

He wondered just how far he could trust Caroline. Reed and Wesley had both been strong for independence; Wesley had shed his life's blood for it. Why then was his widow such an ardent Tory? Or was she?

He glanced back at Caroline. She was sitting as he'd left her, hands clasped in her lap, eyes down. A passerby would think she had nothing more on her mind than the cut and color of a new gown.

She would vex his life beyond belief—he knew it. If he did as she asked, men would say he wed her for her money. And it would be true. Damn it to hell! He wanted nothing more than to fight for freedom. He had no time for a spoiled beauty and her demands. He'd always loved women, but war was no time to take a wife. If he married her, he'd be responsible for her safety. And if he didn't, he'd be hard put to get away from Fortune's Gift with his neck intact.

Straightening his shoulders, he returned to the bench where she waited. "I want a ship," he said.

She smiled. "I have lots of ships. I forget how many, but surely one will suit you."

"Then—"

"Wait," she interrupted. "There's one thing more. You've heard of my sister Amanda?"

"You have no— Oh, you must mean the black girl your father raised. Her name is Amanda?"

"Yes. Amanda Talbot." She stared at him as if daring him to contest the fact.

"What of her?"

"She's black."

He scowled. "I believe we've covered that point. What about her?"

"Amanda is not a slave. She's a free woman."

"Fortune's Gift has never owned slaves. That's common knowledge."

"You have no objections to Amanda?"

"It depends on what she does. I don't know the girl."

"She isn't a girl. She's a woman. And this is her home. She and her son, Jeremy, will continue to live in the house as part of my family."

"So?"

"You don't care if a black woman eats at your table?"

He laughed. "My mother died when I was born. A black woman nursed me, wrapped me in nappies, and taught me manners."

"I allow no black man or woman to be mistreated on Fortune's Gift," she warned.

"Mistress Steele, are you serious about making a bargain with me or not?"

"I'd make a bargain with Lucifer himself to save Fortune's Gift and my people."

"Then I accept your offer. I will give you my name, and you will give me a ship and access to your fortune."

"Within reason," she said.

"Of course." He took her hand. "A kiss of peace to seal our contract, madame?"

"I think not," she replied haughtily. "There will be time enough for that at Oxford Church."

Chapter 5

Oxford, Maryland

It was midafternoon of the following day when Garrett and Caroline stood before the minister in the small frame church in the waterfront village of Oxford. Major Whitehead waited a few steps behind them. In the absence of any of her family members or close friends, Caroline had asked the British officer to stand as one witness. Reverend Thomas's wife, Cora, would sign the marriage contract as the second. The only other people in the church were Mistress Marie Collins, town apothecary and gossip, and the six dragoons who had acted as escort for the bridal party. Mistress Collins, who never missed a wedding or a funeral, was a close friend of the minister's wife.

Nervously, Caroline glanced over her shoulder at the door. Major Whitehead had explained that he'd sent Bruce on patrol with a squad of dragoons at dawn. The major also said that he'd neglected to inform the captain of Caroline's impending nuptials. Still, she couldn't help worrying that her cousin would arrive and put a stop to the ceremony, or that he might have returned to the plantation and caught Mary and Abbie making their escape to Delaware with friends.

This was a very different wedding from the one she'd shared with Wesley before the war. They'd been married in the great hall at Fortune's Gift on a bright May morning. Reed had given her away, and there had been so many guests that dozens of them had stood outside in the garden. The feasting had gone on for three days, and Caroline and Wesley had danced their wedding night away.

Reverend Thomas cleared his throat and Caroline was jerked back into the present. The minister glanced sternly from her to Garrett. "Are you certain you wish to go through with this?" he demanded brusquely.

"We do," Garrett assured him. Her bridegroom had evidently lost all doubts in the night that had passed since she'd presented him with this decision. Today, Garrett was all gallant manners and charming smiles. At this moment, he was gazing down at her as though she were a frosted wedding cake and he was about to take a bite.

"And you, Caroline? Are you certain?" Reverend Thomas had performed the ceremony for her and Wesley, and he was obviously distressed at her new choice of a husband.

Caroline attempted to speak, but the words caught in her throat and she nodded stiffly. Now that she was here and about to become Garrett Faulkner's bride, her courage wavered.

Last night, she had gone to the servants' quarters to tell Amanda to remain hidden until she sent for her. "I'm going to marry Garrett Faulkner," she announced. Amanda had burst into tears as Caroline explained the precarious situation.

"Don't," her sister had begged. "You don't have to do this for Jeremy and me. We'll run away, someplace Bruce can't find us. Bruce can't force you to marry him if he isn't threatening us."

"It's best for all of us," Caroline had insisted. "If it isn't Bruce I'm made to marry, it will someone just as bad. I have too much wealth to be allowed to remain without a husband for long. Garrett Faulkner is a man who will be easily managed. He realizes that if it wasn't for the war, I'd never consider wedding a man of his class. He's only interested in my fortune. I'll make him take us south to the Caribbean where we'll be safe. Once there, I'll get the money to ransom Reed. And when the fighting is over, I'll buy my freedom from Mr. Faulkner. He's already agreed to an annulment for ten percent of my wealth. He's a simple man, Amanda. Give him his race horses, a bottle of good wine, and a tavern girl, and he'll give us no grief."

"I don't want you to ruin your life for us," Amanda argued. "It isn't fair."

"I'm doing this as much for Reed as for you and Jeremy. You know Bruce would never let us buy our brother out of prison. Once Reed's safe, we'll be a family again. It won't matter which side wins the war. If the Americans succeed, Fortune's Gift will be saved because Reed fought for them, and if they lose, I'll keep the land for my loyalty to England. Don't you see, Amanda? It's the only way."

Now Caroline was not so sure. Her stomach felt as though she had swallowed a handful of butterflies. Her hands and feet were cold, and her knees were weak. If she didn't keep her teeth clenched shut, she was certain they'd betray her fear by chattering.

Garrett took her hand in his, and she looked up into his face. He was grinning like a prize fool. His obvious pleasure in this marriage was enough to make her want to run screaming from the church. He had laughed and joked with Major Whitehead all the way from Fortune's Gift. And both men had alluded to the rare pleasures of acquiring both an attractive wife and wealth in the same bargain.

Caroline didn't know how Garrett could keep up such a cheerful front when his wound must be giving him great pain. She had washed and bandaged the injury late yesterday afternoon, again at midnight, and still again this morning. There was little sign of infection—a wonder in itself—and the stitches had held. Still, each step Garrett took must be an effort. And if he stared at her with calf eyes one more time before they left the church, she'd be tempted to swat him in his bad leg with her hymnbook.

They had ridden to Oxford today by carriage, although if it were not for his wound she would have suggested they come by horseback. The roads were a disgrace, one mud hole after another. Twice the carriage had become stuck, and everyone had had to climb down from the vehicle. It had done her heart good to see the major's fancy-dressed dragoons dismount and wade through water and slop to push the wheels free.

She had known how difficult the journey would be, so she'd chosen her second-best gown, a shimmering gray, fygury silk gown with an overlay of silver lace atop a satin petticoat in the palest silver. It was a dress made especially for her in Paris and smuggled into the colony the year before. She had worn it only once, and never since she'd been widowed. The bodice was square-cut and low, cool for the damp church, and too revealing for Garrett's admiring gaze. She wished now that she had come to the altar in her riding habit and coat, or that she had at least had one of the maids sew ruffles across the neckline.

Absently, Caroline put a hand to her throat and fingered the Kincaid diamonds. The cool stones were an inheritance from her Grandmother Bess, and they comforted her. As long as she remembered who she was, the entire British army couldn't get the best of her—let alone some fortune-seeking ne'er-do-well.

"... gathered here in the presence of God and these witnesses ..." the reverend proclaimed.

Caroline kept her eyes on the worn brick floor. This was the church where her parents had been married, the sanctuary where she had been christened. Standing here preparing to make wedding vows to a stranger was one of the hardest things she had ever had to do.

"Do you, Garrett Faulkner, take this woman ..."

At least my bridegroom's hands are clean, Caroline thought. Not like Bruce with his dirty fingernails and grimy wrists beneath his lace shirt cuffs. The minister's words seemed to come from a long way off. Too bad I'm not the fainting kind of woman, she mused. What would they all do if I simply shut my eyes and crumpled to the floor?

"I do." Garrett's affirmation was clearly stated.

Caroline closed her eyes. She could picture Amanda's dark face contorted with dismay. I'm doing this for you and Jeremy, Caroline cried silently. For you and Jeremy and Reed. Not for myself, I swear it.

"And do you, Caroline Steele, take this man ..."

She gritted her teeth. Garrett was so cocksure, so pleased with himself this morning. What would he say when he found out that most of her money was in London, the rest tied up in Bruce's guardianship? Garrett was marrying her for her wealth, but that wealth was tied up in material possessions that she couldn't hope to sell during wartime, when everyone was bereft of cash. In essence she was practically penniless. And if she couldn't convince him to take her to the islands, she wouldn't even be able to raise the ransom to free Reed.

Reverend Thomas cleared his throat again. "Caroline, do you take this man to be your lawful husband, to love, honor, and obey—"

"I take him as my husband," she answered quickly. He can hang from the highest gibbet in Oxford before I swear to obey him, she thought. He needn't take all this too seriously. The marriage is in name only. I'll make him understand that much from the first.

"Darling."

She blinked. What did Garrett want of her?

"The ring," he said.

His deep voice sent chills running down her spine. She looked up into his face and he smiled. Was he laughing at her?

"The ring," he repeated. "Open your hand."

With a start, she realized that her hand was clenched tightly into a fist. Trembling, she allowed him to slide a worn gold band on her finger. It fit perfectly.

". . . man and wife," Reverend Thomas intoned. "What God has joined together, let no man part." He raised his head and spoke to the onlookers. "Ladies and gentleman, I give you Mr. and Mrs. Garrett Faulkner."

"Don't I get to kiss the bride?" Garrett asked.

"Yes . . . of course . . . er . . . you may kiss the bride," the minister said.

Caroline closed her eyes and obediently raised stiff lips for the symbolic kiss.

"My wife," Garrett said with great tenderness. Gently he took her chin between his fingers and tilted her face up to meet his. Her heart began to pound. She would have backed away, but he steadied her with one hand around her waist as his lips met hers.

And then the earth swayed beneath her feet.

Caroline gasped as an electric charge leaped between them, so sudden, so overpowering that she forgot where and who she was. Her eyes opened wide, and she gave a little cry deep in her throat. His warm mouth pressed against hers in a demanding caress of pent-up longing, and she responded with every fiber of her being. Her lips parted and he filled her mouth with the thrusting sweetness of his tongue. Without realizing what she was doing, she slipped her arms around his neck and pulled him tighter. Her mind spun crazily, and she had the feeling of falling off a ledge into deep water. Still, she clung to Garrett and let his kiss carry her farther and farther from reality.

. . . Until he broke away with a low chuckle. "We'd best finish this later," he murmured.

Caroline came crashing back to reality, to the snickers of the watching dragoons and Cora Thomas's muffled sound of outrage. Caroline drew in a deep breath, trying not to look at the red-faced minister or Garrett's smirking grin.

She could still feel the pressure of his lips on hers . . . still remember the taste and texture of his hot mouth. Her breath still came in ragged gasps, and her heart still beat a furious tattoo. She took a step back, amazed by the sensual languidness that held her limbs in thrall, despite her mind's protest at Garrett's mocking audacity.

Shyly, she ducked her head, not wanting Garrett to read what she knew was visible in her eyes. Once, when she was a child, her grandfather had given her a worn curry comb for her birthday. Amid the jewelry, the new gowns, the music box, and the toys, the curry comb had seemed a poor present. Since her grandfather had always doted on her, she had almost tossed his offering away. Then she saw the gleam in his eyes and her pout became a giggle. She turned the old comb over, and on the bottom a single word was scratched. *Stable.* Immediately, she'd run to the barn and found a white-maned pony with a tossing head, dainty hooves, and eyes as warm as melted chocolate.

Caroline shivered. She had taken a man to husband for her own purposes—a man she expected to be nothing but a necessary inconvenience. And now? Delicious expectation teased the corners of her mind. Could she find something with Garrett she had never known before? Would she realize the passion that other women bragged of and she had never felt? The possibility was enough to bring a smile to her lips.

The unexpected turn of events put an entirely different light on the relationship she had supposed she would have with her new husband, and caused her to rethink her strategy for dealing with Garrett.

Caroline had grown up in a world more of men than of women. She had always had the loving care of her mother and grandmother, but the other important people in her life—her father, her grandfather, Kutii, Wesley, and Reed—were all male. Other than her family, Wesley was the only one she had ever really kissed, and she'd never been intimate with any man other than her lawful husband. When she and Wesley had consummated their union, she'd found a warm pleasure . . . a physical satisfaction that had grown slowly throughout their marriage. But not once in Wesley's bed had she ever experienced a tenth of the sexual desire she'd felt in this one moment in Garrett's embrace.

"Darling?" Her bridegroom offered her his arm. She took it gracefully and allowed him to lead her down the aisle toward the door.

Mistress Collins rose to her feet in the back pew, shock written plainly across her face. Caroline smiled sweetly at her and tried not to think of the tale the apothecary would spread around Oxford.

"I have reserved a private room at the Queen's Rose Inn," Major Whitehead said. "I thought it might be nice to have dinner before we start back to the plantation."

"Thank you," Garrett replied. "It was kind of you to think of it. I'm certain the lady must be as hungry as we are."

One of the soldiers opened the double doors and they stepped out onto the brick walk. In springtime, the church would be shaded by old oaks. Now the mottled gray trees loomed barren and cold. The ground was littered with leaves, and patches of ice clung to the edges of the puddles.

To the left stretched a graveyard. Near the church wall, Caroline saw a freshly turned earthen mound that marked a new grave. She wondered who had passed away—an old woman at the end of her life or a young man cut down by the senseless violence of war. So many of the brightest and strongest had died. For a few seconds, she thought of Wesley and her eyes clouded with tears. Then that sadness was replaced with a determination to make his murderer pay for the crime. A rush of fierce emotion filled her heart, and she stiffened her spine as she inwardly vowed that she would find Osprey and seek her own vengeance.

Major Whitehead had begun to chat with Garrett as they neared the carriage. Neither man seemed to notice Caroline's mental withdrawal. Suddenly, her ruminations were interrupted by the thunder of iron-shod hooves. She looked up to see a group of mounted dragoons galloping full tilt down the quiet residential street with her cousin Bruce in the lead.

A gray-haired Quaker who was crossing the street dropped his Bible and scrambled for safety as Bruce's sorrel gelding raced past, spattering the man's black coat and wide-brimmed hat with clods of mud. As the animal neared the church, Caroline's bay carriage horses shied and backed in place. At the last possible moment, her cousin yanked hard on the reins. Bloody foam sprayed from the sorrel's mouth and its eyes rolled white in its head as Bruce sawed at the bit. The exhausted animal reared, then fell back on its haunches as the captain vaulted from the saddle and rushed at Caroline with a drawn pistol.

"What do you think you're doing, you stupid bitch?" Bruce demanded. "You'll not marry—"

"Control yourself," Major Whitehead shouted above the clamor of the arrival of the rest of Bruce's patrol. "You are too late, Talbot. They are already wed."

Swearing foully, Bruce rounded the matched bays and pointed the flintlock at Garrett's chest. "Not for long!"

"Seize that man!" the major ordered his dragoons.

Garrett shoved Caroline away from him so hard that the force knocked her to the ground. She saw a blur of motion as he lunged toward her cousin at the same time that the pistol fired. Flames shot from the barrel of the flintlock; the lead ball whined over Caroline's head, splintering the church door. Men were running, horses snorting.

The carriage rolled back a few feet as the driver fought to control the panicked team.

Caroline rose to her feet and gasped. Garrett had Bruce pinned by the throat to the muddy ground beneath the carriage. The high front right wheel rested against her cousin's head. Another inch of movement, and Bruce's skull would be crushed by the weight of the vehicle.

"Let him up," Major Whitehead said, beckoning to his soldiers. "You're under arrest, Talbot."

"Not yet," Garrett said. "Not until he apologizes to my wife."

The driver spoke soothingly to the bays. Nostrils flaring, they continued to toss their heads and roll their eyes. Caroline knew that the slightest noise could send the animals out of control. Quickly, she moved to the nearer horse's head and took hold of the cheekstrap. "Whoa, whoa," she murmured. "Easy, Brandy. Easy girl." Brandy was the flightier of the two animals; if she could calm her, Rum would settle down.

"I say let him up, Faulkner," the major commanded.

"First, the apology," Garrett insisted. He raised Bruce's head and slammed it down in the mud again. "Loud enough so that the lady can hear you."

"All right, all right," Bruce said. "I'm sorry."

"Louder," Garrett threatened.

"I apologize," Bruce rasped.

Garrett let go of him, grabbed the carriage for support, and hauled himself to his feet. Only Caroline saw the effort it cost him, and the bloodstain seeping through the wool of Wesley's best sky-blue breeches.

Bruce crawled out from under the carriage and was hauled to his feet by two burly dragoons. His face was bruised and swelling. Blood ran from a cut on his lower lip.

Caroline ran to Garrett, blocking the major's view of Garrett's injury with her full skirts. "Are you hurt?" she demanded in a shrill voice. "I was so frightened. He nearly killed you." Then she whirled on her cousin. "How could you? How could you try to kill him on our wedding day?" She turned back to Garrett and threw her arms around his neck. "Your leg," she whispered. "Your wound has opened. Don't let them see."

"I'll escort Mistress Faulkner to the inn," Garrett said.

"Oh, yes," Caroline agreed. "I'm all muddy. My gown may be ruined."

"Of course," Major Whitehead said. "I'll send four of my men with you." He glared at Bruce. "You are in a great deal of trouble, Captain. You disobeyed a direct order of mine."

"I can't believe you let that bastard marry her," Bruce answered bitterly.

"Say nothing more, Talbot. You are burying your career with your own stupidity."

"What would you know of women?" Bruce taunted. "With your tastes?"

The major's lips tightened and white spots of anger appeared on his cheeks. "Sergeant Michaels," he ordered. "You will take charge of the captain's patrol. Take Captain Talbot to the jail here in Oxford and put him in shackles. Tomorrow morning, I want him returned to my headquarters. If he escapes, I'll have you and the rest of the guard detail shot." He glanced back at Bruce. "Perhaps by morning, you will be sober."

Garrett helped Caroline up into the open carriage and stepped in beside her. She covered his bad leg with her skirt as the major sat in the second seat across from them. "Drive on," Garrett instructed the coachman. "The Queen's Rose." As the carriage rolled away, the dragoons who had come from Fortune's Gift with the bridal party mounted and followed the vehicle.

Once they reached the elegant inn, Caroline insisted on being shown to the private bedchamber reserved for important guests. "My new husband and I will be taking this room for the night," she told the innkeeper's wife, Maude Hawkins.

Maude waved away the maid who had come to assist the mistress of Fortune's Gift. "I will tend to her," the older woman said. "See that Major Whitehead and Mr. Faulkner are served some of that excellent Dutch red, and tell the cook to carve the beef." When the girl left the room, Maude closed the door and came close to Caroline. "What service can I give you, my lady?"

Caroline took Maude's hand and squeezed it. Her second oldest son, Tom, had been aboard Osprey's ship when it went to the bottom. "Mr. Faulkner has had an accident. I'll not trouble the physician, but I need the barber, Harley Wiggins. Can someone fetch him here without making a fuss?" Harley was an ardent rebel. The only reason he wasn't with Washington's army in Valley Forge was that he'd lost a leg in the Battle of the Brandywine. Caroline knew that both Maude and Harley could be trusted.

"I'll do it myself," Maude said quietly. "Faulkner won't bring us trouble, will he?"

"I have a feeling he's always trouble, but he's no Tory. I'll stake my life on it." She smiled at Maude. "Still, we'll say nothing that anyone could use against us, will we?"

"No, ma'am, we sure won't," Maude replied. The innkeeper's wife was tall and broad, as round as a plum pudding. Her sensible gray wool dress was covered by a starched linen apron so wide and clean that she could have spread it out for a table covering. Her hands were as large as her feet, and worn red from years of hard labor. Now that the inn prospered and Maude had a staff of twelve girls under her, she still worked harder than anyone else in the Queen's Rose. "It's an honor to serve you, Mistress Caroline," she said with a vigorous nod. "An honor."

Caroline rejoined the gentlemen and forced herself to partake of the excellent dinner Maude had ordered for them. She laughed and talked with Whitehead and Garrett, and shared several bottles of wine, all the while wondering if Garrett was bleeding to death under the table. If he was, he gave no sign of it. He was as jovial as if this were a real wedding and he was a happy bridegroom.

"I suppose we should have invited the minister and his wife to dine with us," Caroline said.

"I think not," Garrett joked. "I don't believe the reverend approved of our marriage."

"No, he certainly didn't. And I don't believe they had much appetite after the bullets started flying," Major Whitehead said. "None of them showed so much as a face outside the church." He smiled at Caroline. "You are to be commended for your bravery. Most women would have fainted or at least pretended to do so."

"I knew I was in no real danger," she replied prettily. "Not with you and Garrett there." She placed a hand on the major's sleeve. "What will happen to my cousin?"

"It depends on his behavior tomorrow. If he sees the error of his ways, he could be let off with a fine. I'd not want to call a court-martial. After all, no one was hurt, and he did have a great deal of provocation."

"You are a wise man," Garrett said. "His Majesty is well served with officers like you in his service."

"I try to be," Whitehead said. "But Talbot demands more patience than I can summon."

"I will ask a boon of you, sir," Caroline said, smiling. "Since it is"—she averted her eyes, affecting shyness—"our wedding night, perhaps you would allow us to remain here at the Queen's Rose, just for tonight."

Garrett's eyes met hers questioningly.

"Please, Major. It would seem so much more . . . private."

"Of course," Whitehead agreed. "You have never been a prisoner. I regret that we've had to detain Mr. Faulkner until word comes from Lord Cornwallis in Philadelphia. It will be no trouble for me and the men to remain here tonight."

The major seemed so eager to honor her request that Caroline wondered if one of the dragoons who had accompanied him was a favorite of Whitehead's. It didn't matter to her. His personal life his own. "Thank you so much," she replied.

"Yes," Garrett said. "Under the circumstances, I'm sure my bride would like to retire early." He smiled roguishly. "And so would I, for that matter."

Whitehead laughed. "I don't blame you a bit," he said, standing and bowing to the lady. "I wish you good night, and I will see you both in the morning."

"Not too early," Garrett warned with a wink.

"No." The major laughed again. "Not too early, indeed." He drained the rest of the goblet of wine.

"Now I shall see if the innkeeper can find a bed for me tonight."

Garrett waited until the British officer left the small parlor, then he turned his gaze on Caroline. "Now what?"

"Now we get you to bed and have that wound looked after properly. I've sent for the barber surgeon. No." She held up a palm. "He can be trusted. You need to have someone besides me tend the injury. Are you still bleeding?"

"No, but it hurts like hell." He grinned at her wryly. "You're certain it was my leg that made you ask to spend the night here?"

"What other reason could there be?" she asked innocently.

"I hate to brag, but you'd not be the first lady who schemed to trick me into her bed. And you did tell me that ours was to be a marriage of convenience."

Caroline's felt her cheeks grow hot. "I can assure you, Mr. Faulkner, that I have no desire to climb between the sheets with you."

"No?" He raised his wineglass in salute. "Forgive me, madame, but from the kiss at the altar, I would have believed quite the opposite."

Chapter 6

Caroline left Garrett in the parlor and went ahead to the bedchamber to see if all was in order. As she entered the room, she saw a serving woman on her knees adding wood to the fire. "Good evening," Caroline greeted her. "Thank you for bringing extra fuel. The temperature seems to be dropping." As she spoke, wind rattled the shutters and swayed the boughs of a tall evergreen outside the window.

"Yes, ma'am." The maid got to her feet awkwardly, and Caroline noticed that her eyes were red and swollen from weeping, and her mouth was pinched. An obvious pregnancy bulged out the front of her threadbare skirt and bodice.

"Ida, isn't it? Aren't you Ida Wright?" Carolina asked. "Your husband made wheels for our carriage last year, didn't he?"

"Not no more he won't," she replied. Ida's shoulders slumped, and her thin fingers worked nervously. The gaze that met Caroline's was sullen—almost hostile.

The last time she'd seen Ida Wright, the woman had been neatly dressed and smiling. Her husband had recently completely his indenture and was setting up in his own business. Jack . . . yes, that was his name. Jack. They were poor as Job's turkey, but his work was solid. "Is Jack sick?" Caroline asked. "He's not died, has he?"

Two fat tears rolled down Ida's chapped cheeks.

"Might as well be," she answered. "He went for a soldier, did my Jackie. Followed Washington up to that godforsaken woods they call Valley Forge. Yes," she said defiantly. "We're rebels. If ye want to scorn us fer that, it don't matter. They're hard-pressed, Mistress Steele. No food, no blankets. They got wood to burn, but it keeps snowin', and that's wet. My Jackie froze his feet in November. Froze his feet in November—can ye believe such a thing? They brought him home to me four inches shorter than they took him."

"I'm so sorry to hear that. And it's not Mistress Steele anymore. I'm remarried. It's Caroline Faulkner now. I do hope your husband's out of danger. Is he healing?"

She shrugged. "Reckon he'll live. If he don't pine away from heartbreak. Not much work for a man without feet. We lost the shop when he went off to fight the British. This job brings in food, but not much else. We're sleeping in the barn out back of the inn." Her lower lip quivered. "My back hurts something fierce, but if I don't work, we don't eat."

"Surely Maude Hawkins won't see you—"

"We ain't charity, Jackie and me!" Ida said fiercely. "Least not yet, we ain't." Her face crumpled. "But now my oldest, little Jackie, has got the soldier fever, and he ain't but twelve. Do they bring him back to me in a box, reckon I'll throw myself in the river and the girls with me."

"Young Jackie's twelve, you say?" Caroline asked. Her heart ached for the beaten woman she knew to be only a few years older than she was. Ida was already missing a front tooth, and the pale blond hair that peeked out from under her worn mobcap was limp and lifeless. Pride was all Ida Wright had left, and Caroline wasn't about to take that away from her by showing pity. "It might be that we could find work for both big Jack and young Jackie at Fortune's Gift. We're short of hands. Most men are gone off to one side or the other."

"We hold fer Washington," Ida said stubbornly. "My Jack wouldn't bow and scrape to no Brits. I hear they's swarmin' all over yer plantation."

"They are," Caroline admitted, "but they're uninvited guests." She held out a hand to Ida. "Talk to your husband. Tell him that Fortune's Gift needs a master carpenter."

"Jackie ain't whole no more."

"Together your husband and son should make more than a whole man. Young Jackie can be his father's feet. Big Jack's hands are whole, aren't they? And his brain's not affected. It's up to you, Ida, but I need the help. If Jack's interested, tell him to come out and talk to my foreman, Mordecai Brown. There's a cabin goes with the job. It's not big, only three rooms, but it's clean and furnished."

"If my Jackie was interested, how would we get out to your place? It's a far piece for a man without feet to walk."

"That's not my problem, is it, Ida? A smart man like your Jack ought to be able to figure out how to get to Fortune's Gift. There's a supply boat that runs from Oxford south to Virginia the first of every month. It stops at our landing. And he can always borrow a horse from Maude. I'm offering work, not charity," Caroline said loftily. "I've always admired your husband's skill, but the decision is yours."

"I'll tell him," Ida said grudgingly, "but I ain't promisin' we'll come work for ye. Jackie don't think much of Tories, and young Jackie's got his heart set on goin' to war."

Caroline sniffed. "You tell them both that the duty to a man's family comes first."

The door opened, and Maude and Harley Wiggins, the barber, came in. "The girls need help in the public room," the innkeeper's wife said to Ida. "There's soldiers want ale and supper."

"Yes'm," Ida said as she picked up her wood basket. She left without another word or look at Caroline.

"A sad case," Maude said. "Widows and weeping mothers. More funerals than christenings in Oxford now. Makes you wonder if this rebellion is all worthwhile."

"Hmmpt," Harley said. "I give a leg and two nephews, and I still know what we're fightin' for. Evenin', Miss Caroline. Now, where's this new husband of yours what had himself an accident that can't be talked about?"

Caroline smiled warmly at the older man. "I'll get him for you. Thank you for coming."

"Little enough I can do for Kincaid's granddaughter. I knew your grandaddy when . . . Well"—he grinned—"let's just say I knew him in the good old days when life was a little tougher than you youngsters know it." He rubbed his stubbled chin, took the bar of lye soap Maude offered him, and began to wash his hands in a large china bowl of water. "Don't think he wouldn't be off with Washington right now, if he was still alive. Lord, but he did hate the British. And fight? That tough old bird was a fightin' fool."

Caroline moved close to Harley. "How does it go for Washington's men? Is it as bad as they say?"

Harley nodded. "Aye, and worse. They're starvin', girl. I seen men with ribs like a picket fence. Any supplies you can spare, our boys can use them. The Marylanders are pretty good about livin' off the land, but food is as scarce as June bugs in a chicken run."

"You know that the British have confiscated most of my livestock, and they keep a tight guard over what's left. But I can do this," Caroline offered. "I'll send two women with a load of wheat for Simon Pine's mill tomorrow afternoon. To get to the mill, they have to pass through that stretch of thick woods in the hollow. It would be a shame if somebody was waiting there to rob them of their flour on the way home."

Harley grinned. "It sure would be, Miss Caroline. It sure would be a shame. I'll try not to mention it to any rascally rebel provisioners what might have an interest in your wheat flour. I don't suppose two women could put up much of a fight to protect that flour."

"Probably not," Caroline agreed solemnly. "Probably not."

"Good. Now let's get this man of yours in here and see what we can do for him," the barber said. "I've never met Garrett Faulkner himself, but I knew of his father. And if you say he can be trusted, that's good enough for me."

"I never said Garrett can be trusted," Caroline answered. "I only said I'd stake my life he's no British sympathizer."

"One and the same," Maude said.

Caroline shook her head and her heartbeat quickened as she remembered Reed and Amanda and all those at Fortune's Gift who depended on her. "No," she replied softly, "not the same thing at all."

* * *

Much later, when Maude and Harley were gone, she and Garrett sat alone before the crackling hearth. They had not spoken for a quarter hour, and Caroline was listening to the soft swish of snowflakes hitting the frosted windows. She was sleepy, but she'd made no attempt to call someone to help her undress and prepare for bed.

There was only one bed in the room. She was very much aware of that fact, and she was certain Garrett was too.

She had remained in the chamber while the barber bathed and treated Garrett's wound. Harley had resewn two stitches that had torn out during the struggle in the churchyard, and he had drenched the whole surface with horse liniment, then covered it with a strong-smelling salve and a clean bandage.

When he'd first uncovered the injury, Harley had leaned close and sniffed the area. "Smells good and ain't leakin' pus," he'd said. "Somebody did good work here."

"Either that, or I'm too mean to kill," Garrett had said good-naturedly. "My father was once bitten by a water moccasin. He said the snake died."

Maude had taken Garrett's stained breeches and shirt. "I'll soak the blood out of the trews," she'd promised. "I'll bring them back in the morning right as rain."

Garrett now wore a blue and white banyan borrowed from the innkeeper's clothes chest and soft leather slippers. The robe was old, but finely sewn of silk brocade and lined with striped cotton. Maude's husband, William, was similar in height to Garrett, but much broader across the beam. Garrett had belted the garment around his waist to cover his nakedness. Caroline glimpsed only a few inches of bare chest and a flash of tanned ankles above and below the old-fashioned night robe.

Caroline still wore her gray and silver gown, her petticoats and shift, and her tightly laced stays, as well as her shoes and stockings. She had no intention of undressing in Garrett's presence, but she was also dubious of finding any comfortable rest in her present clothing.

"You may take the bed tonight," she finally said, breaking the silence between them. "Your leg must heal. You need your sleep."

Garrett eyed her for a long time before answering, so long that she found herself wanting to squirm under his intense scrutiny. "I'd be no gentleman if I let my new bride sleep sitting up in a chair on our wedding night," he said.

Caroline glanced toward the inviting bed. Curtains swathed the four-poster to protect from night drafts, and the feather tick was piled high with quilts and goose-down pillows. The bed glowed in the yellow circle of firelight, and she longed to climb in and snuggle down in the soft depths. "I have no intention of sharing a bed with you," she replied.

"I didn't ask you to."

"I should have asked for separate rooms."

He laughed. "What? And put Maude and William into the servants' beds? You know as well as I do that the Queen's Rose has one private bedchamber. Besides, what would your major think if you didn't share a room with your new bridegroom?"

"He's not my major," she protested. The implications of this marriage were just beginning to settle in. Memories of Garrett's searing kiss tantalized her, but she pushed them away. She must have been momentarily insane if she'd thought of doing anything improper with this man. Theirs was an arrangement, nothing more. She would be wise to keep a distance between them, more so in private than in public.

"If I didn't guess his inclinations, I'd venture that Major Whitehead was infatuated with you himself."

"Stuff and nonsense. Major Whitehead is a decent man, a gentleman, nothing more."

"Rather something more. He's an English officer of dragoons who's quartered in your home. You wouldn't be the first woman in such circumstances to—"

"Nothing has passed between the major and me."

"I said *if I didn't guess his inclinations,*" Garrett said with a chuckle. "It's lucky he does favor you. You'd have poor shift with your cousin."

Caroline glared at him. "The major is infatuated, all right, but not with me—with my ten thousand pounds. He wants the bribe, and I want my brother back alive. Can you understand that, Mr. Faulkner?"

"I think Garrett and Caroline would be better, considering our relationship."

"Our relationship—as you put it—is a business one. I need your protection, and you need my money. Things will be simpler if we can maintain a respect for each other and—"

"Who said I didn't respect you?" He laughed indulgently. "Didn't I just offer you the only bed in the house?"

She unconsciously raised a hand to smooth the stray curls that fell over her face. "I don't want to fight with you," she said.

"Nor I with you, Caroline Faulkner. And you needn't fear me, although you'd try the morals of a saint, sitting all rosy and soft here in the firelight. I've always loved women and they me. But I've never taken one by force and I'm not about to start now."

"That's reassuring," she said, but her mouth was strangely dry, and she could not keep from noticing how a few strands of his wheat-brown hair had come loose from his queue. Garrett's eyes had a way of seeming to undress her without ever being crude. He was no devil, but the thought came to her that if Satan had minions, Garrett might well fit the bill. "It's foolish for both of us to sit up all night. Go to bed."

"You go to bed."

"I've no intention of taking off my clothes with you in the room," she admitted.

"Ah, so you are afraid of me," he teased.

"I am not. I just think we should establish some rules for our relationship."

Rules for me, she thought frantically. All her life she had lived within a boundary of rules. As Caroline Talbot she was expected to do this and that; she was encased in a silver setting of conscience. She had been given many blessings as the heiress to Fortune's Gift, but responsibilities weighed heavy on her shoulders. Now this man dared her to test the limits of her life, and she was afraid.

"You expect us to remain married for five years and never get undressed?"

"Don't try to make me the fool," she said. "At home, we will have separate bedrooms. Naturally, we will—"

"Pretend to be the loving couple," he finished wryly. "Don't think I will sit at your feet like a hound. I've business of my own to tend to. My own land . . . my—"

"No, of course not," she interrupted. "And I am grateful. Reed's safety depends on—"

"Reed's safety. What of yours, Caroline?" His gray eyes were suddenly serious. "Are you such a paragon of virtue that you never think of what you want?"

"You mock me," she answered smoothly. "Do you think that because I am a woman, I can't put my responsibilities ahead of my own wishes?" I know exactly what I want, she cried inwardly, but I dare not give in to those feelings. I dare not allow myself to become controlled by any man . . . let alone you.

He rose to his feet, took a step toward her, and groaned as he put weight on his bad leg.

"Oh," she said. "Your wound. Let me . . ." She slipped her arm around him to assist him to bed. "Let me help you." Suddenly she wasn't beside him; somehow she was standing in the circle of his arms and he was staring down at her.

"Don't," she protested huskily.

"Don't do what?" he asked. "This?"

He lowered his head and his lips brushed the corner of her mouth. Lightly . . . as lightly as a butterfly wing. Desire spiraled through her, and she began to shiver despite the heat from the open fireplace.

"Or this?" He kissed her ear and the curve of her neck beneath it.

She drew in a deep breath and slowly savored the sweet, wild sensations racing through her veins.

His fingers touched the nape of her neck, sliding between her hairline and the high ruffle of her silk gown. "Does this offend you?" he murmured, as his fingers traced minute circles across her skin. "Or this?"

His breath smelled of mint as his mouth covered hers. His lips were warm and firm, his tongue teasing as it glided across the surface of her teeth.

Caroline groaned softly, seeing clearly the trap he'd laid for her, yet willingly flying into it with arms outstretched. What harm, she told herself, as she surrendered to the delicious kiss, what harm can come of a few shared caresses?

His strong fingers slid down her spine, pressing, massaging, finding her cramped muscles and easing their stiffness. His hands were magic, and his mouth . . . Caroline's knees went weak. His mouth was sheer sorcery, and she was tinder to his flame.

Her senses swirled. She felt as though she had been drinking the strongest wine, but she knew it wasn't wine that intoxicated her—it was Garrett's touch.

Boldly, she opened to him, then met his tongue with hers in an erotic dance that took her to the edge of danger and let her glimpse the pleasures that beckoned beyond this lingering kiss.

"Caroline, you are a wonder," he whispered huskily when they paused for breath. "You're all fire and honey." He caught her hand and lifted it to his lips, then nibbled on her fingertips, sending waves of bright desire up her arm. Gently turning her palm, he planted warm, damp kisses on the underside of her wrist.

She could the heated blood pounding in her veins . . . feel her will weakening. I want him to make love to me, she thought. I want him as I have never wanted another man. He is my lawful husband before God. Why shouldn't I—

This is not the time. Kutti's warning came loud and clear inside her mind. *There is great danger. You must flee while there is still a chance.* Caroline's eyes widened. The Incan wasn't here—she knew he wasn't. She and Garrett were alone. Kutii had never intruded on her privacy before.

What harm will this do? she argued mentally.

Kutii's voice in her head was relentless. *This is the man but not the time.*

Garrett's tongue brushed the pulse at her wrist.

"That tickles," Caroline said, pulling back. She swallowed, trying to make sense of her confused emotions, trying to regain the control she had nearly lost.

"Caroline." The husky way he said her name sent shivers up her spine and she sighed.

Kutii's message had broken the spell. Garrett's arms were just as warm, his smell as inviting, but cold reason had returned to guide her.

Another time, she thought. And there would be another time. Unwilling to let the last notes of the magic fade, she stroked his strong jaw and slid her fingers into his silky brown hair. "You are somewhat of a wonder yourself, Garrett Faulkner. I don't know what to make of you. I feel like a hunter who set a snare for a pigeon and caught a hawk instead." She smiled at him. "Pigeons are good for pie, but I'm not yet certain what good a hawk may be."

"I didn't want a wife," he said.

"Nor I a husband."

He glanced toward the poster bed, wondering just how compliant she was prepared to be and how much grief his wound would give him in a delicate situation.

She chuckled, and the sound reminded him of water trickling over rocks. "I don't consider going to bed with you part of our arrangement," she murmured.

He sighed, partly disappointed, but also intrigued that the chase would not end so soon. "You can't blame me for hoping," he answered.

"Nay, I do not." She slipped out of his arms. "I like your kisses. In fact, I think I may say that I like them very much."

"And I like yours." How had she managed to affect him so deeply? he wondered. She was shapely and pleasing to look at, but he had known many lovely women. And Caroline Steele was not his type. He smiled. He hadn't thought she was his type. But now . . . He was glad the folds of the banyan covered his loins.

"You may as well take the bed, Garrett," she said. "You couldn't pay me to sleep there after . . ." She trailed off and he saw that her cheeks were tinted pink. "You are an exasperating man," she continued, "but I suspect I'm telling you nothing you haven't heard before."

He returned to the high-backed chair near the fireplace. "Then neither of us will sleep well tonight," he answered. The ache in his groin reminded him of just how disappointed he was. "It's been a long time since I allowed my actions to be dictated by a woman . . . even a desirable woman such as yourself."

"You're a stubborn man." She rested her hand on the back of the matching chair.

"I've been told that before too."

"Not too stubborn to see reason, I hope."

"Whose reason. Yours or mine?"

She moistened her lips with the tip of her tongue. Her lower lip was full and sensual. He remembered the taste of it, and he began to wonder if even a ship would be worth the trouble she was bound to cause him.

She stiffened. "I haven't been completely honest with you," she said.

A tightness filled his chest. "Go on," he urged. "Don't stop just when it's getting interesting."

"I promised you money if you would marry me."

"You did and I'll have it." He felt his temper rising. What excuse was she going to make to avoid giving him his due?

"I don't have any."

"What?" He leaped up, forgetting his bad leg, and the pain nearly knocked him back in the chair. Gritting his teeth, he glared at her. "What lies are you—"

"No lies, but the truth," she said, putting the chair between them. "I have the money. I just can't get to it. Father never believed there would be a war. Most of our wealth is in London. I can't release it as long as Bruce—"

Garrett swore under his breath. "You led me to believe—"

"Wait!" She threw up her hand. "I never meant to cheat you. You'll get everything I promised. It's just that you will have to take me south to the Caribbean to get it for you."

Black rage clouded his vision. Veins pulsed in his temples. He covered his face with his hands and swore again—a sailor's oath so foul that it scorched his tongue. He'd been had. By a woman. He'd been so eager to get another ship under his feet that he'd been led into the lion's den like a green farm boy. He wanted to hit something. Someone. "Son of a swiving seacook," he muttered. He raised his gaze to meet hers and his fingers clutched the wooden back of the chair. "You've nerve to stay within reach of me," he said between clenched teeth, "when I'd like nothing better than to wring your pretty little neck."

He could read the fear in her eyes. She trembled, but she stood, chin high, small hands balled into fists, and faced him like some ancient warrior queen. "I want control of my money as badly as you do," she said huskily. "If I'd told you before, I was afraid you wouldn't marry me. I can get gold in the islands—I swear it."

"Like you swore before?"

"I didn't lie to you, Garrett. I just didn't tell you everything." Her composure faltered. "Please, you must believe me. I need you. If you'll take me and my sister to Arawak Island near Jamaica—to our sugarcane plantation there—I'll give you whatever you ask." Her voice dropped to a whisper. "Whatever you ask."

"All I've ever wanted from you was a ship."

"I have ships in the Caribbean. Bruce doesn't know of any of our affairs there." Tears welled in her huge dark eyes. "There's no one else I can turn to, Garrett. My cousin raped Amanda, and now he's threatening to sell her south. I need to get her away from Fortune's Gift—away from Maryland. And I need to get my hands on enough of my money to ransom Reed."

"You want me to take you to the Caribbean?"

She nodded. "Me, Amanda, and Amanda's son, Jeremy."

He studied her delicate features. Was she lying again? "How do you expect me to trust you?"

"I'll wager my soul that you've not been honest with me either," she dared. "I'd have to be a complete ninny to believe the story you gave me when you invaded my bedchamber the night the powder magazine was blown."

"You know for a fact that there's money and ships to be had on Arawak?"

"I have gold there. I'm not sure where the ships

are, but my steward will know. They sail the Caribbean on trading voyages."

"How much gold?"

"Enough. Yes or no?"

Garrett considered her offer for several long seconds, then realized he'd probably not get a better one. He'd been a fool not to think her cousin would tie up her ready cash. If she was being honest with him this time, his plans would only be delayed. He could find a crew in the Caribbean. He pursed his lips. Where better to find fighting men who knew a gunnel from a yardarm. With gold in his pocket, he could buy sailors who didn't care what flag they sailed under.

"Please," she murmured. "We must get away quickly."

"I'll take you," he agreed, "but my price has just doubled. Twenty percent. And heaven help you, woman, if you're lying to me again."

Chapter 7

Fortune's Gift Plantation
Maryland's Eastern Shore

The clock on the hall landing had just struck midnight when Caroline slipped quietly out of the house and hurried toward Laborers' Row, the cluster of cabins beyond the orchard where her workers and their families lived.

Two awkward days had passed since her wedding to Garrett Faulkner. When they'd returned to Fortune's Gift the morning after the ceremony, Major Whitehead had found a letter from Lord Cornwallis assuring him of the loyalty of his cousin. Garrett had been released from house arrest and had left immediately to settle affairs on his own land.

Caroline had wanted to seek out Amanda before tonight, but even with Bruce still in custody, she had been unable to leave the house without alarming the sentries.

This evening, the guard at the kitchen door was sound asleep. Caroline's special spiced wine had assured that. She had delivered the drugged spirits to the young dragoon with her own hands, so that if something went wrong none of her servants would be blamed.

The night was icy cold. She shivered and pulled her cloak more tightly around her. Clouds scudded across the sky, hanging low over the plantation, and Caroline smelled a threat of snow on the raw, salt breeze that blew from the Chesapeake. There were no sounds but the dry crackle of frozen grass under her feet and the rattle of branches as she left the path and moved into the total blackness of the orchard. She had never been afraid of darkness, not even as a small child, but tonight she felt a strange uneasiness and wished she had brought a weapon with her.

An owl hooted and she started, then chuckled when she recognized the familiar sound. "Kutii?" she whispered. "Is that you?" When she was young, he would sometimes tease her by imitating birds. Owls were his favorites. "Kutii?"

Nothing.

She waited, holding her breath, straining to hear. Again, all she heard was the wind's eerie song through the leafless branches. A lump formed in her throat as she exhaled softly and began to walk on.

And heard the loud snap of a twig behind her.

"Who is it?" she demanded. "Who's there?"

It could be a deer, or an opossum, or even a family of raccoons, she told herself. Food was scarce in winter. Wild creatures did come near the house when they were hungry. She swallowed; her mouth was dry. Frosty fingers of dread brushed the back of her neck.

Something is there.

Not something, her instincts shouted. *Someone.*

"I'm not afraid of you," she called out boldly. It was a bald-faced lie. She was terrified.

Caroline took a step backward, then another, and heard the unmistakable crunch of a human footstep on the frozen soil.

She wanted to run back to the manor house, but even her courage wasn't enough for that, so she whirled and dashed toward Laborers' Row. Her heart thudded wildly as she fled the lonely orchard, but she heard no pursuit. She kept running until she'd left the apple trees far behind her.

Breathless and feeling somewhat foolish for panicking at noises in the darkness, Caroline slowed her pace to a jog. She could smell wood smoke and barely make out a lighted window in one of the cabins.

A dog barked inside. She heard a man's gruff voice order, "Quiet down!" Firelight illuminated a patch of interior in the small, neat dwelling. She saw a man, naked from the waist up, cross in front of the glowing hearth. Something thumped against the door, the dog yipped, and there was silence.

Not here, Caroline decided. That hut was being used by two brothers who worked with the lumbering crew. Neither of them was married. Amanda wouldn't seek shelter with them. The next cabin was occupied by Willy Jenkins and his wife. Amanda didn't like Willy; she and Jeremy wouldn't be there either. She would hide with one of the black families.

Caroline crossed the rutted dirt road and sought out one of the larger cabins. Mazie Adamma and her two daughters, Ruth and Jane, lived here. Mazie was a skilled weaver. She'd been born on Fortune's Gift, married here, and buried two husband in the family graveyard. Mazie was respected among the bondmen and women, and the free workers. If Amanda and Jeremy weren't here, Mazie would know where they were. Caroline rapped on the low wooden door.

"Who is it?"

Caroline recognized Mazie's voice. "It's Caroline. Let me in."

Caroline heard a rustling, and then the door opened a crack. Outlined in the light from the hearth was a kerchief-covered head and the business end of an ancient wheel-lock musket.

"Miss Caroline? That you?"

"Yes, Mazie. It's me. Put the gun down, and let me in." The door opened wider, and Caroline stepped inside. Immediately, she heard a baby fussing. "Amanda?" she called.

"Caroline?" Her sister's sleepy voice came from the loft. "Is it safe?"

"You think I would have let her in if it wasn't?" Mazie protested. The tall, broad-shouldered black woman dropped a thick wooden bar across the door. "What you doin' here in the middle of the night, Miss Caroline? You got trouble with your new man? Manda told us you was gettin' married over to Oxford with that boy from Faulkner's Folly."

Caroline smiled. "No, Mazie. I don't have trouble with my husband." Not yet, she thought. It was warm and cozy inside, and the cabin smelled of sage and drying tobacco. Sheaths of cured leaves hung from the rafters, along with smoked hams, gourds, and bundles of herbs. In one corner stood a waist-high corn mortar carved from the trunk of a tree. Over the door was a horseshoe with the open end up for luck, and a painted African mask that Mazie swore kept away witches.

"That Cap'n Bruce slinkin' around outside?" Mazie lowered her musket and peered out her single glass-paned window into the cold darkness.

Caroline almost wished it were he. The last man who had tried to force his way into this house had been dropped in his tracks by one ball from Mazie's musket.

"Should I bring Jeremy down?" Amanda asked.

"No, let him sleep." Caroline went to the hearth and held her hands to the fire. Mazie's older daughter got up and lit a candle. The younger, Jane, crawled out of her trundle bed, pulled on a shift and moccasins, and began to heat a kettle of water for tea.

Amanda came down the ladder and hugged Caroline. "I've been so worried about you," she said. She'd braided her black hair in two long plaits down her back, and in the shadowy cabin she looked to Caroline like an Indian. Amanda's eyes were red. She looked sad . . . but then Caroline hadn't seen Amanda smile since Bruce had forced himself on her sexually.

"Is Jeremy all right?" Caroline asked, squeezing her sister's hand. "I've been worried sick about the two of you."

Amanda nodded. "He's fine. He wants his toys, but Mazie's been helping me with him."

The joy is gone out of her voice, Caroline thought. She doesn't sound like Amanda anymore. She sounds old and beaten—like Ida Wright. Damn her cousin. All his life he'd hurt people without ever paying the consequences. Why couldn't it be Bruce who was dead and buried in the graveyard instead of a decent man like Wesley?

"Jeremy ain't no trouble," the older woman put in. "Good to have a man-child crawlin' around underfoot. I raised six boys, and a body don't forget how to look after them."

"He's cutting teeth," Amanda said.

"I need to talk to you—alone," Caroline confided. "I don't want to put Mazie in any more danger than she already is."

"Go on with you, girl," Mazie said, shaking sassafras tea makings into a thick earthen pot. "You young ones don't know what danger is. Jane, Ruth, you two go on up and see to that baby. No sense in fillin' your heads with stuff you don't need to hear." The young women obeyed without question.

Caroline smiled. Mazie Adamma kept a strict house. Her sons were grown and scattered, two with their own wives here on Fortune's Gift. Her four oldest girls had married well and were all living with freemen in their own homes. It was plain that Mazie would keep a tight rein on these last two as long as they lived under her roof. "It's well you hear what I have to tell Amanda," Caroline said. "We're going away, and I'll need your help to keep the other women at their tasks while I'm gone. My new husband is going to take Amanda, Jeremy, and me south to the islands."

"You goin' treasure huntin', ain't you, Miss Caroline? Goin' to Arawak Island and huntin' up that lost Injun gold," Mazie said. "No need to fib to me, I know that's what you're up to."

"What makes you think so?" Caroline asked.

"Ain't you bragged about doin' just that from the time you was knee high to a duck? All I heard one winter was 'Going for the ghost treasure, Mazie. Goin' to buy you a horse and wagon, Mazie.' You think I forgot that?"

"I was a romantic child then. This is real. I need the money to ransom Reed from the British," Caroline explained.

Amanda shook her head. "But that's just a legend, Caroline. You don't know that the treasure actually exists. We can't go all the way down there chasing a ghost tale."

"We can and we will," Caroline answered. She gripped Amanda's hand more tightly. "Garrett married me for money I can't get to. The Incan gold will buy him the ship he wants and free Reed. I know it's real. And I know I can find it if I go there."

"Mother Mary," Mazie intoned. "You tell that new husband of yours that you chasing a ghost story? Caves full of gold and pagan idols! That's stuff for babes still on the teat."

"The gold is there. I know it," Caroline insisted.

"You know it. You don't know anything," Amanda chided.

"Kutii told me," Caroline said. "He wouldn't lie to me."

Mazie crossed herself. "You quit that crazy talk, Miss Caroline. "No wonder ignorant people go callin' you funny. All this talk about ghosts and Injun gold. What happened to my grandmother when she got stole away from her family back in Africky is real. This war 'tween General Washington and the Brits is real. And what some ghost what ain't—told you don't make no sense. And if you done told your new husband you got gold on Arawak Island, he in for one big surprise."

An hour later, Caroline left the cabin. She hadn't been able to convince Amanda that they were doing the right thing, but Amanda would come with her and she would bring Jeremy. Her sister had no other choice. If they remained on Fortune's Gift, they knew that somehow Bruce would find a way to get to her again. And if she left the plantation, she'd be in the same kind of danger that all dark-skinned women knew.

It was all so unfair, Caroline thought. Amanda had listened to bedtime stories on their father's knee, been hugged and spanked by their mother. Amanda was only two years younger than she was, the same age as Reed. There never was a time Caroline could remember that her sister wasn't part of the family.

People might stare on the streets of Annapolis when Caroline and Amanda rode by in a carriage wearing the latest gowns from London. Neighbors might gossip about the Talbots of Fortune's Gift who'd taken a black child to raise as one of their own. But it had never really mattered what other people thought or said. Her parents' wealth and position had always protected them from social ostracism. At Caroline's eighteenth birthday party, even the royal governor had danced with Amanda. And after that, who could pretend that she didn't exist?

In many ways, Amanda had always been the daughter her father wanted. Amanda was kind and gentle, a natural peacemaker. When Caroline and Reed were blackening each other's eyes and pushing each other out the barn loft window, Amanda was learning French, embroidery, and painting. Caroline preferred to spend her days on horseback following Father over the plantation; Amanda wrote poetry and read Latin histories. It was Amanda, not Caroline, who could whip up a heavenly light almond pastry or plan a cold supper for forty guests. If their father had said it once, he had said it a hundred times. "Caroline, you are such a wild Indian. Why can't you be more like your sister?"

In those golden times, it seemed that they all forgot the hue of Amanda's skin, forgot that she was a daughter of Africa, not England. And no one had posed the question, "What will become of Amanda?" until both girls were almost grown.

"Who will I marry?" Amanda had asked that night of Caroline's wonderful birthday celebration. "No white man will ask for my hand, and I'll not go down to live on Laborers' row to get a husband."

Caroline had laughed at the picture that would make—Amanda with her silks and brocades, her dainty slippers and flowered hats, tripping among the log cabins on stylish pattens. "A Moorish prince will come," Caroline had teased. "He'll hear of your exotic beauty—of your hair like black silk and—"

"More like black wool," Amanda had protested between giggles. Her hair was a thick riot of curls that no amount of pins would hold in place. Her nose was wide, her lips full, her eyes as large and shining brown as the new-plowed earth. And her skin . . . her skin was the color of dark, sweet chocolate.

"Anyway," Caroline had continued, "this Moorish prince—"

"I don't care for any Moorish husband," her sister had replied haughtily. "They have their own heathen religion. I could never marry anyone but a good Christian."

Caroline had sighed. Amanda had always been religious-minded as well. "Mama says that no religion is heathen," she'd reminded Amanda. "There is only one God over us all."

"No Moors. If you want to be locked in some sultan's harem, *you* marry a Moor."

"Well then," she had said, "an Indian chief—a handsome Christian warrior with millions of acres of land and hair as black as yours. You can insist that he build you a wonderful brick house and a rose garden before the wedding. I'll come and visit you in the wilderness."

"Why don't you marry the Indian?" Amanda had suggested wryly. "You'd have so much more in common. Then you can live in the woods and I'll come and visit you."

"If I marry an Indian, he'll have to live on Fortune's Gift. After all . . ." Caroline had raised both hands and tilted her head in what she hoped was a regal manner. "I am," she said solemnly, "the heiress."

Amanda had thrown a pillow at her. Caroline had returned the favor, and both had dissolved into laughter. So long ago . . . Caroline mused. It almost seemed as though it had been another lifetime. Before they'd lost Mama and Father. Before the war . . .

Caroline shivered in the night air. Mazie had offered a lantern, but she didn't want to be seen. She'd convinced herself she'd been frightened earlier by a rabbit, or perhaps just the wind. She'd been jumping at shadows. No one had followed her. No one was there in the orchard now.

She left the road and walked across the open field toward the rows of apple trees. She was still terribly worried about Amanda. This rape had shattered her sister. In some ways, she had taken it harder than whatever had happened the night Jeremy was conceived.

Caroline couldn't help but wonder why . . .

Jeremy was a child of mixed race. Even at eight months, no one could look at him and deny his white blood. His skin was a light café-au-lait, his black hair straight, his baby nose and lips much thinner than Amanda's.

Amanda had never spoken of her assault. She had never given the slightest hint who Jeremy's father was. And no pleading from Caroline could get her to tell what had happened. It was Amanda's way to keep her privacy. Caroline had no doubt that someone had forced her sister;

Amanda's morals were without question. But Amanda had gone through her pregnancy and childbirth without revealing her tragic secret. And she had loved Jeremy with all her heart and soul since the moment he was born. How many women, Caroline wondered, could have forgotten the pain and shame the baby's father had caused her? It just proved how sweet and good Amanda was.

Bruce's rape had been violent. Amanda had fought him tooth and nail. He'd blackened her eyes and bloodied her face. Bruce had admitted the attack and shown no remorse for what he'd done. And although her sister's physical injuries had faded, she'd not been the same since. Caroline was afraid that Amanda would never be again.

There would be no child of this assault. Enough time had passed to be certain of that. But even that grace hadn't brushed the shadows from Amanda's eyes.

The orchard loomed ahead of her. She stopped and listened, then entered the shadows. This was the quickest way; if she went around the orchard, it would take her much longer to get back to the house, and she was cold enough already.

She had gone about halfway when she heard a cough—not a human noise, but something more like a horse blowing air through its lips. Caroline froze. "Is someone there?" she asked with more bravado than she felt. "Kutii? Is that you?"

She took another step and collided with a cloaked figure. "Oh!" she cried.

"Caroline. It's me, Garrett. Don't scream."

Her mouth tasted of the metallic bite of terror. She went completely numb.

"It's Garrett," he repeated.

She couldn't hide the sigh of relief that escaped

her lips. "Damn you," she said. "You scared me half to death."

"Who's Ty?"

"Why are you following me? It was you before too, wasn't it? You were here in the orchard when I—"

"Yes."

Her Talbot temper flared. "Why didn't you make yourself known to me? Is this what you do for fun—frighten helpless women?"

He chuckled. "You're hardly helpless, Caroline. I wanted to see what you were up to, sneaking around in the middle of the night. Who's this Ty?"

"Not Ty, you idiot, Kutii. He's a family friend."

"One who lurks about in orchards in the night?"

"You've nerve to talk about lurking around!" She gave him a shove backward. "What are you doing here? What do you want of me?"

Garrett's humor took a definite turn for the worse. "I am your husband. Have you forgotten that so soon?"

"Husband or not, it doesn't give you the right to scare me half to death," she retorted. The more she thought about how frightened she was, the angrier she became. "You're lucky I didn't have a pistol. I'd have shot you."

"Heaven help wandering livestock if you blast away at every shadow that moves." He laid a hand on her arm. "You said you wanted me to take you south to the islands. I've found us a boat, but we have to go now. I was coming to the house to tell you when I saw you come out of the kitchen courtyard."

"Wrapped in this hooded cloak, how could you tell it was me?" she demanded.

"You have a way of walking, but that's beside the point. Do you want to go to the Caribbean or not? And what were you doing out here? It's not safe to wander around. Not for a woman. There are too many—"

"The night I can't walk Fortune's Gift without an escort is the day I want to die," she retorted. "This is my home—these are my people. No one here would hurt me."

"No? Like they wouldn't hurt your Amanda?" He took hold of her other arm and pulled her so close that she could feel his warm breath on her face. "There's a war on, Caroline. Your home is occupied by British soldiers, and the woods are crawling with Tory and rebel raiders alike. There's no safety here for a woman, no matter her age or position."

"I won't argue with you over that," Caroline said. "I went to see Amanda tonight. She's been hidden with one of the—"

"I saw where you went. How long did you suppose you could keep her away from Bruce?"

"It worked."

"I doubt he wanted to find her very badly. He was more concerned with you."

He let go of her, and she found she was still shivering, although not from cold. She wanted to hit him. She wanted him to kiss her again as he had the night of their wedding. Whenever Garrett Faulkner came near her, she lost all rational powers of reason. "What do you mean 'go now'?" she asked breathlessly. "This week? Tomorrow?"

"Not tomorrow, girl. Now."

"I'll have to have things from the house. Jewelry. A little money. Some clothing and—"

"One bag, Caroline. A small one. If we intend to slip out from under the British eye, we'll not do it in a man-of-war. My friend is waiting with a sloop. We'll cross the bay and meet a larger vessel—"

"Tonight?"

"Can I make it clearer?" Garrett's patience was clearly worn thin. "Come back with me to the cabin and tell the woman to go with me. I'll escort her and the child down to the river. Dress warmly."

"Garrett?"

"What is it?"

"I can trust you, can't I? Amanda's not strong. She—"

"She'll have to be strong to make this voyage. Do you think we can reach the Caribbean in—"

"No, you don't understand. Amanda's not sickly. She'll cause you no trouble. It's just that she's been hurt. She's very fragile. If I tell her to trust you and—"

"You think I'd treat her like your cousin did—"

"No. If I believed that, I'd never have taken vows with you. Just be gentle with her. Don't look at the color of her skin. She's a lady, Garrett, a real lady."

"And you, wife? What are you?"

The words *a witch* came to her lips, but she didn't utter them. "I'm not weak," she answered softly. "I can give as good as I get."

"You'd better. For if I risk everything to take you to this island, you'd best—"

"No more threats," she said firmly. "How can we get along if you continually threaten me? If you say we're going tonight, then let's get on with it. If we stand here much longer, my feet will turn to solid ice."

"Do you want me to come into the house with you?"

She shook her head. "No. The dogs would

rouse. Wait for me at the river. I'll fetch my things and meet you there."

"Not at the landing," he warned. "Farther down, around the bend. Come to the sandy beach and I'll carry you out to the sloop."

"Can I ask you something?" she said.

"I don't promise to answer."

"Did you blow up the powder store that first night?"

"Are you mad?" He sounded insulted. "How can you ask that of me, girl? Aren't you a loyal Englishwoman?"

"I just wondered," she said meekly. And it wasn't until she was nearly to the house before she realized that Garrett hadn't answered her question at all.

"You did it," she whispered. "Loyalist, hell. You're a Continental, Garrett Faulkner. And you just don't trust me enough yet to admit the truth."

Chapter 8

It was midmorning of the following day when the courier galloped into Fortune's Gift and handed Major Whitehead's aide a worn leather pouch containing several routine reports and a single slim envelope. The corporal, Milton Jakes, emptied the pouch and stacked the contents in the precise center of the major's desk before returning to the mug of ale he'd been sharing in the kitchen with two fellow dragoons.

Upstairs, the major groaned and lay back on his pillow, waving away the tea and toast the black servant offered. "Nothing," Whitehead said. "My stomach's turned inside out and my bowels are in shreds."

"Just a touch of ague, sir," Toby said. "Tea will help you get your strength back."

"Nothing I said." The officer moaned and drew himself into a fetal position. "Tell my aide that I'm not to be disturbed."

"Yes, sir, Major, sir." Toby hummed inwardly as he let himself out of the officer's bedchamber and carried the tray down the front stairs.

The entrance hall was empty. Toby looked both ways, then walked through the wide corridors to the office. He set the tray with its blue and white Chinese patterned teapot, handleless cup, and plate of toast on a small table, and began to build up the fire.

"Wind sure is fierce today," Toby mumbled to

no one in particular. Icy branches of a bare lilac tapped against the window. From the corner of his eye, he caught a glimpse of a black tail moving between the desk and the hearth. "Cat? Is that you?" Toby looked behind the desk and saw only painted baseboard. Suddenly the small office felt chilly. Quickly, he gathered up two dirty mugs, picked up his tray, and left the room.

A ragged black cat with only one ear, and a scarred nub where the second should be, leaped up on the desk and gazed at the pile of reports. Flames crackled on the hearth and a cherry log snapped.

Outside a gust of wind shook the lilac bush and rattled the branches of the great yellow poplar tree behind it. The house shuddered as a wind devil spiraled down the chimney and sent ashes flying into the room. The cat padded in a tight circle, settled down, wrapped his tail around his body, and began to purr.

Another heavy blast of wind struck the corner of the house. The cat's eyes narrowed to thin yellow slits, and he began to lick his glossy fur.

The crack of a frozen limb giving way was lost in the howl of the winter wind whipping off the bay. The limb swayed, caught briefly on another branch, and tumbled down onto the lilac. One leafless prong hit hard against a single windowpane. The glass shattered and wind streamed through the opening.

Not a single hair on the cat's back ruffled as the reports on the major's desk scattered across the room and one thin envelope spun onto the hearth. At first, the beige paper quivered. Next, one corner blackened and a thin thread of smoke drifted up. In seconds, the envelope burst into flame, twisting and turning until it was consumed by the yellow-red fire.

Kutii stoked the tomcat's head and smiled. Then he strode to the hearth with the swift, sure strides of a warrior and used the sole of his bare foot to grind the last of the sparks out on the wide red bricks.

Footsteps sounded in the hall outside, but when the door opened, the room was empty. All that remained was the icy wind coming in through the broken windowpane and a smell of swirling ashes.

It was morning of the third day when Major Whitehead returned to his regular duties and another twenty-four hours before a bearded Tory scout arrived at his door with a message that shook the commander to the soles of his shiny Hessian boots.

"Opsrey? The devil you say! Garrett Faulkner is Osprey?"

"Did ye nay get me report, Major?" The hard-faced ranger leaned across the commandant's desk. "My informant said we'd have only hours to catch them before they sailed south to the Caribbean. Osprey's found the means to get another ship. If you've let him slip through your fingers, it'll be your ass that burns, not mine. I sent copies of the same message to General Knyphausen's headquarters and to Howe. I'll not take the blame for this, Whitehead."

"You've evidence to back up your—"

"Proof enough to hang Faulkner from the nearest yardarm. General Howe's offered a hundred pounds for Osprey's real name. I had to pay twenty to my informant, and I mean to collect the rest. Ye can still catch him. How far can he get with two women and a suckling babe? If they've escaped ye, ye'd best do somethin' to get them back, Whitehead. When Howe learns of this, you'll spend the rest of the war shovelin' horseshit."

"That remains to be seen, Taylor. Since I never received any such message from you, I must be in doubt that you sent it. Wait outside."

When the blustering Tory was gone, Whitehead searched through his reports to make certain the missing letter hadn't been overlooked. Then he went to his files and removed the collection of information on the privateer captain known as Osprey. He read it through twice, noting the number of British ships sunk and cargo stolen by the traitor. Then he opened the door and summoned his aide. "Release Captain Talbot and send him to me," he ordered. "Immediately."

He closed the door, folded his arms across his chest, and began to pace back and forth. First the woman gone, and now this! How in the name of all that was holy could he have misjudged the pair so badly? Faulkner was a relative of Lord Cornwallis . . . He had influential friends in high places and had served his country honorably at sea. How could a man like Garrett Faulkner be the traitor Osprey?

When Whitehead had risen from his sickbed and learned that Caroline was missing, he'd naturally assumed she was with her new husband. Neither of them was under arrest. He'd had no reason to consult Captain Talbot or even to tell him of his cousin's absence.

He had every intention of freeing Talbot after he'd cooled his heels in the makeshift cellar jail cell. Talbot needed to learn manners. But he'd seen no need for a formal court-martial. A proper public apology from the captain, some extra duties, and a small fine would have satisfied Whitehead.

After all, if he got rid of Bruce Talbot, headquarters might send him someone even less efficient.

Now there was a totally different light on matters. If Talbot had had Osprey and he'd let him escape—no, not only let him, he'd assisted him. God's teeth! He'd even participated in Faulkner's wedding—being one of the witnesses.

A man's career had been lost for far less than this, Whitehead thought, regretfully. He'd been deceived by the prospect of extracting ten thousand pounds sterling from the girl. Now, he'd lost not only the money, but a dangerous traitor as well.

Remembering the missive from Lord Cornwallis, Whitehead went back to the deck and thumbed through his correspondence until he found it. Yes! There it was in black and white. *Mr. Garrett Faulkner is to be released from house arrest.* The major breathed a sigh of relief. He had only acted against his own best judgment after receiving direct orders from his general. He'd make a written statement to that end. Taylor's bungling of the message, and Captain Talbot's involvement, only added pages of complications to the official report. He would issue a warrant for the arrest of Faulkner at once. If the man had left Maryland, it was hardly his fault, after all. The navy should have finished Osprey at Lewes.

Whitehead had banished the last of his panic by the time Bruce Talbot reached the office, and he maintained a cool detachment as he informed the captain of the unfortunate happenings of the past few days.

"Gone? Caroline's gone?" Talbot said. He'd not troubled to shave during his confinement, and Whitehead found the captain's uniform in disgusting condition.

"So it seems," Whitehead admitted. "But you

are still in control of her finances. And since she seems to have married a traitor, I must believe the courts would be unwilling to return Fortune's Gift and Mistress Caroline's other assets to an enemy of the crown." He smiled at Talbot, but the pleasantry extended no further than his lips. His eyes were hard. "I believe what happened between us at the church can be overlooked and we can continue on here as we were. Naturally, I will expect you to permit legal defense of Reed Talbot to continue. Difficult case, I understand. But he is your blood cousin. Even a loyal Englishman would want to see an innocent man get a fair trial."

Bruce scoffed. "You expect me to pay to get Reed out of prison?"

"To get him legal representation. A different matter indeed," Whitehead said loftily. "A long process, I understand. Considering the conditions of the prison ships, it's possible that a man could die while waiting for his trial."

"It's possible," Bruce agreed. "As I understand it, I help you cover your back in this, and you whitewash my military records."

"There's no reason to be crude, Captain Talbot."

"And you expect to drain money from Fortune's Gift?"

"For Reed Talbot's legal defense."

"I think we understand each other, Major." Bruce's face twisted into a grin. He offered Whitehead his hand. The major hesitated for an instant, then reached out and shook Bruce's firmly.

"Now, let us call Mr. Taylor back in here and see what we can do about convincing him that his message was somehow waylaid before arriving here. After all, if one of us goes down, we will all surely fall together. Chain of command, Captain.

Nothing can touch Lord Cornwallis's reputation. It's possible the courier is at fault."

Much later, Bruce returned to his own room on the second floor, his head pounding. He thought he'd come out of this bargain for the better, but he wasn't certain.

Of one thing he was sure—Caroline Steele hadn't gotten away from him for good. Yes, he controlled her finances now, but what would happen when they beat the Continentals? He had no intention of allowing Caroline or Garrett Faulkner ever to lay claim to Fortune's Gift again. There was one sure way to hold total control of the money—his original plan. He must wed Caroline. Only through her could he gain complete and legal ownership of the wealth she'd inherited.

What if she had married Faulkner? She'd been a widow when Bruce had first courted her; she could easily become a widow again. And if they were going to the Caribbean, there was only one place Caroline could be bound for—the family estates on Arawak Island.

Faulkner might believe that Bruce couldn't follow him south, but he was all too wrong. Bruce might not go himself, but he knew of someone far more influential who was already there.

Falconer.

For a hundred years, the Caribbean had been the private duck pond of a influential family business that operated under the name Falconer.

Some said Falconer was a smuggler and pirate. Others accused him of dealing with the French and Spanish. None denied his power. In ports from Jamaica to Charleston to Philadelphia, Falconer's agents listened and reported on the schedules and cargos of ships. Royal governors boasted of having Falconer as a personal confidant, and some—it was said—paid him tolls so that their vessels would arrive with cargoes intact.

For a century, the Falconer enterprise had grown, and like the roots of a mighty tree, the family's interests had wound themselves around the heart of the shipping industry in the New World. And yet, despite the size of the organization, Falconer had remained very human. His friends tended to prosper, his enemies to fall. It was said that Falconer never forgot a good deed to the company or forgave an evil one.

And Bruce possessed a bit of information that he was certain Falconer would like to have. On October 23, 1776, Osprey had fought a running sea battle with one of Falconer's ships, the *Golden Hare,* a square-rigged brigantine out of Jamaica. According to an eyewitness report, a cannon ball fired by Osprey's gunner had struck the *Hare* at the waterline amidships and sent the Falconer vessel to the bottom. All hands but two were lost.

The *Golden Hare* was suspected of piracy, but that was nothing to Bruce; all that mattered was that Osprey was Falconer's enemy. Bruce seated himself at a table, took a quill pen and sharpened the point, dipped it in an inkwell, and began to write.

An hour and three abortive attempts later, Bruce reread his letter to Falconer. First he explained that Garrett Faulkner was the privateer known as Osprey and that Osprey had sunk the *Golden Hare.* Then he stated that Garrett had married his betrothed under false pretenses. Finally, he made his daring offer. If the family would find his cousin, Caroline Talbot Steele—he refused to give her the title of Caroline Faulkner—dispose of her new husband permanently, and return her safely to him, he would hand over half of her inheritance in gratitude.

He sprinkled sand over the parchment to be sure that the ink was dry, folded it, and slipped it into an envelope. He would send the letter to Falconer's representative in Philadelphia. With luck, Falconer would know Garrett and Caroline were coming before they were halfway to the Caribbean. And he would no doubt prepare a unique welcome.

"I'm glad I'm not you," he said softly, remembering a story he'd heard in Chestertown last year. A tax collector—a representative of the crown—had refused to cooperate with Falconer's captains and insisted on claiming a heavy toll from each shipment that entered the port. Then, abruptly, the tax collector had vanished. He was not found until six months later, when a distiller of rum in Massachusetts broached a keg of West Indies molasses and found the missing man. No blame was ever attached to Falconer, but the next tax collector was much more understanding with Falconer cargoes.

Bruce chuckled. Yes, setting Falconer on Garrett's trail was the best solution. Once Garrett was dead, Bruce could handle Caroline. She would either wed him at once or see her dear brother rot in prison. He went to a window and stared out at the gray, bitter day. "Have a pleasant voyage, cousin," he whispered harshly. "And enjoy your bridegroom." He swallowed against the dryness in his mouth. "Do enjoy," he said, "for you'll be widowed again soon enough." He rubbed the frosted windowpane absently and wondered what it would be like to have both Caroline and Amanda share his bed at the same time.

* * *

Some days later, on the deck of the *Gillian Rose,* a half mile off the coast of Carolina, Garrett Faulkner slept fitfully. Sleet mixed with rain kept up a steady tattoo against the length of sailcloth he had wrapped tightly around him.

The raw, biting cold and the ever-present danger of floating logs and hidden sandbars made the night travel even more hazardous than normal. But this stretch of beach was known to be the haunt of wreckers, land-based pirates who lured merchant ships ashore for loot and murder. The black water of the wind-tossed Atlantic offered little mercy to unwary sailors, but what she did give was more than travelers could expect on land.

Garrett had gone for nearly two days and nights without sleep before he finally nodded off. He was as cold and uncomfortable as the crew and captain of the *Gillian Rose,* but what space below that was not filled with cargo was taken up by Caroline, Amanda, and the baby, leaving only the exposed deck for him, his friend Noah, and Noah's brother Eli.

Sleep had not come easily to Garrett since the sinking of the *Osprey* off Lewes, Delaware. Tonight was no exception. Memories of the sea battle that had cost the lives of his friends and crew tore the fabric of his dreams.

. . . The acrid scent of brimstone choked the smoke-filled passage as Garrett fought his way up the narrow ladder to the deck of the Osprey. *He gasped for air and shielded his face from falling shreds of fiery canvas. Men shrieked in agony as iron chain shot whirled through the riggings, then fell, bringing down splintered spars to rend human flesh like hot wax. Cannon roared from the starboard side; seconds later the boom was echoed off the bow. Garrett staggered and fell facedown on the tilting deck, and when he forced him-*

self up, his hands were soaked in the dark red blood of his comrades . . .

"Garrett! Garrett, wake up!"

Someone was shaking him.

He opened his eyes groggily, pushing back the scene of carnage that filled his head. "Who—"

"It's me, Caroline. Wake up. You're having a nightmare." She shook him again.

He was soaked with perspiration. He could still smell the blood. He could taste it. Coming fully conscious, he realized he'd bitten the inside of his mouth. "What is it?" he said, throwing back the makeshift canvas hood. "Is something wrong?"

She crouched beside him as freezing rain soaked through her wool cloak. For once, she was at a loss for words. How could she tell him that she'd awakened from a terrible dream herself—that she had seen the deck of the *Osprey* in her death throes? That she had seen Wesley fall, clutching his shattered chest . . .

That the vision was real, she had no doubt. But how could she tell Garrett that she possessed witchling powers—that she could see past and sometimes future with unerring accuracy? Or that once she had come awake, she had become aware of his distress?

"What are you doing on deck?" he asked. "Have we sprung a leak? Is the vessel in danger?"

"No more than we've been since we set sail in this floating deathtrap," she said, wiggling under the corner of his sailcloth shelter.

"You've no business being up here," he said gruffly, but he slipped an arm around her, wrapping them both in the thick folds of canvas. "You could have fallen overboard. The deck is slick with ice."

Caroline squirmed until she found a comfortable position, knees drawn up under her full skirts, arms crossed over her chest, and head nestled against Garrett's shoulder. "It stinks down below," she said.

"The open deck is no place for a woman."

She shrugged. All her life she'd gone places and done things that were more expected of a lad. She'd found that the best argument against such narrow male thinking was to do what she wanted and not discuss it. That way, when she didn't fall off the spirited horse, drown in the river, or topple out of a treetop and break her neck, the men who'd been protesting didn't have to admit they were wrong. "You were having a nightmare," she reminded him.

"Is the babe well?"

"Sleeping. What were you dreaming about?"

"My dreams are my own affair. Who remembers what they've dreamed of, once they're awake?"

"I do." She took his hard hand in hers. "And I think you do too." Garrett's tone was as frigid as the open deck, but he didn't pull away from her and she sensed his need for companionship.

"'Tis a foul night," he said. "But the captain claims he's run this stretch in every kind of weather. Cape Hatteras is known for sudden storms. This is where the cold Atlantic waters from the north strike the warm Gulf Stream coming up from the Florida coast. Once, we were sailing south from Philadelphia to—"

"Was that when you were in the British Royal Navy?" She felt his muscles tense slightly. When he answered her, she felt—rather than heard—the thin edge to his voice, and she knew she had touched on a subject Garrett Faulkner didn't care to discuss.

"Forgive me." He made a sound of amusement

and became the polished gentleman again. "I should be reassuring you, instead of boring you with old sea stories. I'm sorry if these accommodations aren't what you're used to. A spring sailing date would have been much more pleasant, but once we reach the waters off Georgia, the weather should start to improve."

"How is your leg holding up?" she asked. There was more to this man she'd married than she had first believed, and she was determined to break through his carefully constructed exterior. "You've not had further bleeding, have you?" She'd noticed he still limped when he walked, but the pain lines around his eyes were gone.

"The wound is healing. Your nursing skills are excellent."

"I would have done better with more preparation. You gave me little warning that first night you came to my bedchamber."

"I didn't have a great deal of warning myself."

They sat in silence for a long time, with only the sounds of the rain and water and the creak of rope and canvas. She knew she should have been frightened here in this wild place, but she wasn't. Garrett Faulkner had a solidness about him that made her feel safe.

Gradually, his body warmth seeped through to her, and except for her feet, she was almost comfortable. "You haven't asked me about Wesley," she said finally. "I know you were closer to Reed, but you must be curious about Wesley's death." This time, Garrett didn't tense up. Instead, she felt the wave of pain that washed over him.

Something was wrong. Why should Garrett react so to the mention of Wesley's name? It certainly wasn't out of jealousy. He'd made it plain what he thought of her and their arranged marriage.

"I've put it about that Wesley drowned accidentally," she admitted. After all, if Garrett was an American sympathizer as she believed, he'd know who was for the cause, wouldn't he? "I have something to tell you. I hope you won't hold it against me." She tried to keep her voice meek and womanly. "Wesley died a rebel."

"Your husband was a Continental?" He let go of her hand.

"You can't blame me for that, can you?" she whispered. "He was aboard the *Osprey* with Reed."

"Wesley was a good man," Garrett said noncommittally. "A little hotheaded, but a good man."

"You can say that about a traitor?"

"Why speak evil against the dead?"

"And do you think it strange that I, a good Englishwoman, should have both a husband and a brother fighting for the wrong side?"

"Many families are split. No one could fault you for their sins."

Caroline nibbled on her lower lip. This wasn't going the way she'd expected it. "Why won't you tell me the truth?" she whispered. "I am your wife. I can't be forced to testify against you. Admit that you are a rebel, as well. Admit that you are the one who blew up the powder magazine."

He chuckled. "If I was an American sympathizer, I'd be a fool to admit it to you, wouldn't I?"

"You don't trust me."

"Should I?"

It was her turn to stiffen. Suddenly, she wanted him to trust her—to think highly of her. "Why not?"

"We have been thrown together by circumstances. We aren't even of a class. If it wasn't for your cousin Bruce, tell the truth—would you even have considered my suit if I'd pressed one?"

"I might have."

"I doubt that very much."

She pushed his arm away and squirmed out from under the canvas. "You don't like me, do you?" Pellets of sleet stung her face and hands. "What have I—"

Without warning, Garrett seized her around the waist and threw her hard against the deck. Her outraged scream of protest was drowned by the blast of a swivel gun. Caroline's heart rose in her throat as she saw another ship materialize out of nowhere, directly in their path.

A hair-raising jeer drifted across the narrow gap of water that separated the two vessels. A torch flared on the deck of the black ship, and a coarse voice shouted through a speaking horn. "Heave to or be blown to hell!"

Chapter 9

"*Gillian* under attack!" Garrett shouted. "All hands!" He ducked as a cast-iron ball thudded onto the deck and rolled toward Caroline. "Grenade! Look out!" he warned.

Before she could grab the sputtering fuse, Garrett kicked it over the side. A wave carried the two boats closer together, and Caroline could see shadowy figures of armed men crowded on the deck of the ghostly vessel.

"Get below!" Garrett ordered her.

Caroline's legs seemed to have lost the power to move. Fierce cries rose above the moan of the wind. Howling like beasts, the hellish crew of the black-painted sloop danced and shook their weapons. For an instant, she wondered if what she was seeing was real or some spectral ship from a waking nightmare. Then she saw a wild-haired fiend on the opposite deck lift a musket to his shoulder. Powder flashed in the black night and a solid lead ball smashed into the mast behind her head.

A bearded giant ran shrieking to the plunging bow of the attacking boat and whirled a grappling iron around his head. "Look out!" Caroline screamed to Garrett. She watched in horror as the heavy clawed hook spun through the air toward his head.

To her surprise, Garrett waited until the last possible second, then dodged aside, caught the iron shaft with both hands, and yanked hard on the connecting rope. Gray Beard staggered forward, tried to catch his balance, then was dragged overboard. With a look of stunned fear, he tumbled headfirst into the maelstrom of churning foam between the two boats.

"Hang on!" Garrett yelled. "They're going to hit us!"

Another musket roared, this time from the stern of the *Gillian*. Caroline twisted around to see Garrett's friend Noah behind her, frantically reloading his gun.

"Get down!" Garrett screamed at her.

She flattened herself on the deck as an icy wave broke over the gunnel. Then the two vessels collided with a grinding crack. Before she could rise to her knees, waves lifted the *Gillian*, and an expanse of dark water appeared between the boats. As the bow of the sloop dived again, Garrett leaped across the waves onto the pirate boat, with two pistols blazing.

Pandemonium reigned on the deck of the *Gillian*. She heard the captain shout an order, someone screamed, and bullets flew like hail between the vessels. Caroline saw a flash of steel as a shadowy form swung a cutlass at Garrett's chest. He sidestepped the blow and struck the man alongside the head with his empty flintlock.

Another pirate rushed him, and Caroline lost sight of Garrett in the confusion. Shots were still being fired from both sides. Two men jumped from the deck of the pirate sloop. One landed on his belly on the gunnel; the second disappeared into the sea. One of the *Gillian*'s crew members rushed forward and slashed the boarder across the face with a boat hook. He fell back, clinging with one hand. The sailor stamped on the marauder's clawing fingers, and he slipped over the side.

Then the sailor collapsed, clutching his belly. Caroline began to crawl toward the wounded man when suddenly a half-naked corsair carrying an ax appeared on the bow of the *Gillian*. The pirate lunged toward her and she scrambled behind the mast.

The two boats smashed into each other again, and Caroline could feel the shudder run through the *Gillian*. The man with the ax came relentlessly on. The wet folds of Caroline's cloak weighted her down, so she shrugged out of the garment and inched back on her hands and knees as her assailant laughed and drove his terrible weapon toward her in a shining arc. Her petticoats entangled her knees. Instinctively, she threw up her arms to protect her face and rolled across the wet deck.

The ax plunged into the railing, missing her head by inches. The man's face contorted in glee as he heaved at the handle. Caroline screamed. Just as the raider pulled his weapon free, a familiar dark face loomed up out of the driving rain. Noah raised his musket and fired point-blank. Caroline felt the sting of powder on her cheek as a blackened hole appeared in the center of the ax wielder's torso. With a groan, the man clutched his chest and toppled over the side.

"Get Amanda and the boy on deck," Noah ordered. "The *Gillian*'s sinking."

Caroline's mouth tasted of ashes. Sinking? The boat was sinking? How could they swim with a baby in these waves? Even the terror or the crazed ax-man's attack receded under this new threat. She knew that their survival depended on calm, rational reason—but how could anyone maintain reason in this insanity?

"Move!" Noah commanded her. He swung around to ward off an attack from another pirate, and Caroline crawled on hands and knees toward the cabin. Lying on the deck in front of her was the sprawled body one of the *Gillian*'s crewmen. She recognized him by his knee-high boots and red trousers. Clutched in his hand was a sailmaker's knife.

Gritting her teeth, Caroline pried the knife from the man's stiffening fingers. She could hear Amanda's screams and little Jeremy's cries below. She saw the captain of the *Gillian* raise a musket and fire toward the enemy vessel, but she couldn't tell whether he hit anyone. Another wave broke over the side, drenching her dress.

Without thinking, she sat up and cut the ties of her bodice, slicing away her gown and petticoats. Then, clad only in a shift and corset, she crawled on toward the cabin. Something burned her hand, and she snatched it back and looked at it in disbelief. She was icy cold. What could burn her on this frozen deck?

Then she realized that the mainsail was in flames and pieces of fiery sailcloth were raining down on the open deck. "Son of a bitch," she swore. She was past being afraid. She was mad. "Son of a poxed bitch!" she shouted.

Everything around her seemed to be happening in slow motion. She wasn't sure how long they'd been under attack. She wasn't sure she could trust her own eyes. She didn't know if Garrett was still alive, or if she was a widow once more. The thought was too awful to dwell on, so she let it drift away like the bloody foam washing off the deck. She didn't know if the sloop was going to float until she could reach Amanda. All that was real was the baby's shrill crying. She had to get to her sister and

Jeremy. No matter what—she had to . . . And the crawl that should have taken her only a minute or two seemed to last forever.

Finally, when her hand closed on the cabin hatch railing, she saw the broad back of a bald-headed man and a upraised saber. The pirate reached down and dragged Amanda up by the hair.

Her sister screamed in fear, and Caroline drove the sailmaker's knife into the back of the big man's neck. The saber fell from his hands as he clutched his throat and threw himself backward. Amanda snatched up the sword and slashed him across the belly. Blood gushed from his wounds, and she shut her eyes and turned her head away.

Caroline clambered around his thrashing body to the cabin hatch. "Come on," she said. "Get Jeremy! The boat's sinking!"

The pirate rose up howling and grabbed blindly at Amanda's skirts. She screamed. Caroline struck him again across the chest with the saber. Amanda pulled free and the two women clambered into the cabin, slammed the hatch, and rolled a keg in front of it.

"We can't stay here," Caroline said frantically. "The boat's sinking. We have to get on deck."

The pirate's fist slammed against the hatchway and Jeremy howled in fright. Overhead, the gunfire had slowed to scattered explosions.

Amanda clutched the wailing child against her breast. "Shhh, shhh," she implored him.

"Is he hurt? Are you?" Caroline demanded. Cold water sloshed around her ankles. With each wave, she could feel the unnatural roll of the sloop.

"No. No." Amanda soothed her son. "Hush, baby. It's all right." She stared at Caroline in the flickering yellow light of the single whale oil lamp. "Your clothes . . ." she began. Her beautiful eyes were huge in her frightened face.

Caroline looked down at her blood-spattered shift and the sticky saber she still clutched in her hand. "Take off your petticoats," she said, ignoring the gory sight of her torn clothing. "You can't swim in your skirts. They'll pull you down."

"I . . . I can't swim," Amanda answered with a sob. "You know I can't swim. Papa always said I had a lead bottom." Tears rolled down her cheeks and fell on Jeremy's crown of dark curls. "What will I do with Jeremy?" she asked. "He's only eight months old. And the water's so cold . . . so cold. He's just a baby, Caroline. He can't die like this."

"He won't drown," Caroline insisted. "We won't let him. We'll find a keg—something that will float."

"But the cold . . ."

The hatchway shuddered under the pirate's fist.

"Stay behind me," Caroline said. "We can't stay down here and drown like rats. We're going up on deck, if we have to cut his head off to do it."

"Wait," Amanda said. Quickly, she wrapped the protesting child in a blanket and slipped him into a canvas sea bag. "This is waterproof," she said. "It will keep out some of the water."

Jeremy howled and kicked. "Maa-maa-maa-ma!"

A crash outside the hatch made Caroline's heart leap in her throat. She raised the heavy cutlass and stepped in front of Amanda and Jeremy. She was shaking with cold, her teeth were chattering, and she could barely stand in the low cabin.

"Is your husband dead?" Amanda asked.

Caroline didn't answer. She didn't want to think

about what had happened to Garrett after he'd leaped onto the pirate boat. About what must have happened to him . . . A bottomless abyss opened before her.

No! She pushed back the awful wave of pain. Jeremy and Amanda were all she could think of. Cold reason told her she couldn't take an infant into that black sea. And she couldn't swim and hold up her sister and the baby.

"Did you see Garrett fall?" Amanda demanded. "Noah?"

"No. They're both alive," Caroline answered. They must be—they had to be. "Garrett jumped—" She broke off, suddenly realizing that the deck of the *Gillian* had grown quiet. The gunfire had ceased; no ring of steel or cries of pain rose above the splash of water and the driving cadence of freezing rain.

We should take our own lives before we let them capture us, Caroline thought. Wasn't that what Wesley always said? A woman was better dead than seized by pirates.

Jeremy hiccupped and sniffed loudly inside the seabag.

Caroline's stomach turned over. What was she supposed to do? Kill her sister and her sister's child with a sword? The thought was so awful that she almost threw the bloody weapon away. "They won't take us without a fight," she whispered hoarsely. And the words seemed to give her courage.

"Caroline. Caroline, are you down there?"

Garrett's words rang clear and sweet in her ears. Was it he, or was she hearing what she wanted to hear so badly?

"Caroline!"

"Garrett?" she answered.

"Open the hatch."

"Are they gone?" She bent and dropped the terrible sword in the rising water at her feet. "Are they really gone?" She looked at her hands. They were bloodstained and filthy. Numbly, she rinsed them and wiped them dry on her shift.

"They're all dead, Caroline. It's safe to come out."

Cautiously, she pushed open the hatchway. "How can it be safe if we're sinking?" she asked. She wanted to throw her arms around him. She wanted to tell him how glad she was that he was alive. Instead, she stared at him in numb disbelief.

"Come up, quickly," he ordered, extending a hand.

She glanced back at Amanda. "Come on," she urged. "Give me Jeremy."

"I'll carry him," her sister replied. "No one carries him but me."

Garrett's strong lean fingers closed around hers. "We have only a few minutes," he said. "Quick, now. We're going to the other boat." He passed her on to Noah and reached for Amanda.

Caroline caught sight of Noah's brother Eli holding his arm cradled against his chest. His head was bleeding and one eye was swollen shut.

"I'll grab a few things from the cabin," Noah said when the women were both on deck.

"Be careful," Garrett warned. He looked down at Caroline and realized she was half-naked. He took hold of her arm and pulled her close as black, killing rage swept through his body. "Are you hurt?" he whispered hoarsely. "Did they—"

"No." Her upturned face was dirty but unmarked. Her eyes shone as though lit with inner fires. "I thought we'd have to swim," she said gamely. "I took off my gown and petticoats because I couldn't swim with—"

"God forbid we swim on a night like this," he replied in a rough tone. Relief that she'd not been raped was so great that it shook him to the bone. He wanted to crush her against him, to cover her body from every man's sight, even Noah's. Filled with an overwhelming urge to protect this woman of his, he stripped off his coat and wrapped it around her shivering form. So fierce was the primeval drumming in his blood that he knew that if there were any survivors among the wreckers, he would have slain them with his bare hands.

"We're going to the wreckers' boat," he said. "We've lashed the two vessels together long enough to get us safe aboard—God willing." He put an arm around her shoulders and led her toward the starboard side. "Their sloop has been fitted with an iron bowsprit for ramming. It's the devil's sh—outhouse of a boat, but stout enough to get us ashore."

"The pirates deliberately rammed the *Gillian?*" Caroline said. "How could they rob us if—"

"Not pirates, wreckers," Garrett corrected her. "They know these waters . . . the sandbars, the channels. They disable vessels with their iron beak, murder the crew and passengers, and rob the boat before it goes down."

"There are none still on the sloop, are there?" she asked. One of the *Gillian*'s sailors came forward shyly with her cloak, and she donned it gratefully.

Garrett wanted to kiss her. Most well-born women would have been screaming their heads off after such an ordeal. Instead, she was standing here in the rain in a tattered shift asking questions a man might ask. "They're all in hell," he assured her. "Put your arms around my neck. I'll carry you across."

"I'm heavier than I look," she began. "I can—"

"We've no time to argue," he said. "Noah, help Amanda."

"The baby," Caroline said. "Jeremy's in the bag."

Garrett took the canvas sack from Amanda's arms. "I'll bring him over for you," he said.

"No!" Amanda tried to hold on to her child, but Noah grabbed her arms from behind.

Garrett jumped to the deck of the wreckers' boat with the infant, handed him to the *Gillian*'s captain, and came back for Caroline. Meanwhile, Noah and Amanda had made the dangerous crossing.

"I can do it myself," Caroline said, balancing on the slippery deck. Garrett swept her—still arguing—into his arms and leaped with her to the comparative safety of the raider's sloop.

The women huddled together with the crying baby as the men cut loose the sinking *Gillian*.

Garrett looked at the sloop's skipper. "Where to now?"

"Ashore," the weary man replied, watching the last sluggish rolling of his floundering boat. "Whatever waits for us there sure as hell can't be any worse than what we've just fought our way out of."

Wet and exhausted, the small party of survivors ran the sloop aground on a lonely beach. The captain and two crew members of the *Gillian* had survived, all three with minor wounds. Noah's brother Eli had lost a great deal of blood but was still able to walk. Noah had escaped without a scratch, as had Garrett and the two women.

Because of the bad weather and the danger to

the infant, Garrett decided to keep moving until they found shelter and fuel to make a fire. An hour's forced march took them to a dirt lane, and a half hour after that, they were settled in a farmer's kitchen before a glowing hearth.

"A pity honest folk can't travel the waterways without bein' set upon by thieves and murderers," the thin-faced farmer said. "You're welcome to spend the rest of the night here. In the mornin' I kin take ye to the nearest town in my wagon. My missus can find a pallet fer your lady, but them nigras will have to sleep in the barn. I don't keep no nigras myself. Never could stand the stench of them."

It was the last statement the man made before Noah seized him by the back of his nightshirt and tossed him out the kitchen door and into a brimming mud puddle. Garrett dropped the bar on the door, and Amanda wrapped Jeremy's blanket around both of them, proceeding to nurse the sleepy baby.

"What have ye done to William?" the farmer's wife cried.

"If your barn is so comfortable, madame," Garrett said, "your husband can sleep there himself."

"Ye can't do that!" she protested. "Ye can't come into my house and throw my husband out of his own kitchen on Christmas Eve because of these nigras."

"Hush," Caroline warned. "Another word, and you shall join him."

"I'll have the law on all of ye," the goodwife protested. "We're loyal English folk and—"

"Unlock the door, Mr. Faulkner," Caroline said. "This lady wishes to spend Christmas with her husband."

"No! No! I'll be still," the woman cried.

Garrett dug deep into his pocket and produced a silver crown. "Peace, madame," he said. "It's all we require. That, and a hot meal. If it's not too much trouble?" He raised one eyebrow quizzically and smiled at her.

"Whatever you want," she replied. "Anything." She hurried to a pie cupboard and began to pull out plates of bread, cheese, and cold sliced ham.

Garrett looked around the meager cottage wryly. Christmas Eve, was it? He'd forgotten the date . . . If only the farmer's wife could give him what he really wanted—a quiet spot, alone, with Caroline in his arms—it wasn't likely to be found here. "We mean you no harm," he reassured the woman. "Food for us all." He tossed the woman the coin and she tucked it inside her bodice.

He laid his pistol on the table and replaced the wet powder with dry. "A merry Christmas to you, wife."

"And to you," she replied. "And to all of you." She smiled at Noah. "You saved my life on the ship. I'll not forget."

He nodded. "'Twas nothing, miss."

"Without you and the others, we would all be at the bottom of the ocean." Amanda glanced at the tired men who huddled near the fire. "I thank every one of you for my baby's sake."

"What of me?" Garrett teased Caroline. "Didn't I save your life as well? Admit it, I was as bold as any—"

"Braggart!" Caroline retorted with a chuckle. "You fled the sloop at the first opportunity. I don't see how you can place yourself in the same category as Mr. Walker."

Noah laughed. "It's time my good qualities were recognized."

"Ungrateful baggage," Garrett admonished, and they all laughed together. "You and Amanda get some sleep now. It's the only Christmas gift I can give you tonight. I'll keep watch for our host and any friends he might have."

Raindrops began to spatter against the glass windowpane. Noah took a long-stemmed clay pipe from the mantel, filled it with tobacco he found in a tin can, and settled down to watch Amanda. Caroline spread her wool cloak to dry in front of the fire and nibbled at the corn bread the woman passed around.

Garrett absently rubbed at the engraving on his pistol barrel and tried to figure out where he'd gone wrong. He'd been forced into marriage with a woman he hadn't wanted. And now—now he was afraid everything had changed.

The war with England was what counted. It was his fight as much as any man's. He had no close family alive, no children, no wife to care for—at least he hadn't until a few weeks ago. Wars were meant to be fought by young men without ties. Men who loved were afraid to take chances, and sometimes that made all the difference between living and dying.

He tried to tell himself he'd made that jump onto the wrecker's boat because it made sense, but he knew it was a lie. He'd tried to carry the battle to the enemy—to keep them away from Caroline.

Sweet Jesus! He'd not even slept with the woman. He'd barely kissed her. So why did his arms ache to hold her? Why did his heartbeat quicken at the thought of burying his face in her long red hair?

It had nothing to do with lust. Hell, he was too bone-tired to get it up. He just wanted to hold her . . . to go to sleep with his arms and legs wrapped around her . . . to open his eyes and see her hair spread across his pillow.

Caroline Talbot. She was the last woman he'd ever expect to be love-struck by. Wes's highborn wife . . .

Garrett sighed and brought his palms together thoughtfully. He'd come close to making a clean getaway. He'd had it all figured out. He'd take the conniving wench to her island plantation, get the money for his boat, and go back to the war where he belonged. Now . . .

Caroline caught his eye and smiled at him. He lifted the mug of weak homemade beer in a salute. I suppose a man could do worse if he was to go looking for trouble, he thought. Then again, maybe he couldn't.

Chapter 10

Charleston, South Carolina
January 1778

Caroline sighed with pleasure as Garrett cupped her breast in his hand and teased her love-swollen nipple with the tip of his moist, hot tongue. He slipped one hand down over her bare midriff and stroked her skin with slow, tantalizing caresses. She squirmed under his touch, arching her back, and lifting her aching breasts to be kissed and sucked until she moaned with delight. She tore at his linen shirt, exposing a wide expanse of coiled, hard muscle, and he lifted her in his powerful arms and carried her to the bed.

"You're mine," he said huskily. "You belong to me. I'm going to love to you as no man has ever loved you. I'm going to drive my hard cock into your sweet, tight sheath until you—"

His words were drowned in the heated passion of their kiss as he pushed her back against the heaped pillows and filled her mouth with his tongue. Her arms were around his neck, her body moving against his as he touched her in places that she had not dared to—

"Caroline. Caroline, wake up. Will you lie abed until noon?"

Her eyelids flickered. She opened them wide and saw Amanda's brown face looming over her.

"Caroline?"

Her cheeks flamed as she remembered the dream. Shocked, she pulled the blankets over her head and turned over to keep her sister from seeing her face. Was it only a dream? Her breath came in quick gasps. How could she have dreamed such scandalous things about Garrett Faulkner?

Amanda yanked the covers back. "Lazybones. Get up. You've missed breakfast. I brought you up a tray, but your tea is growing cold. Poor stuff it is too, some sort of Indian herbs mixed with old coarse leaves. Our hostess, I fear, is an ardent rebel."

"You always did prefer chocolate."

Amanda laughed. "With lots of sugar. You know I have a sweet tooth. And speaking of teeth, Jeremy's getting a second. On the top right. One bottom and one top; he'll look like a dragon."

Caroline slid her feet over the edge of the bed and began to pull on her stockings. They were heavy wool, not as fine as she was accustomed to, but they'd brought little clothing with them and most of that had been lost with the sinking of the *Gillian*. They'd been forced to buy additional clothes, but since money was scarce, Caroline had to be content with garments that a tradesman's wife might wear, rather than those of her own class.

Amanda had warmed her petticoats and brocade corset in front of the small hearth. She gathered them up and tossed them to her.

"You're not very good at this," Caroline teased, trying to put Garrett and her disturbing dream out of her mind. "Lady's maids don't throw garments at their mistresses." She put her arms through the corset and tugged at the lacing until it was tight enough to suit her, then tied it.

They had found lodging in a widow's private home. She would not accept gentlemen boarders, so Garrett, Noah, and Eli were forced to sleep elsewhere. Garrett had told the Widow Gordon that Amanda was his wife's serving woman. Caroline had been furious at first, but then reason had prevailed. No white woman would give them a room if she knew the truth of Caroline and Amanda's relationship.

Amanda hadn't complained, but then Amanda never did. Sometimes, Caroline wished her sister would get angry at the injustice shown people of her color. It galled her now to see Amanda in a servant's plain wool skirt and bodice. "I didn't mean that," she apologized. "It was in poor taste."

"Umm-hmmm," her sister replied, shaking the wrinkles out of Caroline's blue chintz gown. "Sometimes I think that Papa would have done me more good had he taught me useful skills instead of French and the harpsichord. At least I could have made a living for myself and my son."

"Don't say that," Caroline protested. "You know you always have a home with us. You will have a handsome dowry when you marry."

Amanda's eyes met hers. She was smiling, but the smile didn't hide the pain there. "Who will I marry, sister? Who will have a black woman raised above her station?"

"Any man with good sense."

Amanda sighed. "Well, I've seen few of them. And fewer yet I'd have for husband."

"Noah likes you. I've seen him watching you."

Amanda wrinkled her nose. "He likes me no better than I like him."

"Garrett told me he's a shipbuilder. He had his own shipyard before the British burned it last year."

"Hmmpt." Amanda took a scone off the tray. "Jeremy, look what Mama has for you." She scooped up the baby, put him in the center of the bed, and made a wall with the quilt to hold him in.

Jeremy grinned and reached for the scone. Caroline saw the gleam of a new tooth as he opened his little pink mouth for the sweet biscuit.

"He'll need a father, Amanda."

"He'll have an uncle when Reed comes home from prison."

Caroline began to brush the tangles out of her hair. The bright room with its wide windows opening onto the busy street, Jeremy's precious face, Amanda's sorrows—nothing could make her forget her dream.

Just thinking of being intimate with Garrett made her a little dizzy. The dream had seemed so real. She averted her eyes so that Amanda couldn't read her thoughts.

Perhaps it was true—what people said about widows—that they were all desperate to get a man into their lonely beds. The wrinkled face of Mistress Gordon popped up in her mind and she barely suppressed a giggle. Not all widows, perhaps . . .

. . . *I'm going to love you as no man has ever loved you.*

Caroline's mouth felt parched. She shifted restlessly. With a little imagination, she could feel his lips against her bare skin . . . feel his hot tongue—

"Caroline! Are you paying attention to me?" Amanda demanded.

"Oh, yes . . . of course I am."

"He thinks I'm loose because of Jeremy," Amanda said.

"Who does? Garrett?"

"Not Garrett. Who's talking about Garrett? *Noah.*"

Does Garrett think I'm loose? Caroline wondered. He would, if he knew what I'm thinking now. He is my husband, after all. Husbands and wives—

"What are you daydreaming about?"

"Nothing . . . nothing," Caroline assured her. "You mean—because of Jeremy. You're afraid Noah will think the worst of you because of Jeremy's light coloring."

"Not that—that I have a child and I'm unmarried. I'm no lightskirts. You know that."

Caroline smiled. "No one who spent an hour with you would believe it. You are the most modest woman I—"

"Now you're teasing me again."

"I'm not. You are simply very—"

"Very what?" Amanda's eyes narrowed and she rested her hands on her hips.

"Very ladylike," Caroline answered. "Who wouldn't ever swim with Reed and me, when we were children, without a shift? And who refused to have the physician from Oxford when Jeremy was born? If I went through what you did to birth him, I'd have wanted a room full of doctors."

"You never blamed me for Jeremy, did you?" Amanda asked.

"No, and I never will."

"And you never pressed for . . ." Her sister blushed. "The details."

"I thought you'd tell me when you were ready."

Amanda nodded. "Someday, maybe I will." She went to the window and looked out. "Will they find a ship soon, do you think? I don't know how long I can play the part of your maid. I was never very good at games."

"Garrett said a Dutch ship anchored in the harbor yesterday. He was going to inquire if they had room for more passengers. We have to be very careful. You know the British navy is boarding ships off the coast and impressing Americans into service. The Widow Gordon said her brother's son was taken in the fall."

Amanda glanced back at the baby, who was happily devouring the last of the scone. "What will happen when we do get to Arawak? Garrett will expect the money you promised him. What will you tell him?"

"The gold is there, Amanda. I know it's there."

"Just as I know a Moorish prince will come and whisk Jeremy and me off to his palace on the hill."

"You make me sound like a child."

"Sometimes, big sister, I think you are. You expect life to have happy endings, just like fairy tales. And most of the time it doesn't."

"You're wrong," Caroline said softly. "I'll find the treasure. We'll ransom Reed from prison, Garrett will have his boat, and we'll all go home and live happily ever after." And I'll stop having such foolish fancies, she thought. Fancies about a man who can only bring me trouble.

"If only you were right. If only it could happen just that way. But sometimes . . ." Tears formed in the corners of Amanda's eyes. "Sometimes . . . I think of Reed and I have this awful feeling that we're never going to see him again."

"Don't say that! Don't even think of it! I'll find the treasure. I'll find so much gold that Jeremy can build his own palace—right there on Arawak Island."

As if on cue, the baby giggled and crawled over the wall of blankets and straight for the edge of the bed. Both women leaped to catch him, and Amanda's face lightened as she kissed Jeremy's nose and wiped the crumbs off his chubby little chin. "Will you build Mama a castle, sweet'ums? Will you?"

"He will," Caroline promised, laughing with them. "He will." And once more—to her chagrin—she found her thoughts straying back to Garrett's hard body pressing hers against the bed and his lips whispering forbidden words in her ears.

"Christ, man, but you're in a foul mood," Noah said to Garrett as they walked back from the dockside tavern and their meeting with the captain of the *Kaatje*. "He agreed to take us to Jamaica, didn't he?"

Garrett's mouth flattened into a thin line and he took longer strides. Noah was right. He wanted Caroline—wanted her so badly that it made him hard just thinking about her

"I've not seen you in such a state since they stripped you of your letters of marque. She's your wife, for God's sake. Bed her and get it over with."

"God has nothing to do with this."

Noah rubbed his close-shaven head. "Since when have you ever had trouble getting any woman between the sheets?"

"We had an agreement, Caroline and me. My name and protection in exchange for a ship."

"So? You wouldn't be the first man to take a rich wife."

"There was nothing in the agreement about becoming involved with each other. A simple marriage of convenience, and after we win our independence from England, a simple annulment."

Noah grinned. "On what grounds? Insanity on the part of the bridegroom?"

"It was her idea. She threatened to tell Major

Whitehead that I'd come into her room the night the powder magazine was blown. I'd have had a hard time explaining the sword wound in my thigh." Garrett stretched his leg cautiously. The injury still ached when he walked, but the stitches had long since been removed and there was no infection.

"That was bad luck, losing the mare. I would have helped you out, but I sort of had my hands full. I never did get back to my horse. I took to the woods like a rabbit with a fox on its tail."

"But we did take out the powder store."

"Aye, right enough. That night cost the Brits plenty. But it's not the same as having a ship under you."

"No, it's not. That's why I accepted Caroline's offer."

"Don't expect that I'll have time to build you a ship in the islands."

"Build, hell," Garrett said. "We'll buy one and a crew. I need you to tell me if she's seaworthy, how much speed we can demand of her, and how many cannon she can carry."

"You've a head on your shoulders—for a white man. It's not like you've never navigated around Kent Island in gale-force winds."

"Some things I know, but I'm not an engineer. You've caulking instead of blood in your veins, Noah. I don't want just any ship—I want a schooner or a sloop that will carry at least eight cannon and four swivel guns. I need a shallow draft to maneuver in shoals and enough speed to outrun a man-of-war."

Noah swore softly. "You don't want much, do you?"

"That's what I want, but I'll take what I can get. The ship and the men to sail her are what's important. I'd have wed the devil's handmaiden to get another command."

"Forced into marriage by a redheaded woman." Noah slapped his leather-clad leg and laughed. "I knew you'd have to marry some woman, but I always thought it would be at the end of an angry father's musket barrel."

"I was waiting for you to get married first."

"I never met the right woman."

"Amanda's been watching you."

Noah's face hardened. "She's not for me," he said. "Too white."

Garrett shrugged. "It's not a statement I'd expect from you."

"Because we're friends?" He shook his head. "Our friendship is one thing. We've known each other since we were in Mama's cradle together. But your granddaddy came from England. Mine came from Africa. He hunted lions with nothing but a spear. My grandmammy on the other side was pure Injun and wild as Eastern Shore whiskey. I'm as American as you, Garrett—maybe more—but I'm no white man. When I marry and raise sons, I want them to be black and to be proud of it. I don't want them to have a mother who thinks she's white."

Garrett looked up at his friend. Noah topped him by three inches and his shoulders were wide enough to make him turn sideways going through narrow doorways. Noah's hands were as big as hams and he could lift a yearling steer. He was fearless in battle and as shrewd as Washington himself. But for the tint of his skin, Noah would have been an officer in the Continental Army. Instead, he wore a common seaman's striped shirt and baggy trousers and had to be content with serving under lesser men. Still, Garrett mused,

Noah had never been one to complain about his lot in life. Usually, he was the most cheerful man Garrett knew. "I never thought you to sound so much like your brother."

"Eli." Noah made a sound of derision. "That fire-eater! He's half the reason I haven't taken a wife yet. Twenty-seven and not settled down. He likes to blame white folks for all his failures. Eli's got good stuff in him, but he wants the easy way—the quick money. You know I've always been more father to him than brother. He's all I've got left in the way of family—besides you. But I see Eli's faults. It would be hard to find a woman who would be willing to put up with him coming home drunk at night or getting into one fix after another."

"Maybe it's time you let Eli go his own way."

Noah's brow furrowed. "I promised Mama I'd look after him. You know how she was. He was her last chick, and she always babied him after he caught that fever when he was six."

"I've got no extra money to bail Eli out of jail if he gets himself in trouble and locked up. The Dutch ship sails in two days, and we all need to be on it. I'm depending on you to keep a close eye on him until then."

Noah grinned. "I'll try, but you know Eli. Trouble naturally finds him."

"And you naturally get him out of it."

"I promised Mama."

"And I promised Caroline I'd let her know about passage on the *Kaatje*." Garrett stopped at the corner of two intersecting streets as a wagon loaded with kegs rumbled by, followed closely by a woman driving a flock of sheep.

Charleston was free of the British military and had been since Sir Peter Parker had been driven out in '76. Commerce flourished and Continental flags hung bravely from many a portside window. The dock was crowded with merchants, seamen, housewives, and peddlers. Slaves moved freely among the open-air stalls with market baskets on their dark arms, and the lyrical cry of "Fresh shrimp! Fresh shrimp!" echoed along the streets.

Dogs scrapped and barked, chasing ragged children of every color and size and being chased in turn. Pigeons and seagulls fought over scraps of fish and produce. Garrett even noticed a small speckled pig rooting along the ditch beside the road.

"Look yonder," Noah said.

On the cross street was a vacant lot wedged between an ordinary and a sailmaker's shop. There, in the muddy strip of sand and crushed oyster shell, stood a rough platform. A slave auction was in progress. A young black man with manacles on his wrists turned around to show off his physique for the prospective buyers.

". . . prime field hand," the auctioneer proclaimed. "Broke to field work. No bad habits. Will work indigo or rice."

Noah flushed. "That's hard to take, no matter how many times I've seen it, or how far I am from that platform. It tears a man to see his own kind bought and sold like livestock."

Garrett nodded. "My own grandfather worked the cane fields on Jamaica. He was bound but as much a slave as that man. I can still remember the whip scars on his back."

"No," Noah replied. "Not like that man. A white man has a term to serve. Most black men have to die to find freedom."

"My grandfather killed to get his. He told me he

cut the throat of an overseer and fled the islands aboard a pirate vessel."

"Not the old man? Perry Faulkner?"

"The same. He always said his mother was an Irish bond servant in the governor's palace on Jamaica. Her name was Keavy. And when she got herself with child by some bigwig, her mistress was so angry that she sent her to the cane fields. She died of snakebite there when my grandfather was seven. She never told him who his father was. Don't you remember he used to tease us that he was a royal governor's woods colt?"

"No, I guess I forgot that. But you spent more time with your grandsire than I did. My mother wanted me to stay in the kitchen and not bother the white folk."

Garrett too his friend's arm. "Come on. There's no good to be done here, and a lot of harm."

"Will it be the same—if we win independence from the Brits?" Noah asked. "Will there be any freedom for my people?"

"We can hope so."

"Hope." Noah frowned. "It's a word that will wear thin after many generations."

"It's your country, same as mine," Garrett said.

"Maybe. Or maybe we're just like the Israelites, and we don't have a country at all."

That evening Garrett invited Caroline to dine with him at the Fox and Hound Tavern, a better sort of establishment near the residential section of Charleston. He wished now that he'd used what money he had to rent them a private room here. Instead, he'd been practical. She was at the widow's, and he, Noah, and Eli, were staying in the loft over a black tradesman's shop.

If they'd had lodging here together as man and

wife, he knew they'd be sleeping together by now. Noah's snoring was poor exchange for Caroline's head on his pillow or her soft curves molded against him.

Since he'd missed his chance to bed her, he at least wanted to treat her to one nice meal before they boarded the ship for Jamaica. Shipboard accommodations would be little better than those they had now. Caroline and Amanda and the baby would share a cabin with two elderly sisters, and he and the Walker brothers would make do with hammocks in the fo'c'sle. Tonight was their last chance to be alone together for weeks, and he meant to make the best of it.

"I'm sorry I can't provide you with the sort of travel you're used to," he said to Caroline formally, "but I brought every penny with me I could scrape up. Prices have risen beyond belief since the war began." He couldn't keep his gaze off her. Her huge eyes were framed with sooty dark lashes, and her lips begged to be kissed.

"It's not your fault. It's that rotten cousin of mine. I couldn't put my hands on much money either. If worse comes to worst, we can sell my personal jewelry."

"I hope it doesn't come to that."

They were seated at a small table in the corner of the parlor reserved for families, away from the raucous clamor of the public room. It was close to nine o'clock, and the weather outside had become even more miserable. The slow drizzle had become a downpour, and rivers of water ran through the streets.

The candle on their table caught a draft from the thick-paned casement window and flickered, casting golden ribbons of light across Caroline's face. She wore her hair simply tonight, gathered at the nape of her neck with a black silk ribbon so that her thick curls tumbled down the back of her green wool riding coat. Perched jauntily on her head was a black beaver cocked hat with the corners turned up. Her riding jacket was a dark forest-green over a paler green waistcoat and white linen shirt with a ruffled cravat. Beneath the hem of the coat, her matching wool riding skirt hung in thick folds.

"You look as though you're about to ride to hounds rather than take ship," Garrett teased as he filled her wineglass for the third time.

She laughed softly, and he noticed how her eyes shone. "Beggars can't be choosers," she answered. "When you buy secondhand, you are lucky to find clothes that fit. We won't be here long enough to have clothing made—even if we did have the money to pay for the seamstress."

"I didn't say I didn't like the look." He placed his hand over hers and caressed her skin with slow, circular strokes. She made no move to pull away. Instead, she leaned closer to him and smiled invitingly. He lifted her hand and brushed her knuckles with feather-light kisses.

She laughed and removed her fingers from his grasp. "You're on your very best behavior tonight, Garrett Faulkner. I want to know why."

"Must I have an ulterior motive?"

"Always." Her smile softened the accusation.

"As long as we're in this together, we might as well be friends." The words sounded good, but they were a lie. He knew it as soon as they fell from his lips. He didn't want to be her friend; he wanted more.

She nodded. "I agree."

A serving girl came, carried away the dirty plates, and returned to ask, "Will ye have a sweet?

We've apple pie, rice pudding, and gingerbread. The gingerbread's four days old, though. Still good, Missus says, but a little dry to my taste. I'd recommend the pie."

"We'll take your advice," Garrett said, wishing she'd go away and leave them alone.

"Pie or rice pudding?"

Caroline laughed. "We'll each have a slice of pie." She sipped at her pewter goblet of wine and watched as the girl hurried away. "The Widow Gordon serves rice with every meal."

Her knee rested against his under the table. "At least we're too far south for snow," he said, making light conversation. He couldn't keep his eyes off the small expanse of throat that showed above her cravat. "You are very beautiful tonight."

She smiled. A tiny drop of wine lingered on her lower lip, and he had the strongest urge to lick it away. "You don't have to say that," she replied huskily. "I've already married you."

"Do you regret it?" He leaned forward involuntarily. His pulse was racing like an untried boy's. Damn, but she was exciting. He smiled back at her and let his gaze slide over the first silver button on her waistcoat to the rise and fall of her bosom. What would it feel like to unbutton that vest? he wondered. To untie her cravat and part her linen shirt so that he could see the curve of her breasts?

"I thought I would, but I don't." Her voice was low and breathy, as if she had been running.

Garrett's coat seemed overly warm despite the chill in the air and the rain beating against the windows. He glanced around and realized with surprise that he and Caroline were alone in the room. He'd not even noticed when the family at the round center table had finished their meal and left.

". . . an unusual arrangement," Caroline said.

"What? I'm sorry," he said. "I didn't—"

"I said that ours is an unusual arrangement."

Her cinnamon-brown eyes were locked with his. Her sensual lips were slightly parted so that he could see a hint of her white, even teeth. It never ceased to amaze him what good teeth colonial women had. In England, most girls began to lose their teeth long before they reached Caroline's age.

She toyed with a button on her waistcoat. "The oysters were very good," she said. "And the venison."

She was eating him with her eyes. He moistened his lips and tried to decide what she smelled like tonight. Lavender and something else . . . vanilla. He wondered if her skin would taste salty or sweet.

"Apple pie." The maid dropped two plates noisily on the table. "Anything else ye be wantin'?"

"Another bottle of wine," he said.

Caroline took a morsel of pie. "Delicious." She took another portion on her three-pronged fork and held it up for him to sample. Laughing, he nibbled at the crumbling crust.

"You're dropping it, sloppy," she teased, catching the bit of apple in midair and pushing it between his lips.

His hand closed around hers and she dropped the fork. He brought her fingers to his lips and tasted them. "Sweeter than the pie," he murmured. He heard her quick intake of breath and felt a tremor run through her.

"Garrett."

No one had ever said his name quite like that before.

"Garrett, don't."

There was no strength in her protest. He turned

her hand and kissed the pulse of her wrist. She made a little sound in her throat, and he nipped gently at her skin.

"Please . . . don't . . ."

"Just a kiss," he bargained. "A kiss of peace between husband and wife." He looked into her eyes and saw her indecision. Before she could speak, he leaned across the table and kissed her lower lip.

"Oh, Garrett," she moaned.

He rose and went to her, pulling her into his arms and kissing her again. Not sweet and slow, but hard and searing. She gave a sigh and slipped her arms around his neck. Her head went back, and the cocked hat tumbled to the floor. He kissed her right ear and whispered her name.

"Oh," she said. She lifted her face and met his next kiss with parted lips, opening for his tongue as naturally as a flower opens to the rain.

He ran his fingers into the mass of hair at the back of her neck and fumbled with the silk ribbon, pulling it loose, and letting her glorious tresses fall like a curtain of dark wine silk.

"Garrett . . . Garrett," she whispered.

He kissed her throat, nibbling and tasting her. She molded herself against him and dug her fingers into his coat. "I want you," he said.

"Yes, yes," she whispered.

The cravat followed the cocked hat and the silk ribbon. He traced the curve of her back with his hand, and the heat grew within him until his loins ached with wanting. "Why do you have so many damned clothes on?" he demanded.

Her back was against the table, and he had her jacket off. She was laughing and crying and kissing him all at the same time. "Not here," she said. "The maid. We can't—"

His breath was coming in hard, deep gasps as

he looked around. To the left, by the fireplace, were two steps and a low board and batten door. "There," he said. Dragging her after him, he crossed the room and fumbled with the wooden handle.

The door swung open to reveal narrow, curving steps leading to the second floor. "In here," he said. He ducked his head and stepped into the stairwell.

Still laughing, she followed him.

Chapter 11

Caroline buried her face in Garrett's chest and clung to him as they stood together in the tiny enclosure. Liquid heat swirled around her as he whispered her name over and over again. Her hands were tangled in his hair, sliding through the silky length and feeling the strong curve of his neck. Eagerly, she ran her tongue over his bare skin, tasting the clean salt of him, reveling in the sensations of his skin on her lips.

She did not know or care if it was the wine or a more potent stimulant that intoxicated her. She felt as though her blood were on fire; she could not get enough of him or of the kisses that drove her wild with wanting.

Garrett pulled the door closed and began to undo the buttons on her waistcoat. "How many of these things are there?" he demanded. She laughed and pulled loose his shirt, boldly sliding her hands up under his garments and feeling the taut, smooth planes of his belly.

"You little minx," he gasped as she reached higher to explore the contours of his wide chest and run her nails lightly over his nipples until they rose to hard nubs under her fingertips.

Caroline knew she was behaving like a wanton, but she didn't care. With each breath, she drew in more of his virile, male scent, and with each moment that passed she shed more of her inhibitions. Never had Wesley or any other man excited her like this. Her body trembled like a willow in the winter wind; her mind whirled with thoughts too daring to be put into words.

And all the while the heat between her legs grew hotter . . .

Her breasts felt heavy and swollen. They strained against the confines of her corset until she could hardly draw breath. Her nipples were so sensitive that she could feel the texture of the linen covering against her throbbing skin.

Touch me, she pleaded silently. *I want you to touch me.*

He lifted her chin and kissed her mouth. Again, the fiery sensations spiraled through her. She could not get enough of him. His tongue was like velvet, his lips as smooth as satin and as hard as his growing desire. His loins were a furnace, and their heat warmed her through the layers of clothing that separated them.

"Oh, Garrett," she repeated, wanting to say his name. "Garrett . . . Garrett. I've wanted you to kiss me like this—to take me to your bed."

"You have the strangest way of telling a man so," he teased, tugging at the lacing on her shirt-front. He kissed her long and hard, then pushed her gently back against the steeply curving stairs. He parted her linen shirt and pressed his face into the rise of her breasts above her corset.

"Mmm," she murmured. "That's nice." Her own hands found the buttons at his waistband and she began to undo them as waves of heat radiated up from the pit of her stomach.

"Witch," he teased. Tremors of pleasure rippled through her as Garrett nuzzled the valley between her breasts.

Then she touched hot swollen flesh, and her

knees went weak. She sat down on the stairs, suddenly unable to stand under her own power.

"Don't stop," he said huskily. "Keep touching me."

His hand guided hers down the length of him. She could not hold back a sharp intake of breath that registered her surprise. Garrett was not an overly large man . . . but here, here in his most intimate parts . . . She felt her cheeks grow warm.

"That's for you," he whispered.

Fear seized her and she began to tremble. What was she doing? She'd been a wife, but she'd never behaved like—

"Touch me," he commanded.

She had no power to disobey him as he straddled her on his knees and kissed her throat and ear, and filled her mouth with his thrusting tongue. The intensity of her own response shook her to her core. The fire was more than she could bear. Only he could drown the heat. She wanted him here and now, and damn the consequences.

Her corset was so tight she couldn't breathe. She brought his hand to her aching breast. "Touch me," she said. She ached for his kiss . . . for the tug of his mouth on her nipples. Unbidden, memories of her dream rose in her mind and she felt herself go wet with desire.

"I want to suck your breasts," he said. "I want to kiss them, and bite them, and fill my mouth with them.

"Mmm," she sighed.

"Shall I do that, Caroline? Do you want me to suck your breasts until your nipples grow hard and throbbing?" he asked.

She could not speak. Instead, she caught his hand and brought it to the knot that bound her corset lacing. The silk cord snapped under his strong pull and one breast slipped free.

"My little wife," he murmured. "Let me taste your sweetness."

She shivered as his warm, wet tongue encircled her nipple. Then he kissed the tip, slowly . . . and she gave herself up to the madness that surged through her body.

"Sweeter than honey." He groaned. His lips tugged at her nipple until she tossed her head and moaned with ecstasy. Only then did he draw the swollen bud into his mouth and suckle with increasing passion.

Her other breast ached for the same caresses. With a little cry of joy, she guided him to kiss, and lick, and nibble at that one too, until she lost all sense of time and place and thought only of Garrett and his hot mouth on her bare skin.

Somehow, one of his hands was on her knee, sidling up the inside of her leg. She laughed and moved her own fingers down to savor again the hot power of his swollen sex.

"Woman," he gasped. "You'll unman me."

She encircled the smooth, tight head with her fingertips, and he gave a low groan of pleasure. "Shall I stop?" she asked softly.

"Witchling." He raised his head and leaned forward to kiss her full on the mouth.

Their tongues touched, withdrew, and touched again. He was velvet and oak. He tasted of wine and apple pie, and his hard body pressing hers was the sweetest weight she had ever felt.

She gasped with surprise as cool night air brushed her legs as he pushed her skirt up around her thighs. She could not lay still. Throbbing hunger made her squirm under his touch . . . made her shudder at his intimate caresses.

Then he crouched down and planted a feather-light kiss on the underside of her knee. She gasped and dug her fingers into his heavily muscled arm. His ensuing laughter was honey to her soul. He kissed her again . . . higher. His fingers stroked her, sliding nearer and nearer to the source of her exquisite sensitivity.

"Garrett," she pleaded. "I can't . . ."

"Oh, you can torture me, but you can't take it?" he teased. His lingering kisses trailed along her inner thigh, and his fingers brushed her love-dampened cleft.

"Garrett . . ."

He slid a forefinger between her folds. She gasped with pleasure. "You're wet," he murmured. "Wet and tight." He withdrew, then caressed her again, this time with two fingers.

"Oh, yes . . ." she whispered. The flame consumed her and only he could put it out.

She felt his lips on her . . . his tongue. Without warning a spasm of sexual delight rocked her body, followed by another and another. She shut her eyes and dug her fingers into his shoulders as she climaxed with fierce abandon.

"Oh, oh," she gasped, when she could breathe again. "I'm sorry. I couldn't—"

"Shhh, shhh." His laughter was soft in her ear. "It's all right, darling. It's all right. I wanted to give you pleasure."

"But you . . ." The waves of rapture still rolled through her. "I wanted to . . ."

"And you will," he promised. "You will, little witchling wife of mine." He kissed the corners of her mouth with infinite tenderness. "That was only the beginning, Caroline," he said. "I've waited too long not to make this a night you will remember."

"Are you sure?" She drew in a ragged breath. "I . . ."

"Shhh," he said, and he rubbed her bare nipple between his fingers. "Sweet little innocent."

To her surprise, the glow radiating through her body intensified. "Make love to me again," she said. "This time, I want to please you."

He laughed and bent his head to kiss her breast and draw a nipple into his mouth. The gentle tugging struck a spark that flared through her veins.

"Surely," she said. "I couldn't—"

His fingers touched her intimately and she sighed. It wasn't possible. She had just . . . But . . . Ripples of desire ran up her spine and she gave her mouth over to be kissed again.

And moments later, when she felt the silken head of his tumescent erection pushing hard against her, she was ready for him. She raised her knees slightly and met the fire of his first deep thrust with eager cries of throbbing need. Her eyes widened as he filled her until she thought she could take no more.

"Oh," she cried. "Oh . . ."

He plunged deep, then pulled back and entered her again, sweeping her along in the searing heat of his passion. His mouth covered hers and they clung together, riding the new tide of wildfire to the ends of the earth . . . letting free the emotions they had held back for so long. And when at last they reached the instant of fulfillment, they leaped over the edge together, giving and taking a love so powerful that each was left with a pounding heart and utter exhaustion.

Caroline lay very still and listened to the rise and fall of Garrett's breathing. She could not speak. There were too many words and not enough. He had taken her where she had never gone before, and now he held her as though she were precious and fragile.

"Is your back broken?" he whispered finally.

She shifted in his arms and closed her eyes. "Mmm," she murmured.

"Am I—"

"What's going on?" The shrill voice of the serving maid filtered through the door. "Mister? Ye didn't pay for the meal. What are ye—"

The door cracked.

Garrett caught it and pulled it shut. "Go away," he ordered.

"What's going on in there?" she shouted. "I'll have the keep on you?"

"Go away, I say," he repeated.

Caroline giggled. What a picture they would make. They must have left a trail of her clothing from the table to the staircase.

A fist banged on the outside of the door. "This is a decent ordinary. None of your lewd ways here."

"Let her in," Caroline said, trying to pull her shirt over her bare breasts and her skirts down. "If you don't, she'll have the whole tavern around our ears."

"I won't let her in. She has a hairy mole on her lip. If I make love to two women, they must both meet my standards," he teased.

"Mr. Stewart! Mr. Stewart!" the maid cried. "A customer has a slut on the stairs."

Caroline burst into laughter. "Get up," she urged Garrett. "You'll have me in the stocks for harlotry."

"Give me a chance to get my breeches up. If she sees how I'm hung, we'll have to bring her in here," he countered.

"Garrett Faulkner, you're shameless," Caroline whispered. "Make yourself decent."

"It's your fault, woman. You lured me into this. On my own, I'm the soul of propriety," he grumbled.

"Open the door, Garrett," she insisted.

He pushed open the door, gave her his arm, and escorted her down the steps and into the family parlor just as the innkeeper entered the room.

"What's amiss here?" the red-faced man demanded. His wig was askew and his shirt out. Caroline wondered if he'd been disturbed in the midst of the same occupation.

"My jacket, if you please," she said to the stunned serving girl. Garrett retrieved her stock from the floor under the table.

"I demand an explanation," the innkeeper roared.

"Look at 'er!" the maid cried. "Just look at the both of 'em! Ye know what they been up to."

Caroline sniffed. "Pay them, Mr. Faulkner," she said in her haughtiest tone. "The service here is somewhat lacking."

"I agree." He tossed a few coins on the table.

"Out!" the innkeeper said. "Out of here!"

Garrett scooped up Caroline's cloak and put it around her shoulders. "Shall we, my dear?" he asked.

"Yes, Mr. Faulkner," she replied, unable to keep a straight face.

"I'll call the watch!" their host threatened. "I'll have the sheriff on you both."

Garrett glanced at Caroline, she nodded, and he grabbed her hand. Together, they ducked through the door, hurried down a shadowy hall, and dashed out nearest doorway into the rain. The innkeeper followed onto the street, shaking his fist and cursing.

"You are the craziest woman I've ever been married to," Garrett yelled in Caroline's ear as they rounded the corner in the downpour.

"I hope I'm the *only* woman you've ever been married to."

He led her a few dozen yards more, then stopped. "Where are we going?" he asked her.

"I don't know." She began laughing again as her hood fell back and rain began to soak her hair.

He pulled her against him. "I've nowhere to be alone with you," he said, threading his fingers through her drenched curls. "And I don't want to let you go." He kissed her full on the mouth. "I've waited too long to be with you like this."

She pulled up her hood and tugged at his hand. "Come on," she said. "I have an idea."

The Widow Gordon's home was only a few blocks from the Fox and Hound Tavern. Still laughing, Caroline led Garrett down one block, through several back yards, across a wide deserted street, and through an alley to the widow's stable. Once they entered the barn, it was pitch-black.

"I haven't been in a hayloft with a girl since I was fifteen," Garrett began. "I got hay burns on my—"

"Shhh," she cautioned. "We're not going to a hayloft. Trust me."

"That's what the recruiter told the country boy," he quipped.

Caroline chuckled and clasped his hand tightly. She had wandered into the stable on her second day as the widow's houseguest and she remembered the simple layout of the low-roofed structure perfectly. Even a blind woman would have known that a cow and calf were penned on the left, the driving horse in a box stall on the left. The air was heavy with the scents of cured hay, molasses, and livestock. For Caroline they were familiar smells of home and childhood.

The gray mare nickered sociably as they walked past, and Caroline could hear the rhythmic nursing of the newborn heifer. Next was a woven willow pen for chickens and the barrels with wooden lids where the feed was stored.

"I know where you're taking me," Garrett said. "A pig pen. I've been whisked off for a romantic evening with a herd of Charleston swine."

"Shhh." She giggled softly. Rain was cascading off the tin roof so loudly that they could have danced a reel without danger of anyone hearing, but sneaking around like fugitives from justice was more fun.

A few steps past the chicken run, she stopped and put out her hand. She felt the paneled door, right where she expected it to be. "Tell the truth," she urged Garrett. "You are a rebel, aren't you? You blew up that powder."

"What are you? The Spanish Inquisition?"

"Garrett. You have to start trusting me."

"I did trust you. I married you, didn't I?" He made a patient sound. "Then you told me you didn't really have the money I married you to get."

"One small misunderstanding."

"From my side, it doesn't look small."

"Are you or are you not a Tory?" she demanded, suddenly serious.

"And if I said I was—would you believe me?"

"No."

He chuckled. "And if I said I was an aide to

General Washington himself, would you believe that?"

"No."

"Then I might as well keep my truth to myself."

"Garrett, you're impossible." Secretly, she was pleased. She wanted him to be on the same side of the war she was on, but she didn't want him to be the kind of man who would forget caution because he'd slept with a woman.

She giggled. They hadn't slept at all. And if she had her way, they wouldn't do much sleeping for the rest of the night either.

Politics was a subject that meant a great deal to her. She was as committed to the cause of American freedom from English rule as she was to ransoming Reed, but as always, Fortune's Gift was her first responsibility. As long as Garrett Faulkner was a proclaimed Tory, her land would be safe if Washington lost his struggle. And if the troops at Valley Forge survived the winter and united the fledgling country, she would be exonerated because of Wesley's heroic death and her brother's service.

Her fingers found the simple wooden latch as she pushed open the door to the servants' quarters. The room was small, snug, and cleaner than the rooms at any inn. And Jane, the widow's cook, had told Mistress Gordon that she would be away tonight attending the birth of a grandchild. "Wait until I strike a light," she said to Garrett. "There was a lamp by the door and . . ." She found the tinder box exactly where she'd seen it before.

The Betty lamp cast a soft glow over the enormous bed. It was crudely made, a simple square of lumber resting on the floor, filled with a homesewn mattress stuffed with corn husks and covered with a bright patchwork quilt. There was nothing in the room but the small table, a sturdy bench, a wooden chest, and a few pegs in back of the door.

Garrett grinned. "The bed is rather *large* for the room, isn't it?" There was barely three feet between the lamp table and the bed, covered by a braided rag rug. Longways, the footboard and headboard touched the opposite walls.

"Obviously, Jane has her priorities," Caroline answered saucily. "And she is a woman of ample proportions." She hung her wet cloak on one of the pegs. "She's away tonight. We won't be disturbed until daybreak, at least."

"You are an amazing woman," he said. "Do you always plan your seductions so carefully?"

"Always." She took his coat and hung it beside hers.

He put his arms around her, tilted her chin up, and kissed her tenderly. "Most women would have gone into hysterics when we were caught on the stairs."

She shrugged. "I don't see why, Mr. Faulkner. We are lawfully wed, are we not? I was only fulfilling my wifely duties."

He kissed the tip of her nose, both eyelids, and the center of her forehead. "Had you chosen another occupation, you would have made your fortune," he teased.

She smiled and looked up at him through her lashes. "You are a delicious surprise," she said honestly.

He laughed. "I've not been called that before." He sat down on the bed, and the mattress crackled under him. He bounced. "It's soft, but noisy."

"We could lie very still." She removed her riding coat and hung it over a worn apron.

"I don't think so," he said huskily.

"It's cool in here."

"Come to bed, wife. I'll warm you."

She shivered then, but not from cold. She turned her back to him and began to undo the buttons on her waistcoat. "Shall I blow out the light?"

"Leave it. I want to see your face."

She glanced back at him. "Only my face?"

"And a few other parts." He removed his boots and stockings. "You have run me a ragged chase, little vixen."

Ribbons of sweet delight tumbled through her veins, and her heart began to hammer like the quick roll of a drumbeat. "You are very nice when you aren't being obnoxious," she admitted, unfastening the last button on her cuff.

"You are nothing like Wesley said," he murmured.

She moistened her top lip unconsciously. "Oh? And what did he tell you about me?"

"That you played a mean hand of whist."

"Is that bad?"

"Only if you beat me."

"You don't like to be beaten by a woman?"

He grinned wickedly. "Only if she's holding a buggy whip."

She sat on the bench and began to roll down a damp stocking. "You, sir, are no gentleman. What gentleman would talk about a widow's last husband on their wedding night?"

He stripped his shirt off over his head, and Caroline's throat constricted. She looked down quickly at the rag rug, hoping he hadn't seen what she knew she must be revealing in her eyes. She wanted him again. Wanted him badly. She began to take off the other stocking.

"He was a good man, and he loved you. I'm beginning to see why."

"What did Wesley say that you didn't like?"

"Did I say that?"

She laid her stockings neatly over the bench. "You implied it."

"He said something about your tongue being as sharp as your foil. You fence, I believe?"

"A little," she admitted.

"More than a little?"

She laughed, feeling the familiar flutter of excitement in the pit of her stomach. "And is that a problem?"

"Most men want only one sword in between their sheets."

"Do they?" She forced herself to take shallow breaths. "I've not had great experience," she said modestly. "You're only the second man that I've—" She began to unlace her corset.

"Come here," he ordered, removing the last of his clothes.

She was very aware of his nakedness. A warm flush flashed over the surface of her skin and her nipples tingled with anticipation. "But I'm getting—"

"I'll do that, Caroline."

She raised an eyebrow quizzically. "Not 'I'd like to do that, Caroline,' or 'Please, darling, let me—' "

"Come here, woman."

Her pulse quickened. She folded her arms over her chest and smiled. "No."

"Caroline."

"Garrett." She squealed as he leaped off the bed and grabbed her, threw her over his shoulder, and dropped her into the center of the heaped cornhusk ticks. Before she could catch her breath, she was half buried in the bedding with Garrett astride her, pinning her thrashing arms to the mattress.

"Do you yield, wench?" he demanded in a masterly tone. His gray eyes, full of devilish mischief, flashed silver in the lamplight.

"Never." She joined his game eagerly. "No torture can make me yield."

"We shall see about that," he murmured. "I am a master at putting disobedient wives in their place." He kissed the corners of her mouth, then outlined her lips with the tip of his warm tongue. His naked loins were pressed against hers; his stiffening rod throbbed through her thin linen shift.

"Mercy," she whispered.

"No mercy."

He cupped her breast in his strong hand, and she gave herself over to the magic of their true wedding night.

Noah awoke at the sound of knocking. He rose from his pallet on the floor, retrieved his pistol, and went to the door leading to the outside staircase. "Who's there?" he asked.

"It's Amanda. Please let me in."

"Good God, woman," Noah growled. "It's the middle of the night and pouring rain. Are you alone?" He hoped it wasn't trouble. Neither Eli nor Carrett had come back tonight.

"I have Jeremy with me."

"You brought a baby out in this downpour?" He lowered his flintlock and swung open the door. "Nobody followed you?" he asked as he lit a lantern.

She shook her head. "There's nobody on the streets. Please, is Mr. Faulkner here? My—Caroline went out to supper with him and she never came back. I was afraid something—"

"She's with Garrett. She'll be fine."

"But she never stays out." The baby stirred in her arms. "I'm sorry to bother you. I couldn't sleep. I was so worried—"

"Here," Noah said. "Look at you. You're soaked through. Damned town is nothing but a swamp."

Amanda's teeth began to chatter. "Caroline doesn't stay out—"

"Take that wet cloak off and wrap a blanket around you. There's no heat in this loft, but there's no need for you to catch an ague. You had no business bringing your boy out on such a night," he scolded.

No female, white or black, that looked as she did would be safe on the streets. Amanda Talbot was a striking woman. Her body was soft and shapely, and she carried herself proudly, like an Egyptian princess. Her eyes were the kind a man could get lost in.

Amanda laid the sleeping baby on a pallet and covered him. "He didn't get wet. He was under . . . under my cape." She was shivering so hard that she could barely speak.

Noah tossed her a blanket. The thought of her and the boy alone on the streets made him furious. He wanted to shake her. Did she think this was the Eastern Shore where a woman was pretty much safe?

Amanda's velvet eyes narrowed. "I don't need this. I'll just go back to the widow's house. I'm sorry to have—"

"Damn it, woman, will you stop apologizing. You're here now. What's done is done." He slid a three-legged stool across the plank floor toward her. "Sit down. I'm not going to eat you."

"There's no need to be rude," she said.

He pulled on a shirt and vest. "Mistress Faulkner seems to me to be a woman who can take care of herself. It's you who was in danger walking the streets so late."

She averted her eyes. "You don't like me very much, do you?"

He shrugged. "I never thought much about you one way or another."

She sniffed. "Good."

"Maybe it's you who are afraid of your own kind."

She raised her chin proudly. "It's not my fault that my family happens to be white. I was an infant when they took me in. If you blame me for that, then—"

He lit a pipe and puffed, trying not to let her see how much she irritated him. "You're jumping to conclusions again. Why should I care if you think you're a white woman?"

"I never claimed to be. Should I reject the people who loved and cared for me because of their skin color?"

"I wasn't thinkin' of that." He motioned toward the baby. Any fool could see that the child was mulatto. "But when you took a lover, I can see what color he was."

"Jeremy's father was white," she agreed.

He frowned at her. "My point."

"It was not my choice."

"You were raped?"

She nodded.

"You're unlucky. Garrett told me that Bruce Talbot raped you two months ago."

"Yes, he did."

"And the boy's father? What was that? A year and a half ago?"

"Yes."

"Same man?"

"No."

"Who?"

"None of your damned affair, Noah Walker." She stood up, threw the blanket off her shoulder, and moved to pick up her son. "I came here only because of Caroline. I thought you could help. I see now it was a mistake."

Noah stepped in front of her. "No, don't go. I apologize." Shame flooded through him. "I had no right to judge you. I'm sorry."

She stood there, back as stiff as a white-oak mast, eyes snapping.

"I said I was sorry," he repeated. "You may as well wait here until the rain lets up. Then I'll walk you back." He picked up the fallen blanket and draped it around her shoulders. "He's a fine boy, and you're a good mother. I didn't mean to insult you."

"Well, you did." She sat down on the stool again.

"Garrett and Caroline, they haven't had any private time alone together," Noah explained. "Garrett got passage for us all on a ship to the islands, but you women will be together and we'll be bunkin' with the crew. Not much of a honeymoon."

"It's not like that," Amanda said. "Caroline doesn't mean to have that kind of a marriage."

Noah chuckled. "What other kind is there?"

"I mean, she doesn't intend to . . ." She blushed. "It's a marriage of convenience."

"That's what he told me too. But he's been as jumpy as a bald bear covered with bees. I think Garrett likes your lady—likes her a lot."

"She's not my lady. We were raised like sisters."

"And naturally, you'll inherit a portion of that big plantation too."

"No, not land. But Reed—that's our . . . Caroline's brother. He doesn't get land either. He'll get money and so will I—when I marry. If I marry . . ."

"If you have a good dowry, I suppose there's men wouldn't mind an uppity wife."

"I don't care to discuss my personal life with you, Mr. Walker."

"No, ma'am. I suppose you don't." He chuckled. "But you're still welcome to spend the night here if you like."

"No, thank you." She stood up. "If you're certain that no harm has come to Caroline, then Jeremy and I will return to the widow's. I'd not keep you from your night's sleep."

"There's no need for you to go. I won't harm you."

"I didn't suppose you would. But what if Caroline comes back and we're not there? Then she'll be frightened. You were right. I shouldn't have come." She put her cloak around her again.

"Stay," he said.

"No." She picked up Jeremy.

"Hell, give him to me," Noah said. "If you're bound and determined to drown us all, I'll carry him back for you."

"I'm much obliged, Mr. Walker," she said sweetly. For the first time, she flashed a shy smile.

"But if I die of pneumonia, it's your fault," he complained. Damn, life wasn't fair. Here Garrett was bedded down someplace with a fine lady, and he was marching around in the wet with one as mean as a bay blue-claw with a cracked shell.

"If you die of pneumonia, I'll personally put

flowers on your grave," she replied with a straight face. "Twice a year."

"That makes me feel much better," he replied sarcastically. "I was awfully worried about the flowers." He opened the door and held it for her, then followed her out into the rainy night.

Chapter 12

The Caribbean
February 1778

Caroline stood on the deck of the Dutch merchant vessel and watched with growing fury as armed British sailors shackled the two young Americans. The mother of one boy—a lad hardly out of his teens—wept and clung to her son. "Don't take him," she pleaded. "For the love of God, don't take my only child."

"Cease your wailing, woman," the lieutenant said. "His Majesty has need of able-bodied seamen."

The hysterical mother, Abbie McGreggor by name, grabbed hold of the British officer's coat. "Not my Will, please. Not my Will. I've lost two boys. He's all I've got left."

The lieutenant shoved her roughly aside and watched as a handful of brutish men in English naval uniforms forced the Americans down the swaying Jacob's ladder. The white-faced Will McGreggor was the first prisoner to reach the longboat. Caroline stared helplessly as the boy looked up at his distraught mother, then over at the British man-of-war anchored a few hundred yards away.

"Will!" Abbie McGreggor screamed. Frantically, she flung herself at the rail. "Will!"

Before anyone could stop him, the boy raised

his chained hands and dived over the side of the small boat. Caroline ran to the railing. Will began to thrash wildly as the weight of the manacles pulled him down.

The lieutenant shouted an order, someone swore, and a seaman in the longboat grabbed the rudder. A sailor cut loose the mooring rope that held the smaller boat to the merchant vessel and others began to row toward the floundering boy.

"Shark!" cried a passenger.

A rifle fired. Then Caroline froze as she saw a dark shadow slice through the clear, blue-green water. Will McGreggor rose partially out of the sea and gave a single inhuman shriek, and Caroline covered her eyes with her hands. When she looked again, the water swirled with black and there was no sign of the boy.

For a moment, there was stunned silence, then Abbie McGreggor began to sob brokenly.

The lieutenant swore again and turned his attention to the struggling black man being dragged from the fo'c'sle by three British seamen. Caroline's mouth went dry as she saw that the prisoner was Noah. Blood trickled down his face from a cut on his temple, and his mouth was bruised and swollen. Sailors clung to each arm, while the third man battered him from behind with a belaying pin.

Noah twisted and broke loose. He seized the wooden club from his tormentor and whirled it around him. The sailors scattered, and Noah backed up until he felt the solid bulk of a mast behind him.

Still swearing, the lieutenant motioned to a seaman carrying a Brown Bess musket. "What are you waiting for, you fool. Shoot him."

"No!" Caroline lunged across the deck, placing

herself between the musket barrel and Noah. "How dare you seek to impress my servant?"

The officer growled an order and the seaman lowered his musket. "Step aside, woman," the lieutenant said.

"What's your name?" she demanded. "Do you know who I am?"

"I only know that you're obstructing my duty."

Caroline glanced back at Noah. "Drop that ridiculous weapon," she said. "This is all a misunderstanding." She looked toward the *Kaatje*'s master, Captain Vander Voort. "Sir, please tell this officer who I am."

"Again, Lieutenant, I must protest," Captain Vander Voort said angrily. "The *Kaatje* sails under the Dutch flag. You have no right to board my vessel, and no right to—"

"Naturally, you must take that up with the proper authorities, Captain," the British officer replied. "I have my orders."

"And your next orders shall send you to Botany Bay if you touch my property. I am Mistress Caroline Faulkner. My husband is first cousin to Lord Cornwallis."

The lieutenant's brow furrowed, and Caroline noticed for the first time that he was barely older than the deceased boy, Will McGreggor. "Naturally, any property will be paid for," he said. "You have but to make a claim in writing to—"

"A claim? A claim?" Caroline laughed sarcastically. "You cannot be serious. "I am to be deprived of my slave while I wait for months—perhaps years—to be reimbursed. I think not." She waved a gloved hand airily. "Go about your business, young sir. I am a good English citizen and I would not dream of interfering in your duties. But doubtless your superior never intended to insult relatives of Lord Cornwallis. Or"—she tried to look heartily offended—"or did he?" She brushed an imaginary bit of lint off her sleeve. "Surely, this is not a personal attack on Lord Cornwallis. Did you board this ship intending to—"

"No, ma'am," the officer said, clearly in retreat. "We have a warrant for a pirate known as Osprey. The search we made of the *Kaatje* was for that purpose. Impressing British citizens for service in His Majesty's navy is only a routine matter. There was no intent to interfere with your—"

"Interfere?" She laughed in what she hoped was a scornful manner. "I should think it is more than that. Deliver my regards to your commander. Return and ask him if *routine matters* meant seizing the property of Lord Cornwallis's family. Doubtless you would enjoy the climate at Botany Bay. I understand it is quite . . . unusual."

"Yes, ma'am, I mean . . . no, ma'am. This has been a misunderstanding." The lieutenant removed his hat and gave a quick bow. "Your servant, Mistress Faulkner. Sir." He nodded to Captain Vander Voort. "My men assure me that the criminal Osprey is not on board. I bid you a good day." Signaling to his men, he crossed the deck and descended the ladder.

Caroline went to Noah. "Are you all right?" She lowered her voice to a whisper. "Where is Garrett?"

"I'll be fine," the black man said. "Thank you."

She shook her head. "That's not necessary. You did more for me on the *Gillian*. Where's Garrett?"

"Hidin' in a better place than me, apparently."

"But why would he hide? Surely he has nothing to fear from the British. It's not as if they'd impress a well-born man like him." She touched the wound on his head. "You'd better let me treat that—"

Noah shook his head. "I'll see to it. I've had worse." He nodded toward Abbie McGreggor. "Best you see if you can do anything for her."

"All right," Caroline answered. "But if you reach Garrett before I do, please tell him that I want to talk to him."

Later, when she'd seen Abbie safely in the care of another woman, Caroline returned to the deck of the *Kaatje.* The British man-of-war had already pulled anchor and was sailing north toward the American coast. Captain Vander Voort had gone below, and the first mate was ordering sailors aloft into the rigging.

There had been no sign of Garrett yet, and Caroline was worried and increasingly annoyed. *Coward.* The word rose in her mind, and she immediately banished it. That was ridiculous. Her husband was no coward. No man who'd fought as he had against the wreckers off the Carolina coast could be lacking in courage. So why then had he hidden from the British boarding party?

And what twist of fate had placed her on a ship suspected of carrying Osprey? And why would the English put out a warrant on him after he had betrayed the American cause and gone over to the British side?

"I wish Osprey was aboard," she whispered, running her hand along the smooth wood railing. "I'd love to have the chance to come face to face with him. I'd send him to hell faster than the British."

"You are bitter."

Caroline's head snapped up and she stared wide-eyed at the vague outline beside her. Swirling colors formed the transparent image of a man, then dissolved until all that remained were two dusty clay-colored feet in a pair of twisted rope sandals. Scarred ankles rose almost to the knee; then there was nothing.

"Kutii," she said sharply. "Don't do that. Either appear or disappear. You know I hate it when you do that."

A flash of copper became a muscular arm without a hand or a shoulder. "I am an old man. You expect too much of me." She was not sure if the sound was coming from the spot beside her, or from inside her head.

"Kutii, where have you been?" In truth, his absence had disturbed her greatly. More than once, she'd wondered if he'd remained at Fortune's Gift, if she was leading Garrett, Amanda, and the others on a wild goose chase to Arawak Island. "Do you know how long it's been?"

"Your time means nothing to me, granddaughter."

"You promised you would help me find the treasure."

"This one made such a promise?"

His soft laughter seemed to surround her, and she shivered. Was he really there? Or was she simply as mad as May butter?

"Kutii told his granddaughter of the gold that the Star Woman brought from the bottom of the sea. This is true."

"You said only part of the treasure was ever recovered. You told me you saw the rest in a cave on the island."

The worn rope sandals rose into the air, ankles folded, and the rest of the Incan began to appear, faint but whole. Caroline blinked twice and saw him clearly, sitting cross-legged on the gunnel. In his hair was a bone comb. He was combing out his waist-length black hair and rubbing it with fragrant oil from a small pottery container. The strange pattern of tattoos on his bronze chest were bright blue, as vivid as if they had been painted only minutes ago. Caroline reached out to touch them, and her fingers found only warm air.

He laughed. "The barriers between us are not so easily crossed, child of my heart." He looked into her face with sloe eyes as black as pitch.

"What do you want?" she demanded.

He looked offended. "This warrior cannot look upon the chosen one without harsh words? Are you with child yet? Your husband has a mighty spear. I thought—"

"No. I am not with child yet." Caroline felt her cheeks grow hot. She and Garrett found little chance to be alone on this ship, but when they did find privacy . . . Her eyes widened. "You've been spying on me," she accused.

Kutii shook his head. "He is a better man than the first, this new husband of yours. I think you should make a child with him. The sooner the better."

"I don't want children," she lied. "At least not now, I don't. And my marriage is my own affair. What was wrong with Wesley?"

Kutii put the lid back on his bowl and tucked the container and the comb into a woven pouch slung over his shoulder. He was wearing a red-cotton wrap around his waist, a gold armband, and a silver nose ring. Now he carefully threaded silver hoops into his ears. Dangling from each earring was a curved jaguar tooth. "He was not worthy of you," he said.

"Wesley died a hero. How can you say that about him?" she protested.

The bosun came toward her hesitantly. "Are ye all right, missus?"

"I'm fine," she assured him. Damn! Anyone watching her would believe she was out of her mind. She glanced sideways at Kutii.

He was watching her with an amused expression. "Do you care what these people think of you?"

She took a deep breath. "How can you expect me not to care? For the love of God. A few years ago, I would have been burned at the stake for being in league with Satan. Am I a witch? A madwoman?"

"You are who you are," Kutii answered in his low, lilting voice. "You carry the blood of your ancestor the Star Woman. And you have her powers."

I didn't ask for this, she thought desperately.

"This one senses a great unease within you, child," Kutii said. "You are descended from a great warrior people. It is right and good that you fight for freedom, but I feel in you a destructive hate for one man."

"Osprey," she whispered. Even his name on her lips was enough to make her tense with seething anger. "I will see him in hell." She owed that much to Wesley . . . to Reed.

The bosun was giving her odd looks again, and she forced herself to *think* rather than speak to Kutii. What news of my brother? Is he all right? Have you seen him?

The Indian shook his head. "My energy is weak so far from you and from the earth where the Star Woman lies. You must seek out Reed yourself. Why do you hesitate? Use what the Creator has given you."

"But I . . ." Her protest died on her lips as she

watched the swirl of colors. One instant she was looking at an Incan nobleman, and the next—air and sparkling sea. Do not stay away so long next time, old friend, she said silently. I miss you. Her lips curved into the hint of a smile. I love you.

"Grandfather," he admonished with gentle amusement. "Have I taught you nothing, child of my heart. Call me Grandfather."

I love you, Grandfather.

Overhead, a black and white frigate bird wheeled and dived toward the ship against a backdrop of sky so blue that it seemed unreal. Fish jumped and seagulls skimmed the surface of the water. It all seemed too beautiful to Caroline to hide the sudden death she had seen with her own eyes.

What was real and what was not? What if Reed was already dead of prison fever? What if he had been executed? She would not know it. To her, he would still be alive. She could hear his teasing laughter, see the way his rusty-brown curls fell back from his high brow and receding hairline. If Reed Talbot was already lying in his grave in New York but alive in her mind, what was the truth? Was he dead or alive?

Not New York.

The words came so clearly that Caroline glanced around to see who had spoken. She was alone on the deck. But the voice had not been Kutii's, had not been any man's; unmistakably, the voice had been a woman's.

"Who are you?" Caroline asked. The only sounds she heard were the swish of water, the creak of rope and canvas, the groan of the ship, and the faint whistling of a seaman high above the deck in the crow's nest.

She closed her eyes and tried to concentrate on

Reed's face. Instead, her brother's plain features were obscured by those of Garrett Faulkner, and that same question returned to plague her. What was real?

All her life, she had been governed by reason, a trait she'd taken from her Grandfather Kincaid, according to her mother. She had married Wesley because they were friends, and she was comfortable with him. She had accepted his proposal because it was the sensible thing to do—the decision most likely to ensure the well-being of Fortune's Gift.

She had never been a flighty female prone to hasty decisions. She had used her intelligence rather than her passions to make important choices. She was a sensible person. And she had been happy in her union with Wesley. Or had she?

This marriage had been completely different from the first moment she laid eyes on Garrett Faulkner in her bedchamber. They shared nothing more than a wild sense of humor and a healthy lusting after each other's bodies. This was a marriage of convenience—nothing more.

She did not . . . could not love Garrett.

But her reality was that she did.

"Noah told me what you did to save him."

Caroline started. Garrett was standing right behind her. "How did you . . . Where did you come from? I didn't hear you—"

"You were deep in thought, Mistress Faulkner. I didn't mean to startle you." He flashed her a devilish grin. "That took a lot of courage—facing down that British lieutenant."

"And where were you?"

He chuckled. "I'll never tell."

"But why would you hide?" she demanded. "You were in no danger of being impressed as a seaman."

He shook his head. "Don't be too sure of that. I was a naval officer once. It wouldn't take much imagination on that lieutenant's part to see me in uniform again."

"So you hid and left your friend to face them alone?" She was relieved that he was safe but also annoyed with him.

"Apparently, Noah wasn't alone. He had you to fight for him." Garrett grinned again and touched his cocked hat in a salute. "Wesley was right. He always said you could take on the whole British navy and come out ahead." His mood grew serious. "None of us thought they would take blacks. They never touched Eli."

"Eli is half the size of Noah," she said. "I suppose they were looking for strong slaves." A horrible thought surfaced in the shadows of her mind. "That lieutenant said they were looking for Osprey," she continued. "Why would they look for him aboard the *Kaatje?*" Her eyes searched his face for any hint of what he was thinking.

Garrett met her gaze levelly. He pursed his lips. "No, I don't know why they would. But if they've put out a warrant for the man, they're checking every ship. It's common procedure."

A cold chill crept up from the pit of her stomach. "How did you know there was a warrant for his arrest?"

"Noah told me. Why? Do you know him, Caroline?"

"Know him? No, I don't know Osprey . . . but I intend to." Her voice took on a thread of steel as she pushed away her foolish thought that Garrett might be the traitor. Surely, if he'd been guilty, it would have shown on his face, she reasoned. He wasn't that good an actor.

"If you're going to be my husband," she said,

deciding to trust him a little, "you might as well be warned. Wesley died because of that bastard Osprey. Wesley died and Reed's in prison. And I'm going to make it my duty to find this Osprey. When I do, I'll turn him over to the British or the Americans, or anyone who promises me that they'll hang him—the sooner the better."

Matthew "Red Hands" Kay held the small cask over his head and drained the last of the fiery island rum into his mouth. "Empty, by God!" he roared, heaving the wooden container against the wall. He staggered back against the bed and slapped the mulatto wench on her bare bottom. "More rum!" he demanded. "More rum!"

Yee giggled drunkenly and collapsed facedown on the stained sheets. Her twin sister, Yaa, slid off the far side of the bed and weaved unsteadily, pendulous breasts swaying, toward the doorway of the large bedchamber.

"And be quick about it!" Matthew ordered. He wiped his mouth with the back of his hand, slid into a gilt Italian armchair, and surveyed his father's room with bloodshot eyes.

The marble-topped table was cracked down the center and littered with spilled food and drink. A delicate carved chair had suffered the loss of one leg; a cutlass was buried in the teakwood mantel, and blood and chicken feathers covered the Oriental rug beside the bed. The rooster—or what remained of it—dangled from one bedpost beside a rusty pair of leg irons. Worst of all, his grandfather's precious portrait of a redheaded woman had been used as a target. A neat hole from a pistol ball pierced the lower corner of the picture, nearly taking off the jade's foot.

"You should see your room now, Papa," he said.

His words struck him as exceedingly funny, and he laughed long and loud. "You always were a sanctimonious pig. Not pig." He belched. "Prig. Peregrine Kay was a sanctimonious prig." His snicker became a snort and then a series of choking coughs that brought a foul taste into his mouth. "Damn you, Yaa. Get back here with that rum. My mouth tastes like bilgewater."

He sniffed. The smell of chicken blood and feces was disgusting. "What the hell did we use that rooster for anyway, Yee?"

The woman on the bed continued to snore loudly.

Matthew snickered again and scratched the hair around his ballocks. He was as naked as the twins. Leaning back as far as he could, he sucked in his gut and admired his thick, red cod. It might be limp now, but by the king's royal arse, it was a mighty weapon when he was primed.

He kicked at the riding crop on the floor with his bad foot. Three toes he'd given to a lemon shark off the coast of Panama when a Spaniard had blown away their mainmast and set the ship aflame. He limped a little since, but pull on a boot with a little leather to stuff the toe, and he was the equal of any man on a dance floor.

"Yaa!" he bellowed. What the hell time was it, anyway? A louse nipped him sharply under the armpit, and he caught the vermin and cracked it between dirty, broken fingernails. He stood up and walked stiffly to the nearest window, then threw open the louvered shutters and let the hot light flow into the room.

Matthew blinked and rubbed his eyes, trying to decide what day it was. If it was Sunday, he'd sure as hell missed Mass. And if he'd missed church again, Mama would be furious with him.

Scratching his head, he went to the prie-dieu in an alcove in the far corner of the room, turned the Holy Mother's face from the wall, knelt, and mumbled a hasty prayer. Now at least he could tell Mama that he had done his rosary this morning—if she asked.

"Red Hands! Where are you, my bull? My ram?" Yaa's husky voice echoed through the room. "The lady been calling for you."

Matthew murmured "Amen," rose, and went back into the main room. "What did you tell her?"

Yaa had put a wrap around her loins, but her huge breasts still hung free for his touch. He caught one and weighed it in his hand, pinched the large dark nipples between his thumb and forefinger. She giggled and grabbed for his crotch.

"No time for that now," he said, snatching the crockery bottle from her hand. He took two long swigs and sighed. "Damn but that takes the tar off a man's hull." His head ached from the back all the way around to his eye sockets. "What day is this, Yaa?"

"Sunday."

"Oh, shit, I was afraid of that." He exhaled softly. "Has the lady been to church?"

"Where else she be this day?"

He grunted and shoved the bottle back into her hands. "Where's my clothes? Got to have my clothes." He looked around the room and realized that what he'd been wearing two days ago was no longer wearable—or even identifiable as waistcoat and breeches. "Where's that damned Juan? Tell him I need—"

"He on his way. Yaa know you need'm." She grinned, flashing a silver-capped tooth.

Matthew scratched at his groin again. "Braid my hair," he ordered. He prided himself on his thick, curling mane, as dark as the twins' hair with the aide of a little lampblack. All of his wigs were black. He'd never favored powdered hair on a man. It made him look too womanly.

By the time the girl had tamed the unruly mass into a single braided club down his back, his manservant had come in with shirt, breeches, and waistcoat. "The lady be in a terrible mad," Juan said, helping Matthew into the white lawn shirt.

"Clean this mess up," Matthew said as he left the room. "And get her out of here." He motioned toward the sleeping Yee. "I never could stand a coarse woman."

Servants stepped back out of reach of Matthew's fist as he hurried through the sprawling house. Damn! he thought. He'd told those girls he had to make Mass on Sunday. He'd have the hides off them if Mama was truly fierce with him. Was it too much to ask, that a man be able to relax on the few nights he spent at home?

He stopped outside a double set of huge paneled teakwood doors. "Mama," he said. His stomach felt nauseous. He hoped she wasn't going to yell at him. He hated it when she yelled. "Mama?" With a rising knot in his throat, he pushed open the door.

Chapter 13

"Matthew." Mama was clad all in black this afternoon with a Spanish lace mantilla over her sparse white hair. She did not rise from her cushioned, high-backed chair, but extended both wrinkled hands to him in the familiar gesture that never failed to bring a catch to his throat.

A huge ruby flashed on one slim finger, a priceless, square-cut emerald on another. Mama's left hand was adorned by only a single gold wedding ring, worn thin with age. Her nails were very long and carefully shaped.

"A good day to you, Mama," he replied, taking her tiny hands in his. She squeezed tightly, showing surprising strength for one of her advanced years.

"Matthew, darling." She turned a withered cheek for his kiss. Her skin was the color of old bronze and cool to the touch; her voice was as crumbly as dried sugar cane.

"Did you sleep well?" he asked. He worried constantly about her health, although he'd never known her to be sick a day in his entire life. His mother was long past the time when most women had gone to their graves, but she was unique enough to be immortal. He didn't want to think about her dying—not ever. In all the world, she was the only one who had ever loved him, and the only one he had ever loved . . . except for Simon.

Thinking about Simon made Matthew's headache worse. His son—his only son—lost to him forever. Unless we meet in hell, he thought wryly. For not even a loving father could imagine Simon in heaven.

Mama frowned. "I did not see you at Mass this morning."

"What?" He watched a small green lizard dart along the windowsill and pretended ignorance. The scent of orchids was almost overwhelming. Mama's garden, just outside the floor-to-ceiling louvered doors, was full of orchids—in every size and color. The heavy smell blended with the odor of citrus and flowering vines.

"Mass. You were not at Mass. Have a care for your soul, Matthew," she rebuked gently. "I fear your sins are . . ."

He smiled at her as a heavy weight lifted from his shoulders. "You pray enough for both of us." She wouldn't yell at him today. Mama might be deadly, but she was never treacherous. If she was angry with him, she said so at once. "I remembered my decades," he soothed. "And I promise my next prize to that convent of yours."

"A pirate cannot buy his way into heaven."

"I am no pirate. Corsair, maybe, or buccaneer." He chuckled. "Who else could Falconer find to do the dirty work so efficiently?"

"You are no longer a young man, Matthew."

He shrugged. "Then I will repent of my sins and take up a life of good works and charity as soon as . . ." He grinned heartily. "As soon as I am too old to enjoy a good swiving."

"For shame, to jest of such serious matters."

"I will change my ways when I am your age and too old to sin."

"How can you speak to your aged mother in such a fashion?" she admonished.

He did not miss the twinkle of mischief in her bright eyes. Once, they must have been as brown as earth; now they swirled with gray and silver. But they were still shrewd eyes, eyes that could bore into a man's heart and ferret out the lies he told himself and others. "You cannot tell me that you do not have your own lusts, Mama? Where else would I have inherited such an appetite? Not from Father, though Lud knows he was besotted with you. Else why would he have married a penniless—"

She laughed, a rustling sound that made him imagine the once vibrant woman beneath the wrinkles and the gnarled flesh. "I was a serving woman in this house, and he was the son of a royal governor," she said proudly. "He came to me in his hour of need and you were conceived. Then I gave him what no other woman could give him—a son. We were married, Peregrine and I, because the church would not legitimize you if we were not." She laughed again. "It cost a king's ransom—even in those days when money went farther than it does today. But Peregrine Kay would not have his son a bastard. His father, Governor Matthew Kay—you are named after him, you know. A great man, Governor Kay, though not so far-thinking as your father. Your father suffered from the falling sickness, but that did not prevent him from . . ."

Matthew shifted restlessly in his chair and wondered if the twins had left the house. He had heard this story of his mother's wedding and his father's genius a hundred times. Matthew's mind wandered as she rambled on. He had promised the crew a week ashore before they set sail for the Brazilian coast, but perhaps—

She rapped him sharply with her ivory fan. "Listen to me when I talk to you."

"I always listen."

"You listen, but you do not heed me. You will go to hell. My only child, burning forever in the fires of—"

"I went to confession only last week, Mama. Surely you can't believe that even I could sin enough to damn my soul in seven days."

Her eyes narrowed. "Do not treat me like a fool. They do not call you Red Hands for nothing. I know of that French merchant, *Paysanne,* you took off Cuba last month. And I heard of atrocities performed on the passengers."

"They would not disclose the location of certain valuables. An unfortunate misunderstanding."

"I am very disappointed in you, Matthew. Your father would never have—"

"I went to confession last week, Mama. My soul is as fresh as a new-washed leaf."

She looked unconvinced. "My maids have been complaining. Remember that you are a guest in my house. Confine your attentions to your common women and leave mine alone."

"You should not listen to servants' gossip. They exaggerate." He smiled at her and drew up a chair. "I brought you back something from Trinidad. Wait until you see. It is—"

She held up her hand for silence. "I did not call you from your whoring to exchange pleasant conversation. There is important news. News that you will want to hear. Falconer has received a letter from the Maryland Colony."

"I do not have all day, Mama. Tell me this message and be done with it."

"It concerns Simon." That had his attention. Annemie forced herself not to show her pleasure. Matthew was a terrible man, but a good son. It was necessary to keep him on a tight rein, lest he regard her as lightly as he did other women.

It had been her lifelong sorrow that the only child she and Peregrine had produced should turn out to be so stupid. Matthew would never be anything more than a vicious sea wolf. He was a man born to hang. She had had higher hopes of her grandson Simon, but he had been cut down before he reached his full potential. For Peregrine's sake, she must put aside her personal desires and convince Matthew to sire more legitimate children to carry on the family name.

"I have the name of Simon's murderer," she said softly. Matthew's dark eyes bulged.

"Give me his name," he demanded. "Be he prince or pope, I'll skin the hide from his living body and make a pouch to hold his heart. I'll burn his—"

"Enough of such childish prattle. Listen to me," she said, seizing his thick hands in hers. The backs of Matthew's hands and his arms were covered with curling black hair. She had always wondered where the trait had come from. Combined with his wedge-shaped body and round face, it gave him the appearance of a bear. "The American privateer Osprey was responsible for Simon's death."

"That tells me nothing," he growled. "We knew as much from other sources."

"Ah," Annemie continued, "but our other sources did not tell us that Osprey is really a colonial by the name of Garrett Faulkner. Or that this same Garrett Faulkner is even now en route to the islands. Or that he has married Caroline Talbot of Fortune's Gift on the Chesapeake."

"Faulkner comes here?"

Annemie nodded. "Her cousin sent word to Falconer. This cousin wished to marry the wealthy widow himself. He has offered Falconer one half of the lady's vast wealth if he will kill Osprey and return the girl to his loving care."

"Where is the girl? Is she with him? I'll spread-eagle Osprey and make him watch while I—"

"You will not."

"I'll have vengeance on Osprey if I have to kill you to do it, Mama. You'll not deny me on this."

"When have I ever denied you anything?" She had no intention of letting him have Garrett Faulkner until she could examine him and find out exactly who and what he was. But Matthew was like a child. She could not tell him everything at once.

She had mused on Faulkner's name since she'd first seen it. Faulkner was so similar to Falconer. A coincidence? She had lived long and seen few true coincidences.

Matthew leaped up and began to pace back and forth. "I'll rip his eyes out with fishhooks, I'll cut his—"

"Yes, yes, I'm sure you will." She sighed and fanned herself. Matthew's pleasures were so disgusting. "You may have Osprey to do with as you will," she promised. "But the girl—"

"Did the letter say what she looks like? If she is an heiress, she will have the face of a sea cook. But her face doesn't matter. I will—"

"You will dispose of the husband and wed the wench yourself."

"Are you mad, old woman?"

"Mad." She laughed. "I am the only sane one in this room. You have no son. Caroline Talbot—whatever she may call herself—is the granddaughter of Kincaid and Bess Bennett and the great-great-granddaughter of Lacy and James Bennett. They are old enemies of Falconer. In your grandfather's time Lacy and James robbed a fortune in Spanish treasure from—"

"Why do you cling to the past? What has this to do with the wench?"

Memories of her dead grandson swept over her, the grandson that Osprey had sent to the bottom of the sea. "Debts must be paid, my son. Friends rewarded, enemies destroyed."

Simon, she thought sadly. My Simon . . . You were my hope for the future. Not slow of wit like Matthew. You were smart, a willing pupil. You would have been a fit candidate to wear the Falconer's mantle.

"This James is long dead. Why should we—"

Annemie raked him with a fierce gaze. "Fool! The land of Fortune's Gift was purchased with gold that should have been Falconer's. By your marriage to Caroline Talbot, you will bring that which was lost back into the fold."

"She is Osprey's wife?"

"Apparently. But marriage is a simple matter to undo. She was a widow when he found her; she will be a widow again when you have dealt with him as he deserves."

"She will hold Osprey's death against me. Why should I be saddled with an ugly, weeping wife?"

"Get a child on her, and you may do as you like. You are no longer young. By marrying Caroline Talbot, you will secure a wealthy wife of high birth and cancel all debts. Will it not be a final blow to Osprey, to take his bride before he is cold?"

Matthew's shaggy black brows drew together. His forehead wrinkled in thought. It was a complicated scheme she had proposed, and Matthew never liked doing more than one thing at a time.

"I can use the woman?"

"Once she is your wife, you may take a husband's right with her." Her ancient voice rang with authority. "But you may not kill her until she has delivered a living child of your loins."

"What if she quickens with a jill instead of a jack?"

"A son would be best. But boy or girl, I care not, I must have a grandchild." I must have a bloodline to continue on, she thought. I am weary of life and long to join my Peregrine in paradise. But I cannot die without ensuring the family—

"You have me," Matthew reminded her sullenly.

"I have you, my lamb," she agreed. "But you take too many chances with your life. I must have a grandchild. And this woman must be his dam."

"Why do they come here, this Captain Osprey and the wench?"

"It matters not why, only that they come," she answered him. But her mind was whirling with possibilities. Peregrine had always believed that there was more treasure on Arawak. "Our informant says their destination is Arawak Island."

"Arawak? No one goes to Arawak. Even the Indians will not live there—they say it is haunted by the ghosts of dead Caribs."

"You are not afraid of ghosts, are you, my son?"

He growled. "I fear only cold steel and hot lead."

"And it is not far."

"Not sixty leagues from Jamaica."

She laughed. "Don't you see? Like a spider I have waited patiently all these months since my precious Simon was killed. And now these two fly into my web as careless as mosquitoes. What do we do with mosquitoes, Matthew?"

"We swat them."

"And destroy them utterly . . . leaving no trace that they ever existed."

"Simon's murderer will take a long time to die. His screams will sound sweet to my ears."

"I'm sure." She tapped his wrist with her fan again. "But you may not kill him until he has been brought before Falconer."

"Why not?"

"Do not question me. I am firm on this. They must both be brought whole and alive. After they have been questioned, then you may have your fun." Once Falconer was clear as to who Garrett Faulkner was, then she could reason with Matthew. After all, when her dear son lied to her so often, why should she bother to be completely honest with him? Matthew was a dangerous weapon that must be handled with extreme care.

"It is unfair that I should do the work of catching him and then have to wait," he grumbled.

"Life is unfair," she said. Sighing, she settled back on the cushion. "I knew when I felt the ocean breeze on my face this morning that it would be a fortuitous day." Her face hardened. "I never guessed just how fortuitous."

It was late at night. Aboard the Dutch merchant ship, Caroline and Garrett stood by the rail in the pale moonlight wrapped in each other's arms. Satiated and utterly content, Caroline leaned against him, waiting for her body to stop trembling and her heartbeat to slow to normal.

Once again, they had been unable to hold back the tides of passion. Here, on the open deck, she had given him what they both wanted so desperately, without heed for propriety. They had made fast and furious love in the shelter of a stack of cargo, and her lips still tasted of Garrett's.

He wrapped a stray lock of her hair around his finger and lifted it to rub against his face. "I think I have the imprint of a cask rim permanently creased in my knee," he murmured.

She laughed softly. "It seems there is never a bed near when we need one."

"If there was, I'd stay between the sheets day and night. You will be the death of me."

She twisted around so that her back and buttocks rested against his chest and loins, and his arms were still locked around her. She didn't want to think, and she didn't want these overwhelming sensations of languid pleasure to stop. Words seemed inadequate for the emotion she was feeling, so she swallowed the lump in her throat and gazed out at the shimmering, velvet sea.

The ocean was as calm as the surface of the river that flowed past Fortune's Gift. Only gentle waves rose and undulated in slow, sensual patterns. The soft salt breeze carried a promise of warm green islands and exotic flowers. The rhythmic sounds of rope and sail and water played a dreamy melody that blended with the Caribbean night until Caroline wanted to weep for the beauty of it all.

"I've never known a woman quite like you," he said, "nor one so vibrant and full of life."

"Save your compliments for the young girls," she answered. She was confused enough without listening to such silken words from him.

She didn't know if what she felt for Garrett was love or lust; she only knew that the moments they were apart seemed desolate. And when she could see him . . . touch him . . . hear his voice—she was happier than she had ever been in her life.

"When we get to this island kingdom of yours," he began, "I will regret the end of this voyage. I . . ."

She deliberately closed her mind to what he was saying. She would not listen—would not try to imagine him going away from her . . . or the lonely nights ahead of her.

I won't let him go, she vowed. He feels something for me, I know he does. We can stay on Arawak after we find the treasure. Once Reed is freed from prison, there's no reason for us to go back to the Chesapeake. I've given enough to the cause. I've lost one husband and I don't intend to lose another.

This war with England could go on for years. Even if she was willing to take the risk and return to Fortune's Gift, how could she justify leading Amanda and Jeremy back into danger?

Garrett cupped her breast possessively with one warm hand and teased her nipple with his thumb until it hardened to an aching nub and her breathing quickened. "Stop," she protested, halfheartedly. Her clothing was all awry; her thighs were still wet from his lovemaking. And already, she wanted him again. "If someone sees us—" she began.

"You weren't worried about that a few minutes

ago," he reminded her. He rubbed against her so that she could feel his growing need.

"My hair . . ." She put a hand up and laughed. She had lost her cap somewhere and her hair was as wild as a gypsy's. "Last night when I went back to my cabin, Mistress Paine—the long-nosed baker's wife—rolled her eyes and called me a common trull."

"Never common."

She giggled. "That's what I told her." She, Amanda, and Jeremy, were packed into a narrow cabin with four other women, as tightly as leaves in a tobacco cask. There were no private cabins on the *Kaatje*. Even the captain shared his quarters with his first officer.

They were both quiet for a long time, and Garrett's next statement surprised her. "Would you go to England if I asked you?"

"England?" she echoed. If he was an American sympathizer, why would he want her to go to England?

"I can think of no place safer. And I want you safe—you and Amanda and Jeremy." He kissed the crown of her head. "I don't want to leave you here alone in the islands, and I can't think of taking you back to Fortune's Gift and putting you within reach of your cousin again."

"You have no responsibility for us," she answered. "That was never part of our agreement." Her mouth felt dry, and a dull ache began in her temple. "I am capable of taking care of myself."

"So you say." He kissed the crown of her head again.

"I won't go to England."

"Things have changed between us, Caroline."

"Perhaps."

He lifted the mass of hair at the back of her neck

and lowered his head to kiss her there. Shivers ran down her spine and she made a small sound in her throat. "I wish we had met another time and place," he said. "It was simpler when I didn't care about you."

She swallowed. "You married me for my money, Garrett. Don't pretend that's changed."

His voice grew hoarse with emotion. "I don't want to see you hurt."

"We could both stay in the islands until the war is over. We wouldn't have to return to the Chesapeake to pay Major Whitehead to arrange for Reed's pardon." The ache in her forehead was spreading. She closed her eyes and saw pinwheels of sparkling light.

"I don't trust the major. How do you know he won't take your money and—"

She opened her eyes and looked at the sea. The moon was only a thin sliver, and there were no stars visible. "What other choice do I have?" she protested, beginning to feel slightly dizzy. "Reed is . . . Reed . . ."

"There are other options," Garrett said. "We can . . ."

Without warning, the boundaries of Caroline's vision began to alter. Crisp, bright images swirled in her mind. One picture after another formed and settled into focus, to be replaced by another and another with the sudden, sharp intensity of a whip's crack.

Reed . . . hardly more than a baby.

Reed's red cheeks glowing, his chubby legs rising and falling as he ran down the furrows of the cornfield shouting for her to wait . . . A slightly older Reed falling from the hayloft and breaking an arm. An earnest young man dressing for his first adult gathering and asking her to tie his stock.

Caroline sighed and her head fell back against Garrett as the pull of the past grew stronger. For a space of time, she was caught between two worlds, and then she could no longer resist the power of her waking dream.

Reed's laughing face . . .

Reed lifting Papa's silver goblet and drinking a toast to Patrick Henry and his bold speech. Reed holding Amanda's hands and boasting of Osprey's victories at sea. Reed, as she had last seen him, the night before he and Wesley went to join Osprey . . .

From far off, Caroline was vaguely aware of Garrett's voice and his touch, of the gentle roll of the *Kaatje* under her feet. But that was not as real as Reed and the events replaying in her mind's eye.

Reed . . . Reed embracing Amanda as he made his farewells.

Caroline watched them with the detachment of a total stranger. Had they always held each other so tightly? Had Amanda's eyes always shone with so much love when she looked at her brother? As Caroline puzzled over those questions, the image of the great hall at Fortune's Gift faded, to be replaced by the terrifying scene of the deck of a burning ship.

Cannon and musket fire shattered the night. The crash of falling yards and the screams of wounded men made Caroline's blood run cold. A fair-haired officer in Continental uniform of blue and white knelt beside a shadowy figure trapped in a morass of tangled rope and burning sails. The young man—her brother, Reed—strained at the shattered mast that held his comrade pinned to the deck until veins bulged out on his forehead.

"Caroline!" Garrett shook her.

She tossed her head, not wanting to look . . . trying desperately to block out the awful vision of pain and death.

*But nothing could drown the shrieks of the flame-shrouded sailor who ran to the gunnel and threw himself into the churning sea. She watched him fall, heard his last cry of fear. And as the waves swallowed his body, the name on the side of the black ship stood out starkly in gold lettering—*Osprey.

"Osprey," Caroline whispered.

Reed drew her back into the fiery deck.

The trapped man groaned. "Help me, Reed. For the love of God, don't leave me to burn." Wesley's voice. She would have known it anywhere.

Again and again, Reed tried to budge the splintered bulk of fallen yards as the fire licked close enough to singe his hair.

"Shoot me," Wesley cried.

"Caroline!" Garrett's plea came from far away.

Tears were running down Reed's face. He cradled Wesley's head in his lap and reached for the knife at his waist.

Caroline whimpered, "No."

Then the deck of the Osprey *tilted. The ship moaned, a terrible sound of cracking ribs and snapping planks followed by the roar of sucking water. Waves rolled over the gunnel. Reed made another frantic attempt to move the heavy mast off Wesley's legs. The water rose as the ship began to slide sideways. With a last glance at Wesley, Reed rushed to the rail and dived overboard.*

The ship rolled and went under. Down, down, down, into the dark water it tumbled, until with a grinding groan, it settled into the black mud of the Delaware Bay.

Caroline tossed her head. She was no longer

staring at the death throes of a ship beneath the waves. The dark, cold water had been replaced by the tranquillity of the brick-walled family cemetery at Fortune's Gift.

A freshly carved wooden grave marker stood near her father's resting place. Caroline could easily read the epithet:

REED KINCAID TALBOT
1755–1778

"No!" Caroline cried. Pain surged through her breast and the pounding in her head became an agony. Blackness whirled around her, and then the pain was gone and she felt only peace.

Garrett caught her as she went limp. "Caroline!" Gathering her in his arms, he took several steps toward her cabin before she stirred.

"Please," she murmured. "Let me . . ."

"Shh, you're ill."

"No." She struggled against him, trying to right herself in this time and place. "Please. This has happened before. I'm all right. Put me down."

Cautiously, he lowered her feet to the deck, steadying her with his arm. "You fainted," he said.

"No." She shook her head. "I never faint." She could not rid her mind of the sight of Reed's grave. Was he dead and buried already? She never knew whether her visions were past or future.

Past, present, future . . . were they so far from each other? And what was real? The *Kaatje* or the sinking of the *Osprey*? Or both?

"You must be fevered," he said. "You must see a physician. I'll call Captain—"

"No. You don't understand," she said. "It's not an illness. It is the curse and blessing of the women of Fortune's Gift." She stared into his eyes.

"I have the sight, Garrett," she whispered. She felt a knife of pain twist in her chest again. "It is a matter I neglected to mention," she said softly. "You are married to a witch."

Chapter 14

Arawak Island
March 1778

"A witch. Well, I'll believe that," Garrett had replied wryly, "if you'll believe that I'm the sheriff of Nottingham."

Now, two weeks later, Caroline could still hear his laughter. He hadn't believed a word she'd told him—not about the sinking of the *Osprey*, glimpsing Reed's grave marker, or even her ability to see across time and space.

"You've a touch of fever," he'd decided. "And the sooner we get you ashore with fresh food and water and a doctor, the better."

The threat of fever aboard the *Kaatje* had been enough to convince the Dutch captain to anchor at the French colony of Saint Domingue on the west coast of Hispaniola. Sailors lowered a longboat and rowed Garrett, Caroline, Amanda and the baby, Noah, and his brother Eli to the dock at Port-au-Prince. Garrett found lodging for them and insisted that Caroline see a physician. Naturally, he had pronounced her as sound as a Dutch *daalder*.

In Port-au-Prince, they were able to purchase an aging sloop and supplies to last them until they reached Arawak. "You'd best produce that fortune in gold quickly," Garrett had warned Caroline. "My pockets are empty."

Noah had spotted the twin mountaintops of Arawak Island early that morning. Now they had sailed close enough to wonder at the sheer limestone cliffs that rose from the sea. Beyond that lay a tangle of green jungle and craggy outcrops of stone heaped in tumbled stairsteps to the rising flanks of the bare-topped mountains.

The contrast of blue-green sea, white stone, and green forest beneath a sapphire sky was breathtaking. Palm trees and lacy vines hung down over the exposed rock, and waves splashed against the cliffs, sending sprays of white foam into the air. Seagulls and frigate birds screeched and circled overhead; tiny schools of fish leaped from water so clear that Caroline could see forty feet straight down to an underwater kingdom of multicolored coral and swaying plumes.

Shadows of fish darted beneath the boat, and a few hundred feet away, a gray form sliced the water. "A shark," Caroline cried pointing. "Look."

"Not a shark," Garrett corrected her as the creature leaped out of the waves. "Dolphin." He smiled at her. "They're supposed to bring good luck."

The dolphin leaped high out of the water, followed closely by a second one. Together they performed a series of spinning dives in perfect unison, and Caroline laughed. "I'm glad they're not sharks," she said, remembering the sudden death of the boy. "I don't care if I never see another shark."

"Where is the plantation house?" Garrett asked. "I don't see any signs of habitation."

"On the west side of the island is a natural cove," she answered, shading her eyes with her hand. "There's a dock and safe harbor between the coral reef and a sandy beach." The sun was hot; even though Caroline was wearing a broad-brimmed hat, the unrelenting heat burned through her wool bodice and made her perspire. "There's a waterfall," she remembered. "We can bathe there. The water is cool and sweet. It comes down from the peaks of the mountains."

"Watch the reef," Garrett warned as Noah guided the sloop closer to shore. "Coral's sharp enough to rip a hull open like butter."

Noah shook his head. "Not this boat. I could sail her in two feet of water. She's shallow draft, made for these islands."

"Papa told me there's a channel through the reef, but it's hard to find. Larger vessels can dock at the landing," Caroline said, "but only if they know the secret of getting in safely."

Noah smiled at Jeremy. "There's one boy who will be glad to have some sand to crawl around in."

The baby giggled and clapped his chubby hands together. "Da-da-da-da," he cooed.

Amanda averted her eyes. "Ma-ma. Say Ma-ma, Jeremy."

"He's a bright boy," Noah said.

Caroline noticed that he had turned his attention to Amanda, and from the slight flush of her sister's cheeks, she knew that Amanda was aware of his gaze. "He'll be walking before he's a year old," Caroline predicted, keeping the conversation safely on the baby.

"I'll be glad to have solid ground under him again," Amanda said. "He's getting heavy to carry, and he'll never learn to walk confined aboard ship. Will you, darling?" She kissed the top of his curly head. "Mama's boy needs solid ground under his feet, doesn't he?" Jeremy giggled and planted a wet, slobbering kiss on Amanda's cheek. Laughing, she bounced him on her knee.

Caroline smiled at the picture the two of them made. Jeremy had been the first to acquire a tan. Only a few hours of the tropical sun had turned his beautiful skin to a golden-tawny shade. He had Amanda's huge liquid brown eyes, but his lips were thin and his nose narrow. Whoever his father was, it was clear that Jeremy would grow up to be an extremely handsome man.

Noah reached over the side and scooped up a handful of water and sprinkled it on the baby. Jeremy giggled and squealed with delight.

It was plain to Caroline that Noah liked the boy and his mother. What Amanda felt toward the shipbuilder was as much a mystery as most of Amanda's thoughts.

Caroline liked Noah. He was open and friendly, a good traveling companion, and someone to depend on—the exact opposite of his brother Eli. She didn't like Eli and she didn't trust him. He was sullen and a constant complainer. She glanced back at him over her shoulder and he stared at her with equal distrust. She sighed and looked again at the island, unable to rid herself of the notion that they should have left Eli behind in Charleston.

Another half hour's brisk sailing took them to the landing spot. There were no limestone cliffs there. Instead, surf rolled gently onto a wide expanse of sloping sand beach. Beyond that, swaying coconut palms rose thick and green, interlaced with gum and pine trees. A huge mossy-backed turtle paused in its slow stroll across the sand to stare at the sailing vessel. The only sign of a dock was a few rotting posts sticking out of the water.

"They must have moved the landing farther along the cost," Garrett said, "but we'll go ashore here. I don't like the looks of those clouds. There may be a storm, and I want to get under a roof before it hits."

They anchored in the shallow water inside the reef, and Garrett carried Caroline ashore. The turtle gave a final stare with round, black, glassy eyes, pulled in its head, and hid in its shell. Nothing moved on the beach but a platoon of fiddler crabs and some long-legged seabirds.

"How far is the house?" Garrett asked.

"Not far." Caroline pointed to a grown-over rutted track that led into the trees. "I think we follow that road."

He looked dubious. "That's a road?"

Noah set Amanda on the sand, and she hurried to take a fussing Jeremy from Eli. The women waited while the men waded back and forth, bringing the supplies and their personal belongings ashore. Then, leaving Eli as a guard, the others set out in search of the manor house.

As they entered the trees, a green and yellow parrot squawked and flew from one branch to another. Something small and brown scampered along the ground and vanished into a heap of rotting palm fronds.

"Let me carry the boy," Noah offered, reaching for Jeremy.

"I can manage," Amanda insisted, shifting him to her hip. Caroline still couldn't get used to seeing her sister dressed as a servant. It seemed strange to see Amanda, who had always worn silk and satin, wearing homespun. Jeremy wore only a nappy and a short dress. He was growing so fast, they could hardly keep garments on him.

The air was cooler here in the forest. Off to the right, among the rocks, Caroline heard what could only be the bleating of goats. She was beginning to feel nervous. Where was everyone? Arawak Hall didn't have as many workers as Fortune's Gift, but there should still be servants, field hands . . . children. Where were they?

No member of the family had been here for years. All business was conducted through their trusted stewart, Angus Frazier. And she'd not heard from him or received a deposit from Arawak since before she and Wesley were married.

"I want a proper bath and a feather bed with pillows and a goose-down coverlet," Amanda said.

"And I want something for dinner that hasn't been salted or dried," Noah chimed in. "A little roast pork wouldn't be bad, or a juicy beefsteak."

They rounded a bend and stopped short. The manor house stood in the center of what had been a sweeping lawn, but was now a morass of vines, banana trees, and waist-high grass. The massive structure was two and a half stories high, of gray brick laid in Flemish bond, with double chimneys at each end of the main house and dormers set into the hip roof. A grand portico with four Greek columns graced the front of the house, accessible by tall French doors on both the first and second floors.

The house was magnificent and completely deserted. Window shutters hung open and sagging; leafy vines wound up the portico and encircled the columns. A shaggy brown and white goat stood on hind legs on the second-story porch, nibbling a flowering plant that grew down from the red tile roof.

"This is Arawak Hall?" Garrett demanded.

Stunned, Caroline nodded. Her stomach did a flip-flop. The awful thought that Kutii might not appear hit her like a splash of icy water. What if he didn't come? Where on this tangled island would she search for the treasure, and what would she tell Garrett?

Amanda stopped dead in her tracks and pointed to a black cat sitting on the front step. "Look," she said. "It's Harry."

"Where?" Garrett said. "I don't see a living soul."

Caroline stared at the black cat. "It's not Harry," she assured her sister. "It's just a stray . . ." But as she watched, the animal stretched and strolled lazily behind a column and disappeared from sight.

"It's Harry," Amanda insisted with a trace of uneasiness. "I know it's him."

Caroline forced a chuckle. "Not likely. We have an old tomcat that looks just like that," she explained to Garrett and Noah. "Amanda doesn't like cats. She's afraid of them."

"Not all cats," she said, "just . . . just that one."

Garrett crossed the shell drive to the front of the house and tried the door. It was locked tight. "I'll go around to the back," he said. "We're bound to find something that—"

Suddenly, the door swung open. Standing in the entranceway was a small brown woman holding an ancient wheel-lock musket. "Get you 'way from dis place!" she cried. "Dis place no belong you!"

Garrett held up his hands. "We mean you no harm," he said. "I'm Garrett Faulkner, husband to Caroline Talbot Faulkner. She owns this plantation."

"Yeah, sure you be," the little woman retorted. "You looks like rich folk, you surely does. And I be de royal governor. Now, get you 'way, 'fore I puts a hole in you a dolphin can jump through."

Garrett glanced back at Caroline. "Wife," he called, "you'd best come and talk to this misguided woman."

Caroline hurried up to the steps. "I am Caroline Talbot," she said. "There's a terrible war in the American Colonies. I'm looking for my steward, Angus Frazier. Is he here?"

"You be Miz Talbot, fer certain?" The woman lowered her gun and a smile broke over her freckled face. "I be Mr. Frazier's wife, Pilar. Come you in. We got *pollo* and black beans for dinner. Come you in and eat."

By evening, the storm that Garrett had expected whirled around the island. Palm trees bent under the force of the wind, and driving rain beat against the windowpanes. In the master bedchamber of Arawak Hall, Garrett sat in a chair beside the huge poster bed draped in filmy gauze and sipped a glass of Jamaican rum. Caroline stood by the window brushing her hair.

"Your steward, Angus Frazier, has obviously been crippled for a long time," Garrett said.

Caroline nodded. Arawak Hall was not what she'd expected. Although Pilar had kept the interior of the mansion in acceptable condition, the rest of the plantation was a disaster. The stables were empty, the horses stolen, dead, or roaming loose on the island. The staff of servants consisted of Pilar and her invalid husband. The cane fields had gone wild, and no other crops had been planted or harvested in years.

"Arawak is haunted with all manner of unholy beasties," the cheerful Angus had told them at dinner. "No freemen will work here, and slaves build boats and sail away."

"De old people," Pilar had chimed in, "de Arawaks, dis be de place where de ghosties live, up there on them mountains. Dey don't scare Pilar. Pilar's grand, she be Arawak—full blood. Dem ghosties, dey don't hurt Pilar or her man, Angus. But I seen dem, yes. Pilar seen dem many a night, dancing on beach and in de treetops. And I hear de drums on the mountain. Arawak drums."

Garrett joined Caroline at the window and took the ivory-handled brush from her hand. "Let me do that," he said.

She sat in a chair and looked out at the rain as he began to brush with slow, lazy strokes. Garrett had not asked about the money yet, but she knew it was only a matter of time. For weeks, she had wrestled with the problem of telling him that she'd brought him all this way to chase down a family legend related to her in part by the ghost of an Incan Indian who'd been dead for a hundred years.

She closed her eyes, taking pleasures from the bristles of the brush dragging across her scalp and down the length of her hair. Garrett would be very angry with her—she knew he would. And that anger would destroy the fragile bonds they had woven with their lovemaking.

To her surprise, she found she genuinely liked Garrett Faulkner. He was funny and smart. He made her laugh, and they were never at a loss for things to talk about. Garrett was one of the few men she'd ever met who respected her ideas, even when he didn't agree with them. In short, he was a perfect match for her—or would have been perfect if he shared her belief in independence for the Colonies.

And she wasn't sure if he did, or didn't. There were many mysteries surrounding her new husband, not the least of which was why he had agreed to marry her. He'd said it was for her money, which made sense. Except that the more she came to know Garrett, the more certain she was that he didn't give a damn about how wealthy she was. And if not for money—then why?

Garrett stopped brushing. "Neither of us had a bath since Port-au-Prince," he said. "I wonder how warm that rain is? I've got so much salt caked on me, I feel like a salt mackerel."

She laughed. "You want me to stand out in the storm?" She took hold of his hand and rubbed the back of his palm against her cheek. She loved the smell of him, and she loved to feel his skin against hers. If they were going to fight over the treasure, they could just as well do it tomorrow or the next day. Tonight, she would sleep in his arms. Or . . . She smiled provocatively. Perhaps they wouldn't sleep at all.

"I only said I wondered if the rain was warm," he said. "I didn't tell you to stand in it." He put down the brush and stripped to his breeches. Then he pulled her to her feet and kissed her.

She laid her cheek against his chest and listened to the rhythmic throb of his heart, all the while massaging his skin with her fingers. "Why go out in the rain?" she murmured.

"Where's your sense of adventure?" he coaxed. "A Caribbean shower-bath is an experience no wife should miss."

"You're serious? You're going out in the rain?"

He kissed her again, slowly, tenderly. He ran a hand down the curve of her back and molded her against him. "Surely you'd not send me out into the night alone?"

Caroline laughed and made no protest as he began to unlace the back of her gown. "You're getting so good at that, there'll be no need for me to have a lady's maid," she said. He kissed the back of her neck and trailed kisses to her ear.

Warmth spread through her at his touch. "Garrett," she whispered huskily. But he already had her halfway out of her gown. She cupped his face between her hands and caressed him lightly. Her eyes never left his.

"You are a rare woman, Caroline Faulkner."

"And how is that, pray tell?"

"Your blood is as hot as any man's."

"Warmer, perhaps." She moistened her lips suggestively and ran her hands down over the taut muscles of his shoulders and upper arms as delicious shivers ran through her. He had only to touch her . . . to murmur her name, and her desire for him overpowered her every conscious thought and reason.

Her breathing quickened as he outlined her lips with the tip of his tongue and then caught her lower one between his teeth and nibbled at it gently. Fire shot through her. Sweet Jesus. Had anything ever felt as wonderful as Garrett's half-naked body pressed against hers? She let her head fall back, and he kissed her throat.

Her mouth went dry as he slowly untied the ribbons on her stays. When she would have helped him, he whispered, "No" and kissed her bare shoulders and the valley between her breasts. "I want to do this myself."

Her stays dropped to the floor, followed by her cotton chemise. "Oh," she gasped as Garrett dropped to his knees and began to slide one silk garter down her thigh. His face was so close to her cleft that she could feel his breath stir her curls. "Ohh." The flame had become a burning that threatened to engulf her.

He kissed her thigh and knee as his fingers unrolled her linen stocking. She swallowed hard and stroked the crown of his head, tangling her fingers in his hair.

"Come with me," he whispered when he'd removed her other stocking and kissed her left thigh, and knee, and ankle. He picked up a bar of French soap from the washstand and took a step toward the double doors that led to the second-story porch.

She would have followed him anywhere.

"I think I like your island already," he said. He paused just long enough to shed his breeches.

"So do I."

A gust of wind struck them as he opened the glass-paned doors. The rain was warm on her naked skin, the air hot and soft. Grains of damp sand and bits of leaves littered the porch under her bare feet, but she didn't care.

The storm was coming from the west, hitting the house straight on. Garrett slipped an arm around her and led her to the front of the portico. The rain struck them in solid sheets, instantly wetting her hair and skin.

"What do you think?" he shouted in her ear.

"I think you're crazy," she answered.

"A little mad, maybe—mad for you."

She circled his neck with her arms, and he kissed her full on the mouth. Her lips parted and he filled her with his tongue. Caroline shut her eyes against the downpour and clung to him while the rain cascaded off their entwined bodies and wrapped them in a velvet cloak of togetherness.

After a long while he began to soap her back. She sighed as he rubbed in slow circles, first her shoulders, then her spine, and down over her buttocks. "Now your hair," he ordered.

Dutifully, she turned and let him lather her hair. The rain rinsed away the soap as Garrett turned his attention to her breasts, lingering over her sensitive nipples before moving lower to soap her belly and thighs.

Finally, he held out the remains of the soap to her. "My turn," he said. She took the soap and did the same for him, paying careful attention to intimate places that made him groan with pleasure.

And still the storm continued. The palm trees bent and swayed, and the water poured from the skies. As a particularly strong gust hit them, Garrett put his hands on her shoulders and pushed her down to her knees.

She knelt before him and with her eyes closed, followed the lines of his legs and thighs with her fingertips. The overwhelming tang of the ocean, musty scents of the jungle foliage, and the taste of the storm lent her a wild courage. She kissed his inner thigh and ran her hands boldly up over his sacs and stroked his swelling manhood.

"Kiss me," he said.

His hair was wiry and wet, his belly as sleek and cool as marble. She laid her cheek against his loins and felt the throb of his sex. He groaned, and she turned her face toward him, brushing his silken rod with her lips.

To her delight, Garrett's staff grew under her touch. She kissed him again, running her mouth along the length of his tumescence, then teasing the hot, swollen head with her tongue. His muscles tensed and he shuddered. With curious wonder, she drew him into her mouth, laving him with her tongue. He groaned again as she took his length deep and gave him the erotic pleasure he so desired.

"Caroline! Caroline," he cried above the driving rain. And she tasted the sweet, salt taste of seed.

Shaken, he knelt beside her and crushed her against his chest. "I love you," he shouted into the wind and rain. "I love you!"

His hands were on her breasts, sliding down over her belly, seeking the source of her femininity . . . of her uncontrollable heat. He lowered his head and took her nipples into his mouth, kissing and biting, suckling until she thought she would explode with desire. Then, when she thought she could stand it no longer, Garrett rose and swept her up into his arms. He carried her back inside, slammed the doors against the wind, and stood her on the hearth before the spitting fire.

"Garrett," she whispered. She was shivering, trembling from head to toe, but she knew it was not from the rain; it was from the storm within.

"Shhh, love," he murmured. "Soon. I promise." He dried her from head to foot with a fluffy towel.

"Now?" she demanded.

"Now." Hand in hand, they ran to the bed and leaped into the center. The posters groaned under the strain as Caroline flung herself back against the pillows and held out her arms for him. He put a hand on either side of her and leaned over her as the single candle guttered and went out. "Are you afraid of ghosts?" he whispered.

"No." Her breathing was heavy, her voice low and throaty. "No, I told you that I'm a witch." She nibbled at his bare shoulder.

"So you did," he said, lowering his head to taste her nipple with his tongue.

She gasped and arched beneath him. His erection rose full and hard again. It pressed against her inner thigh, and she caressed him with her fingers. "I think I'm in love with you too," she murmured.

"Only think?"

"I don't—" Her words were lost as he tugged at her nipple, drawing it into his hot mouth and sucking until she thought she would go mad with wanting him. One of his hands stroked her belly, teasing her damp curls, and sliding down to dip into her folds with a seeking finger.

"Admit you love me, woman." He delved deeper and she squirmed under his touch.

A cry of joy rose in her throat, and she felt the sweet warmth of happiness flow through her. "You love me? Really?"

"I've said so, haven't I?"

"Prove it," she dared.

"Like this? And this?"

She moaned as he sought her breast again. Her nipples ached for him; her cleft was slippery wet with desire.

"Are you ready for me?" he demanded.

"Yes, yes," she cried.

"Tell me what you want."

"I want you," she cried. "I want you filling me with your love."

A gust of wind shook the house and sent the French doors flying open, but Caroline paid no heed. She raised her hips to meet Garrett's first mighty thrust as the fury of their combined passion blended with the wind and rain.

Together, they rode the crest of the tempest, giving and taking, binding each other with invisible bonds of love, until at last they reached a soul-shattering climax and fell into an exhausted sleep in each other's arms.

Later in the night, when the wind had calmed

and the rain fell in scattered showers, they woke, and Garrett closed the doors and added wood to the dying fire. "Where'd you come from, cat?" he demanded.

Caroline rose on one elbow to see a ragged black cat with one ear sitting on the chair licking his front paws. "Harry?" she asked.

"Who the hell is Harry?" Garrett asked.

Caroline laughed. "You saw the cat too?"

"What is this? A game, and I'm the only one who doesn't know the rules?" He stood up and looked around. "Where'd he go?"

"Where'd who go?"

"The cat."

She chuckled. "Did you see a cat? Are you sure it wasn't a goat?" She beckoned to him, and he returned to the warmth of her bed and made slow, deliberate love to her again.

"Do you really love me?" she asked when they lay together locked in each other's embrace.

"Yes, I really love you, Caroline Talbot Steele. I don't know how or why, but I do. Maybe you *are* a witch."

She chuckled. "Maybe. But a little sorcery doesn't hurt from time to time." The purr of a cat rose noisily in the still room.

"Now you can't tell me you don't hear that," Garrett said. He kissed her gently.

"Ummm, just a cat," she murmured.

"It will be light soon."

"Ummm." She curled against him sleepily.

"First thing after breakfast," he said.

"First thing, what?" She burrowed deeper in the featherbed.

His next words shook her fully awake.

"The gold you promised me to buy a ship, wife. First thing in the morning, you'll show me this treasure of yours. I've done what I promised, and now it's time for you to fulfill your half of the bargain."

"I'll try to—"

"No trying, woman. Tomorrow, you'll deliver the gold you promised—or else."

Chapter 15

Caroline slipped from the house in the pearly twilight between night and dawn. As tired as she was, she could not bear to face Garrett this morning and tell him she'd brought him from the Chesapeake to search for a legend.

No one saw her. Pilar and her husband slept in the servants' wing of the mansion; Amanda and Jeremy were so exhausted that they never stirred. As for Noah, she had no idea where he'd spent the night. Caroline helped herself to a banana and a scone from the kitchen and went down to the beach, followed by a small yellow dog with a black ring around one eye.

The sand was smooth and damp near the water's edge and covered with palm fronds and other vegetation farther up. The sloop lay at anchor where they'd left it; the misty sea was blue and empty as far as Caroline could see.

She had come from the house in bare feet, having donned only a shift, her stays, and a gown this morning. She lifted her skirts and waded into the shallow water, laughing as crabs and small fish darted away. The gently rolling waves were as warm as the air, giving no hint of the violence of last night's storm. She walked out until the soft Caribbean covered her legs and thighs. Then she held up her gown and petticoat with one hand and washed herself in the salt water.

Returning to the deserted beach, Caroline bent

and picked up an old conch shell. It glistened in the first rays of purple morning light. In a childish gesture, she held it to her ear and listened, but the only sounds she heard were the birds and the lapping of the water. Then, to her astonishment, she heard a woman's voice.

And how do ye like my Silkie? The words were English, but so heavily accented in old Cornish that Caroline could barely understand the meaning.

Startled, Caroline dropped the shell and stared at the open sea. For one instant, she saw a small two-masted boat with a high pinked stern and a sharp-pointed bowsprit riding the mist just beyond Garrett's anchored sloop. But when she blinked at the glare of light reflecting off the waves, the pink was gone.

Caroline gasped, closed her eyes, and listened, waiting for the woman's voice to come again. Nothing. She tried harder, concentrating with all her will.

"Is that what this one has taught you?"

Caroline opened her eyes to see Kutii sitting cross-legged on the sand beside her. The one-eared black cat was curled up in his lap, and Kutii was scratching Harry's gnarled head.

She jumped back, heart pounding. "Oh, you scared me," she admonished. "I heard a strange voice and—"

"You heard *her* voice—the Star Woman." He smiled. "Your mother's mother's father's mother. That is good. She has much wisdom to give you. Is this the first time you have heard her calling to you?"

Caroline shook her head. "I don't think so. I didn't see her. I just . . ." She gave him an impatient look. "Where have you been? I was afraid you wouldn't come. Now that I'm here, I don't know where to look for the gold."

The Indian regarded her stoically with sloe eyes as black as the devil's well. He was dressed simply this morning in a red cotton loincloth and silver armbands. Two thin braids on either side of his forehead were pulled back to hold the mass of his long hair in place. In his ears were simple shells that tinkled when he moved his head.

"Have you come to help me or not, Kutii? I promised Garrett gold. He's going to be furious with me if I can't produce it."

He closed his eyes and tilted his face to catch the early rays of island sun. Caroline could see the intricate patterns of exotic tattoos on his cheeks and chest clearly.

"This place has memories for this aging warrior," he said, continuing to stroke the cat.

"You aren't aging," she said. This morning he looked younger than she did.

"Once this one was guardian to the royal family of his people. The woman given to him as wife carried the bloodline of a thousand years of rulers."

"I've heard the story." Caroline looked out at the water again. Only the sloop that had brought them from Port-au-Prince was there; she could see no sign of the strange little boat.

"In the high mountains you call Peru," Kutii continued. "The Spaniards came on horseback with armor that gleamed in the sun."

Caroline nodded. She knew this tale almost as well as he did. The Indian had related the tragedy of his family's massacre and his enslavement at least twenty times. She knew how he had fought on alone after his fellow Incan guardsmen had fallen, how he had watched his loved ones die and then been forced to act as a beast of burden. The Spaniards had made him carry part of the treasure he'd spent a lifetime protecting. Bent double with the weight of gold and silver, he had suffered beatings, thirst, and starvation as he traveled with the stolen treasure to Panama City and then along the torturous jungle route to the Caribbean.

But Kutii hadn't remained a prisoner of the Spaniards. Before the overland pack train reached the Spanish port, Sir Henry Morgan and his Englishmen had sacked Panama City, then tracked the caravan and ambushed them. Now a prisoner of the privateers, Kutii was taken aboard the *Miranda*, an English ship captained by one of Morgan's followers, Matthew Kay.

"Henry Morgan betrayed his friends," Kutii said, picking up on Caroline's thoughts. "He wanted the treasure for himself. And when the ship was attacked and sinking, one man stopped to cut Kutii's chains so that he would not drown with the Incan gold."

"James Bennett," she said. "My great-great-grandfather."

Kutii nodded. "He was a good man, the chosen one."

"Chosen to marry my Grandmother Lacy. She was of royal blood, a granddaughter to a king of England. At least that's what my mother always said."

The Incan chuckled. "She was the Star Woman, and she possessed great power. She saved this one—"

"Yes, yes," Caroline said. "You were a slave in a plantation sugar mill and she risked her life to rescue you. I've heard all that a hundred times. But I don't understand why you persist in calling her

Star Woman. My Great-great grandmother Lacy, was from England."

"Her home was the stars," he corrected firmly. "She was the Star Woman of my people's legends—the one who could swim with dolphins and see across time. Once, long ago . . ." He waved a slim hand through the air expressively as he began to relay an old Incan myth.

"The gold, Kutii," Caroline interrupted. "I know all about you and my grandmother, and how you adopted her so that your bloodline would continue. But I don't have time to listen to it again today. You must tell me where the gold is hidden. I have to ransom Reed, and I have to give Garrett—"

Kutii's eyes narrowed to slits. "Is this what this warrior has taught you—to be without respect for your ancestors? Must you be as rude as the young people of your generation?"

"I mean no disrespect to you, you know that, but—"

"Do you always carry on conversations with cats?"

Caroline spun around to see Garrett striding toward her across the sand. "Oh . . ." she gasped. "It's you."

"It seems to be. Who were you talking to? No—" He shook his head. "I'm sure your explanation would be interesting, but what I need now is to know where the money is. I assume your family hid it somewhere in the house or buried it in—"

"Buried," she answered, to stall for time.

He took hold of her shoulders. "Last night was wonderful. Don't ruin it by trying to cheat me of my due. There's too much at stake. I've just begun to trust—"

"Trust me?" she demanded. "You don't trust

me." She jerked free and began to walk quickly down the beach. "You won't even admit to me that you blew the powder store," she said over her shoulder.

"All right," he shouted following her. "I blew up the damned powder."

She stopped short and whirled to face him. "You did?" A smile broke over her face. "You really did? Then you're a spy for General Washington?"

He shrugged. "Hardly. But I will admit to you that I'm not a Tory."

She exhaled softly. "Neither am I."

"Fine," he said, his tone indicating he didn't believe her. "Now that we're both on the same side of this conflict, can we get down to finances?"

Caroline glanced back at the water's edge. Harry, the cat, was batting at a fiddler crab with his paw. Kutii was gone, as she'd expected. "Give me a little more time," she said to Garrett. "I need to talk to someone."

"There's no one on the island but Pilar and Angus. It's obvious they don't know where the money's hidden, or they wouldn't be living poor as Job's turkey." His gray eyes hardened. "No more excuses. It's past time. Where it is?"

"I don't know . . . exactly."

"You don't know." His voice went flat with rising anger. "Go on."

"The treasure exists."

"Now it's a treasure—not just a store of gold, but—"

"It's real, Garrett." She motioned toward the manor house. "Arawak Hall—Fortune's Gift. They were built with Spanish gold. Gold Henry Morgan's men took from the siege of Panama."

"Pirate gold?"

The force of his glare was so virulent that Caroline took an involuntary step backward. "It's a family legend," she said her mouth suddenly dry.

"What!"

"Don't shout at me."

"Shout at you? You're lucky I don't wring your neck. Now, stop all this nonsense about pirate treasure and—"

"No," she said. "It's real. My grandmother saw it, and her grandmother before her. A ship went down off this island carrying—"

"Son of a bitch!" Garrett knotted his hands into fists and kicked a piece of driftwood as hard as he could. "Son of a blue-faced, double-arsed bitch!" he cursed. "Sunken treasure! You dragged me away from the war to dive for an imaginary fortune lost, what—a century ago? For the love of Christ, woman! Are you sane?"

She was close to tears. Her throat constricted, and it was hard to breathe. She'd known that he would be angry when he learned the truth, but she hadn't guessed she'd care so much.

"I went through with this farce," he said acidly. "I married you, and I brought you and your sister down here. I even let myself fall in love with you. I was beginning to think maybe—just maybe we had a chance to really make something of this marriage. To—"

"It's not like that," she protested. "I told you I was a witch. You laughed at me."

"A witch. I could live with a witch—but not a liar and a cheat."

"The gold is real, Garrett."

"Just as real as your saying you loved me last night?"

"I meant it."

He scoffed. "Doesn't it get hard to keep the lies straight?"

"I want the gold as much as you do," she cried. "Maybe more. My brother's life depends on it. Do you think I want him to rot away on a British prison hulk?"

"What are you waiting for?" He gestured toward the sea. "Start diving for this treasure if you're so sure it exists. How deep can it be? Twenty feet? Two hundred? Two thousand? Or maybe we can lower a rope and ask the gold to—"

"Stop it. You're twisting everything. The gold isn't under the ocean."

"No? It was under the ocean, but it moved. Is it under that palm tree? Or here?" He kicked at a hump of sand. "Should we dig here—or over there? It's not a very big island. We should be able to dig it all up in a couple hundred years."

She turned and ran away from him into the jungle, his taunts echoing in her ears. Tears clouded her eyes; leaves scratched her face and arms. "Damn you," she cried. "Damn you, Garrett Faulkner."

She ran until she thought her heart would burst from her chest, until she could hardly lift her legs, until she was panting for breath. And when she stopped, she could no longer hear the sounds of the ocean or feel the sea breeze on her cheeks.

She sank to the ground and buried her face in her hands, but she would not cry. He was being so unfair. She wasn't lying to him. There was a treasure—she knew it. But she couldn't expect anyone to believe the truth of how she knew.

God's flesh! Ha' ye no faith in yourself, girl?

The woman's voice again. Inside Caroline's head. This time, she didn't tense up. She waited. And softly, almost in a whisper, the voice came again.

Aye 'tis time ye showed the sense of an Eastern Shore lass. 'Tis still here, girl, waitin' for ye where I left it.

A flash of blue filled Caroline's mind. Suddenly she was surrounded by an underwater kingdom of living coral, blue and yellow fish, and feathery sea ferns. A crab swam by so close she could have reached out and touched it. For an instant, she was transfixed by the strange beauty. Then she blinked and she was back leaning against a palm tree in the jungle.

My world, the woman said. *I lifted a king's ransom from the ocean floor for James, but I never trusted him. And some, I hid away for a rainy day. You must—*

"Caroline!" Garrett's voice. "Damn it! Where are you?"

"You didn't trust him either?" she asked.

"She did not," Kutii said. He was sitting in a hammocklike loop of a *kaklin* vine about eight feet up from the jungle floor. A green parrot perched on his wrist. The Incan was feeding the bird pieces of banana.

"She said she dived for the treasure," Caroline said.

"Like a dolphin."

"But how?"

Kutii shrugged and flashed a rare smile. "She was Star Woman."

"She didn't tell me where to find the gold."

"Caroline!" Garrett was closer than before.

"I need your help."

"Use your own strength," the Incan said. "You carry her power."

Garrett shoved a leafy vine aside and stepped into sight. "I'll not have you running off and getting lost."

"*You'll* not have!" She stared at him as she got to her feet and brushed off her skirts. "You may be my husband temporarily, but you have no right to tell me where I can and cannot go."

"You don't know this jungle. There may be snakes or—"

"The only snakes I'm afraid of are those that walk on two legs," she said. Then ugly suspicions curled in the back of her mind. "Why do you want a ship so badly?"

"I intend to run the British blockade—bring ammunition and guns in from French and Dutch ships lying off the coast."

She swallowed, trying to rid her mouth of the metallic taste of fear. Weeds of suspicion sprouted at the shadowy corners of her mind. "Dangerous work for a tobacco planter. Who are you, really?"

"Garrett Faulkner."

"Not the man they call Osprey?"

He made a sound of derision. "Hardly."

"I don't know what to believe anymore," she said. "If I thought you were the traitor who killed my husband and left my brother to die, I'd shoot you myself."

"That's a comforting thought," Garrett said. "Didn't a Continental tribunal find Osprey innocent of those charges?"

"How can you defend a coward like that? I'll never believe he was innocent. Never! Have you ever heard of a captain who survived when his ship and entire crew was lost? Use common sense, Garrett. He's as guilty as sin—and I won't rest until I see him hanged for his crimes."

"Suit yourself. But right now I don't give a damn for Osprey or his problems. I want to know why you lied to me."

"I told you, I didn't. I'll find the gold. I just need a little time."

"Two days, Caroline." His voice was cold.

"Show me solid proof in two days or I'm leaving you here and finding a ship some other way."

Annemie's disapproving face was a study in carved amber. "You let them slip though your fingers," she accused. "They spent nearly a week in Port-au-Prince before purchasing a sloop and sailing off—presumably to Arawak Island."

"God's bowels, Mama. Must you come here to shame me?" Matthew sat up in his bunk and shoved the sobbing black child who was with him onto the floor with one vicious kick. "If my crew hears you—"

"Hold your tongue," she warned, pointing a beringed finger at him. "And ask forgiveness of our Lord for taking His name in vain." She sniffed. "This cabin stinks like a harlot's crotch." Scowling, she glanced at the naked girl crouching in a corner, trying to cover her budding breasts with bloodstained hands. "How old is this one?"

"Old enough," Matthew growled.

"Where did you steal her?"

"She's bought and paid for, Mama dear. I gave her mother—"

"Stop whining," Annemie snapped at the child. "And cover yourself."

Still weeping, the girl retrieved a torn shift and tried to wrap it around herself. The attempt proved futile; not enough of the garment remained intact to be of any use. Annemie seized the child by the hair and stared into her swollen face. It was plain to Annemie that she'd been beaten, and she was certain she knew who had done it.

Releasing the girl, Annemie turned to the servant who had accompanied her to the ship. "Wrap her in a blanket and take her to the good sisters."

"She's mine," Matthew protested as the tall liveried mulatto draped a blanket over the child and led her toward the hatch.

"Enough. You've had your shilling's worth and more," Annemie said. "Put your breeches on. Have you no respect for your mother?"

"Doubtless you've seen my pizzle before." He picked up his rum-sodden breeches and stuck a hairy leg into them. "You're naught but a seek-sorrow," he complained. "If they've gone to Arawak, so much the better. The island is small. Where can they hide?"

"They could have come and gone without a by-your-leave," she retorted. "An informer sold news of their passing to Julien Puce in Port-au-Prince. Fortunately, Julien spies against the French for Falconer as well as for the British crown. Falconer's message to be on the lookout for them did not come to him until after Osprey and the woman had set sail, or Julien would have detained them."

"How long ago was this?"

"Several weeks. You will sail on the next tide, Matthew. Falconer will have them in the palm of—"

"I am the captain of this ship. I decide when and where it sails," he said stubbornly.

"Then decide to sail on the tide," Annemie ordered. "And if a hair on their heads is harmed before they face Falconer, you will—"

"I will bring him alive if I can." He smiled. "And it is not her head I am interested in."

"Do not fail me in this," Annemie warned.

"You know best, Mama. As always."

But the gaze that met hers was more defiant than dutiful, and Annemie's heart was troubled. "See that you continue to believe that, my son, lest you too lose your value to me."

* * *

On Arawak Island, the black tomcat padded silently through the underbrush, slipping between the tall ferns and leaping from fallen log to hummock. The sun was directly overhead, hot and molten, but the heat did not trouble the cat. Once a larger, wild cousin saw the sway of leaves and crouched in ambush, but when the tomcat came into view, the native feline sniffed the air, rolled its tawny eyes, and turned to flee.

Harry paid the wild cat no heed. He hurried on, drawn inexplicably to an outcropping of limestone on a hillside within the sound of the breakers. Here the trees were scrubby and clung to the shallow topsoil in sporadic clumps.

For thousands of years, rainwater had gathered into streams on the mountain peaks and rushed down to empty in the sea. Gullies and hollows had been worn into the limestone, some deep, some shallow. And shaded by a tenacious banana tree, Harry found a crack leading deep into the heart of the rock. Without hesitation, he dived into the cool darkness.

Minutes passed, and a small brown lizard scampered across the rock. Afternoon shadows began to lengthen. Clouds drifted overhead, as white and fluffy as meringue. A seagull folded its wings and dropped down on the limestone to preen and strut. Then a black furry head emerged from the crack, and the bird squawked and took off into the air.

Harry trotted out into the bright glare of afternoon, and the sunshine reflected off the tiny gold guinea pig clutched in the cat's mouth. Harry dropped on his belly and released his prize. He extended a scruffy paw and batted playfully at the intricately carved statue, then watched as it tumbled down the limestone incline and came to rest against a fern. Yawning, he closed his eyes, stretched out on the warm rock, and began to purr contentedly.

The gold guinea pig with the turquoise inlaid eyes lay motionless in the island sun.

Chapter 16

Amanda patted Jeremy's leg and sang softly to him as the small hammock swung slowly back and forth on the side veranda of the manor house. It was late afternoon, and she'd put the baby down for his nap. Here, shaded from the hot island sun, the air was heavy with the scents of wild orchids and lemon blossoms. Amanda's eyelids were heavy and she found herself on the verge of drifting off to sleep as she continued to hum and sing the old lullaby.

". . . can there be a chicken that has no bones?
How can there be a cherry that has no stones?
How can there be a story that has no end?
How can there be a baby, with no cryin'?"

Jeremy whimpered and she soothed him, rubbing his sturdy little back. "Shhh."

"A chicken when it's peepin', it has no bones.
. . . cherry when it's bloomin', it has—"

Amanda started as a man's hand closed over her breast. "What are you—" She twisted around and Eli caught her by her shoulders, yanked her to her feet, and kissed her roughly. "No! Stop that!" she shrieked, shrinking away from him. "Take your hands off me!" she cried, trembling with a mixture of fright and rage. Her eyes widened in shock as she stared at Noah's brother. "You have no right," she protested.

Eli laughed. "You know you liked it. What you goin' around pretendin' you're better than me for? Anybody can see that light-colored boy of yours. You laid down for some white man. Why a fine-lookin' woman like you so standoffish with your own kind, Manda?"

"No!" she insisted. "Get away from me!" Her first thought was for Jeremy, but he was sleeping soundly. Shaking, she moved to stand between Eli and the baby's hammock. "Don't touch me," she said hoarsely.

"No need to act like that," he said, grinning.

Amanda's stomach knotted. Eli was nothing like his brother. He was short for a man and wiry; his skin had a yellow cast, and his eyes were small and slightly bulging. His hair was shoulder-length and greased back against his narrow head. With his long teeth, he reminded her of a weasel. "Leave me alone," she pleaded.

"Noah said you've givin' him a little sugar—why not me? Eli teach you something fine, sweetness. All the women like Eli." His left hand shot out and grabbed her arm.

"No! Not again!" She tried to twist free, but he was surprisingly strong for his size. He squeezed her flesh until she winced.

"Don't be that way," he coaxed. "You and me, we got to get to know each other better." He brought his wet mouth down on hers. When she tried to turn her head, he grabbed her hair and forced her around.

Amanda gagged as Eli's thick tongue thrust between her lips. She bit down hard. He cursed and slapped her. She fell back against the hammock, and Jeremy woke and started to cry.

"Damn you," Eli cried, wiping the blood off his mouth. "You'll not—"

At that instant, Noah came charging down the porch, spun his brother around, and struck him in the face with the back of his hand. Eli went flying. He slammed his head against a table; it tilted and showered him with crockery. He groaned once, his eyes rolled back, and he lay still.

Noah turned to Amanda and his dark eyes searched her face. "Did he hurt you?"

She gathered the baby against her breast. "No . . . no, I'm all right." Huge tears rolled down her cheeks.

He held out a broad callused hand to her. "I'm sorry, Amanda." Eli stirred and moaned. "Lay there!" Noah snapped. "You move from there, and I'll knock your teeth down your throat."

"Don't," she murmured. "Don't hit him." She swallowed as her stomach churned. "I hate violence," she said. "I hate it. I don't want you to hurt your brother because of me."

"The little shit—" Noah ran a hand over his shaved head. "He's my brother, but I don't understand him. I'm sorry, Amanda." He turned back to Eli, grabbed him by the back of his shirt collar, and hauled him to his feet with one heavily muscled arm. "Apologize to the lady," he said.

"I only kissed her," Eli whined.

Noah drew back a meaty fist.

"I'm sorry," Eli said. "I'm sorry."

Noah gave him a shove. "Now get out of here. I don't care where you go, but stay out of my sight."

Still trembling, Amanda rocked Jeremy and patted his back. "He said that you said you and I . . ." She hesitated. "You didn't tell him that we . . ."

He shook his head. "No, Miss Amanda, I did

not. I wouldn't do that. Not with a lady I wasn't doin' it with, and not with one I was. There's a mean streak in Eli. I don't know why. It's like he gets a thrill out of sayin' things that hurt folks. I raised him, so I guess part of the fault must be mine."

"I can't believe that," she said, putting the baby back into the hammock and pushing it. "Shhh, Jeremy. Go to sleep," she crooned. "You're a good man, Noah Walker, and I can't imagine you teaching your brother anything bad."

"He won't bother you again. I'll make sure of that."

"Thank you." She wiped the tears from her face and stroked the baby's back lovingly.

"Could I sit here with you for a while?" Noah asked.

"I'd like that . . . but . . ." She felt her cheeks grow warm. She liked this kindly giant, but he wasn't Reed. And it wasn't fair not to tell him that her heart was already set on another man. "I appreciate your help, but I wouldn't want you to think—" she began.

"To think you were encouragin' me?" he teased. He sat down on a bench, took out his pocket knife, and began to whittle on a piece of pine.

"There is someone else," she said shyly.

"Figured there must be."

"You're a good man."

"You said that already."

She laughed. "I guess I did."

"You're not much what I first thought you were."

Their eyes met. "No?"

"Nope. I told Garrett you thought you were a black white woman." He grinned. "Or a white black woman, I'm not sure which I said exactly."

"I feel that way sometimes," she admitted.

He concentrated on the block of wood, which was beginning to take the shape of a boat. "Family always meant a lot to me," he said. "Eli's all I got left. I always wanted my mother to see my sons, but that's not possible."

"You don't think the people who love us can see down from heaven?" Amanda asked.

"Not sure there is a heaven—or a hell."

"I am."

"You and my mother would have a lot in common."

A parrot shrieked in the tree overhead. A bee buzzed, and Amanda kept pushing the hammock to and fro. Jeremy's regular breathing told her that he was sound asleep. "When he was born, I wondered what he was," she confided. "White or black? After awhile, I realized he was just a baby."

"Eli's got it in his head that he's goin' to get a potful of money and go back to Africa and be some kind of African prince." Noah chuckled. "I hear Africa is a big place. And somehow I can't see Eli huntin' lions or leadin' men he can't even talk to in their own language."

"He wants to go back to Africa. What do you want, Noah?"

He thought for a moment. "I want to build the best boats I can. And I want to raise a houseful of kids. I want a wife to come home to and friends to laugh with."

"You mean you wouldn't laugh with your wife?" she teased.

Noah rubbed his nose. "I guess you got me there." He began to shave thin strips from the hull of the wooden boat. "A man shouldn't take a wife unless they're friends," he said. He held out the toy. "Maybe he'd like it to chew on. It's pine. It won't splinter."

Amanda fingers brushed his as she took the boat. "Thank you. He'll love it. We had to leave all his toys behind at Fortune's Gift."

"A boy needs something to play with. If I can find some leather, I'll make him a ball tomorrow."

"Noah?"

"Yes."

"If I asked you a question, would you tell me the truth?"

"Depends on what the question was."

"Is Garrett Faulkner Osprey?"

Noah slipped his knife back into its sheath. "Would you tell her if he was?"

She smiled at him. "No. I wouldn't. She loves him, you know. She won't admit it, but she does."

"Garrett's a fine man—none better."

"Then what they said he did—"

"Garrett or Captain Osprey?"

"Osprey."

"No." Noah shook his head. "He didn't do those things. He didn't take British gold to drown his crew, and he didn't lead them to their deaths. I carried him off that burning deck myself. Whatever happened there—it wasn't the captain's fault. And that ship took part of him to the bottom with it."

"You're certain?"

"Certain enough that I stood before Washington's court and said so." His brow furrowed. "But they didn't pay heed to me. Virginia men, they were. 'A black man's testimony is inadmissible in this court.' That's what they said. Like I was nothin'." The skin grew taut along Noah's heavy jawline and she read the lingering sorrow in his dark eyes. "But I'm a man as much as any of them. I know what I know, and there's no changin' the truth. Osprey did nothin' to shame hisself or the cause."

"You're his friend. Maybe that was why—"

"They would have listened if I was a rich white planter . . . or maybe just white."

"They must have believed you or they would have hanged you both."

He shrugged. "Maybe they did . . . a little. But the words stung—they still do."

"Are you going back to the war, if you get a ship?"

"Garrett is. The war don't seem so important to me now."

"But I heard the British burned your boatyard."

"They did that, all right. Turned ten years of work into ashes in one night."

"Don't you hate them?"

"Nope. I'm not sure I hate anybody anymore. Life's short to waste time hatin'. You should know that."

"I do," she admitted. "I do." She smoothed her hair. "Would you like some lemonade, Noah? Pilar said she had some in the kitchen."

"That would be nice, Miss Amanda, real nice."

"Just Amanda." She smiled at him. "Just call me Amanda."

He'd lied to her. Garrett poured himself two fingers of rum, brought the glass to his lips, and sat it on the library table untasted. By the nails that pierced Christ's hands! He had become as much a liar and a cheat as any pirate.

He rose and went to the bookcase, then ran his fingers over the moldy leather spines of books that had not been disturbed in fifty years. Doubtless they would crumble under his touch if he tried to take them from their resting places. He'd come to the library this evening in the hope of finding some clue to whether Lacy's tale was true or simply a story for children.

He'd not seen her since their argument early that morning, but neither had he ceased to conjure her face every time he shut his eyes. Her accusing words cut him over and over as deeply as the lash of a cattle whip.

. . . Traitor . . . killed my husband and left my brother to die . . ."

How many times had he replayed that night in his mind? How many times had he heard the agonized screams of dying crewmen and smelled the charred wood and human flesh? And how often had he wondered if Noah had done him a favor when he'd carried him on his back from the cabin and kept him afloat until they'd reached the deserted Delaware beach?

Images of his dead men rose to twist his gut. Billy Carter . . . Joe Commegys . . . Daniel Carney . . . Jack Emmerson . . . They'd believed in him, trusted him, and he'd lived to see them all at the bottom of the Delaware Bay along with the ship he'd loved as some men love a woman.

His ship *Osprey* had led a charmed life until then. She'd taken a few cannon balls through her rigging, and once a British snow had nearly rammed their bow. But for the most part, the *Osprey* had played ring-a-rosy through the English blockade. They'd left a trail of sunken enemy ships behind them, and even managed to take a few pirate vessels in the process.

Then he'd been wounded in a fiery exchange off the mouth of the Chesapeake Bay. A fragment of lead had lodged in his shoulder, and infection had set in. For nearly a week, he'd been delirious with fever. Wesley, second in command aboard the *Osprey,* had insisted on getting a surgeon. They'd slipped into the Delaware Bay and up the St. Jones to Dover, where a physician had operated on the wound and removed the lead.

Dover was unsafe, so they'd sailed out of the river and south down the bay to the town of Lewes. There, Wesley had gone ashore and met with Eli, who provided him with information about an English vessel, supposedly off the Coast of New Jersey, bound for Philadelphia. Spies claimed the *Perserverance* was a fat merchant ship, weighed down with loot, unescorted, and fair prey for the *Osprey.*

He'd been suspicious from the moment Wesley had related the news. Able Collins, a free black farmer, had always been their contact in Lewes. But Able had gone north to Washington's army with supplies, and Able's wife had directed Eli to another source, a miller by the name of Johnson. Garrett didn't know Johnson, and he'd been unwilling to trust him, despite Wesley's enthusiasm for the endeavor. He'd ordered Caroline's husband to take the *Osprey* south to the Chesapeake.

Wesley hadn't listened. He'd been so certain that he could take the *Perserverance* that he'd convinced the other officers, including Reed, to stalk and attack the merchant ship despite the bad weather.

Garrett had been flat on his back and as helpless as a spring lamb when the first British cannon opened fire. A simple story to confirm—if more of his crew had survived. Perhaps impossible now . . .

The decision to take the *Perserverance* hadn't been his, and he shouldn't have felt guilty, but he did. All his life, pride had been his greatest fault. It was hard for a man to keep a sense of honor when even children sullied his name in their games. He'd heard little girls singing as they jumped rope . . .

"Captain Osprey was a mighty man,
Drove English ships upon the sand,
Chased the redcoats off the sea,
Made Maryland safe for you and me."

"Captain Osprey was a mighty man,
Drove English ships upon the sand,
Until the night our captain bold,
Sold his ship for British gold."

"Captain Osprey was a mighty man,
Drove English ships upon the sand,
Watched his crew drown one by one,
Put his country to the gun."

Eli had taken revenge on the false miller. He'd cut the man's throat from ear to ear, but that hadn't brought back the crew or the ship, and it hadn't erased the stain on Garrett's soul. The only way he could do that was to find another fighting ship and take enough British ships to help drive the king's men out of America.

If there wasn't any gold on Arawak Island, he and Noah would have to steal a ship somewhere. And even then, they couldn't sail it alone, or fight the British. He needed a seasoned crew, cannon, ammunition, supplies. He needed money to pay his sailors.

He was far worse off here than he'd been on the Eastern Shore. But he'd been taken in by the curve of a woman's stern and the cut of her jib. He'd done what he'd always sworn he'd never do in wartime—marry. And he'd cut out his heart and offered it to her on a pewter platter.

Garrett picked up the glass again and swallowed the rum. It burned a channel down his throat and warmed his insides. Two days, he'd given her. If she didn't produce evidence in that time, he and Noah would set sail for—

"Do you think to find a fortune in the bottom of a rum bottle?" Caroline's sarcastic remark made him stiffen. He turned to see her standing in the doorway.

"I thought to see if there was anything here about your *family legend.*"

"Nothing in the rum but headaches," she replied, coming toward him. Her eyes were suspiciously red, but her demeanor was as haughty and self-possessed as ever.

Garrett started to pour himself another drink.

"Don't," she said. "You've probably had enough."

"Enough?" He scowled at her. What right did she have to comment on his drinking? "How do you know how much I've had? I've just started." In reality, he rarely drank and never alone, but no newly acquired wife was going to tell him when and where he could have a glass of rum.

"I've come to offer you a—"

"No more bargains, Mistress Caroline," he said. "I've had enough of your agreements." He'd not be swayed by the threat of a woman's tears. "I've played the fool, but that's over."

Her lower lip quivered, and he had the damnedest urge to take her in his arms and kiss the hurt away.

"You were right to think there was evidence in a book," she said. "This is what you're looking for." She held out a water-stained journal. "This is my great-great-grandfather's. It tells in his own hand of the siege of Panama City, and of the sinking of the *Miranda* off Arawak Island. He also tells how my great-great-grandmother dived down to the sea floor and retrieved part of the gold before the ship it was in fell into a crevice and was lost forever."

"Let me see this," Garrett said, holding out his hand. "Where did you find it?"

"It was here, in the library. I came straight back to the house this morning and asked Angus if James Bennett's journal was still here. I've read through it twice. Some of the pages are torn out, and the ink is faded, but you can still make out the words." She handed him the old, leather-bound diary. "Don't you see? If the story about Morgan and the *Miranda* is true, the rest has to be true. I know part of the gold is still here. Angus believes it too. He said he spent years looking for—" She stopped, as if realizing what she'd said.

"So Angus has looked for it for years, and you expect us to find it in two days."

"Maybe not in two days," she answered, "but I'll find it, I know I will."

"Why are you so sure?"

She swallowed. "I have help."

He made a sound of derision. "Wait, let me guess. If you're a witch, you must have a familiar."

"Garrett, please . . ."

"The black cat. What did you call him? Harry?" His tone took on a caustic sting. "Your cat will help you find the treasure."

"Save your sarcasm," she said. "You're here

now. You need a ship. What can it hurt to give me a few weeks to—"

He swore a foul French oath. "Are you deaf as well as obstinate? I told you two days, and two days you shall have. After that, our arrangement is at an end."

Her voice dropped to a whisper. "And if I have a child from our *arrangement?*"

"Do you have reason to think you might be—"

"No." She shook her head. "Not yet, but we—"

"If I've fathered a child on you, I'll take responsibility." For the briefest space of time, he allowed himself to imagine Caroline swelling with his seed. A son? No, he decided. He wanted no sons to die on the decks of ships as he'd seen other fathers' sons die. A daughter, then . . . a babe with red-gold curls and eyes like—

"I thought you loved me," she said.

"Love and lust are often mistaken for each other." He wanted the barb to cut deep and it did. She took a step back from him, her face as pale as if he had slapped her.

"So I have been told," she answered.

Damn but she had nerve, he thought. He gave her no time to recover but followed up with a coup de grace. "It wasn't you I wanted," he lied. "It was the money. If you remember, this marriage was your idea. You knew what I was from the beginning. I never lied to you."

"No, you didn't."

But I did, he thought. I'm lying to you now.

She raised her eyes to meet his, and he nearly lowered his colors and surrendered his sword. But then a stern voice in his head reminded him that parting was the best thing for them both. *She's lost one husband. She doesn't need to weep over another.*

"If I was in need of a wife," he admitted, "you'd be my first choice." My only choice, he cried inwardly. But he'd do her no favors by telling her how he really felt. His first commitment was the solemn oath he'd sworn to fight for the Colonies' freedom, and a privateer's life was worth less than nothing. If he went into battle thinking of Caroline, he'd be too cautious. He'd end up killing himself and maybe another crew.

"Will you read the journal?"

"What?" He looked into her unwavering gaze.

"Will you read this journal?" she asked.

"I'll read the damned journal."

She picked up his glass and drank the rum herself. Her cheeks flushed as she sipped the potent liquid.

"Rum is hardly a lady's choice."

"But I'm no lady, according to you," she flung back. "A liar and a cheat, I believe you called me."

"Aye, I said it. And I've heard nothing to change my mind." A frisson of heat washed down his backbone. The air between them seemed charged with energy. He could almost smell the sulphur and brimstone of a lightning strike.

He loved her. Plain and simple. Honest woman or liar, rebel or Tory, he loved her. And there was no chance for them at all . . . Not when she found out that he'd lied to her about being Osprey . . .

"Damn you to a coward's hell, Garrett Faulkner," she whispered. "You love me and you're afraid to admit it."

He shrugged. "Not likely."

Her stubborn chin firmed. "What will you say if I do find the treasure in two days?"

"I'll say I was wrong."

"Will you stay with me?"

"I can't."

"Can't or won't?"

"It comes to the same thing."

"No." Diamonds sparked in her eyes, then one single tear trickled down her left cheek. "No, it's not the same," she argued.

"Our alliance was doomed from the start, Caroline. We're nothing alike, you and I."

"You're wrong," she said with a tremor in her voice. "It's not that we're so different—it's that we're so much alike." She took a step toward him and extended her hand. "Please . . ."

"Is this what you want?" he demanded, seizing her and crushing her against him. He bent his head to hers and their lips met, as the glass fell unnoticed from her fingers and smashed against the floor.

He branded her mouth with a scalding kiss of possession as he pressed her back against the library table. His hands moved over her, and his breath came in deep shudders. She arched against him, meeting his fevered embrace with a white-hot ardor, fanning the flames of his rising desire.

The smell of her, the feel of her body under him, drove him nearly mad with wanting her. Her skin was like silk; her breasts—

If he didn't release her now, there'd be no going back. Summoning every ounce of willpower, he let go of her and stepped away.

Trembling, she stared at him with eyes as large and liquid as a wounded doe's. "Why, Garrett?"

Her husky voice slid through him like a blade of polished steel. "Find your treasure," he said with hard, cold precision. "Find the treasure, and then we'll see if there's anything left between us besides lust." After picking up the rum bottle and the journal, he strode from the room, leaving her staring after him in stunned disbelief.

"Damn you," she called after him. "Damn you to everlasting hell."

He had no doubt that her wish would be granted.

Chapter 17

Caroline sank to the floor and covered her face with her hands. No physical blow could have stung her as deeply as this assault on her pride. She was mortified—but a part of her still wanted to be in Garrett's strong arms. Her mouth still tingled from the pressure of his lips; her blood still pulsed fiercely with his name. "What have I done?" she whispered hoarsely.

Her only answer was the lazy droning of a bee in the warm, still air.

I've let myself be deceived by hard thighs and a devil's smile, she thought bitterly. I've given myself—heart and body—to a man who only married me for my fortune.

She shut her eyes and rubbed at the dull ache in her temple, then gave a cry and jerked back—the picture of Reed's fresh grave imprinted on her mind's eye. "Reed?" She glanced quickly around, then forced herself to concentrate, to close her eyes, and to try to summon up her gift of prophecy. The awful thought that her brother was already dead threatened her sanity, but she would not consider that option. Reed had to be alive. And if he was alive, there was still time to do something to save him.

She let go, sinking down and down into the trance state until the shadowy outlines of the cemetery took shape. She could see the raw earth—the newly carved marker with Reed's name spelled across it. And again, the sight was too bitter to hold.

She fled the waking dream, with heart pounding . . . opening her eyes to see the cruel face of a leering, black-bearded brute standing over her with an upraised cutlass. Instinctively, she threw up her arm to protect her head from the impending death blow. A shriek of absolute terror formed in her throat, but when she tried to scream, she had been struck mute.

Fear worse than anything she had ever known washed over her. She was frozen in the blink of time between realization and finality.

No! Denial rose from the depths of her soul. No! She would not go as a lamb to slaughter. Fury lent her strength, and she drove her fist into the monster's crotch. And through it . . .

She gasped as the sweaty image faded to shadow, then vanished. "I'm going mad," she murmured through dry lips.

"No, child. You are not." Kutii's friendly face loomed over her. He held out a bronzed hand. Cupped in his lean palm was a miniature gold llama. "The treasure waits for you," he said. "It rests where your great-great-grandmother placed it for a time of need."

"I need it now," she said, getting to her feet. "Reed is in danger."

Kutii nodded. He was dressed simply in a purple loincloth and silver armbands. A bow and a quiver of arrows were slung over one shoulder. Feather earrings dangled from his earlobes, and his long hair was wound on top of his head and fastened with a silver pin. He seemed years older than when she had last seen him; his black hair was streaked with gray, and his face lined. Old scars crisscrossed his chest and shoulders, and marred his sinewy wrists.

She could not touch him, of course; she knew that her hands would go right through his image as easily as her fist had gone through the hideous pirate specter. But Kutii didn't frighten her. Instead, she found his presence calming.

"You were wrong about Garrett," she said. "He's not what you thought. He's nothing but a fortune-hunter."

The Incan smiled with his eyes. "What have you come to this place for, child?"

She sighed. "To hunt a fortune." She felt foolish. "Kutii, why can't you tell me where the gold it?"

He shook his head. "It is hard to break old habits. For time out of time, the warriors of my blood have stood guard over the treasure of the royal family. Even for you, this man cannot forget his duty."

"But you said I could have it," she reminded him. "You said I had the right—"

He nodded. "Prove that you carry her power. Take the gold and it is yours." He tilted his hand and the tiny, shimmering object dropped into her palm.

Caroline gasped at the weight of the gold. "It's real." She touched it. "It's—" Her fingers were empty. "Don't play games with me, Kutii," she said. "I thought for a moment that—"

"The llama is real," he replied. "It is just not in this room."

"Is it on the island?"

"Quickly," he said. "Find the treasure of my people quickly. Danger comes."

"I saw a man with a cutlass. Is he—" She broke off as a white, swirling mist enveloped Kutii and he disappeared as suddenly as the gold figurine.

"Kutii?" Caroline gritted her teeth in exasperation. "Men! You're all alike," she said. "Completely undependable!"

The sun rested on the waters of the sparkling blue-green sea, then sank slowly beneath the western horizon, leaving a molten caldron of orange and red and violet bubbling across the ever-darkening sky. Amanda and Noah stopped walking and stared, transfixed by the beauty of the sunset.

"Red sky at night, sailor's delight," Noah said.

Amanda smiled shyly at him. "Red sky at morning, sailor take warning." They laughed softly together.

Noah shaded his eyes and gazed far out to sea. Beyond the island reef, the Caribbean was as flat and calm as a mirror. The only movement was the ever-constant wheeling and diving of the seabirds, the only sounds, the gentle lap of waves against the shore and the shrill calls of seagulls. " 'Tis a queer place," he said. "Nothing like home, but it seems familiar."

Amanda sat down on an outcropping of limestone and drew her knees up under her skirt. Her simple rose-colored servant's gown had no side hoops, and she was enjoying the freedom of movement it gave her. She and Noah had spent the whole day talking, and the morning that had begun with Eli's assault had become a pleasure. It had seemed only natural to accept Noah's invitation to stroll with him along the shoreline as evening approached. Jeremy was safe with Angus's wife. The good woman had assured her that she'd feed the toddler his supper, give him a bath, and tuck him into bed.

"Do you suppose some ancestor of yours lived

beside the warm sea under a coconut palm tree?" Amanda asked Noah.

He laughed. "Where do you get these notions, woman? You are the beatin'est for comin' up with fancy thoughts."

She felt her cheeks go warm and she ducked her head. "It was you who said you were at home here." She cupped her hands and scooped a double handful of air to wash her face with. "Have you ever felt such softness? Or smelled such flowers? I'm drunk on the scent of them. This island is a paradise."

Noah shook his head. "Women."

"Do you miss the cold at home? It's raw yet and the nights can be bitter."

"No," he admitted, taking out his pipe and puffing on it. "I was never overfond of winter."

"Why hasn't a nice man like you found a wife and raised a family?" she asked him boldly.

"Maybe 'cause I've not met a wench like you before."

Amanda felt a shiver of regret ripple down her spine. "I told you, Noah," she began. "I like you but—"

"But there's someone else."

"Yes." Someone she had loved as long as she could remember—someone forbidden to her, both by the rules of society and by family ties. How many nights had she lain awake wondering if Reed was alive or dead? Wondering if he was sick or hungry? Wondering if there was any place on earth where the two of them could find happiness together?

Noah turned his pipe upside down and tapped the last of the tobacco out on the sand, then ground out the embers with his foot. "I'm lonely, Amanda."

"I know." Why was her heart beating so fast? Why was it suddenly hard to breathe?

"I think you're as lonely as I am."

She shook her head, knowing the truth of what he was saying, but refusing to admit that she wanted . . . wanted . . . What did she want of this big man? Friendship, or something more? "I have my son," she lied. "I have Jeremy and—"

"A child can't fill a woman's needs in the dark of night."

"I've promised—"

"Promised yourself to this man?" Noah shrugged. "Where is he, Amanda? You're lonely and so am I. Would there be any harm in takin' a little human comfort—"

She got to her feet and started walking away from him. "What you're suggesting is sinful," she said. "I'm not that kind of woman."

He went after her and took hold of her arm. "Amanda."

Tears filled her eyes as she looked up into his face. He lifted her chin and kissed her, a gentle kiss of longing, and she slumped against his chest. His arms closed around her, and for the first time in many years she felt safe.

"Not so great a sin," he said. "Not for two lonely people."

She'd never wanted a man's touch—never trusted any man but Reed or her father. But Noah's embrace felt right, and his lips were warm on hers. Excitement churned in her belly as he kissed her again and again.

"Let me love you," he said huskily in her ear.

"No." She shook her head and pulled away, staring into his eyes. "Not this way. Never again without the blessing of the church. I've had bad things happen to me, but I'm a good person. And

I won't willingly give myself to a man who is not my lawful husband."

"And if I did ask you to be my wife?"

"I'd think on it."

"You do beat all."

She smiled up at him. "Is that an honorable proposal of marriage?"

"It is."

She smiled as he pulled her against him and cradled her head against his chest.

Garrett returned to his bedchamber and read until the candle guttered in its silver stand. Except for the pages which had been torn from the journal, it was intact and clearly written. Near the end of the book, the handwriting changed from an elegantly masculine script to a woman's flowing lines.

> *For any who come after me who would doubt the truth of James Bennett's account, let me state that in the year 1725 my husband, Robert Kincaid, and I traveled to the jungle of Panama and recovered part of the treasure hidden there by my Grandfather James. So great was this store that we were unable to carry out all of the gold and silver, and were forced to leave a goodly portion in its watery resting place.*
>
> *Elizabeth Lacy Bennett Kincaid*
> *Fortune's Gift, Maryland*
> *December 1, 1740*

The last few pages, Garrett read standing on the balcony by the light of the moon. And when he'd finished, there was no doubt in his mind of the truth of most of what James Bennett had written.

What concerned Garrett now was not what was recorded, but what hadn't been.

James said nothing of any of the gold being hidden on Arawak Island, only that Lacy Bennett had dived to the ocean floor to recover the treasure from the sunken *Miranda*. The diary proved Caroline's story, and yet proved nothing.

What was it she had said? *If the story about Morgan and the* Miranda *is true, the rest has to be true.*

But did it? All legends had some basis in fact. Who was to say that the original source of the family's wealth didn't provide the seeds for a fanciful tale of buried riches? Still, he couldn't help wondering. And wishing . . .

James Bennett was a man Garrett could understand. A man he'd like to have served with, and one who would have understood the importance of the Colonies' bid for freedom. No wonder Caroline was the woman she was, Garrett thought. She came from daring stock.

Was it possible that he'd misjudged her? That Caroline was telling the truth when she said she supported the American side? Was it possible she could be trusted to understand why he had to leave her?

He brushed a hand over his eyes, then started as he heard a slight rustle behind him. He tensed as an odd pricking feeling raised the hairs on his arms, but when he spun around prepared to face some sort of unknown danger, all he saw was the black cat stretched out on the balcony railing.

"Are you back?" he said to the tomcat. He didn't bother to chase the animal. As long as he stayed out of Garrett's bedroom, he could prowl around and catch all the lizards he wanted.

Absently, Garrett rubbed the worn cover of the journal between his thumb and forefinger. James

Bennett had never said anything about his childhood or where he was raised. It was obvious the man was educated. His script and choice of words made that evident. He began the account by saying he had left his home to make his career on the sea.

As Garrett had. At nineteen, when Garrett was fresh from the College of William and Mary in Virginia, the Eastern Shore and his father's tobacco plantation had seemed too small for him. There had been two other sons, Alfred and Charles, to take up farming, and ever since Garrett was twelve, he'd had his heart set on a commission in the Royal Navy.

His father had sold off two hundred acres of prime land earlier to pay for that commission, and had petitioned the Cornwallis branch of the family for assistance. Garrett had gone directly into His Majesty's service aboard a Royal Navy snow.

And realized within six months that he'd made a terrible mistake.

He'd never led a sheltered life. When he was four, his brothers had overturned a boat in the river. He hadn't known how to swim, but he'd learned. He'd come up under the boat and had hung on for what seemed like hours before he'd gotten up enough nerve to let go and swim out. At eight, he'd broken an arm riding a wild horse, and when he was nine, he and Alfred had cornered a pig-killing bear in the swamp. At thirteen, he'd shot his first man—a renegade who came into the plantation kitchen and threatened his mother.

But nothing had prepared him for the brutality of life aboard one of His Majesty's ships. Month after month, he'd witnessed men flogged, even hanged for minor offenses. He'd seen mutilations and brandings, and the seizure of American colonists for service aboard naval ships.

By the time he was twenty-five, he'd had a bellyful of English justice, and had resigned his commission and returned to his father's plantation. Within a year, he'd begun meeting with other Marylanders and Virginians who thought the Colonies would be better off if they declared their independence from England.

For eleven years he'd been involved in the struggle for freedom. And not once in all those years had he felt as useless as he did now. One way or another, he had to find a ship and return to the action.

With a sigh, Garrett went back inside and placed the journal on a table next to the bed. The house was quiet, and he realized he'd not heard any sounds from below in some time. He wondered where Caroline was. He hadn't expected her to join him in their bedroom tonight. He would miss her head on his shoulder . . . her warm body curled next to his.

A movement on the balcony caught his eye and he tensed, ready to spring. For the space of a heartbeat, he saw the profile of a native standing just outside the door. The Indian had a jutting hawk nose and waist-length hair that blew in the wind.

Except that there was no wind.

Garrett's mouth went dry, and the hair on his arms stood up. "Who are you?" he asked. His voice sounded hollow to his own ears.

The Indian turned his head and stared directly at him. *Guard her well.*

Garrett tried to move, but his feet seemed frozen to the floor; his body seemed carved of solid wood. His breath caught in his throat. "For the love of God," he began. "Who—"

But the voice in Garrett's head would not be stilled. *Danger comes. Guard her well, chosen warrior.* The moonlight was on the Indian's back, yet his eyes glowed like twin coals.

"Who are you?" Garrett repeated. A curious prickling sensation ran down his spine.

The Indian shook his head. *Guard her well.*

Garrett charged the shadowy figure, but when he plunged through the open doorway, the porch was empty.

"What the hell—" Garrett cried. He scanned the lawn below for any sign of a man. Nothing.

Then he realized how quiet the surrounding jungle had become. No night birds called out; no parrots screeched. No small rodents rustled in the underbrush. Garrett heard absolutely nothing but the rasp of his own breathing.

The feeling that his skin was too tight for his body had left him . . .

"I saw a swiving ghost." He shook his head. That was crazy talk; he must have been dreaming. That or some native had been sneaking around trying to see what he could steal. Garrett ran his fingers over his scalp. Dreaming . . . that's what he'd been doing.

He was a man who'd survived by his wits. He'd been afraid for his life many times, but he'd never known a feeling quite like the one he'd just experienced.

"Just a nightmare," he muttered to himself. It made sense, he reasoned. This island, this old house, the journal—it was enough to give a man nightmares. This was 1778. Only fools and children believed in ghosts nowadays.

He leaned out over the porch railing and looked

up. It was possible that the Indian had climbed up a rope to the roof, or maybe up into a tree instead of jumping to the ground. But Garrett knew better. He hadn't taken his eyes off the intruder long enough for him to jump or climb anywhere. He'd simply vanished.

Which meant that Garrett had been dreaming . . . or perhaps still was . . . The Indian's voice hadn't been normal. His speech had been perfectly clear, yet it had come from inside Garrett's head.

A dream . . . or too much rum. He went inside and latched the doors behind him. He glanced back at the journal. It was lying open. And from somewhere far off, Garrett heard the sound of gentle laughter.

Chapter 18

Annemie's sedan chair arrived at the Kingston dock almost before the sailors had secured the anchor on Matthew's ship. Her two huge, turbaned bearers barely broke a sweat in the hot morning sun as they lowered the covered conveyance to the street, folded their arms over their wide black chests, and stood erect and motionless between their carrying poles. An equally colorful running-footman pushed back the heavy satin drapery, and the old woman peered out.

"Bring him to me," she ordered. Rings flashed on her withered hand as she waved toward the longboat being lowered over the side of the brigantine *Reprisal*. The blackamoor bowed deeply and hurried to the end of the dock, dodging conch shells, fruit and vegetable vendors, barking dogs, and two laborers rolling an enormous cask toward a waiting boat.

Matthew saw his mother's chair and swore a French oath so foul that the nearest seaman throwing his weight into the longboat's oars winced. Matthew knew why Annemie was here—she'd come to accuse him in front of his crew. He started to make the sign of the cross over his chest, then stopped, balled his right fist into a knot, and drove it into the palm of his left hand.

Jesu! How to tell Mama what had happened . . . A storm. He glanced back at the battered rigging, the shattered yards on his flagship, the *Reprisal*.

How to tell her that they'd sailed from Kingston on a calm sea under perfect conditions for a swift journey to Arawak Island—smack into a black maelstrom of rolling clouds, high winds, lightning strikes, and short, choppy waves that rose to twenty feet and more.

Matthew shut his eyes as chills ran through him. Forty years at sea and he'd seen nothing like the violent bolts of white light that had seared an impassable wall of fire in front of them or . . . His stomach churned and sour bile rose in his throat. Or the green fluorescence that had leaped from masthead to masthead like the unholy flames of hell, until his men had panicked and begged him to turn back.

He'd refused, shooting John Dagget through the head at point-blank range and splitting Long Tom's skull with a belaying pin for daring to contest his orders.

Until he'd seen the ghastly phantom of an Indian brave holding a severed head in one hand and glowing with a terrible blue-white radiance, standing on the bowsprit of the brigantine.

Matthew's mouth had gone as dry as coconut husk. His muscles had turned to water. He had soiled himself as disgracefully as any coward put to the sword. And he had turned back . . . because of a ghost.

He swallowed the bitterness in his throat and tried to concoct a lie that would satisfy his mother. But when he climbed out of the longboat and up the ladder to the dock, her knowing eyes bored into him and he felt overwhelming shame.

"Where are they?" she demanded. "One woman and one man. Surely that shouldn't be so difficult for the scourge of the Caribbean—for Red Hands Kay."

"The weather—" he began mildly.

"Do not give me excuses, Matthew," she said. "Give me Garrett Faulkner and the girl."

"I'll bring you his severed head in a vinegar jar," Matthew promised.

Annemie frowned. "Alive. I warned you, they must be alive. Your wife-to-be cannot be harmed, and Falconer would speak with this Garrett before you part his head from his body."

"I will sail on the next tide," he said. "On the *Reiver*. The brigantine needs too many repairs."

She shook her head. "You disappoint me, my son. Again."

"You'd be disappointed if I didn't, Mother," he replied.

She shrugged, a delicate movement. "Your father would never have let so small a thing as a storm turn him back."

"My father was a gibbering idiot."

Annemie's hand shot out and her ivory fan cracked across his knuckles. "Show respect for your father," she cautioned. "And for me." She rapped the fan against the frame of the chair. "Home," she ordered.

Obediently, her bearers lifted the poles.

"Don't let me see your face again until you have them," Annemie warned her son, then let the curtain fall.

Seething, Matthew watched the swaying chair until it vanished around a busy corner. "She wants them, I give them to her," he growled. "If I have to sail through hell to get them."

After the argument she'd had with Garrett in the library, Caroline had lain awake half the night unable to sleep. She'd gone to Amanda's room. The baby was there, but her sister hadn't come in until the case clock struck one. The two women talked quietly for a few minutes, so as not to disturb the baby, and then Amanda fell asleep. She hadn't said where she'd been so late, but Caroline suspected it had something to do with Noah.

Caroline was so tired when she did drift off that she didn't stir when Amanda and Jeremy crept out of the room in early morning. The first thing she knew was when Garrett shook her rudely awake.

"Are you going to sleep all day?" he demanded. "Amanda and the baby have already finished breakfast."

Caroline pulled the linen sheet up to her chin before she realized how foolish that must look. Garrett had seen far more of her than her breasts. "What are you doing here?" she snapped.

"Get up. I need to talk to you."

She turned her back to him. "I have nothing more to say to you."

"I'm sure you'll think of something. Get dressed."

"Not with you here." She held on to the sheet stubbornly. "You've no right to be in my bedchamber."

"Caroline, I've no time for this. Just get dressed—please."

"Just leave—please."

"I'll meet you on the beach in ten minutes," he said impatiently.

"As you wish, sir."

After Garrett was gone, she slipped out of bed, washed in cold water from the pitcher, cleaned her teeth, and pulled on the gown she'd worn the day before. She ran a brush through her hair, secured it casually with a ribbon, and went out to the necessary beyond the manor house, carrying her shoes and stockings like any common serving maid.

When she finally reached the beach, Garrett was waiting for her at the water's edge. "Well?" She fixed him with a defiant glare. "I'm here. Now what do you want of me? I remind you that you told me I had two days to find the treasure. My time's not up yet."

Garrett's hair was damp; she supposed he'd started the day with a swim. He wore black breeches, a white linen shirt, and a silver and black waistcoat. Between the time she'd last seen him in Amanda's bedchamber and now, he'd strapped on a sword and tucked a pistol into his waistband. He looked like a man about to go to war.

"Caroline, I've a few things to say to you, and I'd appreciate it if you'd be silent until I've finished."

Curious, she waited, shoes and stockings still in her hands. The sand felt warm on her bare feet, and she was still not fully awake.

"First," he began, "I want to apologize for last night. There is no excuse for my behavior. I—"

"You're right—there isn't."

He silenced her with an upraised palm. "Wait, there's more. Something happened to me last night, something I can't explain."

"That's a first. You seem to have the answer to everything."

"I saw a ghost. Hell, I just didn't see one—I talked to it." He exhaled softly. "It made me think about—"

"You saw a ghost," she replied sarcastically. "I've been seeing them all my life. The best advice I can give you is to keep quiet about it. Otherwise, people think you've taken leave of your senses."

"You're not making this any easier for me."

"Kindly get to the point," she urged. "I'm hungry. I haven't had my breakfast." Damn him. She didn't care if he'd seen Kutii or the two-headed ghost of Annapolis. If he thought she'd forget last night's shame, then he had another thing coming. It would take more than a few honey-glazed words to—

"I lied to you. I've lied to you from the first night I came to your room at Fortune's Gift. I'm the man the British were searching for. I blew up the powder store."

"I knew that."

"No"—he shook his head—"there's more. I'm a privateer—or at least I was. I engaged in acts of war against the English—"

Caroline moistened her lips. This wasn't what she'd expected. "Why are you telling me this now?"

"Be still!" he ordered. "Damn it, woman, can you never hold that raven's tongue of yours? I'm trying to make an abject confession here."

"Confess away."

"I've just told you enough to have me hanged twice over."

"Not a bad idea," she said.

His eyes narrowed. "You asked me if I was Osprey."

"And you said you weren't. You are, aren't you?"

He nodded. "Yes, Caroline, I am."

"You bastard!" She stared at him in astonishment for what seemed an eternity before a white-hot fury swept over her. Without thinking, she heaved a shoe at his head with all her might. He ducked and she threw the other one. The second shoe struck him in the chin, and she followed it up with a blow to his chest. "You bastard!" she cried again, punching him as hard as she could. "You told me—"

He seized her wrists and wrestled her, kicking and struggling, to the sand. They landed half in and half out of the water.

"Let me go!" she screamed. "Let me go so I can kill you!"

"Stop it," he said. He loosened his grip on one wrist, and she reached out and scratched a furrow down his cheek. "Stop it, I said," he protested. "You'll hurt yourself."

"You misbegotten, yellow-backed—" Words failed her as she twisted in his arms and tried to bite his shoulder. "You let me marry you . . ." She gasped for breath. ". . . knowing that you were the one who killed—"

"All right, Caroline, you asked for this," he said. He stood up, threw her, kicking and punching, over one shoulder, and waded out into the cove.

"Let go of me, you son of a bitch!" she cried. "Put me down!"

"Yes, ma'am," he replied and tossed her into the sea.

She hit with a splash. Salt water closed over her head and filled her mouth and nostrils, stinging her eyes. She came up sputtering and thrashing, tripped, and fell back under again. This time, Garrett pulled her to her feet.

"Had enough?" he asked.

She gasped for breath and rubbed her smarting eyes. "How dare you?" she cried. "I—"

"You needed cooling off."

"You . . . you bastard."

"I believe you're repeating yourself, darling."

She glared at him with as much dignity as was possible under the circumstances. Blood was trickling from his nose, and his right eyelid was beginning to puff. The welts on his cheek stood out like scarlet stripes against his tanned face.

"Feel better, now that all that's out of your system?"

She pushed her dripping hair from her face. "You loathsome toad." She looked around for her lost ribbon, but it was nowhere to be seen. "I hate you," she said.

"Now you're starting to sound like a spoiled child."

"I do. I hate you."

"It didn't seem like that to me last night."

She knotted her right hand into a fist.

"No more of that," he said mildly. "I had it coming for lying to you, but only a besotted fool would declare his treason to a Tory bride. And you did proclaim your allegiance to Mother England loudly enough."

"Garrett." Caroline took a step toward him. If she had the strength, she would have cheerfully held his head under water until he drowned.

"My patience is fast coming to an end," he warned. "You hit too hard for a woman. It's time to get on with our purpose here."

She was still coughing up water . . . still trembling with anger. She wanted to hurt him. "You lied to me," she said.

"And you lied to me when you said you were loyal to England."

"That was different." Her lower lip quivered and she was afraid she was going to burst into tears. "I . . . I thought you . . ." *Loved me*, she cried silently. *I thought we had a chance.*

"I was wrong when I pushed you away last night," he admitted. "I did it because I knew we were both on the verge of something very different than we agreed upon when we married."

Different? she thought. I would have died for you. Is that different? I would have put you before Fortune's Gift—before my own life.

"Now stop bristling and listen to reason," he said. "I am the captain they call Osprey, but I didn't betray the Continental cause or my men. I was too badly hurt to be at the helm that night. Someone else was commanding the ship."

"Who?"

"It's not important."

"You expect me to believe that?"

"You expect me to believe you're some kind of witch, don't you? We're in this fix together, Caroline. If we can't believe in each other, whom can we believe in?"

"I don't want to believe in you," she said shakily. "I want to see you hanging from a gibbet."

"I'm sure." He took her hand and led her back to the shore. "I don't expect you to believe this, but I do care for you, Caroline. Under any other circumstances, I'd consider it an honor to be your husband, and I'd make you my life's work."

"You're right," she answered wryly. "I don't believe it."

"I never lied to you when I said I loved you." A crooked smile played over his lips.

"Don't, Garrett," she pleaded.

"We just met each other at the wrong time."

"For you and me, it will always be the wrong time." She looked up into his gray eyes and her heart leaped. Damn him for a lying rogue, she thought and steeled herself against his easy charm.

"We came here to seek a treasure," he reminded her.

"And . . ." She waited.

"And whatever happened to me last night—madness or ghostly Indians haunting us—makes me think you might just be able to find that gold. I want to help. What can I do?"

She lifted her skirts and began to wring the water out of them. "I don't know," she said truthfully. "I don't know how my gypsy's sight works, and I don't know how to find my grandfather's Spanish treasure."

He sighed. "You're not trying, woman. Is there something you're supposed to do—some spell or ritual? I'm new at this sorcery."

"I'm not a witch, not really," she protested. "I just have dreams, sleeping and waking. I see and hear things. Sometimes they are events in the future; sometimes they are in the past. I can't tell the difference."

"The journal said the *Miranda* lay off the limestone cliffs. Would it help if we walked along those cliffs?"

She shrugged. "I don't know. It might."

"What have we to lose?"

"Nothing, I suppose. But why should I want your help in anything, least of all in finding the treasure? I'll never be able to trust you again."

"Truce, Caroline. We still need each other for all the same reasons we did in the first place. Because I am Osprey—"

She let him run on, but she was really lost in her own thoughts. She's suspected him for a long time—suspected and hoped it wasn't true. But now that she knew for certain . . . He was right. She didn't hate him.

What was wrong with her? This was the man she'd sworn vengeance on. She couldn't have been wrong about him from the start, could she? The idea that he might be telling the truth seemed too farfetched to be real.

"... never took you for a quitter," he said.

The word *quitter* struck a chord deep inside her. "I'm not," she replied.

"Then let's go and find your treasure," he dared.

"All right," she agreed. "Give me leave to change into something dry, and we will."

For three days they trudged across the island, climbing over rocks, sliding down vine-covered hillsides. At dark they returned to eat and sleep in separate bedrooms, but every morning, Garrett was waiting for her when she came downstairs. They spoke to each other with guarded politeness when they spoke at all, but Garrett made no mention of his original two-day time limit.

Again and again, Caroline felt drawn to the area above the limestone cliffs. But each time she went there, her familiar sensations evaporated like mist over the morning sea.

On the third night, she couldn't sleep. She rose, put on her clothes, and went back to the cliffs alone. After she'd reached the rocky outcrop, she curled her legs under her and sat still in the pale moonlight, staring out to sea.

She sat there for hours, waiting. Waiting for Kutii ... for the return of the voice in her head ... for anything. But all she heard was the crash of the waves, and all she saw were the stars blinking fainter and fainter until the first rays of morning struck the white stones.

Discouraged, she stood up and glanced back toward the direction she thought the house lay in. She stretched to ease her stiffness and listened to the wakening jungle noises, so different from those at Fortune's Gift.

Something moved at the edge of the forest. She stared intently and made out a man's lean form in the purple dawn. Garrett. How long had he been there watching her?

He raised a hand and waved. She waved back and began walking over the uneven surface of the bare rock. It was hard going; the limestone was strewn with smaller pebbles and loose dirt. Then, caught in a root, she saw a glittering object. "Oh," she gasped. Something small and golden glowed in the sunlight. She bent to pick up the golden guinea pig and lost her balance as the gravel under her feet shifted. Before she realized what had happened, she was slipping down into an outgrowth of shrubbery.

"Caroline!" Garrett shouted. "Be careful—"

She grabbed hold of the leafy bush, but the plant tore out of the shallow earth. To her shock, she didn't come to rest in the tangle but dropped through a crevice in the limestone and fell screaming into pitch blackness.

Chapter 19

Caroline smacked the ground hard and tumbled down a dirt embankment. She rapped her head against something solid and lay there for a moment, stunned, hardly able to catch her breath.

"Caroline! Caroline!"

Garrett's voice seemed to come from a long way off. Not off . . . up, she realized. She'd fallen into a deep crevice in the rock. Tentatively, she reached out a hand and felt only cool air around her. Not even a crack in the rock, she corrected herself—a deep hole—and evidently much larger than an animal burrow.

She blinked and twisted around, trying to adjust to the darkness. Then she noticed a shaft of sunlight striking the ground a few yards away. The source of the light was high over her head. "Garrett," she called weakly. "I'm down here. Help me!"

"Caroline? Are you all right?" His head appeared at the edge of the hole. "Is anything broken?"

"I don't know." Everything hurt, and she felt dizzy. Cautiously, she flexed her arms and legs. One knee ached worse than the other one, but she didn't think it was serious. She tried to stand up, but immediately began to slide down the hill again. "Get a rope," she called, pressing herself flat on her stomach and trying to hold on to the loose gravel.

"Where are you going?" he said.

"I'm trying not to." She slid down a few more inches.

"I said don't move! There may be snakes down there."

"Snakes?" She shuddered. She hated snakes. And down here in the blackness . . . She didn't want to think about it. "Come get me out of here!"

"Just stay still."

She heard rustling and the sound of falling earth and stones. The circle of light grew larger, and the surrounding darkness darker.

"I think it's too deep to climb down without a rope," he said.

"That's what I said to do."

"Stay calm. I'll have to go back to the house and get help."

"Fine, you go, I'll wait here," she quipped. She shivered. It was much cooler down here than up above. "Take your time," she said. "Don't hurry on my account."

She closed her eyes and began to count backward from one hundred. She'd reached thirty-one when she found nerve enough to open her eyes again. This time, she was careful to look away from the light.

At first, the hollow seemed stygian; she could make out nothing but black emptiness. But gradually, walls began to take shape. "I'm in a cave," she said aloud. Her voice echoed. ". . . In a cave . . . in a cave . . . in a cave . . ."

She listened, but heard nothing. "Kutii," she whispered, "this would be a good time for you to drop in for a chat." Still nothing.

Nothing could be as frightening as waiting here—

expecting that at any second she might topple into a bottomless pit. The seconds became minutes. How long, she didn't know, but she couldn't stand it. Little by little, she began to inch down the slope, always feeling with her toes to be certain there was something solid underneath her. Her pulse was thudding in her ears, her muscles protesting, and her mouth full of sand. Still, it felt better to be doing something than to be hanging on like a gecko to a sunny rock.

She had no way to judge distance or how far she'd come, but after a time, the floor leveled out. She sat up, felt around her, and cautiously stood. When she reached over her head as far as her arms would stretch, she still couldn't touch the ceiling.

She looked back up the long incline. To her dismay, she could no longer see the small patch of sunlight. Subdued, she sat down, drew her legs up under her, and waited for Garrett.

She heard him before she saw him. "Caroline! Where the hell are you?"

"Here!" she shouted. The words echoed down through the stone passageway. "I'm here!" she repeated.

And when he finally came scrambling down beside her with a lantern in one hand and a rope wrapped around the other, she threw herself against his chest and held on for dear life.

"I thought you hated me," he said.

"I do, but I hate snakes more." She didn't cry—she wouldn't cry. She had known she wasn't trapped down here, that Garrett would come back and get her out. Still, she was so glad to have him beside her that she almost forgot how angry she was with him.

He held the lantern high so that the light shone

into the corners of the natural tunnel. "Snakes? What kind of snakes have you seen?"

She averted her eyes from the light. "How do I know what kind there are? You're the one who told me to watch out for snakes."

"So you haven't actually seen any?"

She sniffed. "How could I see anything? It's dark down here, or hadn't you noticed."

"Garrett!" Noah's voice bounced off the walls of the cave.

"I've found her. She's fine," Garrett shouted back.

His deep voice echoed louder and longer than hers, but Caroline wasn't nearly as frightened, now that she wasn't alone.

"Are you coming up?" Noah called.

"Not yet. I want to look around down here." Garrett held the lantern over her head. "You're not hurt?"

"No. Just bruised."

He began walking deeper into the cave. "Stay here," he ordered her. He dropped the end of the rope that led up to the surface.

"Not likely," she said. "Where you go, I go."

"It may be dangerous."

"More dangerous than falling down here? More dangerous than staying here without a light and waiting for snakes to devour me?" She hurried after him. "How do you know you won't get lost or fall down another pit and need me to rescue you?"

After they walked downhill about fifteen feet, the passage grew smaller and the ceiling angled down so that they had to stoop. Next, they came to a division. Three openings loomed in front of them, one narrow, one low, and the third half closed by falling rock. Garrett took the right-hand path, the one so compressed that he had to turn sideways to get through.

"I don't like this," Caroline said. Dark caves were the stuff of nightmares. "What if the lantern goes out. What if—"

"Shhh," he said.

Her "what if's" echoed through the cavern, followed by his hushed "shhh." Caroline took hold of the back of his waistcoat and held on with a death grip.

"I think I hear water," he said.

A few more twists and turns, another long slide, and the cave widened again. They entered a small chamber with limestone stalagmites growing up from the floor. Beyond that opening was a pond, so still and clear that it might have been made of white glass. Garrett put his arm in the water, but he couldn't touch bottom. "Stay close to the wall," he warned her. "The water's cold. I don't want to have to pull you out."

He led her along a broken ledge that ran around the edge of the underground lake into a second chamber, larger than the first. Here were columns of stalagmites and stalactites, some as thick as her waist, some as thin and delicate as knitting needles. The floor here was no longer made of dirt, but solid rock.

"Let's go back," she said. "I don't like this. What if you forget which way we came?" She tried to remember if the opening to the lake room was directly across from the ledge or off to the right. The weight of the island pressing down overhead seemed oppressive. "I want to go back, Garrett," she said again. "I mean it. I—"

He stopped short. The way ahead was blocked by loose debris. He raised the lantern and let the light fall on the two feet of open space at the top of the rock slide.

"All right, this has been fun, but it's time to leave," she said. "Enough is enough."

"Wait." He climbed up and peeked over the top. "Here," he said. "You hold the lantern." He shoved the light into her hand and began rolling aside rocks.

"I said, we've seen enough," she began. "I don't—" Stones and dirt rained down around her shoes.

"Look in there," he said, catching her by the waist and boosting her up.

Caroline gasped with wonder. Just beyond the cave-in was a chamber many times larger than the two they'd passed through earlier.

"Listen," he said.

She held her breath and heard the unmistakable sighing of the sea. Giant icicles of stone filled the vast room, and in a raised basin between two huge stalactites lay a great heap of shining gold and silver antiquities.

Garrett set the lantern down on a flat rock and scrambled over the top of the barrier. "Leave the light," he said. "You won't believe this."

Before she could protest, he was on the far side and holding out his hands to her. "Come on," he said. "You have to see this." Heart in her throat, Caroline followed him over.

It was true. The stalactites and stalagmites glowed with an inner ice-blue fire, and the arched ceiling was studded with cold twinkling stars.

Caroline could smell the briny tang of the ocean on the damp, cool air. She moved close to Garrett and looked around her. Not far away, in a corner of the room, human bones were scattered and a skull lay imprisoned in the base of the stalagmite.

She shrank from the sight, imagining the fate of the trapped victim and the years of lonely solitude that had encased the bone in limestone.

Garrett slipped an arm around her shoulders. "Look," he said. "Look at it."

She was afraid to look, afraid not to. She pinched herself to see if she was hallucinating. Together, they took a few hesitant steps toward the priceless hoard of treasure.

Precious stones set in gold and silver jewelry lay strewn across the floor. Gem-studded goblets, incised silver bowls, and gold statues of animals and birds spilled over the natural depression. Masks and headdresses of beaten gold were piled one upon the other, along with emeralds, pearls, and armbands of gleaming gold set with crystal and jade.

"Your grandfather's prize," Garrett whispered hoarsely.

"No," she replied, suddenly certain, "my grandmother's fortune." She dropped to her knees and buried her hands in the ancient Incan relics. "It's true. It's all true—or we're dreaming."

"If we are, we're both dreaming the same thing," he said, picking up a silver and gold inlaid necklace that must have once graced the throat of a prince.

A feeling of sadness swept over Caroline. Tears formed in the corners of her eyes, and prickly sensations irritated her throat. One by one, she reverently lifted the objects and examined them. So old, she thought, so old and yet as new as the morning sunrise.

"The memories of a people," Garrett said. "I've read that there are pyramids in Egypt, built in biblical days." He cradled a silver spearhead in his hands. "This piece is as ancient," he ventured. "All that's left of a civilization that existed from the dawn of time."

Oh, Kutii, she whispered inwardly. I didn't know I'd feel this way. I thought I'd find the gold, but I never thought I'd feel as if I were stealing memories.

His answer came back as swiftly and naturally as her next breath. *Through you, they live. Through your blood, nothing is lost.*

"I won't take it if you don't want me to," she murmured. "If it's stealing . . ."

"What do you mean you won't take it?" Garrett said.

But she was listening for Kutii's reply.

She left it here for you. It is yours to do with as you wish.

Caroline glanced at Garrett. Hadn't he heard Kutii's voice? How could she hear the Indian so clearly and Garrett not hear at all?

". . . not take it?" Garrett scoffed. "You'd best believe we're taking it."

"Is there enough here to ransom Reed and buy your ship?" she asked him. Kutii's presence was fading. She could feel his essence drifting away.

"Sweetling, there's enough here to ransom King George himself." Garrett pulled her against him and kissed her hard. "You did it," he said. "I never thought you would, but you did it."

"*We* did it," she corrected shakily, pulling away. "We did it." Why had he kissed her? She'd been in control until he'd kissed her. She scowled at him, but he grinned mischievously. "You had no right to do that," she reprimanded him.

"We found it," he said. "You found it." He clapped her on the back so heartily that she bit her tongue. "You had to fall down a rabbit hole to do it, but you found it."

"I told you it was here," she reminded him, trying to recover her dignity . . . trying to remember who he was and who she was.

"You did that. I'll never argue with a woman's intuition again," he promised.

"I doubt that."

Garrett picked up a gold cup set with turquoise and freshwater pearls. In the bottom, the face of a jaguar stared up at them, the eyes glowing emerald-green. It was so heavy, it took two hands to lift it. "Mother of God," he said. "If this was part of the treasure, how much was there to begin with?"

"Three times as much," she said, cupping a beaten-gold nose ring in the palm of her hand. Her lips tingled from where he'd kissed them, and her blood was still running hot. "There's enough here for us to share," she said.

"I want enough for my ship and crew, no more," Garrett assured her. "The rest is yours and you're welcome to it."

"I never expected so much. I'll free Reed and have enough left—"

"Enough to make yourself and your heirs wealthy for time out of time," he said.

"It was really here all these years, waiting for us." And then she remembered Wesley and his plans for Fortune's Gift—plans he'd never get to carry out now. "But this changes nothing between us," she reminded Garrett.

"No, nothing," he agreed. "You shall have your annulment."

"That and my brother's freedom is all I've ever wanted."

"Fair enough. But I'll not rob you of your share."

"No . . ." She hesitated. "I didn't think you

would." Her stomach felt suddenly full of fluttering birds' wings, and her excitement was tempered with a real sense of loss. She had won. Against impossible odds, she'd found the treasure she'd set out to seek. "I don't know what to think about you, Garrett Faulkner."

"I didn't lie to you when I said I loved you," he said huskily.

She shook her head. "It doesn't matter. I've hated you too long to forgive—"

"I'm not asking for your forgiveness, Caroline. As I said before, we met at the wrong time and the wrong place."

"I'll honor my part of the bargain if you'll honor yours," she said. A lump rose in her throat and another tear fell. What was wrong with her?

"You may not believe it now," he said, "but you'll stop mourning Wesley. You'll meet another man someday—someone right for you."

But I already have, she thought with quiet desperation. I already have . . .

That night at Arawak House, they held a celebration. Caroline and Garrett had each carried one Incan relic out of the hidden cavern. He had chosen the cup with the jaguar's face in the bottom; she had looped a heavy gold necklace set with emeralds and pearls around her neck. Now, the precious objects rested in the center of the table as Carolyn and Garrett shared the evening meal with Amanda, Jeremy, Noah, and Eli.

Angus's wife, Pilar, was too aware of her position in the household to sit and eat with them. She contented herself with rushing back and forth, bringing one delicious-smelling dish after another to the table while Angus looked on proudly. Noah and Garrett had carried him into the dining room and propped him on a couch along the wall. Angus's withered legs were hidden under a throw, and with a stout mug of rum in his hand, he felt as much a part of the success as anyone.

Jeremy bounced excitedly on Noah's knee, and opened his mouth like a small bird for each morsel of roast pork to be popped in. Noah and Garrett were full of talk about the ship. They discussed at great length the size and type of boat, how many cannon it would carry, and what might be the best port to purchase a likely vessel. Only Eli was his usual sullen self. He sat at the far end of the table, shoveling in food and scowling at everyone.

Amanda forgot her manners and leaned on the table to stare at the pagan treasure. Caroline couldn't help but notice how happy she had looked the last few days. Her eyes held a sparkle Caroline hadn't seen for years, and she had tucked a wild orchid into her frilly lace cap. "Tell me about the underground passageway," Amanda begged. "I can't believe you weren't afraid, Sissy. I would have been terrified."

"I was," Caroline admitted. How long had it been since Amanda had called her by that pet name? Ages. It warmed Caroline's heart to hear it again, and for just a few seconds, she could picture two little girls—one white, one black—running through a meadow. Amanda's short, chubby legs would be flying up and down and she'd be shouting "Wait up, Sissy, wait up!"

"You always were the brave one, Caroline," Amanda said, using a napkin to wipe Jeremy's chin. "Remember that time Reed dared you to ride Papa's bull? And you tried?" The baby squealed and she turned to him. "Here, let me take Jeremy," she said to Noah. "He's an awful mess."

"Leave the boy be," Noah replied with a grin. "He's learnin' men's talk. You women spoil him."

Jeremy grinned at his mother, exposing three shiny white teeth, two on the bottom and one on top.

"You're a rascal," Amanda said to her son. "It's time you were in bed."

Jeremy retorted with a string of baby chatter and a squealing laugh. Noah tucked a spoon into the toddler's hand and he began to pound it on the table.

Garrett and Noah laughed, and Pilar refilled everyone's goblets. The ladies were drinking a light red Spanish wine, very old, from the wine cellar below the house. The men had finished off one bottle of Haitian rum and were starting on a second.

"I can't imagine icicles of limestone," Amanda said. She was wearing an old-fashioned, peach-colored gown of watered silk with a fall of Irish lace at the neckline. Caroline was certain Amanda had never looked lovelier.

She's in love, Caroline thought. For an instant, she had to look away. No one deserved it more than Amanda, but still . . . An empty aching rose in Caroline's chest . . . a sorrow for what might have been.

She wished they hadn't found the treasure—that they still had the search before them. Anything to keep Garrett with her a little longer. Because it didn't matter anymore who he was or what he had done.

I'd love him if he were the prince of England, she thought . . . if he were Cornwallis himself.

All her hate, all her plans for revenge, had

drained away—stolen by a kiss from a man who clearly didn't want her.

"Caroline." Amanda repeated her name. "Caroline?"

She blinked. "I'm sorry, what did you say?"

Amanda giggled. "No more wine for her, Pilar." She smiled at Caroline teasingly. "I asked you how you knew the gold was in the cave."

Caroline shook her head. "I didn't. I wanted to turn back, but just when I thought I had Garrett convinced—"

"That's when we found the treasure chamber," Garrett said. He slid the gold cup down the table to Noah. "What do you think that will bring?"

The black man shook his head. "I wouldn't even want to guess. More than enough to buy a few cannon."

"You can't very well trade gold for a ship," Caroline said. "You'll have to sell these pieces somewhere."

"Jamaica," Noah and Garrett said together. Everyone laughed. Garrett said something about the benefits of a brigantine versus a schooner, Noah countered with a good argument for the speed of a snow in choppy water, and they were off again.

Caroline finished a final bit of plantain fried with honey, and Pilar tried to put more dessert on her plate. "No," Caroline protested, "not another mouthful. It was wonderful, all of it." She stood up. "If you gentlemen will excuse me, I think I'll bid you good-night."

"And so shall we," Amanda chimed in, lifting Jeremy neatly out of Noah's lap. "It's long past his bedtime, and mine."

Garrett flashed Caroline a look, and she knew he was daring her to come to their bedchamber tonight. But she couldn't. Not anymore. The game was finished. All that remained was to pick up the playing pieces and count their winnings and losses.

With cool dignity, she murmured the correct responses, thanked Pilar and Angus for their kindness, and followed Amanda from the dining room.

In their room, Amanda changed the baby, washed his face and hands, and nursed him. He fell asleep in her arms, and she placed him carefully in an antique cradle. "Watch him for me," Amanda asked. "If you'll be here, that is."

"You're meeting Noah?"

Amanda nodded. "He's asked me to marry him."

"What did you say?"

Amanda looked away toward the floor-to-ceiling louvered shutters. In the flickering circle of candle flame, she looked to Caroline like a dark Madonna.

"There's someone else, isn't there?" Caroline asked.

"I'm thinking about Noah's offer."

"It's Reed, isn't it? You love Reed." Goose bumps rose on Caroline's arms. "You've always loved Reed."

Amanda swallowed. "We all love Reed."

"But it's different for you, isn't it? You love him as a woman loves a man." As I love Garrett, she wanted to say but didn't dare.

"Don't ask me about Reed," Amanda said.

"Is Jeremy Reed's son?" Caroline took hold of her sister's hand. "Is that who his father is?"

Amanda jerked away and her face went taut. "Don't ever ask me about that! Never. Never, do you understand."

Before Caroline could calm her or beg her pardon, Amanda fled the room. Caroline stared after her, troubled by more unanswered questions than ever before.

Chapter 20

Two hours after Amanda and Caroline left the dining room to retire for the evening, Noah and Eli carried Angus to his bed in the servants' wing and went their separate ways. Noah had promised to meet Amanda; Eli mumbled drunkenly that he was tired and wanted to sleep. Garrett had remained at the table after Pilar cleared away the dishes, telling Noah that he intended to examine the Incan pieces closer.

Noah left the house with a lighter heart. It was a cloudy night, and there was little moonlight. The evening air was heavy with the scent of jungle flowers and seaweed, and he was looking forward to a few stolen hours in Amanda's company. Even though she wouldn't allow him to make love to her, he found just being alone with her exciting. He was certain that with a little more urging, she'd agree to become his lawful wife.

Earlier, the two of them had discovered a sparkling waterfall in a natural hollow, less than a mile from the manor. They'd decided upon that hidden spot for their tryst. But when he reached the cascade, Noah found it deserted.

At first, he thought Amanda had had trouble slipping away from the baby. He waited for a few minutes, called her name again, then started back, expecting to come upon her on the overgrown trail. Again, he was disappointed. But as he neared the house, he caught sight of a figure on the beach. "Amanda?" he said, lengthening his stride.

Instead of answering, she waded into the surf.

"Amanda?"

"Stay back, Noah."

He stopped short, realizing that the person he saw wasn't Amanda. It was his brother. "Eli? What are you doing out here? I thought you were going to bed. Are you sick?"

"Mind your own business."

Noah noticed that his brother had a sack over one shoulder. "What are you doing?" Noah repeated, starting forward. "What have you got there?" Something didn't sit right. He pulled off his shoes and waded into the water. "Eli?"

"Stay the hell away. I mean it!" Eli was up to his waist in the waves, walking toward Garrett's moored sloop bobbing at anchor a hundred feet from shore.

"Have you done something stupid?" Noah began to run. Eli splashed away, evidently struggling under the weight of whatever he had in the bag. "Eli!" Noah called. His longer strides closed the distance between them quickly. "Where do you think you're going? And what—"

His brother turned abruptly. Noah saw a flash in the moonlight and felt something cold bite into his flesh. "What—what?" He put his hand to his side and drew it away, sticky with blood. "Eli?" He felt sick and wanted to sit down . . . But how could he sit in the water? His mind was playing tricks. He was suddenly tired, and his eyelids felt heavy.

"Damn you! Damn you to a bloody hell!" Eli screamed. "I warned ye! I warned ye, but ye wouldn't listen! Ye didn't pay me no mind—like always! Do ye think that because they let you sit at the same table with them, they think you're as good as they are? It's a trick—a trick to use you."

Noah blinked. Was that a knife in Eli's hand? He clutched his ribs and swayed on his feet. "Did you knife me, brother?" he asked in disbelief.

"Ye coulda come with me—ye coulda shared. But no!" Eli's thin voice rose in twisted fury. "It was always him!" He shook the sack at Noah. "I've got somethin' now. I've got something that will take me back to Africa and make me a king!"

"Miss Caroline's gold. You stole Miss—"

"Hell with 'em, Noah. Hell with 'em all." He laughed. "Ye were as stupid as he was. Who do ye think told the British who he was? Who do—"

"It was you, wasn't it?" Noah answered. "You. And you in Lewes. You lied when you said that merchant ship wasn't guarded. It's your fault the *Osprey* went down."

"Right, brother. And your fault you're stupid enough to shed your blood for white men who don't give a shit about us."

"I should have drowned ye long ago," Noah replied hoarsely. "I knew you were no good. But you were my brother, and I promised—"

"You're a fool. A knee-bendin', white-ass-lickin' fool. And you're welcome to whatever slop they feed ye." Eli flung the bag into the boat and climbed aboard. "Goodbye, brother. Don't forget to kiss Massa Garrett's foot when ye tell him his gold is long gone." He began to pull up the anchor.

"Eli . . ." Noah seized the trailing end of the bag and yanked hard. With a splash, it fell into the sea.

"Damn you!" Eli yelled. He grabbed an oar and slashed it at Noah. "I'll kill you!" he screamed.

Noah dodged the blow and fell forward into the

water. He came up coughing and grabbed for the hull of the boat. Eli slammed the oar down again.

A musket shot rang out from the beach. Noah looked back to see Garrett running toward the water's edge. "Garrett! Garrett! Stop him!" he cried. "Eli . . . Eli . . ." and then his knees buckled, and he slipped under the waves again.

Garrett pulled Noah from the water and dragged him to the beach. It took all his strength, plus that of Caroline and Amanda, to get the black man back to the house and up on the dining room table, so that they could treat his knife wound. Garrett had nearly finished bandaging Noah when Caroline noticed that not all of the blood on the floor and table was Noah's.

"Garrett, you're hurt," she cried. Red soaked the back of his hair and ran down his shirt. "Your head."

He nodded. "Eli struck me from behind with something. I think it was the rum bottle. That's how he stole the treasure."

"It's my fault," Amanda said. "If I'd only met Noah when I—" She broke off and blushed. "I mean that we . . ."

"Where were you?" Noah asked weakly. "I went to the falls, but—"

Amanda placed a hand on his forehead. "Shhh, don't try to talk. I never left the house. I was upset over something Caroline and I—"

"Discussed," Caroline finished. "It's all right, Amanda. I shouldn't have asked you what I did."

"Eli's gone with the boat and the gold," Noah managed. "I'm sorry, Garrett. I didn't . . ." Tears filled his large brown eyes as he related the extent of his brother's treachery. "You were right," he said, when he was through. "I was too soft on him. I should never have—"

"Eli's sins sit on his own shoulders," Garrett said, clasping his friend's hand. "The deaths of those good men lie on his soul, not yours. I should have been more wary of him. I suspected that he wasn't trustworthy, but I still let him sneak up behind me and nearly split my skull."

"Lucky for us all that it's such a hard skull," Caroline observed. "It shouldn't be hard to find the missing pieces of treasure in the morning. As heavy as the gold is, the tide shouldn't carry it far. But even if we lose it, it doesn't matter. There's much more still below ground. But what do we do now without a boat? How do we get off the island?"

"All in good time," Garrett said. Caroline reached up to touch his bloody head and he flinched. "Ouch, don't touch it," he said.

"Don't be such a baby. You've just sewn up Noah's side and he didn't make that much fuss."

"You're fortunate the knife struck a rib and glanced off," Amanda said, stroking Noah's forehead. "You could have been killed."

"I'm sure Angus and Pilar know where there's another boat," Garrett said. "Will you leave my damned head alone, woman," he said to Caroline, stepping back.

"It needs cleaning," she said, "and maybe stitches."

"I'll wash it in salt water and wrap it," he replied. "I've suffered through one bout of your sewing. I'll not stand still for another."

The three of them moved Noah to the couch. "Leave him to me," Amanda said. "I'll get his wet clothes off him, wash away the brine, and watch to see that he doesn't start bleeding again." She glanced at Pilar. "Bring me warm water, more soap, and towels."

"It looks as though you're in good hands," Garrett said. He rubbed his head. "I think I'll get some sleep myself."

"Not without having that cut looked after," Caroline said firmly.

"You begin to sound like a wife," he teased.

"I need you in one piece," she replied tartly. "We still have to get the rest of the treasure out of the cave, and you still have to get us back home to Maryland."

"It can't happen soon enough to suit me."

She grimaced. "Then at least we're agreed on one thing." She pointed to a chair and reached for a clean rag to begin tending his injury. "And who knows, this may be the beginning of—"

"Don't set your cap for it," he said. "For you are the most contrary female I've ever had the misfortune to meet."

"From you, I consider that a compliment."

"Enjoy it then. It may be the last you get from me," he grumbled.

She soaked the cloth in rum and began to pat the swelling on the back of his head with gentle fingers. "Be still," she cautioned. "I may have to shave off some of your hair."

"The devil you will."

She couldn't feel any broken bone, but the gash was a nasty one. "I should sew this," she said.

"Just bandage it," he answered through clenched teeth.

"Some privateer captain you are," she said, "to be run aground by one puny man."

"He came at me from the back when I wasn't expecting it."

"Excuses, excuses."

"You're enjoying this," he accused.

"I am not," she said. But she couldn't help smiling, just a little, as she poured the remainder of the rum over his torn flesh.

Once he was free of Arawak Island, Eli turned the sloop's rudder in what he hoped was a northwest direction in an attempt to return to Port-au-Prince. But the wind and currents kept sweeping him south.

By dawn, he realized how much trouble he was in. The bag Noah had pulled into the sea had contained not only the two pieces of treasure, but food and fresh water. Garrett's sloop contained neither. All that day, he watched the clouds and the horizon, hoping for rain or sight of land.

Just before evening, Eli lowered the sail and began to fish, using a bit of cloth as bait. He caught nothing, although he could see fish jumping all around the boat. After dark, he moistened his lips with salt water, then drank a few sips. When he felt no ill effects, he allowed himself a half cup. Minutes later, his stomach rejected the briny liquid, and he was violently ill.

At noon on the second day—hopelessly lost and suffering from hunger and thirst—Eli spied a sail and waved his shirt to flag down the passing schooner. At first, he was afraid the ship wouldn't stop, but at the last moment, the vessel came about. As the larger schooner approached, Eli saw that she flew a Spanish flag.

"Help me!" he cried, when the ship was close enough to make out figures on the deck. "I need water! Something to eat!"

As the distance closed between them, Eli noticed the dark faces of many of the crew. Some were merely tanned from sun and sea; others were half-caste or as black as Noah. He spoke no Spanish at all and hoped someone aboard the schooner understood English.

"I'm trying to reach Hispaniola. Port-au-Prince! Do you understand?" He guided his sloop close to the Spanish ship and caught the line that a sailor threw him. A black-haired man in officer's garb smiled and called a greeting in Spanish.

"I need help to reach Hispaniola," Eli repeated, feeling more confident now that the Spanish appeared friendly.

Two crewmen dropped a rope ladder over the side, leading down to Eli's lower boat, and the officer motioned for Eli to lash his sloop to the ship and come aboard. The sea was calm, but Eli wasn't sure of his ability to do as the Spaniard requested. "I'm alone here," Eli shouted. The sloop was difficult for one man to maneuver.

The officer gave an order in his own language, and the two seamen who'd dropped the ladder scrambled down it. One went to the tiller; the second took hold of the line that joined the two boats and secured it.

The breeze was blowing toward the sloop, and Eli caught a whiff of something foul. He wondered what cargo the schooner was carrying, and hoped there was no sickness aboard. "No sickness?" he shouted? "No plague?"

"No! No!" the officer replied. Using gestures, he repeated his invitation for Eli to come aboard.

Too thirsty to argue further, Eli climbed the ladder to the schooner's deck. "You'll be glad you stopped," he said. "I'll make it worth your while. I can tell you where there's an island with a store of gold. More gold than—"

The black-haired officer gave an order in Spanish and several seamen rushed forward and seized Eli.

"What are ye doin'?" he cried as they ripped off his shirt and breeches. Two men hoisted him off the deck while another yanked off his shoes and stockings. "Stop that!" he shouted. "Why are ye—"

A heavy wooden club slammed into his head and he lost consciousness momentarily. When he opened his eyes, an open hatch yawned before him, and the terrible stench he'd smelled earlier enveloped him. "What . . . What . . ." He groaned as his bare feet were dragged along the splintery deck. "What are ye doin'?" he cried. "I'm a friend. I can lead ye to gold!" Then he screamed in terror as they swung him high and tossed him into the hold.

The sailors dropped the hatch cover in place, oblivious to Eli's howls of terror or the resounding moans and cries of a hundred damned souls chained below.

The two seamen aboard the sloop made a quick search for valuables, then returned to their ship. Someone loosened the lines, and the sloop drifted slowly away. Within minutes, the slaver *Guadalupe*, nearing the end of a fortuitous voyage from the Guinea Coast to Cuba, continued on course.

On Arawak, Noah's injury made it impossible for him to go down into the cave to recover the treasure with Garrett. Amanda and Noah remained aboveground while Garrett and Caroline made trip after trip along the narrow passageways to carry out the gold and precious artifacts. This time, after Garrett and Caroline brought up the treasure, Noah and Amanda buried it in the rich earth among the tangled growth near the house, taking care not to let Pilar and her husband see them. The servants seemed trustworthy, but Garrett didn't want to take any more chances with the remainder of the find.

While Caroline and Garrett were making the descent, Amanda and Noah had time alone to talk. On the second day, Noah repeated his proposal of marriage.

"I've a mind to remain in the islands," he said. "I like the climate, and I feel freer here than I ever did at home." He took her hand in his. "I'd like you to stay with me, Amanda—you and the boy. I'll be a father to him if you'll let me."

"You'd stay here?" she said. "Not go back to the war?"

"It's not my war. Eli was right about that."

"Does Garrett know?"

Noah nodded. "I told him as much. He doesn't blame me for what Eli did, but I still blame myself. It sickens me, Manda. I knew he had bile in his belly, but I never thought it went that deep or that black. On Osprey's ship, it was different. A man like me might have to step off the walk for a white man in Chestertown, but not at sea. On the water, I was as good as any of 'em."

"Not just on the sea, Noah Walker," Amanda answered shyly. "Anywhere. You're a better man than most."

"Anyway, I was thinkin' of young Jeremy. Maybe here he'd feel better about his own self. These islands . . ." He looked far off, trying to find the right words. "They feel like a place where people like us can put down roots."

"What will you do here?"

"What I know best—build boats."

"For white men or brown?"

"For any what has the silver to pay and an eye for a seaworthy vessel."

"You're a dreamer."

He grinned slowly. "Aye, maybe I am. But a man has to dream a thing before he does it."

"Perhaps." She liked the sensation of his hand around hers. She laid her head against his chest. "I'm a Christian woman. Remember, if you marry me, there'll be no jumping the broom. It will have to be a real ceremony with a ring and a man of God to say the words."

"Whatever pleases you, Mrs. Walker."

She laughed, and they sealed their promise with a lingering kiss.

A hundred feet below the surface, Caroline and Garrett walked along the ledge than ran beside the underground pool. This was the third time they'd made the trip today. Garrett had run a cord from the ladder that now led down from the entrance hole to the treasure room so that there was no danger of becoming lost in the labyrinth of connecting passageways.

Still, Caroline was uneasy underground. She'd always hated being closed in. The air in the cavern was damp and musty until they reached the chamber where the gold was stored. Garrett had left her there and followed the passageway in the opposite direction until he'd come to the underground river that led to the sea.

"That's the way the treasure was brought in," he'd said when he returned from his exploration. "I'd swear to it. But I don't know how deep we are. I'd venture that the mouth of the river is forty feet below the surface. If it was your great-great-grandmother who left it here, she must have been some swimmer."

But Caroline's thoughts had not been on the gold or even on her Grandmother Lacy. A far more personal worry troubled her and made the process of recovering the treasure more difficult for her. For the last two days, she had been sick to her stomach and had suffered from recurring dizzy spells. This morning, she had awakened to find her breasts tender.

She could no longer deny the possibility that had plagued her since she had missed her women's cycle this month. She was carrying Garrett's child. There was no doubt in her mind. Her sudden weakness and her loss of appetite could not be disputed. She'd always been as regular as the rise and fall of the tides, and now—nothing. Nothing but the certainty that she and Garrett were about to become parents, and that an annulment had become an impossibility.

A few childless women in the colony had annulments and went on to marry again. Of course, their reputations were always slightly tarnished, and they were hardly ever received by the best families. That had never seemed an obstacle to Caroline. Her wealth and position were such that she was above censure by ordinary people.

The coming child would change her marriage of convenience to Garrett Faulkner to a real union that only death could sever. And no fear of what he would say could dim her secret, fierce joy that she would always have a part of him.

"Watch your step," Garrett said, bringing her back from her reverie to the narrow stone ledge clinging to the rock wall. "It's slippery here."

He held the lantern in one hand and offered her his other. The only way to traverse the path along the lake was sideways, with your back against the wall. That meant the bag of artifacts had to be swung around to the front, throwing you off balance.

"Steady," he coaxed. "One step at a time. Keep pressed against the wall. Mind the water here."

The lantern swung to and fro; the yellow-white light reflected off the pool and ceiling. Caroline found the motion distressing. She swallowed as perspiration broke out on her forehead and concentrated on putting each foot down with care.

It was Garrett who slipped. He let go of her hand and swore an oath as he fell into the icy water with a splash. At the same instant, the lantern went sailing through the air, hit the surface of the lake, and plunged the chamber into total darkness.

"Garrett!" she screamed. She froze, molding her body to the wall until she felt the imprint of the stone. She heard him gasp as he came up. "Garrett?"

"I'm all right," he said. She heard more thrashing in the water, then his hand touched her foot. "Don't move," he ordered her.

"I can't," she said. She was glad she hadn't eaten anything that morning. As it was, her stomach threatened to betray her. She closed her eyes and took deep breaths. "Drop the pack," she suggested. "You'll never get back up on the ledge with that weighing you down."

"Hell," he muttered. "I'll never get back up anyway." He groaned. "This water is freezing."

"Are you hurt?"

His teeth were chattering. "Stay where you are," he said. "I'm going to make my way along the wall to the far side and go for another lantern. Don't try to walk the ledge in the dark. Wait for me."

"Let go of the bag," she urged him.

"It would be too hard to get it back. I don't know how deep this damned lake is."

"Garrett—listen to reason. You—"

"Stay where you are, woman. I'll come back for you."

She held her breath as she heard him moving away. The sound of his movement through the water grew fainter and fainter until she was left in total silence.

Seconds dragged into minutes. Caroline fought to control her faintness, knowing that if she slipped into the water, she might not have the strength to swim to safety. Wondering if Garrett was alive . . .

She could taste the acrid fear on her tongue, feel the throb of her blood pulsing through her veins. And then, when her despair was greatest, she heard an oddly accented woman's voice beside her and felt a warm hand take hers.

"What's wrong, lass? Lose your nerve? Any Cornwall lad of six could walk this path. Where's your pluck?"

Caroline's senses reeled. It was the voice she'd heard before on the beach when she'd seen the strange little boat. Her mind was playing tricks on her.

The lean fingers tightened. "There's a fine broth of a man you've chosen, though he's not so tall or broad as my Jamie. He needs ye, an' you're standin' here like ye had all the time in the world."

"I can't," Caroline said. "I can't walk the ledge without a light."

"Stuff and nonsense! Course ye can. Hold my hand. I'll help ye. 'Tis easy."

"Garrett needs me?" Caroline's muscles were

locked. She knew she couldn't move them if she wanted to.

"Aye."

"All right." Caroline swallowed and took one step.

"There ye go. Easy as paint on a harlot."

"I can't see."

"Look with your head, not your eyes. Eyes can be tricked." The Cornwall tang was thick in the woman's speech, but Caroline could understand every word.

"Are you . . ." She tried to swallow again, but her mouth was too dry. "Are you Lacy Bennett?"

Laughter. Merry as fresh-popped corn.

"Did Kutii send you?" Caroline asked. The hand was warm and alive—as real as any hand she'd ever clasped. "Are you my great-great-grandmother?"

"Ye mind that land, girl. Love it. Stand firm for it, and teach that boy ye carry to do the same. Land not worth sheddin' blood for isn't worth havin'."

Caroline took another step.

"You've not seen a black cat around, have ye? A one-eared rascal, missin' part of his hair?"

"Harry?"

"Oh, so ye have seen him. Damned cat. Can't keep track of him. Came with us on the *Silkie*, ye know—all the way from London Town. Fond o' him, I be."

Another step. Onto a wide, solid surface. Startled, Caroline felt around her in the darkness, then realized that no one was holding her hand. "Lacy?" she called. "Grandmother Lacy?"

Her voice echoed through the passageways. *Lacy . . . Lacy . . . Lacy. Grandmother Lacy . . . Grandmother Lacy . . . Grandmother . . .*

Caroline dropped to her knees, shrugged off the pack, and began to feel the cave floor. After a few seconds, she found the cord Garrett had strung, got to her feet, and began to follow it.

She hadn't gone a dozen feet when she tripped over something in her path and fell headlong over Garrett's cold, wet body.

Chapter 21

"Garrett!" Caroline began to shake him. He was soaked to the bone and his skin was icy to her touch. "Garrett!" He groaned, and she lifted his head into her lap. "Garrett, wake up," she said urgently. "You have to wake up." His hair had come loose from its queue and hung around his face and neck like wet silk.

A violent shiver racked his body. Grabbing his arm, she rolled him over onto his stomach and pressed against his back hard. He coughed and choked up water. "What are you doing to me?" he gasped weakly.

"Get up," she pleaded with him. It was pitch black. She couldn't see him; she could only feel his unnaturally cold skin. She knew she couldn't drag him far, and it was still a long way to the cave entrance where Noah and Amanda waited. "You have to move or you'll freeze," she said. Between here and the surface lay the tight fissure of rock that could only be traversed standing upright with your back against the wall. It would be impossible to carry an unconscious man through that slender crack in solid limestone. "Please," she begged. "You have to get up and walk."

Garrett choked again, and his teeth began to chatter. "I'll be all right," he said. His voice was a strained whisper. "Just leave me alone."

Desperate, she yanked a handful of his hair and slapped his face. "Get up, I said!"

Gasping, he pushed himself up on his hand and knees, and swore at her.

"I said, get up!" she repeated, punching his arm with her fist. "Put your arm around me and walk!" She'd lost the cord that showed the path out—she'd even lost all sense of time. All she could think of was reaching the warm sunshine above.

He staggered to his feet, and she fumbled with the heavy bag around his waist. But the ties were wet, the knots stretched tight. She couldn't unfasten them. Instead, she reached into the bag and removed the gold and silver, one piece at a time, and dropped them to the floor. When the bag was empty, she wedged her shoulder under his arm and began to help him walk. She hadn't gone two feet before she struck something hard. "Ouch!" she cried.

Feeling with her free hand, she found a stalagmite growing out of the cave floor, and realized they must still be in the small chamber near the pool. And if she was there, then she needed to keep close to the wall to take the correct tunnel leading out of the chamber. But which wall?

Garrett groaned again and swayed. She was afraid that if he fell, she wouldn't get him up again. He was so cold. How could anyone be so cold and still be alive? "Your blood must have ice crystals in it," she said.

"What?" he asked drunkenly.

"Keep walking," she ordered. She tried to remember the correct sequence of inclines and openings ahead of her. Right entrance going in, she mused. Would that be left coming out . . . or . . . It was no use. She was too frightened to use logic. She'd have to rely on her instinct.

"Just let me rest awhile," Garrett said.

"No! We're going to walk out of here." Sounding braver than she felt, she took one step and then another. Please, Kutii, she whispered inwardly. We could use some of your ghost lights now. But the cave ahead of her still loomed as dark as the devil's soul. She closed her eyes. Somehow, the blackness wasn't as overwhelming if she didn't have to stare into it.

Her right hand struck a solid wall. "We're all right," she soothed Garrett. "Keep walking. Just a little ways this way, then . . ." She remembered that the passageway was low. "Duck your head."

The floor began to rise steeply. The incline, she thought. I remember the incline. His weight made the climb difficult, but it seemed to her that Garrett was gaining strength. He'll have to, she cried silently. I'll never get him through the narrows unless he can walk on his own power.

Perspiration beaded her forehead. Turn, step. How long? she wondered. Garrett didn't ask if she knew where they were going, and that frightened her even more. The tons of rock and earth above them seemed to press down on her like a great tomb.

"That's right, keep going. You're doing fine," she told Garrett.

The compressed passage was a nightmare. They crept through it an inch at a time, while demons of doubt danced at the back of Caroline's mind, crying, *What if you took the wrong turn? What if you're leading him deeper into the mountain instead of out?*

When she opened her eyes and saw the patch of sunlight ahead, she shouted for joy. "Look," she said. "Look there!"

Garrett shook off her arm and squatted down to catch his breath. "I'm all right," he said. "I can walk on my own." He was still shaking, but the walking had gotten his blood moving. He was able to make the distance to the ladder and climb it on his own.

"What the hell happened to you?" Noah demanded as Garrett set foot on the grass. "Been swimming?" He began to strip off Garrett's shirt.

"Something like that," Caroline said. She was almost as wet as Garrett, but the hot sun on her bare arms and face soon warmed her.

Garrett sat on a rock while Amanda used her apron to dry his back and hair. Noah got the bag unfastened and threw it aside. As it struck the rock, Caroline heard a thud. She retrieved the sack and turned it inside out. A gold llama tumbled into her hand—the same exquisite statute that Kutii had shown her earlier.

"Oh," Amanda said. "That's beautiful."

Caroline held the tiny llama up so that the sun reflected off it. "This piece I'm keeping for luck," she said, and tucked it into her gown pocket.

"I was about to send Noah down after you," Amanda said, looking from Caroline to Garrett.

"He fell off the ledge," Caroline explained. "And he was too stubborn to let go of the gold he was carrying. He nearly drowned."

"I didn't 'nearly drown,' " Garrett protested. He still had the shakes and his face was pale, but Caroline knew he was all right.

"I should have come down," Noah said.

"No," Garrett answered. "No sense to it. You're too big. You'd never fit through the narrow crevice."

And no one could have carried you out, Caroline thought. "You could have died down there," she said. "It's too dangerous. Let's take what we have and leave the rest."

Garrett shook his head. "No, two more trips will

do it. One to bring back what we only got part of the way out, and another to get what's left in the treasure chamber."

"I don't want to go down there again," she said, looking around her at the vivid greens of the grass and trees, the blue of the sky, and the white of fleecy clouds."

"Then stay here," Garrett said stubbornly. "But I'm going. Too much depends on—"

"I'm not letting you go down there alone," she said.

"Wait until tomorrow, at least," Amanda suggested. "You both look like you could use something to eat."

Garrett shook his head. "I won't go back along the lake, but I'm bringing out what we dropped." He threw Caroline a challenging glance. "Coming or not?"

He lit the spare lantern and started down the ladder. She shrugged and followed him. "This time, I'm not letting go of the cord," she said.

"You worry too much, woman," Garrett replied. And his words echoed down the long corridors and raised the hairs at the back of her neck.

On the way back to the house, Noah told Garrett and Caroline that Amanda had agreed to marry him, and that they both wanted to stay in the Caribbean.

"But you can't," Caroline said. She was tired and dirty and wanted nothing more than to bathe and crawl between clean sheets. She and Garrett had made the return trip to the chamber beside the underground lake without incident. There they'd found Caroline's pack and the pieces she'd emptied from Garrett's bag, and brought them back to the surface. Garrett had agreed to wait until the following day to make the final trip. "If you stay here," she continued, "Jeremy won't grow up on Fortune's Gift. It's his right."

"It's his right to grow up where I want him to," Amanda corrected her. "Noah thinks this will be a better place for all of us. Jeremy needs a father."

"You haven't said anything about love," Caroline protested. "Reed—"

"If anyone can free Reed, you and Garrett can do it," Amanda said. She clasped Noah's arm. "I do love Noah. He's convinced me that we belong together."

"We'll miss you," Garrett said. "There's no man I'd rather have serve beside me on the deck of a fighting ship."

Noah put a big arm around Amanda's shoulders. "From now on, the only wars I'm going to fight are my own. I'll help ye find a ship, like I promised, but I like it here."

"I'll give you Arawak as a wedding gift," Caroline said. "Amanda's due a dowry."

"I want no handouts," her sister said.

"We'd like Arawak fine," Noah replied with a grin. "I could build me a new shipyard right in the cove, if you'd let us have a few acres to go with the house."

"No," Caroline said. "I mean I'll give you the island. It's the least—"

"Not for Jeremy's sake," Amanda said sharply. "I won't let you—"

"For *your* sake," Caroline corrected her. "For Papa and Mama. You are my sister—you'll always be my sister, even if a little ocean divides us."

Amanda's eyes gleamed with liquid. "Thank you," she said simply.

"And I'll give you enough money to start your shipyard," Garrett said.

"You'll *loan* me enough," Noah said gruffly. "I'll pay back every shilling."

"Only if I can be best man at the wedding," Garrett agreed.

"Done."

Then Jeremy came toddling around the corner of the house with Pilar in hot pursuit. "He walks," she cried excitedly. "Little man walks."

Noah caught the baby and swung him high over his head, to Jeremy's delight. He squealed and kicked his bare feet. "My first son," Noah declared. Then he winked at Amanda. "But he'll only be the first of many."

"Not too many," Amanda replied primly, "or you'll find yourself sleeping on the beach."

Even Pilar and the baby joined in the following laughter. And Caroline's distress at the thought of parting from her sister and Jeremy was eased by the happiness that beamed from Amanda's round face.

Supper was hot conch soup, cold pork, fruit, and hot bread. Caroline ate a little of the soup and nibbled at a biscuit. She didn't taste her wine. Her warm bath had made her sleepy. All she wanted now was to go to bed. When she wished Amanda and Noah all the best and left the table, Garrett followed her into the entrance hall.

"Thank you for what you did today," he said.

"It was nothing," she answered stiffly. "As you said, you would have gotten out without my help."

"Probably," he said, "but maybe not. I was careless, and it could have gotten us both killed. You used your head and didn't panic." He rubbed his cheek. "You've got a hard right for a woman."

"I didn't punch you, I slapped you."

"Admit it. You enjoyed it," he teased.

"It's not funny, Garrett."

"No, I suppose it isn't." He took her hand and raised it to his lips. "I want you to come back to our room." He turned her palm over and brushed his lips against the pulse at her wrist.

"No." The touch of his lips made shivers run up and down her spine. God, but she wanted him to want her! Not just for a night—but forever.

"I won't touch you, if you don't want me to. You have my word of honor on it. I miss you, Caroline. It's lonely without you."

Her throat tightened, and her bones felt like jelly. I'm carrying our child, she wanted to tell him. I'm pregnant, and I'm glad of it. But she didn't. She only shook her head. "It's best if we leave things as they are," she said. "You'll get your boat, and I'll get my brother."

"Caroline, I wish it could be otherwise with us." His gray eyes beseeched her.

"No," she said firmly, pulling her hand back. "It's better for us both, if we—"

"Have it your way," he answered frostily. Turning on his heel he walked away, leaving her to ascend the wide staircase alone.

The sound of splintering wood and the shrill terror of Pilar's screams woke Caroline from her sleep. She sat up in the wide poster bed, heart thudding wildly. Jeremy was whimpering. By moonlight, she could see that he was sitting up in the cradle with his arms outstretched for someone to pick him up.

"Amanda? Amanda, are you here?" she called.

Glass shattered downstairs, and she heard the heavy tread of men's boots in the entrance hall. Pilar shrieked again. Her cry was cut short by the unmistakable roar of a musket.

Caroline's door banged open, and terror spilled through her body. She leaped out of bed and stood between the cradle and the shadowy male figure in the doorway.

"Caroline!"

Her knees went weak with relief. "Garrett. I'm here."

"We're under attack. Come with me. Now!"

Grabbing up Jeremy, she dashed to the hearth and took down a fencing foil that hung over the mantel. "Where do we go?" she asked. From below came the crash of overturned furniture, the sounds of breaking china, and men's coarse laughter.

"Quick! Our room," Garrett said. "We can't use the stairs."

He grabbed her arm and dragged her into the hall. Pounding feet on the steps made her twist around. The window at the head of the staircase illuminated the face of a bare-chested stranger with an upraised cutlass in his hand. Garrett whirled and fired his pistol. The explosion momentarily deafened Caroline. The baby began to howl and kick. She didn't wait to see if Garrett had hit his target, but kept running down the passageway with the terrified baby.

Garrett tore open the door to their room. "Inside, quick," he said. She obeyed without question, and he pushed an upright chest-on-chest in front of the door and went to the corner of the room for his musket. Jeremy wailed in total panic.

Caroline put the baby on her shoulder and began to pat his back. "Shhh," she soothed. "Shhh."

"Can't you keep him quiet?" Garrett hissed as he dumped a measure of powder into his pistol barrel and tamped down wadding and a ball.

Jeremy shrieked louder.

"He's scared. If you think you can do any better than me, you take him," she replied hotly. A door crashed open down the hall. She heard a shout, then another shot, much closer.

"The balcony," Garrett whispered. "We can't let them trap us in here."

"I can't jump two stories with a baby."

"I didn't say you had to. Get out on the damned balcony." He slung a powder horn over one shoulder and strapped on a sword.

She stumbled over a footstool in the darkness.

"Caroline!"

Her hand closed on one of Garrett's shirts, hanging over the back of a chair. Quickly, she knotted the shirt around the squirming baby's chest, then tied the arms together to make a sling.

"In here!" a man shouted. Something heavy struck the bedroom door. Wood cracked and the door buckled.

"Caroline, go!" Garrett ordered.

She turned the handle on the French doors.

"Careful," Garrett warned. "I don't know how many of them are outside." Then he raised his musket and fired through the splintered doorway. A man trying to force his way in screamed and fell.

Caroline dropped to her hands and knees and crawled out onto the porch as she heard a lead ball pierce the paneled door and ricochet around the room. There was more shouting and an ax split the door.

Garrett fired his pistol in the general direction of the pirates, then followed her onto the balcony. "Put your arms around my neck," he said. "I'm going to lower myself from the porch and drop."

"You're crazy," she said.

"Got any better ideas?"

"We could go up on the roof."

"And be trapped up there if they fire the house?"

"Who is it?"

"How the hell do I know? Now shut up and put your arms around my neck and hold on."

"Can't you jump to a tree?"

"With you and that squalling brat on my back? What do you think I am?"

"If I was a man—"

"Well, you're not. So shut up and do as I tell you!"

The chest-on-chest toppled to the floor with a crash, and Caroline flung herself onto Garrett's back and held on with a death grip. Jeremy dangled from her side, sobbing loudly and struggling to get free.

"Get rid of that foil," Garrett said. "You'll kill us both." She tossed it over the porch railing.

"Great! Now I'll land on the friggin' thing," he said as he lowered himself down over the decorative woodwork with Caroline clinging to his back.

Her heart rose in her throat as Garrett swung from the landing, then dropped. They hit the ground hard, and she and Jeremy rolled away. Almost instantly, even before she'd had time to catch her breath, a barrel-chested man with a beard ran toward them from the trees. A flintlock flared in his hand.

She staggered up and began to run, snatching up her foil as she fled. She saw Garrett launch himself at the bearded man. He raised his empty pistol and brought the long barrel down to smash against Garrett's head. Garrett grabbed his wrist and the two began to struggle.

Caroline saw two men coming over the railing of the second-floor porch. She dodged a sailor rushing at her from the front entrance steps, ran toward Garrett, and drove the point of her foil into his assailant's shoulder.

The bearded man howled and fell back, and she and Garrett dashed for the trees with musket balls flying over their heads. They ran a few hundred yards into the jungle, changed direction, and crawled into a thicket of overgrown vines. Garrett pushed her down flat on the ground. "Keep Jeremy quiet," he warned. He began to load his pistol again.

She put her hand over the baby's mouth, but he continued to whimper. "I can't," she said.

"I'll distract them. I want you to crawl out and—"

"No. They'll kill you. They won't kill me. I'm a woman with a baby."

"Don't be stupid, Caroline. There are worse things for a woman than death." His hand closed around her shoulder and gripped so tightly that she felt his fingers dig into her flesh. "I want you to back out of this thicket and run like hell. Hide in the jungle, far enough from the house that they can't find you. Find water and follow it up the mountain. Now go!" He gave her a shove, and he crawled out and ran in the opposite direction.

She heard Garrett's flintlock go off, and she dug her way out from under a vine and ran as fast as she could with Jeremy clutched against her breasts. Suddenly, a man blocked her path.

"What 'ave we here?" he cried.

Caroline shifted the sling to her shoulder. Ignoring the baby's howling, she grasped her foil in her hand and backed up a few steps into the shadows of the trees.

"Where to so fast, wench?" He fumbled with the

button fly of his wide-legged trousers. " 'Ow'd ye like to 'ave a taste of ripe beef afore the crew—"

She lunged forward and executed a perfect direct riposte, plunging the point of the foil into the left side of the scoundrel's chest. He grabbed the naked blade with both hands and fell back onto the ground. An awful bubbling sound came from his throat, and his death cry was drowned in a tide of blood.

Caroline seized the hilt and tugged, but the foil was caught between muscle and bone. She shuddered, then shut her eyes, put her foot on the dying man's chest, and yanked the sword free.

"What's this?" another man shouted. He burst out of the trees and ran toward her swinging a boarding ax. She gasped in fear as the moonlight glinted on the steel blade.

A branch snapped behind her, and she whipped her head around to see a second attacker in the shadows—a giant of a man—carrying a machete. She raised her weapon to defend herself, knowing full well that against two of them she had no chance. "Stay back!" she warned.

The ax man laughed and lifted his terrible weapon over his head. The giant took one great leap forward and brought his machete down across the other man's neck. He fell mortally wounded. The baby whimpered and Caroline turned to run.

"Wait! Miss Caroline! It's me, Noah," came the frantic whisper from the big man with the machete.

She sagged with relief at the familiar voice. "Thank God, it's you." She was numb with fright, too terrified for tears. "Where's Amanda? Is she safe?"

"Aye. I hid her in the cave. She's hell-bent on

gettin' to this babe of hers." Noah wiped his machete on the grass and reached for Jeremy. "Give me the boy. He's heavy for you to carry."

"Garrett's back there somewhere," Caroline said. "We climbed down from the porch and—"

"Shhh," Noah warned.

Harsh voices came from the direction of the house.

"I don't know who they are," Caroline whispered.

"Pirates, most likely," he said. He nudged the first dead man with his foot. "You kill this one by yourself?"

Caroline nodded.

Noah laughed softly. "Guess he didn't know what kinda woman he was facin'."

"I think they killed Pilar and Angus," she said.

"We got to go. There's no time for weepin' over the dead."

"But Garrett—"

"Garrett will give good account of hisself—never you fear, miss. I'd be more worried about what I'd say to him, did I let you come to harm, now that I found ye."

"Caroline Talbot!" Her name echoed through the trees. "Caroline Talbot! Come out or you'll carry your husband's head to his grave in a basket!"

"What's that?" she asked Noah. The voice was strange, almost inhuman.

"Speakin' trumpet," the black man replied. "Masters use 'em on ships. They carry a man's voice in the wind."

Or through the jungle, she thought. What had he said? They had Garrett?

"Come out, woman! This is your last chance!"

Noah tugged at her arm. "Don't listen to them. It's a trick. Garrett will be all right."

Caroline handed him her foil. "Take this," she said. "Take it, and get Jeremy safely away from here. You look after Jeremy and Amanda."

"I won't let ye give yourself over to them," Noah said. "Don't be a fool. He may be hidin', or he may be dead. You surrenderin' yourself won't help him."

"Caroline Talbot!"

Jeremy began to cry.

"Run!" Caroline said to Noah. "Quick, before they catch you." She pulled free and darted back toward the house and Garrett.

Chapter 22

Caroline froze for a moment at the edge of the clearing. The jungle was strangely quiet. No night birds shrieked; no small mammals rustled through the undergrowth. The slight breeze was from the mountain, and it carried with the heavy scents of exotic flowers and rotting leaves. She had never felt more alive than she did at this moment—or so close to dying.

Kutii's voice came faintly from the far recesses of her mind. *Do you know what you risk?*

"I have to do this—don't you see?" she whispered. She desperately wanted to protect the spark of life within her womb, but she couldn't leave Garrett to the mercy of these raiders.

"Caroline! Don't listen to him! Run—" Garrett's shouted warning was cut off abruptly.

"Don't hurt him!" she called out. "I'm giving myself up."

Furnishings from the house had been dragged outside onto the lawn and set aflame. The light from the fire illuminated the black-bearded captain standing on the front steps of the manor and his motley band of hard-faced followers. There was no doubt in Caroline's mind as to who the leader was—or that the swarthy devil in the red and gold coat and cocked hat was the man she'd run through with her foil.

Heart in her throat, she searched frantically for Garrett with her eyes. Then she saw him near the corner of the house, held fast by two burly pirates. "I'm here," she said. Stepping out of the tangled vines, she stiffened her spine and walked toward the corsair captain with her chin high.

"Caroline, run!" Garrett cried. One of his captors struck him brutally across the head with the hilt of his sword and he slumped forward, unconscious.

Caroline held her breath and kept her eyes focused on the commander. He looked as broad as he was tall; the seams of his coat strained with every breath, and the backs of his hands were covered with curling black hair. No doubt he had cloven hooves as well, Caroline thought as she drew closer. His was the evil face of Lucifer himself.

The thick smoke from the bonfire made her eyes water. The heat from the flames scorched her skin, but the leering stares of the pirate crew seared hotter still. They closed in around her, laughing coarsely and taunting her with filthy, unspeakable threats. She could smell the sour odors of unwashed flesh and stale beer; she could see their bloodshot eyes and green-scummed teeth. She kept walking, determined not to give them the satisfaction of seeing how terrified she was—hoping her thudding heart wouldn't burst through the bodice of her torn shift.

They hemmed her in, jeering, bullying. She bit the inside of her mouth until she tasted blood, but she didn't flinch. Then one wraith of a man with a twisted scar where his nose should have been grabbed her arm and spun her around. She screamed and beat at his face with her fists as he groped for her breasts with blood-encrusted hands. His foul mouth descended on hers, and she nearly fainted from the overwhelming stench.

With unbelievable strength in his bony arms, he threw her to the ground and seized the neck of her shift to rip it away.

Suddenly, her assailant was gone. Through waves of dizziness, she heard an inhuman howl of pain. She struck out at the weight on her chest, realized that it was a hand and six inches of arm, and went cold with shock. She blinked, trying to maintain her grip on sanity, as she realized that the captain stood straddle-legged over her—a bloody cutlass in his hand.

The hollow-cheeked brigand who'd attacked her was standing six feet away, staring gape-mouthed at the stump of his severed arm.

"Blast ye for witless dogs!" the black-bearded captain shouted. "Will ye let a fellow crewman bleed to death?"

Some of the men began to mutter among themselves. One, a Carib Indian, wrenched a flaming chair leg from the fire, while two sailors took hold of the injured man and wrested him to the ground. Caroline turned away as the Indian lowered his glowing torch toward the hemorrhaging wound, but nothing could block out the sound of the injured sailor's screams.

Determined not to look at the tortured victim, Caroline concentrated on the small tuft behind the captain's feet and noticed a gleam of white almost hidden by the tall grass. It was the bone-handled knife she'd seen tucked in the gaunt pirate's belt, just before he'd pushed her down. Cautiously, her fingers closed around it and pulled it close to the folds of her shift.

"On your feet!" The captain leaned over Caroline. "Will ye miss the fun?" He took hold of her arm and dragged her up. "Gordo offended ye, did he not?" He raised his voice to a bellow and turned back to his crew. "This crotch-festered hulkscraping laid hands on what is mine," he bellowed. "He dared to disobey my direct orders."

His touch made Caroline's skin crawl. She shrugged off his grip, keeping her hand holding the knife hidden from sight. Her stomach was turning inside out. Any moment she'd disgrace herself by retching all over his boots. "Hell spawn," she accused.

He roared with laughter. "Hell spawn, am I?" He swept off his velvet cocked hat and executed an exaggerated bow, to the delight of his audience. "Captain Matthew Kay, at your service, madame," he shouted above their raucous catcalls. He rocked from one foot to the other, still chuckling. "Hell spawn, she calls me. Bold talk for a bride-to-be."

Bride-to-be? What in God's name was he talking about? she wondered. But God had nothing to do with this abomination. He was a lunatic. She glanced back to where she'd last seen Garrett, but he was hidden from view by two ugly brutes.

Like a pack of stray dogs circling prey, the ruffians drew closer. Their scarred faces were not so much amused as wary, Caroline decided. They studied their captain with the eyes of men who expected random violence and had seen it many times before.

Kay ran a hairy hand possessively down her arm and she shuddered with revulsion. Once, in the stable at Fortune's Gift, she had reached into a barrel for grain and a large black rat had run across her hand. She felt the same way now. "Keep your hands off me," she snapped. "And release my husband at once."

"Your husband?" Kay flashed crooked yellow teeth as he smiled. Then he laughed. "Not for long. Osprey will be gelded and gutted by sunrise, and you'll be a widow again." He winked at her. "But not for long."

"What do you want of us?" she demanded. "We haven't done anything to you." She wondered if she had the strength to drive the small knife into his black heart before they killed her.

"Haven't you?" Kay answered. "Haven't you? But first things first." His scowling gaze moved over his follower. "Gordo disobeyed his captain," Kay continued mockingly. "He tried to take what was mine. Thus, I struck off the offending hand that tried to steal from me." He smiled, then the piggish eyes narrowed slyly. "But he touched my bride-to-be with both hands, did he not?"

"Aye!" shouted a wiry mulatto in knee-high boots and Scots kilt. "Both hands!"

Caroline's throat constricted. This was a nightmare of hell—it must be. She'd wake in her own bed and find Amanda and the baby beside her. "No . . ." she uttered softly. "Don't do this."

"Shall one hand pay the price of mutiny and the other go free?" Kay demanded. "Or shall we teach him the cost of disobeying Red Hands Kay?"

"Both hands! Both hands!" cried a villain in a striped bandanna.

"Cut him!" shouted another.

A thickset albino surged forward waving a cutlass. "Make crab bait of 'im!" he howled.

Gordo crawled across the grass toward his captain, begging, blubbering, clutching his charred stump of an arm against his chest. "No. No. Mercy, Cap'n. Ain't I always been loyal? Ain't I always—"

"Off with his other hand!" Kay shouted. He thumped Caroline on the shoulder. "Watch! Watch and see how I'm going to make him pay for touchin' what was mine. And then think what I'll do to Osprey—that bastard husband of yours what killed my only son."

This time, when Kay lifted his bloody cutlass over the writhing seaman's head, Caroline tensed to slip the blade between the captain's ribs. But before she could plunge the knife home, she heard a man shout and the clash of steel on steel. Gordo staggered up and tried to run; Kay dashed after him and buried the cutlass in the man's back. Caroline used the diversion to flee up the steps toward the main entranceway of the manor house.

When she glanced back over her shoulder to see if she was being pursued, she saw a knot of crewmen beyond the firelight scatter. Someone cried out; the albino fell facedown into the fire, and Garrett hacked his way through the circle. "Run, Caroline!" he yelled. A blackamoor rushed at him with a pike. He dodged aside, slashed the man in the striped bandanna who was coming at him from the right, and ran straight at Captain Kay.

A marauder caught sight of Caroline backing toward the front door and ran forward to grab her. She stabbed his outstretched hand with the bone-handled knife. When she looked up again, Kay had drawn a pistol, cocked the hammer, and taken aim at Garrett.

She screamed Garrett's name as the gun spat fire and lead. He twisted sideways, and the pistol ball cut a furrow along his chest. Garrett turned and thrust at the captain.

Kay blocked the attack with his cutlass. "Kill him!" he roared.

"I said, get the hell out of here!" Garrett shouted to Caroline.

She flung herself at Kay's back. He sidestepped and dealt her a stunning backhanded blow that sent her spinning back against the porch. She hit the railing hard and slid down until she was sitting on the ground. She started to rise, but a seaman in red stockings put a knife to her throat.

"Stay where ye are!" he warned.

Three men with cutlasses moved in around Garrett and backed him blow by hacking blow toward the house. Again and again, he blocked and parried, but Caroline could see he was weakening.

"I said kill him!" Kay bellowed. "Give me that musket!" He yanked a Brown Bess from a burly onlooker and raised it to his shoulder.

"No!" Caroline screamed and tried to leap up. The sailor standing over her smashed his fist against her temple. Her world exploded in a shower of stars. And, as everything went black, the last thing she heard was the boom of cannon fire echoing across the water.

"How dare you follow me here?" Matthew demanded of his mother. Annemie had been carried ashore from her ship and was now resting comfortably in the master's high-backed chair in the north downstairs parlor.

Annemie waved a liveried footman to bring the branched candlestand closer. "More candles," she instructed. "At my age, I need all the light I can get."

"You have no business here," Matthew scolded. "To sail from Jamaica to this godforsaken island. What can you be thinking of? What if you were to take ill?"

She pursed her lips and made a smacking sound. "Then I should likely die," she said. "I am, after all, long past the age for it." Matthew was nervous; she could see the sweat on his upper lip. The fool could never hide what he was thinking from her. It confirmed her decision to take Falconer's personal vessel, the brigantine *Black Princess,* manned by the some of the best fighting men in the Caribbean, and come after her son.

After her visitation . . .

She had gone from the Kingston dock, where she had met Matthew, directly to the church to pray. And while she was there, kneeling, a miracle had occurred. She knew it was a miracle. After all, hadn't she spent a lifetime waiting for one?

She had been deep in prayer when she'd heard the angel's voice. Not soft and sweet as she'd always imagined, but firm and clear, ringing with authority. A strange accent, granted, like none she had ever heard. But how would an angel learn to speak properly in heaven?

Your son is an abomination, the voice had said.

It was not a statement she could argue with; it was truth, pure and simple.

"He is all I have left of Peregrine," she answered.

No. Another, more worthy, awaits your coming.

"Where? How?"

Osprey.

"He is our enemy."

Matthew is your enemy. He will shame his father's name. He will destroy the house of Falconer. You must stop him, before it is too late.

She had waited for nearly an hour, waited until her old bones were stiff from kneeling, but the angel spoke no more. She had called her servants and had them carry her back to the harbor, where she had laid eyes on the *Black Princess,* and she had known then what the angel wanted her to do.

The *Black Princess* now lay anchored broadside to Matthew's schooner *Reiver.* By now her captain, Nathan McCarthy, would have control of the *Reiver.* Matthew had not expected trouble from the sea; he'd brought most of his crew—including his gunners—ashore. The *Black Princess* carried more cannon and more men than the *Reiver*. Whether he knew it or not, Matthew had been outsmarted and outgunned by an old woman.

"I am weary, Matthew," Annemie lied. In truth, she required little sleep and was rarely tired. "Where is Garrett Faulkner?"

"Osprey? You promised him to me," Matthew reminded her.

"Yes, yes, I did, but only after I was finished with him. I have the right to face my grandson's murderer—do I not?"

"If you'd not interfered, he'd be dead by now."

"You were instructed to bring him to Falconer before disposing of him."

"Stop it, Mama. Why must you keep up this ridiculous pretense? My father has been dead for nearly half a century. There is no Falconer. It's only you. You give the orders. You make the decisions. It's past time that this playacting was at an end."

"Who then should take Falconer's place? Your father created an empire. Would men continue to obey his wishes in Boston if they knew a woman ruled? In Galway? In Lisbon? How many ships does Falconer command, Matthew? Where are our funds deposited? What contracts for shipping do we control? How many sugar plantations do we own? In short, my son and heir—how much do you know of Falconer's affairs?"

"And whose fault is it?" he demanded. "Who has deliberately kept me in the dark? Who treats me like a hired servant?"

"Your father, Peregrine—"

"To bloody hell with my father! May he rot in his grave. And you with him! I'm sick of your foot on my neck. I have Simon's killer and I will do with him as I please."

"And the woman, Caroline Talbot?"

His reply was so crude that Annemie's wrinkled cheeks grew hot and she looked away in shame. She closed her eyes, covered her face with her hands, and rocked to an fro in silent misery. If only Peregrine were here. He would know what to do with Matthew.

The angel's words came back to her. *He will destroy the house of Falconer.* And: *Another, more worthy . . .* She raised her head slowly and looked at the only living descendant of the man she had loved with all her heart and soul. "May God forgive you for your sins," she said. "Does the Bible not say, 'Honor your father and—' "

"Enough, old woman." Matthew stood up so quickly that he overturned the delicate French chair he had been sitting in. Angrily, he kicked it aside, and the toe of his boot cracked one of the rungs.

A waste, she thought. Such a pretty chair with all that gilt trimming . . .

Her thoughts drifted back to her grandson, Simon. Annemie had had such high hopes for Simon, but he had proved as stupid and as heartless as Matthew. How could she and Peregrine have produced such worthless offspring?

"It grows late," Matthew said, "and my bride awaits my coming. Talk to Osprey if you wish. I will deal with him in the morning." He paused in the doorway. "When we return to Jamaica, you will content yourself with your religious concerns, and I will take Falconer's chair."

"You will take it? From me?" She asked the obvious to make certain she understood the extent of his disrespect.

His answer was a muttered curse and the slamming door.

Annemie clapped her hands. "Bring me the prisoner," she instructed her servant. "At once." She waited, tapping her fan against the chair arm, impatient as only the very old can be, when they know each minute is precious. And when they dragged Osprey before her, she looked long and hard into his angry gray eyes.

Caroline strained at the ropes that held her wrists to the bedpost. Her head throbbed fiercely, and a trickle of blood ran down her cheek from the place where she'd been struck.

Worse of all, she did not know if Garrett was dead or alive. He had been on his feet and fighting when she'd last seen him, but no swordsman—no matter his skill—could survive attack by three or more armed men. If he was already dead . . . She shut her eyes and tried to summon up her powers of sight.

"I hope you're not asleep," Matthew said, coming into the room and closing the door behind him. "A bridegroom expects better on his wedding night."

Her eyes flew open. "I am not your wife," she cried. "I will never be your wife!"

He shrugged off his tight red and gold damask waistcoat and dropped heavily into a chair. "Are you fertile?" he asked. "My mother wishes me to get you with child." He tugged at one of his boots. "Would you do this for me if I untied you?"

Caroline lowered her head to hide her eyes. "Remove your boots?" she whispered.

"Yes, remove my boots. What the hell are we talking about?"

"Yes."

"You will?"

"Yes."

"That's better." He rose and walked stiffly over to the bed. Using a knife, he cut her bonds. "Don't try to run, little chicken," he warned. "My men are everywhere."

"There is blood on your shirt," she said. He smelled like a hog wallow.

"You should know. You cut me." He settled back into the chair and held out his foot.

She forced herself to take hold of his boot and pull. The stench of his filthy stocking made her ill. She gritted her teeth and removed the other boot. "Your wound should be bathed and tended," she said. "Otherwise it will fester in this heat."

He laughed and groped crudely at her backside. "One would think you are reluctant to perform your marital duties, little chicken," he said.

"No." She raised her head and looked into his dull brown eyes. They seemed lifeless, like those of a fish. No, she decided, they were goat's eyes. "I am a practical woman, Captain. If I am to be yours, then my interests lie with you."

"Sensible." He smiled with his lips, but the goat's eyes remained flat, without any hint of amusement. He raised the bottle of rum he'd brought with him and drank deeply, then wiped his mouth with the back of his sleeve.

"I take it that my husband is dead."

"Enough talk." He grabbed her arm and pulled her into his lap. "Give us a kiss."

She knew it was useless to fight him. She knew the logical thing was to pretend to give in and watch for a chance to kill him, but she couldn't. She balled her fist and drove it into this wide nose with every ounce of her strength.

Blood flew. Matthew backhanded her and she

tumbled onto the floor. He was on her before she could move. He slapped her once, hard, and then ripped the front of her gown from neckline to waist.

Caroline screamed.

Matthew lowered his body onto her and cruelly squeezed one breast until she cried out with pain. "Bitch!" he growled. "I'll teach—"

He broke off as a bolt of lightning shattered a massive tree branch outside the window and shook the whole house. Matthew gasped and scrambled back as a ball of white light materialized in the corner of the room. "Mother of God!" he muttered. Caroline crawled away and put a table between her and Matthew Kay.

The ball of energy exploded through the nearest window, and a gust of wind extinguished the lamp, plunging the room into darkness.

"Where are you?" he shouted.

She held her breath, afraid to breathe.

The door burst open. "Caroline!"

Garrett's voice. She drew in a deep breath. "Be careful," she warned.

As soon as she spoke, Matthew lunged for her. The table saved her. He struck the edge of it, slipped, and fell facedown. She was on her feet and running across the room. She threw herself into Garrett's arms.

He crushed her against him for an instant, then pulled her away from the vulnerability of the doorway and into the hall. "Did he—"

"No. I'm all right," she managed. "But be careful. He's armed." Then she realized that Garrett had a sword in his hand. "How did you get loose?"

"No time for that now." He pulled her down the hall and thrust her into the first bedchamber they came to. "Go inside and lock the door," he ordered. "Don't come out until I—"

Matthew appeared in the hall, a pistol in his hand. He raised it and cocked the hammer. "You're a dead man, Osprey," he said, taking aim at the center of Garrett's chest.

It seemed to Caroline as if time had stopped. She heard the sound of the hammer snapping into place. Then a Brown Bess rifle roared; a second later, the explosion was followed by the crack of Kay's pistol. Splinters of wood and plaster sprayed across the hall. For what seemed an eternity to Caroline, Garrett and Matthew stood staring at each other, then the captain clutched at the saucer-sized hole in his chest, staggered against the wall, and slid down with open, sightless eyes.

Behind Kay, standing at the top of the stairs, Caroline saw a tall liveried blackamoor in a red turban holding a smoking rifle.

Garrett took a few steps toward the stairs, and the blackamoor lowered his Brown Bess and held up a broad palm. "No trouble, monsieur. Madame give order Jantje shoot *Capitaine*," he said.

"Who is Madame?" Caroline asked. "And why . . ."

Garrett took her in his arms. "Falconer," he said, as he covered her face with kisses. "Falconer is a lady, and—" He held Caroline at arm's length. "Are you certain he didn't hurt you?"

"He knocked me around," she answered. "And yes, that hurt like hell, but he didn't have his way with me. That lightning storm—"

"What lightning? What are you talking about?" He rubbed the lump on her temple gently. "You've taken a beating, Caroline. It's only normal that you'd begin to imagine—"

"A lightning bolt took a limb off a tree right outside the house. You didn't hear it?" she asked in disbelief. "Ball lightning rolled right through the room. It scared Kay—"

"Honey, you need to be in bed."

"Kutii," she said softly.

"It's all right," he soothed. "You'll feel better after a little rest. I'll look for your sister and Noah—"

"They're at the cave. They're safe. At least, I hope they are. But the rest of the pirates—Kay's crew—what about them? They—"

Garrett picked her up in his arms and carried her into the nearest bedchamber and laid her down on the bed. "It's all right, Caroline. It's all right. Falconer is here. Whatever power Captain Kay had, it wasn't as much as Falconer's. She promised us safe passage home to the Colonies."

"But why? How? She held on to Garrett's hand with a death grip, fearful that he'd vanish. Afraid she'd wake up and find that this was the dream.

"Shhh, trust me. I'll call Pilar to stay with you for a while until I can—"

"Pilar? But I thought she was dead."

"No." He shook his head. "Kay's men killed Angus. Pilar was hurt but she's alive. She's tough. I just saw her a few minutes ago, downstairs."

"This Falconer is a woman, you say?"

"Yes. A very great lady, and Captain Kay's mother."

"But that man just said—"

"That she ordered him shot." He exhaled softly. "I don't understand that part, but I believe it. I'll talk to her about it."

"You? How do you know her?"

"Her men saved my ass when they came ashore."

"But why?" Caroline demanded.

"My grandfather, Perry Faulkner, was a bond slave on Jamaica. He cut sugarcane on one of the plantations there before he escaped and came to Maryland. His mother, Keavy, was from Dublin, but he never knew his father.

"Falconer—Mistress Annemie—claims that her husband, Peregrine Kay, mentioned an Irish bond girl named Keavy whom he once loved when they were both in their teens," Garrett continued. "Peregrine said the girl told him that she was pregnant with his child, but that she vanished without a trace, and he thought his mother had gotten rid of the wench.

"Mistress Annemie believes old Perry Faulkner was her husband's bastard by Keavy. Peregrine Falconer Kay was the only son of the royal governor. Mistress Annemie thinks Keavy gave my grandfather the name Perry Faulkner because she was afraid to call him Peregrine Kay."

"But the names aren't quite the same."

"My grandfather couldn't read or write. I'm sure his mother couldn't either."

"So you are related to Falconer?"

"So she says. It makes me her step-great-grandson, or something like that."

"He carries Peregrine's blood," came the dry whisper from the doorway.

In the light from the hallway candlestand, Caroline saw an old woman leaning on a cane. "It seems we have much to thank you for," Caroline said. "You saved us both from—"

"I knew it when I laid eyes on him," Annemie continued. "Pergrine's son's son's son. He has the look about him. It's the Kay eyes." She glanced back over her shoulder at the prone body on the floor. "Matthew never had them. I'm not sure who he took after."

Garrett turned toward her. "Why did you order him killed?" he asked. "Your own son?"

"Matthew was a great disappointment to me," she answered. "But he was all I had. Now I have you."

Chapter 23

On April 23, Caroline and Garrett witnessed the marriage of Amanda and Noah by a French priest in the garden of a rented house in Port-au-Prince. Amanda wore a brocaded silk Polonaise dress of pale rose with a petticoat of deeper pink and a wide straw hat adorned with a band of island flowers. Noah was decently dressed in a gentleman's azure-blue coat, waistcoat, and matching fawnskin breeches; and the baby, Jeremy—securely held in Pilar's capable arms—wore identical garments.

Amanda, Noah, and Jeremy had come to Port-au-Prince to assemble a household and purchase a seaworthy sloop and supplies before returning to Arawak Island to establish a boatyard. Since finding skilled craftsmen, tools, and trained servants might take time, Noah was prepared to spend several months there.

After the brief wedding ceremony, local musicians played instruments and native women danced gaily as the bridal party was served a ten-course wedding supper beneath the flowering trees. Caroline sat beside Garrett and watched her sister's happiness with mixed emotions.

"I wish you were coming home with us," she said, placing her hand over Amanda's dark one, adorned with its shiny new gold wedding band. "Jeremy should grow up on Fortune's Gift."

Amanda smiled mysteriously and shook her

head. "No. He should grow up here on the shores of this warm sea. Don't you hear the old songs of Africa in the drums and castanets? In the guitars and flute? Jeremy is a person of color. It is best for his future and that of the children Noah and I might have together that we stay here."

"But I will miss you all so."

"And I will miss you . . . and home." Amanda squeezed Caroline's hand. "I worry about you, going back into a war."

"I'll be fine." She glanced at Garrett and Noah, who were deep in conversation about the new ship.

Cassandra was anchored in the harbor, awaiting Garrett's orders to sail north. Falconer—Mistress Annemie—had given Garrett a half interest in the brigantine and had put the crew at his disposal. It was a generous gift, since the brigantine was only four years old and carried the finest German-made cannon and swivel guns. No amount of money could have purchased a better vessel in the Caribbean for Garrett's purposes.

"It is in our interest that the American Colonies win their independence from England," Mistress Annemie had pronounced solemnly before she left Arawak Island to return to her home on Jamaica. "I would prefer that, as my heir, Garrett remain here in the islands until the war is over. But since he is as stubborn as my Peregrine . . ." She trailed off, smiling proudly at Garrett. "Since I wish to protect you, naturally I want you to command the best ship in Falconer's fleet."

Mistress Annemie had also arranged for much of the treasure to be converted to good Spanish doubloons, louis d'ors, and English guineas. And to Caroline's surprise, the old lady had refused payment for the *Cassandra*.

"I have more than an old woman needs," she had told Caroline. "I am a simple woman with few wants beyond my charities. However, it would please me immensely if you should decide to name your firstborn son after my dear Peregrine."

"If we ever have a son, I will name him Peregrine," Caroline had promised. She hadn't told anyone except Amanda about her suspicion that she was already pregnant. She had been afraid that if she did tell Garrett, he would insist that she remain behind in the islands instead of going home.

This morning, a message had arrived from Falconer in Jamaica informing Garrett that France was about to recognize the independence of the Colonies, and that Sir Henry Clinton was rumored a prime choice to replace Howe.

. . . If that happens, Mistress Annemie wrote in her spidery script, *Washington must march north with all his troops to attack the British forces in New York. He will need all the support possible along the coast. Vital that you proceed north to the Chesapeake immediately . . .*

"I'll sail at the end of the week," Garrett had told Caroline. "There are a few more arrangements that I need to make."

Since Matthew Kay had invaded Arawak, Garrett had treated Caroline with the greatest consideration, guarding her as though she were the fortune. He had barely let her out of his sight. At night, if she awoke, she found him sitting close to her bed. But they had not lived as man and wife.

Now with fresh news of the conflict, it seemed to her as if he had already left her. The Garrett Faulkner beside her at Amanda's wedding feast was not the man who had held Caroline with such passion that night on the balcony of Arawak House. He was the captain of the *Cassandra*—very much a military officer—and not the husband and lover she wanted so badly.

Even when the musicians began to play an English country dance and Garrett took her hand to lead her out onto the grass, his touch was that of a gentle stranger. She smiled at him, dipped and turned and laughed as bright blossoms rained around them like warm snowflakes. But all the while, her heart was aching.

At quarter after ten that evening, Noah accompanied Garrett to the town dock. Garrett shook his friend's hand a last time and wished him happiness and success with his new business. Garrett turned to climb down the ladder to the waiting dory, then stopped and looked at the big black man. "It's not too late to change your mind and come with me," Garrett said. "I'll make you my first officer."

Noah laughed and shook his head. "No more fighting for me, Garrett. I've had my share. Just remember me when you need a solid sloop built."

"I'll remember you."

"And me you. For a white man, you'll do."

"Take care of my Caroline, and God keep you all." Garrett's voice cracked, and he threw his arms around his friend. Then, without speaking again, he scrambled down to the small boat where two brass-bound chests were already waiting and signaled for the seamen to row him to the *Cassandra*.

Able Conner, the first officer, had already given the commands to make the brigantine ready. The tide was changing, and Garrett intended to sail on it. If the British decided to evacuate Philadelphia, he knew the *Cassandra* could take an active part in freeing the Chesapeake.

Caroline would be furious to be left behind, and she would consider his decision to go without her a betrayal of their agreement. He meant to make Fortune's Gift his first stop on the bay, and he would do everything in his power to secure Reed's release from prison, but he wasn't taking Caroline back to the war. When it was over—if he survived—they would see if they could put their marriage back together. Until then, he owed it to her to provide for her safety.

Knowing he planned to leave her behind in the Caribbean, he'd not slept with her again. It would have been more than human flesh could bear—to hold her in his arms night after night, realizing that they would soon be separated, perhaps forever.

The deck officer, Mr. Bridger, waited by the gunnel as the sailors brought the dory alongside the *Cassandra*. The bosun piped Garrett aboard with proper ceremony. Garrett returned Mr. Bridger's salute, then watched as the two chests were brought on board. He gave a few last-minute orders concerning the departure, then commanded that the chests be delivered to his quarters.

Captain McCarthy, the previous captain of the *Cassandra*, had taken control of Matthew Kay's schooner *Reiver*. McCarthy had left the *Cassandra* at Arawak in such haste that many of his personal belongings were still aboard in the master's cabin. Garrett made a mental note to be certain the items were returned to McCarthy when possible.

Garrett thought he should have been in a better mood tonight. After all, hadn't he achieved all he'd set out to do when he'd fled the Chesapeake with Caroline? He had a stout ship underfoot, ten cannon better than he'd ever hoped to find, and a hell of a crew to take into combat.

He hesitated for a moment outside the hatchway that led to his cabin and looked back over the moonlit water at the few lights still burning in the town. Faintly, over the water, came the strains of an old French sailors' drinking song. He took a deep breath, savoring the familiar ship odors; the warm, moist air was laden with the scents of salt, new hemp and canvas, and tar.

Bloody hell! It was good to have a deck under his feet again. He'd been too long ashore, and too long away from hunting English ships.

He swallowed, trying to think of the action to come . . . trying not to think of Caroline, or the way damp ringlets of her hair had escaped from her cap and curled at the back of her neck as she'd danced with him . . . fighting the memories of her silken body molded against his . . . And once again he wished that they had met at some other time and place.

Garrett blinked away the film of moisture that clouded his vision and descended the ladder to his cabin. He threw open the door and swore softly.

Caroline was sitting on his bunk dressed only in her shift and stockings with a glass of red wine in her hand. "Good evening, sir," she called to him. "I was afraid you'd miss the tide."

The days sailing northward toward home and the Chesapeake were not what Caroline would have wished. Garrett had been furious that she'd come aboard without his knowledge. He hadn't admitted it, but they both knew he'd intended on leaving her behind with Noah and Amanda.

Because the crew and ship were new to him, Garrett insisted that she remain a virtual prisoner in the cabin unless he escorted her up to the quarterdeck for a breath of fresh air. "A fighting ship is no place for a woman," he'd admonished her. "You jeopardize my effectiveness with the men merely by being here."

Despite her obvious invitation the night they pulled anchor in Port-au-Prince, she and Garrett had not been intimate. The captain's cabin contained two narrow bunks; Garrett slept in one, and she in the other.

"This has nothing to do with you," he'd explained brusquely. "What we have between us must wait until after this war is over."

"And if it won't wait?" she'd asked him. His only reply had been a shrug and the regret in his eyes.

She had come so close to weakness then; every feminine instinct had urged her to proclaim her condition. But she hadn't. She'd been as stubborn and unreasonable as Garrett. And every day, she'd tried to harden her heart against him.

He's right, she argued with herself. I will have my hands full with Fortune's Gift. I won't have time to worry about another man at sea during wartime. If I don't allow myself to care, I'll not be hurt again if he dies as Wesley did.

It was a lie. She knew it in her blood and bone. What she felt for Garrett Faulkner compared to what she had felt for Wesley was the difference between a glowing emerald and a piece of cheap green glass. Still, the lie helped her to sleep at night and made it possible to think of Reed's safety, and the prospect of planting the river fields in late corn this year.

Fortunately, Captain McCarthy had been a reader, and he'd left two books in the desk. One was a copy of Jonathan Swift's works, the other,

Essays on Husbandry. Without the books, she would have gone mad. Garrett was on deck before first light until long after sunset.

Since he'd taken command of the *Cassandra* on Arawak Island, Garrett had driven the crew relentlessly. He'd ordered sails raised and lowered, cannon loaded and fired, decks scrubbed, and brass polished until the *Cassandra* shone like a June bride. He was a fair commander, but hard. He demanded instant obedience, and once, when a seaman was insubordinate, he gave the fellow six lashes and put him ashore at the first fishing village.

Yet, with all the work, Garrett realized that the crew needed good food, hearty drink, and time to relax. Often, Caroline would drift off to sleep to the thumps of dancing feet and the wail of the hornpipe coming from the deck above.

By the time the *Cassandra* reached the banks of the Carolinas, Garrett had earned the confidence of his men. The ship crossed the path of a British Royal Navy snow, exchanged cannon fire, and made the English ship turn tail and run.

Garrett shared his breakfast with his officers; the noon meal he took alone on the quarterdeck. Only at suppertime did he return to the captain's cabin to sit and eat with Caroline. And if nights were strained times between them, the evening meal was a good time.

Supper was simple, often fish, hot bread, cheese, and fresh or dried fruit. She would listen as he told her of what the crew had accomplished, of the distance the *Cassandra* had traveled in the last twenty-four hours, and what the weather conditions were. Then they would discuss Caroline's plans for the plantation, and finally, politics.

Garrett had a shrewd, logical mind, and if he

had the typical arrogance of a man, at least he was willing to listen to her ideas. Often, they argued over obscure points of colony law or what Caroline felt was the unfairness of the treatment of women.

One evening, when they had finished eating and were sharing a bottle of wine, she asked him what he intended to do when the war was over.

"I don't suppose I've thought that far," he said, crossing his legs and propping his feet on the lid of one of the treasure chests. "There's always farming. I have the land. Since my oldest brother married the Flaherty girl and went to Ireland to live, and my second brother is settled in New Castle on the Delaware, managing the family plantations is my responsibility. Faulkner's Folly is mine, left to me by my Grandfather Perry, but it's small compared to Fortune's Gift—barely self-supporting. The earliest tobacco fields are wearing out, and I need to clear more virgin forest."

"I don't think you need to worry about money, Garrett," she replied. "Your share of the treasure—"

"I have what I want—the *Cassandra*. The rest is yours, Caroline, to do with what you will. It was always yours."

He started to pour her a second glass of wine, but she waved it away. "No, thank you. I've no head for drink lately," she said. In truth, since she'd quickened with child, even a glass made her sleepy, and she'd all but given spirits up. "Mistress Annemie said that she will make you her heir. If she controls as vast a shipping empire as she says, then—"

He laughed. "I'll waste no night's sleep on an old woman's promises. If she could order her only son shot, who knows what she might do? It's enough for me that she put the *Cassandra* at my command. I'm not greedy. I've never wished to be rich."

"But if Falconer's estate does come to you?"

He grinned boyishly. "I'm not so much a fool to turn it down."

"It could make you more powerful than a royal governor."

"Could, and would, and should, honey." He laughed again. "Together they didn't fill the sailor's empty sleeve."

"It is a possibility," she insisted. "You could become a very wealthy man."

"Perhaps. But if I did, it's more likely that it's you who would become the rich widow. This war is just beginning, Caroline. It may run for years." He exhaled slowly. "And I intend to be in the thick of it—as long as it takes, as much as it takes."

"You're not the man I thought you were when I first met you," she said softly. "I thought that Garrett was more interested in a warm wench to tumble and his next card game."

"A few years earlier, and your estimation would have been right. I was hot for independence. I once sat in on one of Patrick Henry's speeches during a Virginia convention. Something he said stuck in my mind. 'The battle . . . is not to the strong alone, it is to the vigilant, the active, the brave . . .' I suppose most young bucks are eager enough for the excitement of war. But it wasn't until the *Osprey* went down that gunpowder ran in my veins. I kept thinking that if we didn't win this thing—if we didn't drive the British from our shores—then Wesley, John, Will, and the others would have died for nothing. I just couldn't live with myself if I let that happen."

"But what of Noah and Amanda and Jeremy?

Will there ever be a place for men and women of color in this new country? A time when they can be free, regardless of the hue of their skin?"

"God will it so," he answered. "But slavery is an evil that's been with us since biblical days."

"It doesn't make it right."

"No, it doesn't. It just makes it harder to root out."

"Will it change in Jeremy's lifetime?"

"Maybe. Or maybe in his son's or grandson's."

"It makes no sense to me," she replied ardently, "why so many men can fight willingly for their own freedom and deny it to a man like Noah."

"Human nature."

"It's not right."

"Keep saying so, little hothead, and maybe, after a while, some will begin to listen." He covered her hand with his. "For now, we must concern ourselves with freeing Reed. I've found it best to fight one battle at a time."

And to her great dismay, Garrett's mention of her brother's name brought back the memory of her vision of the fresh grave at Fortune's Gift. She shivered. "What if we're too late to save Reed?"

For that question, he had no answer.

Chapter 24

In the early hours of morning darkness on May 1, the *Cassandra* extinguished all lamps and muffled every sound aboard ship. Garrett took the wheel and whispered a prayer as his brigantine passed within two hundred yards of a British man-of-war to slip silently into the mouth of the Chesapeake Bay.

An hour later, he went below deck to his cabin and woke Caroline. "We're home, sweet. That's Chesapeake air you smell."

"Already?"

She sat up and he heard the faint rustle as the linen sheet fell away. He couldn't see her in the blackness, but he could smell the scent of gardenias in her hair. He felt his groin tighten as he imagined what it would be like to run his hands over her . . . to slide into the bunk next to her.

"Garrett?"

Her voice was low and husky. His name on her lips sent a shiver down his spine. "The Tories hold Tangier Island and the surrounding area. Once we're safely past the island—"

"We can't go to Fortune's Gift," she said, seizing his forearm. "I have to get to Chestertown."

Her nails bit into his skin. "Please. Reed's there. I can't tell you how I know, but I know it. And if we don't get to him right away, he'll die."

Garrett sat on the side of her bunk. "Use sense, girl. You wanted to go home. Now I'm taking you.

You've been on this ship since we sailed from Port-au-Prince. There's no way you could know where Reed is any more than I could. The last word we had, he was a prisoner in New York."

"He might have been there, but he's not now," she said urgently. "I saw him in a dream. For months, I've been seeing his grave. But this was different. First I saw the grave, then I went back—before. He's not dead yet. He's in Chestertown in the cellar of the Customs House."

"Caroline, you've got to listen to me," he reasoned. "You're losing your grip on reality."

"I found the treasure, didn't I?"

"Yes, you found the damned treasure. But that doesn't make you a witch, and it doesn't mean you can—"

"I'm not telling you the truth," she admitted. "Reed is in Chestertown, but I didn't dream it. Someone told me."

"Who?"

"You wouldn't believe me."

"Who?"

"Kutii."

"Caroline . . ."

"Call him a ghost, call him a spirit—call him anything you want. I don't pretend to understand it, but I know he's as real as you and me. He told me about the treasure and we found it. Now he's telling me I have to go to Chestertown if I want to save Reed."

Garrett stood up and turned away from her. "If I take you to Chestertown, if I prove to you that Reed's not there, then will you go back to Fortune's Gift and stay there?"

"What about my cousin Bruce?"

"I'll handle Bruce."

"What happens to us once you take me to Fortune's Gift?" she asked him. She had never felt more vulnerable than she did right now. Her resistance to Garrett—to giving herself to him completely, body and soul, seemed to melt away in the shared darkness of the cabin.

"What do you want to happen?" He heard her feet touch the floor, then she was in his arms.

"I want to be your wife, Garrett," she said with a burst of pent-up emotion. "I don't care if it's for two hours or two days. I want us to stop all this pretending that we don't care. I love you more than my own life. I want to you to be my husband."

"And if I get killed in the war?" Suddenly all his arguments for keeping an emotional distance from Caroline seemed weak. Had he been a fool to waste what time they had? "I can't stay with you. I have to do what I can to help in this struggle against the English."

"I'll take my chances, the same as every other wife of an American soldier or sailor." Her arms went around his neck, and he groaned as she pulled his head down. Their lips met, and for a long minute, he lost himself in the intensity of their kiss.

It took every ounce of his willpower to step away from her. "I'll take you to Chestertown," he promised. "Damn me for a fool, but I'll do it."

"I love you."

"In spite of Wesley and the *Osprey?*"

"I believe in your innocence, Garrett. I think I've always believed you, deep down inside. And it doesn't matter anymore what happened that night the *Osprey* sunk. It wasn't your fault any more than it was Wesley's or Reed's. I'm sorry I ever blamed you for it."

Someone rapped on the cabin door. "Captain,

it's your second, Bridger. Mr. Conner needs you on the quarterdeck, sir."

"I have to go," Garrett told Caroline.

She ran to him and kissed him again. "I mean every word, Garrett," she whispered. "I do love you."

"And I love you," he said. "Heaven help me, but I do."

"You'll give our marriage a second chance?"

"Captain, sir?" Bridger called again.

"Coming," Garrett answered.

"Garrett?" She held her breath as she waited for his answer.

"There's no need for a second chance," he said. "I never stopped loving you since the first night I climbed through your window."

Two days later, Caroline walked down High Street in the riverfront port of Chestertown. She crossed over to the brick building that housed William Myers and Son—Transporters and Investors, went inside, and inquired whether Mr. James Myers was in the office. James, grandson of the long-dead William who'd founded the firm, had remained firmly on the fence in the matter of independence for the Colonies. Despite that, Caroline's father had done business with both James and his father, and she was certain she could ask questions of James without putting herself at risk. Unfortunately, the clerk informed her that James was in Annapolis.

Caroline left Myers and Son and continued on down the hill toward the Chester River and His Royal Majesty's Customs House. There were few people on the street, and she noticed far fewer ships at anchor than normal. An official British port of entry for many years, Chestertown had been recently losing much of the shipping to the growing town of Baltimore on the bay.

The *Cassandra* was anchored in a hidden cove a few miles away. Caroline and Garrett had come to the outskirts of the town with a handful of men. It had been Garrett's idea that they go to the Customs House in daylight and try to find out if Reed was actually there, before planning a jailbreak. And Caroline had insisted that she was the logical one to do the reconnaissance.

"I suppose you expect to knock on the door and ask if they're holding any traitors prisoner in the cellar," he'd said.

"Don't be ridiculous," she'd replied. "I'll ask the town gossip. If Mattie Lee doesn't know, no one will."

"And if someone recognizes you?"

"What difference would that make? The authorities aren't looking for me. I'm a loyal subject of the crown, remember?"

Mattie Lee lived only two doors down from the Customs House. She had been a cook and housekeeper for her employers for over forty years, and she knew every resident of Chestertown and all their secrets. Furthermore, Mattie's grandson, Plato, was a shepherd on Fortune's Gift.

As she neared the Customs House, Caroline noticed two British soldiers standing at attention on either side of the entranceway. She kept her eyes averted beneath her wide straw lady's hat as she walked past.

Her heartbeat had just slowed to normal when she heard someone shout her name. Startled, she turned to see her cousin Bruce.

"Stop that woman!" he ordered the two guards.

Caroline's stomach lurched. Bruce! The last person in the world she'd wanted to meet. She resisted the urge to run, knowing she'd only look foolish, and tried to maintain her dignity as the two tall redcoats dashed toward her.

"You'll 'ave to come with us, mistress," the older of the two said sternly.

The younger, blond and fresh-cheeked, didn't speak. He flushed a dark red and his prominent Adam's apple bobbed. He would have taken hold of her arm, but Caroline fixed him with such a fierce glare than he snatched his hand back as if he'd been burned.

Bruce came trotting up behind them. "Well, cousin," he said sarcastically. "You're as tanned as a field hand. Where have you been?"

"What business is it of yours?" she replied.

"Corporal, this is my ward. I am responsible for her safety, and she has been quite ill." He tapped his round forehead with one ragged fingernail. "Mistress Steele has a nervous condition."

Caroline's eyes narrowed in disgust. Bruce was as slovenly as ever. Even the new red coat he was wearing was spotted with wine stains, and his sash looked as through dogs had been sleeping on it. "You have no right to detain me," she said. "I am not Mistress Steele; I am Mistress Garrett Faulkner. My husband has legal jurisdiction over me, not you, *cousin.*"

He smiled. "I think not. Where is this *husband* of yours? Another traitor. You are dangerously close to arrest yourself. Is he with you, I hope?"

"He abandoned me in Charleston," she lied.

"A pretty story. And why, pray tell, are you here in Chestertown instead of at Fortune's Gift?"

"Has Major Whitehead forgiven you for—"

"The good major left Fortune's Gift two weeks ago, transferred to New York with all his men. I have been assigned to Chestertown, and until our new commander arrives, I am the senior officer here." He motioned toward the Customs House. "Bring her inside. It's best we don't make a dog-and-bear show for the locals.'

"I'm not going with you," Caroline said.

"You will come, or you will be carried. Which is it, Caroline?" He smiled again. "I hope you've brought Amanda and her whelp back with you."

"No," she answered quickly.

"No, you won't walk, or no, your pet nigra has abandoned you as well?"

Having no desire to be dragged through the public street, she gave in and followed him without further protest. "My sister and her son stayed in Charleston."

"A pity," Bruce said. "You see, Corporal, Mistress Steele is so distraught, she believes that she is sister to a black slave wench."

"Amanda is free," Caroline replied.

"We'll see about that."

As they neared the entrance of the Customs House, the blond soldier quickened his step and opened the door for them. Caroline nodded her thanks and entered the cool, austere building.

"Resume your posts," Bruce told the guards. "Under no circumstances are you to permit my ward to leave the building without me." He glanced back at Caroline. "So why exactly are you in Chestertown?"

She gathered her courage. "I've come to see my brother." Bruce blanched. "I know he's a prisoner here," she continued. "I demand to see him."

"You are in no position to demand anything from me."

"Please, Bruce." It galled her to ask anything of him, but she must find out if Reed was really here and if he was all right. "It's been so long."

"How did you know he'd been moved to Chestertown?"

"It doesn't matter. What matters is that I see him." She tried to play the role of a distressed woman. "Please. What can it hurt?"

"You must know that I intend to annul your marriage to Faulkner. After that, he will be arrested and hanged for high treason. I am shocked at you, Caroline, to marry the man responsible for your husband's death. Faulkner is the notorious Captain Osprey. Did you know?"

"I learned of it. And when I did, I confronted him with his past. It was the reason we fought, and the reason he left me," she lied glibly.

"I am responsible for having Reed brought to Chestertown. Despite his sentence, it may be possible to have him released in my custody. He lost an arm—did you know that? A one-armed man is little danger to anyone. With the right bribes, I may be able—"

Reed had lost an arm! Caroline tried to keep from breaking down. "Please," she said. "You must let me go to him."

"I intend to be your next husband," he said.

"I don't wish to marry, ever again."

He shrugged. "You will marry me if you don't want to see Reed sent back to one of those prison ships. Have you heard of conditions on the *Jersey*? They say the men who die are the lucky ones."

"I don't believe you. I don't believe anything you say. Let me see my brother, and then we'll discuss my future plans."

"As you wish. Private Starr!"

A young soldier appeared in the doorway leading to the next room and snapped a salute. "Captain, sir."

"Take the lady down to the cellar. She may visit

the prison for ten minutes. No more. And they are not to touch. If there is any physical contact, the visit is at an end. Do you understand?"

"Yes, sir!"

Reed was imprisoned in a small room in the dampest part of the cellar. He was unshaved and dressed in rags, and it was plain to Caroline that he'd not had a bath or a decent meal in many months.

"Reed!" she cried.

He rose off the pile of dirty straw until the ankle chain pulled tight. "Caroline! For God's sake, don't come any closer. I'm crawling with lice."

She glanced at the soldier. "Leave us some privacy, can't you. He said I couldn't touch him; he didn't say anything about talking. This is my brother, and I haven't seen him for over a year."

Starr backed off. "You leave the door open, and stay clear of him," he warned.

She turned her attention to Reed. He was skin and bone, his cheeks as hollow as a starvelings, his eyes sunken. "How are you?" she asked.

"You can look at me and ask that?" His voice was thin, but the old Reed hadn't changed. He was always ready to laugh, especially at his own woes.

"You look beautiful to me," she said and meant every word.

"Have you talked with our loving cousin?" Reed asked her.

"Yes."

"He wants Fortune's Gift—all of it."

"He said he may be able to get you paroled."

"When the devil sprouts wings and a halo. He wants me dead—and you. After he weds you and gets an heir from your body."

What? Another monster wants me to bear his heir? she thought with a sinking heart. "I'm already remarried," she told him. "And with child."

He smiled. "Congratulations. Don't let Bruce know that if you can help it. Who's the lucky man?"

She held her breath. "Garrett Faulkner."

"Garrett?" His smile broke into a wide grin. "You couldn't have done better for yourself, little sister. He's a man I'm proud to have as a brother-in-law."

"Are you, Reed? Even after what happened?"

"Hell, sis, you can't blame Garrett. Wesley was in command that night. He—"

"Wesley?" She stared at him in disbelief. "Wesley took the *Osprey* into that fight?"

"You didn't know that?"

"No." She shook her head. "I know Garrett is the captain they called Osprey, but I didn't know Wesley was at the helm. Garrett said it wasn't his fault. They tried him for treason, you know. They dismissed charges for insufficient evidence, but everyone still suspects—"

"Well, high command won't think it for long. I was afraid something like that might happen. I made a full report to a Methodist minister when the British surgeon amputated my arm last winter."

"Last winter? Then you didn't injure your arm in the fire when the ship went down?"

"Yes, I did. Along with my hip, my leg, and a few ribs. But the damned arm never healed right. They didn't give me proper medical treatment or even clean bandages. When it started to stink, they found some butcher to cut it off. I thought I was dying, and I called for a man of God to confess my sins to. Reverend Gates wrote out what I told him, and I signed it with my left hand. He hid it in his Bible. He promised to see that the letter went to the nearest Continental unit with orders to send it directly to Washington himself. Don't forget his name," Reed cautioned her. "The Reverend Thomas Gates from Morristown, New Jersey. A deathbed statement from a hero like me should stand up in any court."

"It's hard for me to accept that Wesley was in command that night," she said. "I never dreamed that he was the one at fault."

"You'd best believe it. You know what a hothead Wes could be. Garrett told him not to go after that merchant ship. It was too easy a prize. Not even the Brits would be stupid enough to try running up the Delaware without an escort. But Wesley was hell-bent on proving he was as good a captain as Garrett, and he convinced the men to try. You know the results."

"Time's about up, miss," the private called.

"Just another minute," she pleaded. She looked into Reed's eyes. "Don't give up hope."

"Worry about yourself. Bruce can't be trusted."

"We'll get you out of here," she promised.

"It doesn't matter."

"Of course it matters. We'll get you home to Fortune's Gift and get you a physician—"

"Caroline, listen to me. I don't have long to live, no matter where I am."

"Don't say that."

"Miss!" the soldier said.

"Reed, you won't die,' Caroline whispered. "I won't let you."

"I have consumption," he said. "I'm coughing up blood. "I've lost an arm, and I have a belly wound that won't heal. What happens to me isn't important. It's you and Fortune's Gift that—"

"And Amanda," she cried. "What about Amanda?"

"Her too."

The guard approached them. "You'll have to go up now, miss. Orders from Captain Talbot."

She ignored him. "Amanda married Noah Walker," she said to Reed. "They're going to live on Arawak Island."

"Maybe that's for the best," her brother answered hoarsely.

"Come along quiet, miss." The soldier took hold of Caroline's arm.

"You have a son, Reed," she said. "A beautiful son." She yanked her hand out of the guard's grasp. "His name is Jeremy." Private Starr reddened and reached for her again, and she threw him a withering look. "Have you no decency? One more minute, and I'll go."

Reed was staring at Caroline as though she'd grown a second head. "I have a what?"

"A son," she replied.

"And who is the mother?"

She felt her cheeks grow hot. "You don't know? Amanda."

"She told you that?"

"No . . . but . . ." Caroline hesitated. "She didn't say who the father was, but I thought that you and she . . ."

"Loved each other," he continued. "We did, but we both knew it could never be. I knew she was with child, Caroline, but I'm not the father. Amanda and I never were intimate."

"Who then?" she demanded.

"He was drinking and he found her bathing, Caroline. He told me that it was his fault and that he was sorry. She said it would break your heart if you found out he raped her, so we kept it a secret."

"Who?" Caroline asked.

"Let it go, sis. If Amanda didn't tell you—she didn't want to hurt you."

"Who did it? Who raped her?"

"It's not important now."

"I have as much a right to know as you do. Who was it?"

"Your husband. Wesley."

Chapter 25

Bruce dismissed the guard. "I wish to interrogate Mistress Steele," he said. "Under no circumstances am I to be disturbed."

Caroline went to the window overlooking the Chester River and stared out into the twilight. For hours, her cousin had rambled on, making threats and heaping her with insults, but she'd paid him little mind. All she could think of was Reed, chained below in the cellar like a wild dog, hungry and thirsty. Reed . . . and what she'd learned about Wesley.

How could she have misjudged her husband so? She'd believed him to be an honorable man. With all her intuition, why hadn't she guessed how weak he really was? Raping Amanda was unforgivable—foul. If she'd only known the truth, she would have driven Wesley from Fortune's Gift at the point of a sword. He'd forced himself on her sister and then led an entire crew of good men to their graves through his own willful arrogance.

Both Amanda and Reed had protected him from her anger. They'd done it to protect her from the knowledge of what Wesley was really like, but it hadn't been a favor. Far better if she had known the truth; she wouldn't have wasted so much time mourning him or blaming Reed for getting Amanda with child.

Further angered by her continued composure

in the face of his tirade, Bruce had dragged her here to his temporary quarters on the second floor of the Customs House. The room was small, containing a desk, a single camp bed, and one window.

". . . this doesn't have to be unpleasant for you."

What was Bruce saying? Caroline was torn from her state of shock and reverie when she realized Bruce's tone had changed. She glanced back at him and an icy chill washed through her.

"Many women have said that I am rather . . . well endowed."

Her throat constricted as she realized the danger she was in. Bruce was ogling her with an expression that could only be out and out lechery, and he was removing his coat and stock.

"Why am I here?" she demanded, refusing let him see how frightened she was—not so much afraid of what he might do to her, as of what she might be forced to do to him. Don't make me kill you, she cried inwardly. No matter how rotten he was, he was a Talbot, and it sickened her to think of living out the rest of her life with her cousin's blood on her hands.

"You're not stupid, Caroline. We are betrothed. I'm only going to sample what I should have had long ago."

"You wouldn't," she said, trying to regain her dignity.

"Save your playacting for one who will appreciate it," he said, pouring himself a cup of port. "You will not scream or fight me—" He smiled slyly. "Well, perhaps you can struggle a little. It adds spice to a man's palate."

"You expect me to allow you to—"

"I'll kill him, cousin. I can do it. One order from me, and our good Corporal Jakes will go to the cellar, put a cord around Reed's neck, and strangle him like a Christmas goose."

"What good will Reed's death do you?" she bargained. "You stand to gain much more by his living."

"No, you have the wrong of it. When Reed is dead, everything falls to you."

"And when I'm dead, you'll inherit," she dared.

He drained the tin cup. "You wound me," he replied. "You have only to behave as a proper wife, and we shall enjoy a long and contented marriage."

A shout rang out from the stairway. Bruce turned toward the door and Caroline's fingers closed around the neck of the wine bottle. She swung it with all her might, and struck him squarely in the groin.

Bruce howled and bent over, clutching his genitals, and she smashed the bottle over his head. He crumpled forward like a poled ox.

Caroline wrested his sidearm from his body, opened the door cautiously, and stepped out into the hall. It was empty. Hiding the pistol in the folds of her skirt, she walked quickly down the first flight of steps. To her surprise, there was no guard at the foot of the stairs.

She knew she should try to escape. If the blow hadn't killed Bruce, he'd come to and sound the alarm. But she couldn't leave without Reed. She kept walking, down the corridor to the small doorway that led to the cellar.

Halfway down the twisting wooden steps, she heard men's voices and stopped short. She turned to run back the way she'd come, but it was too late. A man's form loomed up in the shadows of the cellar.

"Put up your hands," she ordered, twisting

around and using both hands to cock the flintlock pistol. "Move an inch and you're a dead man."

"Caroline!" Reed's voice came from behind the man she was trying to take prisoner.

Then a familiar chuckle made her limp with relief.

"By the king's arse, woman, will you decide for once which side you're on?"

"Garrett!" she whispered. "Where have you been?"

"Where's Bruce?" he demanded.

"I broke a bottle of port over his head," she said, throwing herself into his arms and leaving out the part about her first blow. "There are at least three guards."

"Below in my cell," Reed said.

"All of them?" She held tight to Garrett, fighting the giddiness that threatened her consciousness.

"Your math is a little off, Caroline," Garrett teased her. "We locked up five of His Majesty's finest."

"Someone shouted. It gave me the chance to get the best of Bruce," she explained.

"You're mistaken," Garrett said. "They didn't get a chance to utter a sound."

"But we both heard . . ." She broke off. "It doesn't matter." She let go of Garrett and went to her brother and hugged him. This time, she couldn't hold back the tears. "Reed," she murmured thickly. "Reed."

He patted the crown of her head. "There, there, sis, you'll be all fleas and stink. Here, give me that pistol, if you don't mind. It's been a while since I've held one."

She saw then that the two were not alone. Four sailors from the ship crowded hard on Reed's heels. "You took your sweet time," she admonished Garrett. "I thought—"

"We'll argue later," he said. "This isn't the place." He passed her on the stairs, opened the door, and stepped out into the hall. "Come on," he whispered. "Quick, now."

Then were nearly out the far door when Caroline heard Bruce's shout. " 'Ware the watch! Beware the watch! Prisoner escaping!" He came stumbling down the wide staircase with a rifle in his hands.

"Caroline! Look out!" Reed shouted, taking instant aim with his pistol.

Garrett shoved Caroline aside and raised his own gun, but Reed was between him and Bruce and he couldn't get a clear line of fire. Bruce's rifle and Reed's pistol went off as one explosion. Both bullets struck their targets with killing accuracy. Bruce pitched headlong down the steps, and Reed sagged sideways against the wall with his cousin's musket ball through his chest.

"Reed!" Caroline cried out.

Garrett gathered her mortally injured brother up in his arms, and they ran outside to the street. Two men were waiting there with horses. In seconds, they were mounted and pounding down the river road out of Chestertown toward the waiting ship.

"Will we be pursued?" Caroline asked as she climbed the ladder to the deck.

"I doubt it," Garrett replied. "Chestertown's hot for the rebellion. Besides, I doubt if Bruce made any friends there while he was commander. His remaining troops are probably glad to see him dead."

* * *

Reed lived for three days, and died peacefully in his bed at Fortune's Gift. And as Garrett had predicted, no one came to search out the escaped prisoner or his accomplices.

"The British are pulling out of Philadelphia and heading north just as Falconer told us they would," Garrett said as he stroked Caroline's hair. She had not slept or eaten since they'd ridden out of Chestertown and he was deeply concerned about her. "You needn't be afraid. There's so much confusion, I doubt if anyone will look for Bruce's murderer."

"It's not that," she sobbed to Garrett. "I'm not afraid. It's just . . ." She paused and sniffed. "Reed's dead. We didn't save him. I feel as though it was all for nothing."

"No," Garrett answered softly as he rocked her against his chest. "Not for nothing, woman. Reed died a free man, on his own land."

Teardrops sparkled like diamonds on her long, dark lashes. "Do you think that makes a difference?" she asked.

"It would to me," he answered firmly.

They buried Reed in the family brick-walled cemetery, and Caroline could not remain dry-eyed as she watched the carpenter erect the wooden monument over her brother's grave . . . the same one she had seen so often in her dreams.

Afterward, when friends and neighbors had all gone home, Caroline and Garrett walked hand in hand along the river. Green fields spread around them, and water sparkled on the surface of the water. High above, an osprey soared. The air was heavy with the scent of honeysuckle and apple blossoms.

"When will you leave?" she asked him. Her

tears were cried out now, and she had come to terms with Reed's loss.

"A few days," he said. "Now that the French have recognized our independence, and Washington is on the march, I'm needed more than ever. I'm needed, Caroline. No matter how much I want to stay with you, I have to go."

"Only part of you goes," she answered. "Part, I get to keep with me." She squeezed his hand tightly. "In late fall or early winter, we'll have a child."

"You're pregnant?" He took hold of her shoulders and stared into her eyes. "For certain?"

"Are you happy, Garrett?" she asked. "I want you to be happy about it."

He crushed her against him, tilted up her face, and kissed her tenderly. "If we have a son, I suppose I'll have to come back teach him a thing or two, won't I?"

"Or a daughter." Her heart was thudding wildly. He was pleased. She'd been so afraid that he'd blame her—that he'd think it was a way to trap him into staying away from the war.

"A daughter of yours will need my hand more than a son," he said.

He kissed her again, so long and hard that it nearly took her breath away. She raised his callused hand and laid it against her cheek. "I've been thinking about the treasure," she said, "the chests of gold we brought back on the *Cassandra*."

"I thought the best thing for you would be to bury them. Now that Bruce is no longer a threat, and the main British army is moving out of the area, you should be safe here. But I'd not want to risk leaving so much gold—"

"Take it to General Washington," she said.

"What?"

"For Reed, and for Grandmother Lacy. Fill Washington's war chest with Kutii's—"

"But what of our child, Caroline?" he asked. "Are you willing to risk beggaring—?"

"Our children and grandchildren can build their own future. If Kutii's gold can help make the Maryland and the other twelve colonies free of British domination, then it can't go for a better cause."

"But if you give up the treasure, and we lose the war, you could lose Fortune's Gift," he warned.

"This land is a dream," she said. "And dreams don't die so easily."

"You are my dream, Caroline Faulkner."

Her eyes widened in amazement. "You can say that . . . after all I've put your through?"

He grinned that special crooked smile of his that always made her heartbeat quicken.

"Do you love me, Garrett—really love me?"

"Aye, woman, as the preacher said, 'For richer for poorer . . . until death do us part. . . .' "

"And then?" Her voice dropped to a whisper.

He groaned. "You know how to make a man cut out his vitals and lay them on a table for you, don't you?"

"I just want to hear you say the words, Garrett . . . just this once. Forever and ever?"

"From hell to heaven and back again," he answered huskily. "No matter where I drop anchor, or what star I sail to, I want you beside me."

"You'd best mean it," she replied, "because I intend to hold you to it. I do love you, Garrett—with all my heart and soul."

"You do?"

"I do."

"Then why are we wasting what little time we have left in talking?"

"You're the one doing all the talking."

"Caroline."

She laughed and raised her face to meet his slow, tender kiss.

Epilogue

Fortune's Gift
October 31, 1781

"No bedtime!" Peregrine protested. "Want to stay up. Hungry. Want cider. No bedtime, Mama."

Caroline took her small son in her arms. "I'll put him to bed, Susan," she said to his nurse.

"Thirsty," the boy repeated loudly, then flashed a smile that melted his mother's heart.

"Have a drink of water," Caroline soothed. The nurse poured a little from a pitcher into a pewter goblet and handed it to her. She gave Peregrine a few sips.

"Hungry, Mama."

"You have had a long day. No nap this afternoon, remember?" She'd taken him with her on horseback to the river cornfield where they'd watched the men cut and stack long, straight rows of corn shocks. "I told you that if you went into the fields with me, you'd have to go to bed early."

"Want Harry." He pursed rosebud lips into a pout.

Susan produced a much-loved stuffed cat with button eyes. "Here you go, my lamb."

"Not that Harry." He threw the toy. "Want the other Harry."

"Be nice," Caroline said, "or no bedtime story." She rolled her eyes at Susan. "I'll take him up. I think we've all had quite enough of this young gentleman's antics today." As she started for the stairs, a spotted hound unfolded its long legs and trotted after them.

"Flirt chases Harry," Peregrine informed her.

Caroline looked down into the cherubic face that reminded her so much of his father. Peregrine's huge gray eyes sparkled with mischief. "Flirt chased Harry up on the highboy, and Harry jumped through the wall. Poof! All gone."

"Through the wall, hmmm?" Caroline nuzzled his sweet-smelling cheek and neck.

"Is it tomorrow yet?"

"Almost." She carried on a daily battle, trying to explain the concept of *tomorrow* to Peregrine and failing miserably. He couldn't understand why tomorrow was always the next morning—but when morning arrived, tomorrow had jumped *poof* to the next day. Tonight, she was too tired of the subject to allow herself to be drawn into the discussion.

"My Papa come home tomorrow?"

"I hope so, but I can't promise," she said. Since word had come of Cornwallis's surrender at a little place in Virginia called Yorktown, she'd hoped for Garrett's return. Every day, she watched the river for sails, and every night, she prayed for his safety.

She and Garrett had had so little time together in the last few years. Garrett's ship had engaged the enemy time after time, sinking English vessels in the Chesapeake and up and down the east coast. It hadn't taken the British long to learn that Osprey was under sail again, and they'd doubled the price on his head. Garrett had outwitted the English naval captains in New York, Charleston, and Savannah. Once, he'd even captured a naval snow carrying pay for enemy troops in South Carolina. She had every reason to be proud of him, but she'd feel even better once he was back in her arms.

Already, two locals boys, Frank Bennett and Alfred Thompson, had come home from the southern campaign. Both had served with the Maryland militia, and neither had any word of Garrett.

"Sleep in your bed," Peregrine said when Caroline had finished the night's story.

"You're a big boy," she said, "too big to sleep with Mama. You have Flirt for company, and I'm just down the hall." The hound curled up at the foot of the boy's small poster bed.

"I want Harry," he said.

"Good night, Peregrine."

"You forgot prayers."

"I didn't forget them. Say your prayers."

A few minutes later, she tiptoed out of the room. As she paused in the doorway and looked back, she saw the hound's ears go up as a black cat leaped onto the bed. "Harry, don't you dare wake him," she warned. From somewhere far off, she heard the gentle sound of Kutii's laughter. "You either," she said, firmly closing the door. "Anyone who wakes that little hellion can just sing him back to sleep."

She went down the hall to her bedchamber and pushed open the door, then froze in shock as she saw a man's figure in her open window. "Put your hands up!" she cried, trying to frighten him away with a ruse. "I warn you," she bluffed. "I have a gun here, and I'll shoot."

"Lord, woman," Garrett answered. "If I put my hands up, I'll fall out the window."

"Garrett!" She ran toward him. "What in the world? I've been watching the river, and—"

"The *Cassandra*'s docked in Annapolis. I stole Guy Wiggin's sloop and crossed the bay to get here." He grinned at her as his boots hit the floor. He opened his arms, and she flung herself at him. She kissed his mouth, his chin, his eyelids, and then his lips again.

"You've been drinking," she accused when she stopped to catch her breath. "Are you drunk?"

He laughed. "No. Just had a few drinks with my friends. We were having a bit of a celebration. You heard about Yorktown, didn't you? By God, we showed them a thing or two. You should have seen the lobster-backs' faces. Cornwallis didn't even have the guts to surrender his sword; he sent O'Hara to do his dirty work."

"It's over, then? Really over?" She tightened her arms around his neck. He swept her up in his arms, groaned loudly in jest, and carried her to their bed.

Their lips met again; this time a spark of desire flared between them and they clung to each other as though their lives depended on it.

"Over for me," Garrett answered huskily. "I think it's time I came home and gave our son a brother or sister for company." The tip of his tongue brushed her lower lip, and Caroline shivered with anticipation.

"It's been so long," she said, pulling loose the ribbon that held his hair in a braided queue. "You're in need of a bath, husband."

"You don't like sweaty men in your bed?" He dropped her onto the heaped feather ticks and knelt beside her, nuzzling her breasts.

"Are you mad to climb in my window?" she asked. "What if I'd taken you for a Tory scoundrel and shot you?"

"With what? You didn't have a gun." He proceeded to unlace the bodice of her gown with one hand, all the while running his other under her petticoats and up her thigh.

She giggled. "Well, if I'd had a gun, I could have shot you."

He pulled the top of her gown off one shoulder and trailed kisses down her bare skin. "You smell like heaven," he murmured.

"Why did you come in the window?" she insisted.

"If you must know . . ." He raised his head and winked at her. "I didn't want to see anyone but you tonight. I didn't want to talk to anyone. I just wanted to tumble you."

"Like any dairymaid?"

"Mmm." He kissed her long and hard, and she tasted the sharp bite of rum on this tongue. "You talk too much, woman."

She closed her eyes and inhaled the scent of him. He was all tar and gunpowder, tobacco and spirits. "Are you here?" she asked him. "Really here, or have I dreamed it again?"

"I'm home, Caroline. Home to stay."

"To be a farmer?" She gazed at his unshaved face and thought how lucky she was to have him. He tugged at his shirt and pulled it off over his head. Her heart rose in her throat as she saw the raw furrow of another fresh scar across his chest. I won't ask him about that wound tonight, she thought . . . but she wanted to kiss it and take away the memory of the hurt.

"I've a mind to try growing tobacco," he answered hoarsely. "And with Falconer's help, I'd like to try to help make these Colonies into a whole. The war was only the start," he said. "The real work of forging a country lies ahead."

"Falconer?"

"I received a letter months ago, and I've just spoken with a barrister in Annapolis. Mistress Annemie is dead. She passed on last July."

"And—?"

"And she left it all to me."

"All of it? The Falconer empire?"

He grinned. "I don't know whether to cheer or be sorry. It's one hell of a responsibility."

"And not all Falconer's endeavors are honest ones."

"Yes, I'll have to straighten that out."

"So you are Falconer now?"

"You could say that."

"I think I prefer to keep you as Garrett Faulkner. But what will this inheritance mean to us? Can you stay here on the Chesapeake, or will you have to go to Jamaica?"

"I told you, darling, I'm home. I intend to stay right here with you and Peregrine. Those who want to do business with Falconer can come here."

"Nothing would make me happier," she murmured, unable to take her eyes off him. "Wait until you see that son of yours. He's grown so—"

"Tomorrow," Garrett replied, stripping out of his breeches.

She laughed. "Tomorrow."

"What's so funny about that?" He began to unlace her stays.

"Ask Peregrine," she teased.

"What are you talking about? Ask Peregrine what?"

"You'll see."

He cupped her breast in his strong hand and leaned down to kiss it. She sighed with pleasure as sweet sensations raced through her blood and she reached to stroke his swollen manhood. "Have I ever told you that I love you?" he asked her.

"I think I remember you saying something like that," she teased, "but I'd like to hear it again."

"I love you."

Then he pressed her back against the heaped pillows, and she forgot everything but the feel of the man in her arms, and the sweet, bold promise of what lay ahead.